Street Magic

...TABLE OF CONTENTS...

Jackpoint Login 5	**Advanced Magic Rules** 28	Psionics 45
The Awakened World 6	Material Links 28	Miracles 46
Magic in Daily Life 8	Sympathetic Links 29	Madness 46
Popular Beliefs and Media-	Acquiring Geasa During Play 30	**Building a Magical Tradition** 46
Fueled Misconceptions 8	Tweaking the Rules 31	Step 1: Concept 46
Myth vs. Reality 9	**Paths of Magic** 32	Step 2: Spirits 47
The Magical Child:	The Many Paradigms of Magic 34	Step 3: Drain 47
Growing Up Awakened 11	The Practice of Magic 34	Step 4: Rounding Out 47
Magic and Education 12	Possession-Based Traditions 34	**Initiation & Metamagic** 48
Magic and the Law 13	Faith, Belief, and Magic 34	Initiation 50
The Other Side 14	**Alternate Magical Traditions** 35	Beyond the Doors
Magic and Religion 14	The Aboriginal Tradition 35	of Perception 50
Christianity 15	The Aztec Tradition 35	Group Initiation 50
Eastern Religions 15	Black Magic 36	The Initiation Rite 50
Islam 15	The Buddhist Tradition 36	Initiatory Ordeals 50
Judaism 16	Chaos Magic 37	Metamagic 52
Neo-Paganism 16	Christian Theurgy 37	Learning Metamagic 52
New Religions 16	The Druidic Tradition 38	New Metamagic 52
Magic and the Corps 16	The Hindu Tradition 38	Advanced Metamagic 58
Corporate Mojo 16	The Islamic Tradition 39	**Magical Groups** 62
The Big Players 17	The Norse Tradition 39	Social Circles 64
Small but Mighty 17	The Path of the Wheel 40	The Magical Group 64
Magic in the Shadows 19	The Qabbalistic Tradition 40	Purpose 64
The Awakened Character 20	The Shinto Tradition 41	Customs 64
Creating an	Traditional or	The Group Bond 65
Awakened Character 22	Hedge Witchcraft 41	Individual Strictures 66
Metatype 22	The Voodoo Tradition 42	Group Strictures 67
Attributes 22	The Wiccan Tradition 42	Group Benefits 67
Skills 22	The Wuxing Tradition 43	Group Resources and Dues 68
Qualities 23	The Zoroastrian Tradition 43	Patrons 68
Magic and Technology 23	**Paths of the Adept** 44	**Finding a Group** 68
New Awakened Skills 24	The Athlete's Way 44	Joining a Group 69
Arcana (Logic) 24	The Warrior's Way 44	Founding a Group 69
Enchanting (Magic) 24	The Invisible Way 45	Creating a Group 69
New Awakened Qualities 24	The Shamanic Way 45	Sample Magical Groups 69
Positive Qualities 24	The Speaker's Way 45	Bear Doctor Society 69
Negative Qualities 26	**Magical Oddities** 45	Benandanti XXV 70

Street Magic

Table of Contents

Brotherhood of the Iron Crescent	70
Dead Warlocks	70
Gladio	71
Hermetic Order of the Auric Aurora	72
Illuminates of the New Dawn	72
Jamil Islamyah	72
MCT Research Unit 13	73
Mystic Crusaders	73
Pathfinders	73
The Rat Pack	74
Sisterhood of Ariadne	74
Sons of Thunder & Sea	74
Magical Goods	**75**
The Ins and Outs of Talismongering	76
Doing Business	76
Inside the Alchemist's Lab	78
Game Information	79
Enchanting 101	79
Enchanting Tools	79
Getting the Goods	79
Practical Alchemy	81
Artificing	82
Advanced Foci	84
Vessel Preparation	86
Unique Enchantments	87
Spirits of the Sixth World	**89**
The Nature of Spirits	90
On the Intellect of Spirits	90
On the Forms of Spirits	90
Free Spirits	92
Wild and Aberrant Spirits	93
New Spirit Rules	94
Astral Movement	94
Disruption	94
Long-Term Binding	94
Spirit Combat	94
Spirit Services	94
Spirits and Edge	95
Spirits and Vessels	95
Spotting Spirits	95
New Spirits	96
New Spirit Powers	98
Ally Spirits	**103**
Conjuring an Ally	103
Ally Spirit Abilities	105
Enhancing an Ally	105
Losing an Ally Spirit	105
Free Spirits	**106**
Born Free	106
True Names	107
Free Spirits and Karma	107
Binding a Free Spirit	108
Spirit Pacts	108
Banishing a Free Spirit	109
Free Spirit Powers	109
Greater Powers	110
Wild Spirits	**110**
Astral Space & the Metaplanes	**111**
The Mirror World	112
Astral Topography	112
The Living Earth	114
Astral Phenomena	115
Alchera	115
Astral Shallows	116
Astral Rifts	116
The Nature of Mana	117
Background Count	117
Mana Anomalies	119
Astral Security	122
Wards	123
Wards with a Twist	125
Tools of the Trade	126
The Metaplanes	128
Worlds beyond Possibility	128
Metaplanar Quests	130
Goals of a Metaplanar Quest	131
Magical Threats	**134**
Things that Go Bump in the Night	136
Using Threats	136
The Dark Paths	136
The Darkness Within	137
Paths of the Twisted and Corrupted	137
Twisted Agendas	137
Twisted Adepts	139
Blood Magic	139
Toxic Magic	**141**
The Toxic Path	141
Toxic Agendas	141
Toxic Mentor Spirits	142
Toxic Metamagic	143
Toxic Spirits	144
Toxic Spirit Powers	146
Shadows Spirits	**146**
Shadow Spirit Types	147
Extraplanar Menaces	**148**
Evanescence (Weakness)	148
Insect Spirits	149
Hive Insect Spirits	150
Solitary Insect Spirits	151
Insect Spirit Types	152
Queen and Mother Spirits	153
Insect Spirit Powers	154
The Shedim	155
Grimoire	**156**
Spell Design	158
Spell Formulae	158
Designing New Spells	159
New Spells	**164**
Combat Spells	164
Detection Spells	165
Health Spells	169
Illusion Spells	170
Manipulation Spells	171
New Adept Powers	**174**
New Mentor Spirits	**180**
Mentor Spirit Archetypes	180
The Many Faces of Mentor Spirits	183
Sidebars	
Magic-Related Urban Legends	11
Magical Terms & Slang	12
Tweaking the Rules	31
Sense Link Power	54
A Note on Attuning Animals	54
Metamagic Techniques	55
Anchoring Trigger Conditions	60
Optional Rule: Aid Enchanting	79
Magical Goods Form and Function	82
Magical Compounds in Your Campaign	88
Spirit Appearance	96
Inhabitation Merges	100
Possession and Vessels	102
A Quick Aside About Mana	112
On Location: The Deep Lacuna	116
On Location: The Watergate Rift	117
Flexible Aspect	119
On Location: Crater Lake	120
Domain Examples	121
On Location: Cermak Blast Zone	122
On Location: The Maya Cloud	124
Metaplanar Gazetteer: Crystalwell	128
Metaplanar Gazetteer: Emergence Lake	130
Metaplanar Gazetteer: The Hive	131
Friends in High Places	132
The Perception of Evil	136
Playing the Twisted	138
Radiation Elemental Damage	145
Toxic Spirit Quick Design	147
The Insect Tradition	149
The Limits of Sorcery	159
Unaware Resistance	162

Elemental Effects	164
Spell Design Examples	167
Other Elemental Combat Spells	168

Credits: Street Magic

Writing: Lars Blumenstein, Rob Boyle, Robert Derie, Robyn King-Nitschke, Jason Levine, Jon Szeto, Peter Taylor, Frank Trollman
Editing: Rob Boyle, Jason Hardy, Michelle Lyons, Peter Taylor
Development: Rob Boyle, Robyn King-Nitschke, Peter Taylor
Art Direction: Rob Boyle
Layout: Jason Vargas, Matt Heerdt
Cover Art: Michael Komarck
Cover Layout: Jason Vargas, Matt Heerdt
Illustration: Ed Cox, Thomas Dooley, Alex Draude, John Gravato, Fred Hooper, Abrar Jamal, Mike Rooth, Anne Rouvin, Klaus Scherwinski, Chad Sergesketter, Mia Steingräber
Inspiration: Atari Teenage Riot and Muted Logic (dev-editing music)
Shout-Outs: Steve Kenson—who wrote the magic rules in previous editions and pumped a lot of his ideas into *Shadowrun*—deserves special thanks and credit. Similarly, Michelle & David Lyons deserve recognition, as they did the bulk of the hard work putting the *SR4* magic rules together. We'd also like to thank Elissa Carey, Christian Lonsing, Heiko Oertel, Olivier Thieffine, Malik Toms, and Costan Sequeiros for additional input. Finally, Jason Levine gets a big cheer for stepping up to bat on short notice.
Playtesters: Steppen Adams, Natalie Aked, Rob Aked, Yassil Benamer, Joseph Bohms, Anthony Bruno, Thibaut Carloz, John Dunn, Frederic Duwavran, Ortwin Escher, Torsten Germer, Rene Hess, Jochen Hinderks, Martin Janssen, Daniel Juhnke, Matthias Kleen, Brian Leist, Peter Leitch, Matt Marques, Chris Maxfield, Margarete Muhle, Jon Naughton, Maxime Noël, Fabien Pérès, Fiona Petiet, Thomas Rataud, Helge Saathoff, Geoff Skellams, Mark Somers, Olivier Thieffine, Martijn Weezepoel, Jakko Westerbeke, Jason Wortman

Copyright© 2006-2010 The Topps Company, Inc. All Rights Reserved. Shadowrun, Street Magic, and Matrix are registered trademarks and/or trademarks of The Topps Company, Inc., in the United States and/or other countries. No part of this work may be reproduced, stored in a retrieval system, or transmitted in any form or by any means, without the prior permission in writing of the Copyright Owner, nor be otherwise circulated in any form other than that in which it is published. Catalyst Game Labs and the Catalyst Game Labs logo are trademarks of InMediaRes Productions, LLC.

Corrected Third Printing,
Second Printing by Catalyst Game Labs
Printed in the USA.

Find us online:
http://www.catalystgamelabs.com
 (Catalyst Game Labs website)
info@shadowrunrpg.com
 (Shadowrun questions)
http://www.shadowrun4.com
 (official Shadowrun website)
http://del.ico.us/shadowrun
 (cool links)

```
Connecting JackPoint VPN ...
... Matrix Access ID Spoofed.
... Encryption Keys Generated.
... Connected to Onion Routers.
> Login
****************************
> Enter Passcode
****************************
... Biometric Scan Confirmed.
Connected to <ERROR: NODE UNKNOWN>
"Disbelief in magic can force a poor soul into believing in government
and business."
```

JackPoint Stats
42 users currently active in the network

Latest News
* <sticky> This private p2p MoSoSo network is still in beta-test, so pardon the mess and report any glitches to me. —FastJack
* <031670> Sorry about that AR spam virus that got loose in the network. The SpamWitch filter zigged when it should have zagged. If anyone wants to kick me in the head for it, be my guest. I think that's the only way I'm going to get that jingle out of my brain. —FastJack

Personal Alerts
* You have 47 new private messages
* You have 6 new re-routed, anonymized, sanitized messages from "<unknown>"
* You have 1 priority message from "Mom"
* You have 4 new responses to your JackPoint posts
* 2 personal profiles in the immediate vicinity meet your search agent's parameters

First Degree
Netcat, Beaker, and Nephrine are online and in your area

Your Current Rep Score: 38 (97% Positive)

Current Time: April 11 2070, 0403

[PREFERENCES] [FEEDS] [TASKS] [LINKS] [HISTORY]

Welcome back to JackPoint, omae; your last connection was severed: 4 hours, 15 minutes, 16 seconds ago

Today's Heads Up
Scan the Street Magic tag for a refresher course on how magic makes our lives safer and simpler—or is that more deadly and complicated? [Link] [Guests]

Incoming
* Clockwork and Picador are scraping together some fun facts on the latest guns, toys, and vehicles. [Tag: Arsenal]
* Just back from a working vacation in a nice, quiet, secure, gated community? Review your fave biz zones here. [Tag: Corporate Enclaves]
* Ready for an upgrade? Before you risk your parts with that shady cyberdoc again, check out our upcoming primer on personal technological enhancements. [Tag: Augmentation]

Top News Items
* Gaeatronics is denying reports that sabotage was the cause of a power outage that struck parts of Seattle and the Salish-Shidhe for several hours last week. Other sources indicate the clean energy corp has doubled security around its new geothermal taps in the Olympic peninsula. Link.
* The great dragon Rhonabwy signed a contract with Evo's MetaMatrix to publish a new daily music review blog, "Soothing the Savage Beast." Link.
* Yet another researcher has died in an attempt to explore the "Dunkelzahn Rift" in Washington, DC. Doctor Miguel Echavarria astrally entered the rift in a bid to claim a Draco Foundation prize yesterday, confident that he had devised a "fool-proof" way to return to his body. Several hours later, when he failed to return, his body entered a coma; he was pronounced dead this morning. Link.
* Russian officials have been indicted in the cover-up of a missing floating atomic power plant. According to reports, the vessel carrying the reactor has been missing for "well over a year," spurring outrage among environmentalists who fear this may lead to a "floating Chernobyl." Link.
* There's a buzz brewing in the Nexus over some new secret research project cooked up between Manadyne and Mangadyne. What do a magic research outfit and a Matrix design and security corp have in common? Link.

[CHAT] [MESSAGES] [FILES] [POSTS] [NEXUS] [SEARCH]

Active — ComStar Firewall ✓
Active — Jack-in-the-Box Antivirus ✓
Active — SpamWitch Filter ✓
On/Receiving — Commcode
Excellent — Signal
Active — Hidden Mode ✓
Local Map

Street Magic
Invited Guests
<none>

Posts/Files tagged with "Street Magic":
* The Awakened World
* Magical Goods
* Spirits of the Sixth World
[More]

[CONTINUE] [ADVANCED SEARCH] [SAVE]

...THE AWAKENED WORLD...

Jose's head ached, like someone had jabbed an icepick through his eye and into his brain. His vision reeled with indistinct shapes and colors. Patterns resolved with agonizing slowness into the familiar crumbling alley and the faces of his fellow Chulos. They were all staring at him.

They stood in a semi-circle a few meters away, their expressions identical masks of shock, incredulity, and—fear? Quickly he whipped his head around to verify that no threat was behind him, but the area back there was empty and dark save for the stinking dumpsters overflowing with refuse from Amelia's Cantina. He turned around, confused, pushing himself up with his arm. Two of the gangers—one was his brother, Carlos—took steps back. None of their eyes left him. Then he saw the bodies.

There were three of them, lying on the garbage-strewn street just behind the Chulos. All three wore the red jackets of the Rusted Stilettos, and none of them was moving. And he remembered.

His eyes grew wide and he stared down at his hands, spreading out his fingers as if he'd never looked at them before. Then he looked up at the Chulos. His friends. His brothers. "I—" he began.

"What did you do, man?" Carlos's deep voice was reduced to a harsh whisper. Carlos, who was two years older than Jose and nearly a head taller. "What did you do?"

"I don't—" *I don't know!* His face grew hot as the images returned: the Stiletto slipping up behind Carlos, the raised knife, his own voice crying out, and then the flash of light, the screams, the explosion of pain behind his eyes—

"You did magic!" It was Gato, his brother's best friend. His tone was loud, accusing, shot through with trembling fear that Jose could feel in his bones.

"I didn't—"*That's crazy! I can't do magic! I'm just a kid!*

"They were gonna stick Carlos, and you—you—yelled something, pointed at 'em, and they all screamed and went down!" Gato came forward, practically screaming in his face now. Then, as if realizing how close he'd gotten, Gato staggered back. He pointed a shaking finger at the boy. "Don't you dare fuckin' read my mind, man, you hear me? You do and I'll—"

Gato suddenly pitched forward, spraying blood. The alley behind him echoed with gunfire. Jose screamed and scrambled up as red jackets filled the alley. Shouts of "There they are!" filled his ears.

"Get 'em, Jose!" Carlos was yelling, an edge of desperation in his voice. "Magic 'em again! Jose!"

Jose felt his heart pounding, sweat breaking out all over his body. Everything was loud, everything was moving. How had he done it before? What had he done to make it happen? He couldn't remember! He—

Carlos yelled something as his head jerked sideways and his body spun in an obscene dance before dropping. His dead eyes stared accusingly at his brother.

Jose ran for his life, his eyes burning with shame. What good was being able to do magic if he couldn't control it—if he couldn't use it to save his own brother? Hot tears streamed down his face.

Though he was right in front of them, the Stilettos never saw him go.

Street Magic

> **WORD ON THE STREET:**
> **WHAT DOES MAGIC MEAN TO YOU?**
> (asked at: Aurora Mall, Seattle)
>
> **Mary, 24, *New You* Employee, Seattle:** Magic is scary. I mean, those people can do whatever they want to you. They can read your mind, fry your brain, or watch you when you're taking a shower or having sex. And you can't even tell who's magical and who's not.
>
> **Franklin, 18, Student, Seattle:** What does it mean to me? It means power. I'm from the wrong end of town, but I got tapped by the Mitsuhama college recruiting program and I'll have a great job waiting when I get out, just because I can summon spirits and cast spells. It means respect. It means nobody messes with me.
>
> **Ethan, 54, Middle Manager, Chicago:** It's unnatural. Miracles and magic are the province of God, not of man, and one of these days all of these blasphemers are going to find out just what kind of fire they've been playing with.
>
> **Li, 42, Mystical Consultant, Hong Kong:** Magic is a gift. It's a way to be closer to the natural forces around us—to work in harmony with them to bring about beneficial change. Magic is not a thing to fear, but a thing to embrace.
>
> **Corrine, 40, Lone Star Officer, Seattle:** Frankly, magic is a pain in the ass, especially when it's on the wrong side of the law. It's hard to stop, hard to catch, and hard to deal with once we *do* catch it.
>
> **Rain, 22, Eco-Activist, Seattle:** Magic is a way to be one with nature, to see firsthand what the corps have been doing to our mother Gaia. Anybody who's magical and doesn't support the fight against the rape of our planet doesn't have a heart.
>
> **Tetsuo, 20, Athlete, San Francisco:** Never mind spells and spirits. Magic is about being in tune with your body. When every muscle is under your complete control, singing with the mojo, letting you do things that mundanes can't hope to match—man, who needs drugs? It's the ultimate high.

- Magic. What do you think of when you hear that word? Blazing fireballs? Invisibility? The spirit world? Mind control? Even though magic in its various flavors and incarnations has been around for close to 60 years now (some would say even longer), the average nonmagical person has at best a flawed and media-fueled understanding of its methods and capabilities. Before we can talk about slinging the real powerful mojo, I thought a primer on the basics would be a good starting point. I've gathered together a few sources, relying primarily on a nice little set of files I've found useful in the past when teaching mundanes about the Higher Mysteries (some from other authors, some I've written myself). Please, as always, feel free to chime in with your own experiences.
- Winterhawk

MAGIC IN DAILY LIFE
From *Magic: A Survival Guide for the Mundane:*

Come on, admit it: everything you know about magic, you know because you saw it on the trid, heard it from a friend of a friend, or slotted some sim with too much electric green and way too many exclamation points. Sure, you've probably met or may even know someone who is "Awakened," and maybe you saw some real illusions at a Cirque du Soleil show—but have you ever actually seen anybody use magic on the street? If not, you're not alone.

Fact is, even in our modern times, real magicians are rare. Everybody's heard the statistics that say approximately one percent of people are magically active, but like most statistics, that's not really accurate. For one thing, that number encompasses everybody who has a shred of magical talent, from minor-league adepts all the way up to spellslingers with enough mojo to give dragons a second thought about snacking on them. Just because one percent of people are magical doesn't meant that one in every hundred people you see on the street is secretly reading your mind.

Still, for all its rarity, magic is pervasive in daily life, from the lowest slum to the highest corporate boardroom. Why, then, have you never seen anybody fling a lightning bolt, summon a fire elemental to burn down a building, or command a horde of zombies to take over the nearest small town? Simple. In reality-land, where most of us spend our time, magic is a tool, not a weapon or a source of entertainment. Just like a vehicle, a cyberarm, or a twenty-story-tall crane, magic in everyday life is pressed into service to make life easier (and more profitable) for its practitioners.

- Fact is, a lot of Awakened types prefer to keep a low profile. People treat you differently when they know you're a mage. Partly it's fear, like the mage-o-phobes who are afraid we'll rape their minds and enslave them. Partly it's ignorance, like the people who get mad when you can't cure their cold or cast some spell they saw in a sim. But the worst are the fanboys who won't stop pestering you to levitate them or "show them" how to summon a spirit, like it's something anybody can learn.
- Haze

POPULAR BELIEFS AND MEDIA-FUELED MISCONCEPTIONS

Ask the average person to describe magic to you, and chances are good that one of two expressions will cross his face: excited fascination or abject fear (or sometimes a combination of the two). Magic holds a particular allure to mundanes, and no wonder: even though most people don't have much familiarity with the real thing, the media and popular culture are positively awash in it. While this can make for compelling entertainment, the downside is that the people

who create the entertainments in question rarely bother to consult with actual magicians to verify that the mystical feats they're portraying are actually possible.

Let's look at it from another standpoint: suppose an extraterrestrial being were to enter orbit around Earth and attempt to learn about magic using nothing but our mainstream, pop-culture entertainment sources. What might he discover? A few possibilities:

- Magicians fall into four basic types: beautiful human women wearing too little clothing; square-jawed human men with oddly-colored eyes; metahumans of both genders who are either sly or bumbling, and usually evil; and ninjas. A little more research might get you cold-eyed Asians or dark-skinned zombie masters, but let's stick with the highlights for now.
- Magicians are quite fearsome; they can sling powerful spells all day long with no adverse effects (unless, of course, the plot calls for the magician to suffer a setback, in which case a simple stun spell will drop her to her knees immediately).
- Magicians can do whatever they need to do in order to get the job done: summon powerful spirits, read minds, compel people to kill their own children, or teleport from one side of a town to another.
- Magic requires elaborate gestures, recitation of complicated incantations, or other showy accompaniments. In the same vein, magic always results in a massive display of pyrotechnics, even if the spell in question is as prosaic as simple healing or invisibility.
- Magicians always use the showiest, most powerful, and most damaging spell that fits a situation. Magicians are proud of being magicians and are *never* subtle (except when they're invisible).
- Magicians can spy on your every move astrally or with spirits, no matter where you're hiding.

It all sounds rather silly when you read it here, doesn't it? But you'd be surprised at the number of people who believe a lot of that nonsense. In the interests of trying to dispel a bit of ignorance, let's take a look at the reality of magic in the Sixth World.

MYTH VS. REALITY

First things first: there's no particular "look" for magicians. Just like everyone else in the world, they can be male, female, young, old, fat, thin, tall, short, beautiful, or ugly. They can be of any race, nationality, or metatype. Some of them like to emphasize their Talent by wearing magical symbols or runes on their clothing or by carrying elaborate wands, staves, or other props; others dress in nondescript styles and try not to draw attention to themselves. The only foolproof way to identify a magician is to look at his or her aura on the astral plane—and many of them can even mask that so they look completely mundane. In fact, in many cases, the people who look the most like magicians are likely not to be—"mystical" runes and arcane symbols are popular in current fashions.

Secondly, magic isn't always easy, even for powerful magicians. In highly simplified layman's terms, casting spells requires opening your senses to the mana—magical

> **SUKIE REDFLOWER IS BACK—AND THIS TIME IT'S PERSONAL!**
> The renegade corporation SolarTech is at it again—this time kidnapping a promising young scientist to acquire access to cutting-edge research worth millions. Turns out they're getting far more than they bargained for: the scientist in question is none other than the niece of spell-slinging powerhouse Sukie Redflower! Join seductive and tough-as-nails Sukie as she hand-picks a team of hard-core shadowrunners in Amazonia to once again take on her corporate arch-rivals. You can bet SolarTech's in for some heavy-duty magical punishment in *Sukie Redflower 3: Mojo Rain*! Available for download April 27!

energy—that surrounds us, channeling that mana through your own body, and then shaping that energy or directing it at a target. Not an easy prospect, especially if the spell is a powerful one. Using one's body as a conduit for "magical power juice" can have all sorts of deleterious effects: everything from headaches and dizziness up to real (and serious) physical damage if the magician overextends himself. While there are items and spirits that can aid a magician in casting, those methods have their own potential drawbacks, and it's best not to rely on them overmuch. The point is, despite what they might show in the trids, it's not practical (and rarely *possible*) for a magician to sling spells all day long with no adverse effects.

Surely, you say, magicians can cast whatever spells they need at the moment, even if they can't do it at world-shaking power levels, right? Not even close, I'm afraid. The methods vary by tradition: a shaman might learn a technique from a totem or mentor spirit, a mage from a digital spell formula, or an adept by physical practice, but in any case the process is the same—the magician must *learn* a technique before she can use it. "But what about spontaneous manifestations?" you ask. "Like when children first discover their abilities?" True, it does happen, and there have been many documented cases—but it's rare, and almost never controlled.

While we're at it, let's get a few more things straight about magic, specifically about what it *can't* do. No matter how many times you see it in simsense or how many friends of friends assure you that they've personally witnessed it, magicians can't teleport. Not at all. Not even dragons (unless they aren't telling us something). They can't time-travel, either. They *can* read minds, but it's not nearly as easy as the media wants you to think it is, especially if they want to get something more than surface impressions and emotions. Trust me—you're not going to accidentally lay bare your deepest thoughts to the guy sitting next to you on the subway (unless, of course, he's a dragon in disguise—in that case all bets are off).

Are you beginning to see a pattern here? Think about it this way: the popular media is going to make magic as showy and dramatic as possible, because their purpose is to *entertain*, not to *instruct*. One more example to support my point: how many times have you seen a magician in a trid show cast a spell by yelling some incomprehensible phrase in Latin, dancing around chanting in a faux-Native American tongue, or performing what looks like a complicated Tai Chi routine? "They do *too* do that!" I can already hear some of you exclaim indignantly. "I've seen that one *myself*!" And right you are—except that you should replace "do" with "can" in your first sentence. Yes, many magicians employ chants, incantations, or physical gestures in their spellcasting and spirit summoning. It is, in fact, fairly common. But the point is, it's not usually *necessary*. I, for example, am perfectly capable of casting any spell in my repertoire without uttering a word or making a move. All I have to do is *concentrate,* focusing my mental energy on the appropriate pattern or formula—and this is true for the majority of magicians, what they choose to do notwithstanding. So if you've managed to comfort yourself that you're safe from magical effects because nobody near you is dancing around or performing Gregorian chant, I'm afraid you'll have to alter your outlook a bit.

That makes a nice segue into another topic I'd like to bring up: the dark side of magic. My examples thus far have been somewhat lighthearted, and with reason: I wanted you to see the sheer amount of misinformation that's circulating around regarding magic and its practices. A great deal of prejudice and fear is based on these mistaken assumptions, but I'd be remiss if I didn't point out that some of this ill-feeling, a real and dangerous part, is based on perceptions that are much more frightening because they've got a foot in reality. Magicians *can* kill people with little effort, especially unprotected mundanes. They *can* spy on your activities from astral space, either on their own or with the aid of spirits. They *can* cause untold destruction (just last week, a mage in a small town summoned a fire spirit to exact revenge on a business owner, lost control of it, and ended up responsible for the destruction of a significant part of the downtown area, not to mention four deaths and countless injuries). Media misconceptions aside, magic and magicians can be very dangerous—it's just unfortunate that some groups take their paranoia a bit too far and use this fact to advocate all sorts of injustices against the Awakened.

Let's talk about these injustices for a moment, shall we? Many people believe that magicians have the world by the tail: they get the best jobs, they can learn spells to help make their lives a lot easier, and they have access to advantages that mundanes can only dream of. This can be true—but they (especially law-abiding, everyday-citizen types) also have to contend with restrictions and inequities that mundanes never have to suffer. For example, certain groups (such as some rad groups and fringe religious organizations) hate and fear anything to do with magic and are constantly seeking to limit magicians' rights and liberties (by legal and illegal means—while some push for laws to restrict the use of magic, others are quite content to take more immediate and physical action if they can get away with it.) In many places, law-abiding magicians must register their talent and any gear they possess

with local authorities, and many very useful spells, spirits, and magical items are outright forbidden. True, many of us find ways around these strictures, but the ongoing climate of misunderstanding and fear has produced an environment where it's very difficult to remain law-abiding as a magician—even if you work for a corporation.

Oh—one more thing, lest you think the life of magicians is all fast cars and willing spirits: magic is *expensive,* in more ways than one. Most magicians, regardless of tradition, tend to spend large parts of their available funds on purchasing magical gear, spell formulae, training, and other things necessary for advancement in the Arts. This is in addition to the time and—for lack of a better word—life energy that's required from anyone who wants to be more than a dabbler. The proportions of these vary a bit by tradition, but I can almost guarantee that if you show me a magician who cares about her art, I'll show you a person who has little time for any other significant nonmagical pursuits. Magic is a rewarding but exacting taskmaster.

THE MAGICAL CHILD: GROWING UP AWAKENED

Excerpt from *My Child Has the Talent: Now What?*

You'd swear little Johnny disappears in your house even though you know he's there. Maria is so much better than her peers at sports that it's not even fair. Tran is just "a little odd," though you can't put your finger on why. Congratulations! There's a good chance that your child has magical talent, and that will open up many new opportunities!

Children usually manifest magical talent around puberty, though it's been known to show up in children as young as eight (on very rare occasions even younger, especially in some metahumans). Often it's discovered during play or during stressful situations (for example, a child might lash out with a low-powered spell when bullied or distressed). Usually, however, children are tested around their tenth birthday, and those who show signs of magical ability are offered additional training. This training, whether special courses in a corporate educational system, apprenticeship with a tribal shaman, or something else appropriate to the child's tradition, usually continues throughout the teen years until the child is a young adult and can claim his or her valued place as a practitioner of magic. Many lucrative careers are open to magically talented children of all traditions, both magicians and adepts.

• This is bullshit. 'Hawk, why are you feeding us this corp-sponsored crap, anyway? "Oh, sure, little corp kids who show a spot of magic get their asses kissed until they're old enough to sign up as just another wage mage working for the Man, and everything is all flowers and nuyen forever." Let me tell you about how it really works: most street kids don't even find out they've got magic, let alone have people falling all over themselves to teach them how to use it. If they do find out, they're lucky to latch onto a street mage or shaman who'll take them on as an apprentice—and believe me, not all these relationships are healthy ones. A lot of these kids end up seriously messed

MAGIC-RELATED URBAN LEGENDS

Magic and magical phenomena aren't exempt from their share of urban legends. Here are a few popular examples, all of which happened to a "friend of a friend":

The Disappearing Village
Driving in unfamiliar territory late one night, the victim stops off in a small village to grab a bite to eat. The place seems eerie, the townspeople either somehow "off" or strangely familiar. He finishes his meal and leaves the town. When he arrives home, he tells his friends about the strange village. "But there's nothing on that part of that road," they assure him. Consulting a map, the victim discovers that he's right. Doing a bit more research, he finds that numerous people have disappeared or suffered fatal accidents on that stretch of road. He counts himself very lucky and wonders why he was spared…

The Evil Babysitter
A single mother has an appointment she can't miss. Her regular babysitter isn't available, so she's forced to allow a friend of a friend to watch her child. The young woman seems normal and trustworthy, so the mother reluctantly agrees. When she returns home, both the child and the babysitter are gone. Frantic, the mother finds a note on the kitchen table, covered in magical symbols and written in blood: "Thank you for providing me with a perfect sacrifice. The spirits will be pleased." Neither the child nor the sitter is ever seen again.

Bloody Mary
This urban legend, which predates the Awakening by many years, states that if you enter a completely dark room that contains a mirror and you chant "Bloody Mary!" three times (the exact chant varies widely by version) while looking in the mirror, a vengeful spirit will appear and kill you (or drag you into the mirror, or simply glare menacingly at you). The legend got a shot in the arm when magic reappeared; many people swear that friends or acquaintances actually experienced the phenomenon. If they're telling the truth, mischievous free spirits or practical-joking magicians are the likely culprits.

up. Yeah, okay, a few of them manage to get into some kind of corp program, and I'll give the corps one thing: they're so short of magicians that they'll take just about anybody who wants in, regardless of background. But is that really better? The end is the same: the kid ends up as a mage-drone in a tight-assed

MAGICAL TERMS AND SLANG

Band-Aid – *n.* Shadowrunning magician who specializes in patching up teammates with healing spells.

Burnout – *n.* Magician or adept who has lost all or part of her magical ability (for example, due to too much cyberware).

Christmas Tree – *n.* Magician who relies heavily on foci and thus lights up on the astral plane.

Floaters – *n.* Watcher spirits.

Ghost – *n.* An astral form.

Gode (m.)/Gydje (f.) – *n.* A magician who follows the Norse tradition.

Groggy – *n.* or *adj.* Derogatory term for an aspected magician (from "half Awakened").

Hitmage – *n.* Magical assassin.

Houngan (m.)/Mambo (f.) – *n.* A magician who follows the tradition of Voodoo.

Kannushi/Miko (f.) – *n.* A magician who follows the tradition of Shinto.

Koradji – *n.* A shaman that follows the Aboriginal tradition.

Manatech – *n.* or *adj.* Technology that interacts with magic.

Mundane – *n.* or *adj.* Person who does not possess magical ability; the state of being non-magical.

Nahualli – *n.* A magician who follows the Aztec tradition.

Ping – *v.* To detect a target with magic.

Poindexter – *n.* Derogatory term for a hermetic magician.

Shoes – *n.* The body left behind when a magician astrally projects ("I left my shoes in the car").

Sleeper – *n.* or *adj.* Mundane.

Spellworm – *n.* Magician.

Theurgist – *n.* A magician who follows the Christian tradition.

Wage mage – *n.* Magician employed by a corporation. The expression is also used as an insult for a magician with no real talent or potential.

Wizzer Gang – *n.* Gang consisting of (usually young) magicians.

Wizpunk – *n.* Musical genre popular with young magicians; it employs illusions and astral components to heighten the experience.

Wizworm – *n.* Dragon.

Wujen – *n.* A magician who follows the tradition of Wuxing.

X-men – *n.* or *adj.* Derogatory term for adepts.

Yogi (m.)/Yogini (f.) – *n.* A magician who follows the Buddhist tradition.

---

corporate environment. Me, I'd rather take my chances with the streets.
• Axis Mundi

• That's not all true, at least not in the larger sprawls. Most of the megacorps retain recruiters who keep their ears to the ground (usually by paying off area locals) so that they're the first ones to hear when some Barrens kid starts acting a little strange. You're right that corps are always desperate for new talent, and street kids are usually so dazzled by the offers of training and cred that they don't look back until it's too late. But the fact is, the corps can't afford to screw over their magical talent. As long as they don't mind being good corporate citizens, these kids have a shot at a far better (and most likely far longer) life than they'd have enjoyed if they'd stayed on the streets.
• Ethernaut

• What really sucks is the poor kids who have the bad luck to be born into a society where everyone thinks the Talent is evil, like some religious extremist groups. Yeah, they're getting rarer, but even here in modern-day 2070 I've heard stories of kids who've been put to death as "evil" or "of the devil" just because they manifested magical abilities at the wrong time.
• Frosty

MAGIC AND EDUCATION

We've covered how magically active children are identified, as well as the early stages of their schooling. No doubt I'm biased, but I think the topic of magical education deserves a bit more discussion.

Most people, when the subject comes up, immediately think of the classic hermetic paradigm. Widely employed in North America and Europe, it consists of a rigorous and scientific course of study designed to train classical hermetic magicians, giving them a grounding in both the theory and application of the major magical areas: spellcasting, conjuring, counterspelling, astral space, and ritual magic. Once a student has the basics, she can choose to specialize (for example, in theoretical magic or paranormal animal studies) or to pursue the more esoteric disciplines (such as enchanting or alchemy). In any case, the classic hermetic education by its very nature treats magic as a quantifiable science that can be mastered. Thus, university programs in magic (and even some high school programs) are similar to a scientific education, albeit a great deal stranger and more potentially dangerous. If the program is of any value, it is also inherently unforgiving; the percentage of students who fail to complete university-level magical programs is quite high. You probably won't be surprised to find out that the stress levels one experiences in such programs tend to lend themselves to rather … interesting … outlets. Pranks by magical students are matched only—perhaps—by those of Matrix programming students, and for much the same reasons.

• I remember hearing about a class of magicians that arranged (with the help of some hacker friends) to convince an entire class full of freshman English students that they didn't have to come to class one day—and the magicians, using Mask spells, took

their places. They drove the professor so crazy casting annoying little spells when he wasn't looking that he nearly quit, and nobody found out until the next day when the real class returned and got an earful from the department head.
• Jimmy No

• Oh, that's nothing. Over at the University of Prague, some of the student pranks have been masterpieces of magical innovation—I've heard that Schwartzkopf, the great dragon who teaches there, gives extra credit for anything that manages to impress him. So far not too many have succeeded, but they keep trying.
• Winterhawk

• Speaking of Europe, the "study circle" concept that's been popular over there for years (basically an initiatory group recruited from the students in a particular university magic class or program) is starting to catch on more in North America. People are beginning to realize that continuing studies with a group you're already familiar with (and can agree with!) gives you a leg up on things.
• Lyran

• Corporations have their fingers all over the academic magic programs: not only are they constantly watching for potential recruits to lure into their magical research programs, but they also fund more "independent" research projects out of the universities than you might suspect. If you think that academic scholars are free of corporate influence, you're hopelessly naïve. The corps and the universities are so incestuous that it's amazing that they're not producing three-headed kids.
• Jimmy No

So where does this leave the other disciplines? Despite unfortunate and lingering prejudices at the university level (while most schools have nature magic programs, many don't view them with the same level of respect as those for hermetics), many other, more "nontraditional" (in the hermetic sense) avenues exist for the education of shamans, houngans, and other more nature-based schools of magic. Often, this sort of education comes in a more one-on-one fashion, where a more experienced practitioner takes a student under her wing and teaches her what she needs to know, usually requesting some period of service or other payment in return. Also, we can't underestimate the importance of mentor spirits, particularly in traditions such as shamanism where they take a vital role. It's rare, but possible, for a young shaman to learn magical techniques wholly from his mentor spirit if no other education is available to him. These shamans tend not to be as well rounded as those who have been taught by more experienced practitioners, but they are often more powerful and focused in the areas that the spirit deems important.

• Many Asian magical schools (such as Wuxing) follow a middle ground with regard to magical training, combining formal studies with direct mentor-student relationships.
• Jimmy No

• A lot of street kids of all traditions who never got a "classical" education join gangs or other groups where they can help each other and hopefully gain access to a spellslinger or two who've been around the block a few times. It's entirely possible for a young magician to get a perfectly acceptable education on the streets, even if they don't know all the names of the techniques and which graybearded old coot first came up with them.
• Lyran

MAGIC AND THE LAW

Ever since magic reared its head, criminals with the Talent have embraced it as a way to make their jobs a little easier. Unfortunately for them, law enforcement agencies weren't long in playing catch-up, and these days Lone Star and their security brethren (both private and public) sport an impressive array of offensive, defensive, and investigative magical tools to help them make life difficult for shadowy types like us.

Let's start with how the law views magic. When you get right down to it, many of the laws governing magic and its use are fairly simplistic, at least in North America; for example, any felony committed with the aid of magic is automatically considered to be a premeditated act. If you kill someone with magic, you're looking at Murder One. If a spirit you summoned gets up to mischief and, say, burns down a few buildings or goes on a killing spree, you're considered responsible—even if the spirit had broken free of your control. Possession of some magical goods, particularly foci and other offensive items above a certain power level, without valid documentation (which is, of course, nearly impossible for anyone without a SIN to obtain) is a criminal offense even if you haven't committed any other crime with them. And if you think that's restrictive, try traveling outside of North America—in some other countries, such as Great Britain, being a magician requires that you register yourself with the government and keep a tissue sample on file. Times are tough all over for the shadowrunning magician.

• Not necessarily. In some of the Awakened nations, most people won't bat an eye at magic use, as long as you don't infringe on anybody's rights with it. Sometimes not even then.
• Kay St. Irregular

They get tougher still if a spellslinger is ever captured and delivered into the tender mercies of the legal system. Law enforcement fears magic because it's so insidious and difficult to counter, and thus they're often prone to taking draconian and inhumane steps to ensure that their magically active guests don't cause any trouble. Depending on how enlightened the legal system is, these steps can range from magemasks (designed to keep the wearer from speaking, hearing, or even concentrating) and special cuffs designed to prevent astral jaunts all the way up to psychoactive drugs, implants, and even the permanent destruction of the prisoner's magical abilities. These methods vary widely by jurisdiction, so anyone contemplating using magic to commit a crime should study up on the local laws and political climate before making a decision.

THE OTHER SIDE

While you're our there busily trying to make a living in the shadows, the other side hasn't been idle. Modern-day law enforcement agencies possess a wide array of magical techniques useful in many areas of crimefighting, including forensics, apprehension, interrogation, incarceration, and rehabilitation.

Because the UCAS and the CAS still retain major bits of the former US Bill of Rights in their legal codes, methods like mental probes and aura reading can't be used to gather evidence, since both violate Fifth Amendment prohibitions against self-incrimination. Even without these, however, magical means still provide many avenues to obtain evidence: for example, astral signatures have become as widely accepted as fingerprinting and DNA evidence for establishing the presence of a particular magician at a given location. Almost every law enforcement organization of reasonable size maintains a forensic thaumaturgy department, the members of which work hand-in-hand with the nonmagical forensics technicians and concern themselves with things like bodily fluids, hairs, astral impressions, psychometry, and any evidence that exists in astral space. Forensic magicians are considered analogous to the coroner or medical examiner, and they are almost always consulted when any evidence of a magical nature is introduced in a court of law.

In the UCAS, spectral evidence (that is, evidence or testimony provided by spirits) isn't admissible in court, so magicians can't do things like summon up the spirit of a murder victim to finger his or her killer—because there is no way to prove definitively that the spirit in question is in fact the victim. That doesn't mean, however, that spirits haven't been useful to investigations in the past, and in many cases, ghosts and spirits have led investigators to evidence crucial to convicting a suspect of a crime.

• This happens more often than you might think. A few years back I read something about a case where the spirit of a murdered woman haunted a small area of out-of-the-way woods. When the story eventually found its way to the ears of the local police chief, he brought in a big-city forensic thaumaturgy expert who went out to find the spirit. She led him right to where her body was buried, and some of the evidence on the body helped them nail her boyfriend for the crime. After that, she was never seen in those woods again.
• Kay St. Irregular

In more Awakened-friendly jurisdictions, however, spirits often have their say. Under some NAN tribal jurisdictions, for example, shamanic judges have been known to not only accept the testimony of spirits, but to actively consult them for advice in legal matters. In other countries, the judge might even *be* a spirit.

Another area where magic and the law come into conflict is when they're dealing with the rights of Awakened creatures. While great dragons (thanks to the late Dunkelzahn and his brief term as President) are considered sapient and can achieve citizenship in the UCAS, the status of other Awakened creatures such as sasquatches, free spirits, and ghouls remains murkier. All three groups (and more) have been actively campaigning for increased political and social status for years, but the gears of government move very slowly—especially in areas where the issues still aren't wholly understood. The fact is, some Awakened entities that are deemed dangerous to society not only are not afforded legal rights, but in some cases must fear bounties from corporations and countries. Shapeshifters and toxic magicians are two such entities.

• Note that this is a very North American/European view—many nations where the Awakened are more common (Amazonia, Yakut, and parts of China, for example) have more flexible views regarding rights and who gets them.
• Jimmy No

When dealing with all the potential legal issues relating to magicians, civil law isn't a subject that tends to come up right away. However, a large body of law exists to govern purely civil magical matters, such as spell copyrights. Under present UCAS law, the designer of a spell can copyright it and receive payment or royalties from its sales. This law is designed to discourage formula piracy, but in practice it's nearly impossible to prove in court. While it's considered a violation of the law to reverse-engineer a spell formula, in reality these cases are almost never prosecuted because the spell itself (as opposed to the formula) is considered an expression of natural law and therefore not subject to copyright. For example, if a magician sees another magician cast a fireball spell and then goes off to create her own fireball spell, who can say whether the second magician copied the first? Fireballs are fairly standard fare, magic-wise. Still, a lot of lawyers make a lot of nuyen going through the motions of filing suit in these cases, even if the magicians rarely see any benefit from it unless the spell in question is particularly unique or esoteric. In practice, secrecy is the best tool to keep one's spell formulae from prying eyes—they're rarely published, which naturally means that there's a thriving market in industrial espionage to gain access to them.

• I know some corps are looking for secret ways to protect their proprietary formulae, like "encrypting" them with some sort of magical key or even inserting "mystical traps" into the formula to surprise the unwary. There's also been talk of researchers looking into ways to insert "back doors" into a formula, so that a spell sold by Mitsuhama can be more easily dispelled by a Mitsuhama magician. Luckily, magic wants to be free just as much as information does.
• Haze

MAGIC AND RELIGION

In these Awakened times, the way magic and religion interact depends largely on the flavors involved, the cultural background in which they operate, and the society at large. Religion's reaction to magic and its practitioners ranges from "It's heresy! Burn them!" all the way to "Thank (fill in relevant deity, force, or expression of Nature) that magic has finally returned and assumed its rightful place!" Naturally, if you

look hard enough you can find just about everything in the middle as well.

By now everyone who's interested in this topic knows about the early highlights, including the reaction of many churches to the Awakening (some considered it the Apocalypse, while most were a bit more adaptable); the Pope's "In Imago Dei" (In the Image of God) papal encyclical declaring that metahumans have souls and that magic itself isn't inherently evil; and the early scrambles of the various world religions to incorporate this new power into their worldviews (or, in some cases, to simply condemn it). Instead of covering old territory, let's instead look at how some of the major and minor religions of the world currently view magic.

CHRISTIANITY

Most Christian churches followed Rome's lead, accepting magic to at least some degree and incorporating it into their doctrines and practices. The Catholics, though they accept the existence and practice of magic, declared that some practices such as conjuring touch on so many questions of faith and doctrine that church members may not practice them without permission. Some, like the Methodists and Unitarians, took a more liberal view, embracing magic and the good works it could enable. Only the most rigidly fundamentalist of Christian denominations (including more than a few evangelicals) completely resisted magic and all of its trappings.

- Some churches even maintain separate groups of magicians—for instance, the Catholics have an entire priestly order, the Order of St. Sylvester, that's nothing but spellslingers. You do *not* want to get on the wrong side of those folks.
- 2XL

EASTERN RELIGIONS

In most cases, the major Eastern religions (such as Hinduism, Buddhism, Daoism, and Shinto) embrace magic—since its existence only supports and reinforces beliefs that have existed for thousands of years, its reintegration into Asian society has been a relatively painless one. The flavor of magic practiced varies greatly by faith. For example, the priests of Shinto focus on summoning and communicating with spirits, while the Daoists of China seek knowledge that will aid them in their next lives through mysticism and alchemy. Even so, it's rare to find an Eastern religion that does not accept, revere, and make use of the magical arts in one way or another.

ISLAM

The way in which Muslims view magic depends upon which sect a believer belongs to. Largely, Islam reluctantly accepts magic, and its scholars spend much time studying it and its manifestations. The exception is the more conservative factions of both the Shi'ite and Sunni sects (including the Wahhabis), which maintain that the Qu'ran strictly forbids the practice of magic—in fact, it is a capital crime to do so in many areas these groups control.

• At least in the Middle East, those Muslims who are accepting of magic have a powerful ally—the great dragon Aden. He doesn't take kindly to anti-Awakened Islam, to the point where he wiped out Tehran back in the day in response to the Ayatollahs' call for an anti-Awakened jihad.
• Goat Foot

• Of all the flavors of Islam, probably the most accepting of magic is Sufiism, a non-sectarian sub-tradition that embraces ecstatic mysticism.
• Lyran

• Even some of the more conservative Islamic sects have occasionally been known to look the other way if the practice of magic helps their aims (especially in the cases of holy warriors). It isn't common, but these Awakened mujahedin believe they can expiate the evil they were born with by placing themselves at the service of Allah and dying in the holy cause.
• 2XL

JUDAISM

The three main theologies of Judaism accept magic as a divine gift. Orthodox Judaism allows it only for healing and defense against harmful magic and spirits. Some esoteric, ultra-Orthodox theologies with qabbalistic traditions don't restrict magical activities, nor do Conservative and Reform Judaism. All three theologies forbid magic on the Sabbath, however, and consider it a sin to use it for evil purposes. Jews consider metahumans and the Awakened to be fully equal in the eyes of God.

• When we're talking about Jewish magical traditions, we need to differentiate between Orthodox qabbalistic tradition (which is kept strictly within the faith) and the more modern, "New Age" variety that keeps turning up in the media and that pretty much anybody can pick up.
• Axis Mundi

NEO-PAGANISM

The neo-pagan religions (Wicca or witchcraft, Druidism, Asatru, Native American spirituality, and similar faiths) experienced a significant resurgence following the Awakening, due at least in part to the fact that the magic and wonder-working that formerly had to be taken on faith by many believers now became visible and tangible to all. These days, you can find neo-pagan adherents almost everywhere, including most of the formerly monotheistic lands of North America and Europe. Neo-pagans embrace magic and Awakened beings, and most of them are active in metahuman rights, magical rights, and eco-activist organizations.

NEW RELIGIONS

Many new religions have popped up in the wake of the return of magic and while many of them appear and disappear so quickly that they barely have time to gather converts, some have exhibited remarkable staying power. Examples of some of the more long-lived of these organizations are the Church of the Whole Earth (a liberal, pantheistic organization focused strongly on Gaia, the Mother Goddess), and the Children of the Dragon (who appeared following the assassination of the great dragon Dunkelzahn and who worship the "Great Dragon Spirit").

MAGIC AND THE CORPS

Magic is a fact of life in the corporate world, like it or not. Though as a whole they prefer to focus on things that are easier to quantify (and control), no large corporation can afford to turn its back on the magical arts—not with as many lucrative opportunities as these arts offer to those who make an effort to understand and employ them. Like individual people, though, corporations vary in their view of magic—some embrace it, sponsoring cutting-edge research and employing its methods to help them achieve their aims, while others view it as almost a necessary evil, a useful tool but essentially an afterthought when compared to the corporation's more important pursuits. As you might guess, most megacorporations fall somewhere in the middle of this spectrum.

First, let's discuss what corporations *do* with magic, and then we'll have a brief overview of some of the notable megacorps and their magical pursuits.

CORPORATE MOJO

Magic has many uses in a corporate environment; the most pervasive is in the area of security. Even those corps that don't concentrate much on magic know that it would be foolish to ignore potential magically-based threats from outside influences (like shadowrunners, industrial spies, and saboteurs), so almost every corp retains or out-sources a small staff of Awakened employees whose purpose is to keep these threats out. Common magical security techniques include spirits and astral patrols, wards and natural barriers (such as plants) to prevent entry by astral means, and the use of paracritters as guard animals around building perimeters. In addition, the magicians themselves are quite effective in dealing with intruders directly with their spells (lethal or otherwise, depending on things like extraterritoriality laws and how charitable the corp is feeling that day).

• It might be worth mentioning the sorts of things it's reasonable to expect nonmagical corpsec grunts to know about magic, since the reality is that many sec-teams don't even include a magician. Most of these teams (at least the ones working for the big corps) are trained in basic magical threat response, things like staying out of line of sight, limiting visibility, not clumping together to make themselves sitting ducks, and identifying the opposing magician(s) so they can take them out first. Some are even trained to spot the signs of spellcasting and recognize the "shiver" of an astral form passing through your aura. Teams well versed in magical theory are rare, but it's reasonable to expect that the bush-league stuff isn't going to catch them by surprise.
• DangerSensei

Security is by no means the only way corps employ magic, however. Those who have a stronger presence in the magical arena rake in serious nuyen from producing magical goods, distributing formulae, and providing thaumaturgical services of all types. Most of major players maintain secret labs where they

conduct cutting-edge research into magical techniques and goods (always with an eye on the bottom line, of course).

- One thing to point out here: This makes it sound like magical stuff is produced on an assembly line by a bunch of robots and factory workers. Nothing could be further from the truth. The production of any magical gear worth its price is a slow and careful process demanding skilled labor. Any corp that figured out a way to automate it would make a fortune (at least before the market got flooded), but so far nobody's done it yet.
- Lyran

- As far as corp magicians go: if you're good and you can stomach working for the Man, most of these folks have it made. It's said that a talented magician is harder to replace than a senior exec, and I believe it. That's why corp magicians are so often the targets of extraction attempts—and many of them don't mind, since all they care about is their research. They don't care who signs the checks as long as they get to keep their cushy lives.
- Cosmo

- This file kinda implies that corporate magic is all cloak-and-dagger secret-lab stuff. There are a *lot* of magicians out there, and most of them want to buy stuff—formulae, foci, talismans, metamagical techniques, fetishes, manatech goodies, and all sorts of other everyday magical products. Somebody's got to produce them, and it's not all weird old women in their attics. Magical goods are big business, and corps are always racing to develop the next big thing.
- Fatima

One other sector where magic is big in the corporate world is the entertainment and fashion industries. The trid and sim trades are constantly scouring university magical programs looking to snap up talent to feed their never-ending need for bigger and better special effects. In many cases it's cheaper to pay a few magicians to toss around some showy effects than it is to produce them virtually, but that doesn't mean the magicians don't make a good living.

THE BIG PLAYERS

Every megacorporation focuses on magic to a greater or lesser degree, depending on their priorities and the wishes of their top management. All major corporations also subsidize and sponsor research think tanks and university programs in exchange for options on R&D developments and the first pick of promising talents. Here is a brief rundown on the top magical megas and their *mojo operandi*:

Aztechnology

AZT is probably one of the two names that come to mind when you think of corps that focus heavily on magic. The Azzies have their fingers in just about every magic-related pie: magical security, mystical goods, general magical services, entertainment magic, and research. Expect a good chunk of your lore store supplies to have been produced by an Azzie subsidiary.

Saeder-Krupp

Nobody's dumb enough to believe that a corporation headed by a great dragon isn't going to be a heavy hitter in the magical arena, right? S-K's magical research labs are nearly unrivalled in the corp sector, and they're also known for their high quality magical aids: spell formulae, metamagical techniques, and enchanting processes. They also sponsor initiatory groups and, while they focus on hermetics, they employ a surprisingly high number of shamans and other "nonstandard" (in a corp environment) magical types. Subsidiaries Awakened World Research and the Spellweaver Consortium are leading lights in various fields of thaumaturgical development.

Mitsuhama

One of the undisputed leaders in the area of magic, MCT is the second-largest producer (after Aztechnology) of magical goods and services. Though they are primarily seen as a technology corporation, like AZT they're involved in almost every area of magical commerce. Mitsuhama's Thaumaturgical Research Division is behind some of the most significant breakthroughs in metamagical development in recent years, and Pentagram Publishing leads the pack in licensing proprietary spell formulae as well as academic and professional publications.

Wuxing

Though they started life as a finance and shipping concern, Wuxing has made a reputation as the "mystical" corporation. This transformation owes largely to bequests from the great dragon Dunkelzahn and events surrounding the Year of the Comet—since then, this Chinese corp has turned its focus more and more toward things magical while still remaining strong in its original pursuits. Wuxing's top projects include alchemical materials and supplies, telesma distribution, and security and general services. They are also the driving force behind many non-hermetic research and publishing groups.

- These are indeed the major players, but don't let this imply that the others aren't active in the magical realm. It's rumored, for example, that Horizon is investing heavily in magical applications for entertainment and marketing, while Shiawase has recently launched a new operation around the containment of dangerous magical byproducts. And with Celedyr in charge of R&D for NeoNET, you'd be a fool to believe that they aren't working on some projects. Transys Neuronet was doing heavy-duty research into the magic-technology interface pre-merger, and I doubt that's stopped just because the Big C has a different logo on his business card.
- Ethernaut

SMALL BUT MIGHTY

Despite what you've read above, don't go away with the idea that everybody who's anybody in magical research works for a corporation with three A's in its rating. The fact is, more than a bit of the cutting edge work in the field is coming out of the labs and testing facilities of some of the smaller fish in the pond, including these bright lights:

Alchemix

This little Czech corp came out of nowhere a couple of years back, introducing the market to no less than two entirely new metamagical foci and a handful of patented mana-technologies. Alchemix has since made a name for itself as the brand to trust for reliable and quality alchemical supplies—and sorcery foci as well. Capitalizing on its contacts in parascientific and academic circles, it has scooped up several supply contracts for universities and independent corporations with its reputation for innovation and unique magical applications.

o Rumor has it that the founders are old Charles University alumni and former students of Prof. Schwartzkopf (yes, the great dragon). That might explain where the initial investment and cutting-edge R&D is coming from.
o 2XL

Manadyne Corporation

Headquartered in Boston, UCAS, Manadyne has the advantage of proximity to some of the best magical universities in North America, including MIT&T, Harvard, and many others in and around the Boston megaplex. They must be doing something right, since they've been coming out with a steady stream of spell designs, metamagical techniques, and other thaumaturgical tricks for years with no sign of slowing down any time soon. Following dual financial shots in the arm a decade or so ago resulting from their success in dealing with the insect spirit problem and their inclusion in Dunkelzahn's will, they've been pushing the magical envelope ever since.

o Nobody ever found out what was up with their former CEO, Dr. Carolyn Winter. Rumors flew for years, saying that she was everything from a free spirit or a dragon in disguise to an insect spirit (I even heard that some people claimed she'd died and been possessed by a master shedim) but following her disappearance in 2069 nobody's been able to track her down. Too bad, really—I'd like to have known the details.
o Cosmo

Xerxes Positive Research

Xerxes was in limbo for a while following the disintegration of its parent megacorp, Cross Applied Technologies, but the oddball "pure research" company is back in business and churning out weird magical goodies (among other things) at its Mendocino labs under the wide umbrella of former rival Ares Macrotechnology.

o I don't know how reliable this is, but I've heard vague rumors that Xerxes is working with the Welsh "Sea Dragon"—something to do with the "Neptune's Net" bequest they received form the late-president Dunkelzahn. I haven't been able to get even a whiff of what they're doing or what the net is all about, but given those bedfellows it's not hard to make guesses.
o Snopes

MAGIC IN THE SHADOWS
by Fatima

Okay, so we've spent a lot of time getting the skinny on magic and its applications in various areas of society, but we all know why you're really here. Let's get to the good stuff: what can magic do for you as a shadowrunner?

Short answer: Plenty.

Maybe I'm biased, but magic is such a versatile ally for a shadowrunning team that I would never even think of going on a run without magical backup. Think about it: almost everything that the other members of a team can do, a magician can duplicate. Need super strength? A spell can take care of it. Spying? Spirits can infiltrate just about anywhere that's not warded. Reinforcements? Spirits again. Firepower? Granted, your local shaman might not be as good with the guns as your favorite samurai, but can the sammy throw lightning bolts?

Now, before anybody thinks I'm a magic snob, let me say this: everybody, whether they be samurai, hacker, rigger, adept, or whatever, has their role on a team, and a whole lot depends on the individual talents (I'd much rather run with a mediocre hacker than an incompetent mage, f'rexample). But the fact remains that when you work the shadows, mojo can mean the difference between life and death.

- Okay, that's true a lot of the time, but remember this: most magicians are more than a little strange. Everybody has their quirks, but spellslingers tend to have more than others. I don't know whether it's just all that "things man wasn't meant to know" crap or just that they know they can get away with it because they're so useful, but be prepared when you take on a new magician—and the more out-there the tradition, the weirder things are likely to get.
- 2XL

Let's take a look at some of the common areas where magical types can be useful to a shadowrunning team, as well as a more overlooked area: the shadowy infrastructure that supports (and is supported by) them.

Before the run even starts, your magical type (I'm going to call her a "mage" for brevity's sake, but just assume I mean one from any tradition) can help you by setting up astral recon around the meet site, using spells like Clairvoyance and Clairaudience to see and hear things that the team might find useful, and astrally perceiving during the meet to get a better idea of whether Johnson is planning to screw you over.

During the run itself, the mage's abilities come in even more handy: she can disguise you or your vehicle to look like something else; make you invisible; levitate you over fences, walls, and potential threats; spot hidden traps and lurking bad guys; provide offensive magic to take down your opponents and defensive magic to make sure they don't take *you* down first, and deal with spirits—both hers and the other guy's. And oh, yeah: she can heal your ass if you get it shot up. Sure, not all of them have all these spells, but good shadow-magicians will have a basic complement of them plus a lot more interesting ones besides. And I haven't even talked about adepts yet: the strength, agility, and combat capabilities of a good street samurai without all that pesky metal that keeps setting off security detectors or getting hacked by the opposition's security forces.

Once the run is over, your friendly neighborhood spellslinger shows her usefulness in other areas: keeping you out of the hospital or at least shortening your stay with her healing spells; changing your appearance (temporarily or permanently) to take the heat off you; and even manipulating the mind of the Lone Star cop who's pulled you over as you make your getaway (and if she's good, you'll get off without even a ticket).

- We need a clarification here, before people start thinking that magicians are some kind of super-versatile jacks-of-all-trades who can do everything but clean your oven. Since time and resources are limited, most shadowrunning magicians focus on one or two areas of expertise: surveillance, conjuring, healing, offensive abilities, subterfuge, or some other magical skill that's useful to a team. It's very rare to find magicians who can do everything, and those who can usually don't do any of it very well. Keep this in mind when you're looking to hire a spellslinger for a job—make sure you're not expecting a healer and getting a spy.
- Ethernaut

So now that I've (hopefully) convinced you of the usefulness of magicians on shadowrunning teams, let's talk about infrastructure. I'll bet you never even thought about the fact that there's a whole shadowy economy around magic (and especially illegal magic), did you? It's a nice little symbiotic relationship, actually: the talisleggers acquire the raw materials and smuggle them to alchemists, the enchanters put the stuff together and create magical goodies, the talismongers buy the goodies and sell them to magicians. Runners, of course, work both ends of the pipeline. Talisleggers hire runners to obtain the rare, valuable, and sometimes dangerous raw materials, and sometimes have them smuggle the telesma into/out of areas that restrict or control them. Runners are also sometimes a talismonger's best clients, both for purchasing and also unloading any magical goods or curiosities they've "acquired" during the course of their work—whether from fallen opponents, illegally accessed research labs, or as payment from Mr. Johnson. Shadowrunners provide a steady stream of the more interesting magical items that make talismongers salivate with barely controlled avarice. It's a mutually beneficial relationship.

Finally, looking at things on a bit more of a macro level, I think we need a brief mention of the magical groups out there—or at least the ones that might be of interest to shadowrunners. Initiatory groups run the gamut from fairly single-purpose (the Bear Doctor Society, which accepts only Bear magicians and focuses on the healing arts, or the radical feminist Sie, which allows only female magicians) to broader-based (the Illuminates of the New Dawn, a magocratic organization heavily involved in politics). Whatever floats your magical boat, there's a group out there somewhere for you—and if by some chance there isn't, you can always start your own. There are definitely advantages for shadowrunning magicians to be involved in a magical group, even if it does mean paying dues and attending a few boring meetings. The first time things go to hell and you have a few loyal group members to fall back on will make all those payments and meetings worthwhile.

...THE AWAKENED CHARACTER...

"Done yet, Alex?" Janatia glanced nervously back and forth, keeping watch like a metronome.

"No!" snapped Alexandra, looking up from the loose-leaf notebook. She absently reached down and brushed the golden ankh hanging from her waist as she glared back down at the book. "Another couple minutes, Janet. The fucking sleeper spell-hack didn't exactly take organized notes. It's taking me longer to scan his scribblings than I thought."

Janatia's response was to mutter under her breath, step over the dead researcher's body, and cast a spell. The back of Alexandra's neck tingled—she wasn't sure what the shaman was casting, but it was powerful, and she hoped it didn't trigger any magical defenses. Just because the dead man was a mundane didn't mean he couldn't write a good spell, or that he wouldn't have some mystic defenses around his office. *It always takes the young ones so long to discover the value of subtlety,* she sighed to herself. *You don't always call up the most powerful mojo at your disposal just because you can.*

She'll learn soon enough, thought the street witch as she resumed scanning the contents of the notebook into her commlink. She kept fingering her ankh with her free hand, drawing comfort out of the cold metal. Nothing had gone right since she came back to Seattle, and this latest bit of business was no different. *Please gods, let something go right ...*

Brax suddenly cocked his head and drew his pistol. "We got trouble, boss," the ork said sharply. "System's on alert. It won't be long before they send—" The echo of gunfire in the hallway cut him off.

So much for the power of prayer, Alex thought. Before she could get a word out, Pilgrim exploded into the room, guns out, moving so fast he bowled over Janatia.

"They're here!" Pilgrim yelled. He grabbed a desk and heaved, leaping over it as it crashed into the floor. He snatched Janatia and pulled the shaman back with him. A stampede of bullets from beyond the doorway followed, splintering Pilgrim's shelter.

Alex was already moving, the notebook splayed at her feet, her hand firmly on her ankh. She snapped it from her belt and held it high, a spell forming in her mind.

The rites spun through her mind like a cyclone, but just as she was about to release the power she had called to her, a bullet cut a sharp trail of ice across her hand, and the ankh fell. The threads of mana she had been weaving evaporated, the formula fled her mind, and she abruptly felt as vulnerable as a squirrel on a highway. *Oh, shit ...*

She dropped down on all fours, hands scrambling for the ankh. More bullets zipped past her as Pilgrim and Brax fired blindly into the hallway to provide cover. She closed her eyes as she fumbled on the floor, letting the ankh tell her where it was. Her right hand made a sudden lunge, guided by something beyond conscious thought, digging under a credenza until it touched familiar metal. A fire behind Alexandra's eyes flared into life. She sprang up, and the words of incantation exploded from her mouth. She pointed at the guards down the hallway, and they immediately fell to the ground before her in stunned unconsciousness.

Well, she thought, as she surveyed her handiwork, *at least that* eventually *went right.*

Street Magic

Awakened characters aren't just another kind of shadowrunner. Their perspective on skills, magic, Karma, and general limitations is different from that of other *Shadowrun* characters. This chapter expands on several points players should keep in mind when creating and developing their Awakened character. It also provides a general overview of the new magical skills in this book and introduces some new qualities that may pertain to an Awakened character.

CREATING AN AWAKENED CHARACTER

Players create Awakened characters using the Build Point system, same as any other character. To be Awakened, a character must possess either the Adept, Magician, or Mystic Adept quality. When creating an Awakened character, players should keep two things in mind.

First, the Awakened comprise the smallest minority of the world's population. Less than one percent of the Sixth World's populace even has the potential to use magic. Of that one percent, only a fraction has the training, focus, or discipline to use it effectively; the rest either go mad trying or spend their entire lives ignorant of the power at their fingertips.

The rarity of the Awakened makes them valuable, but it also makes them feared; they are Different with a capital "D." A corporation will put up with a lot of crap from a wage mage that would normally be grounds for termination (employment or otherwise) for even a high-ranking mundane employee. Since Awakened employees are hard to come by, corps and other organizations (the governments, the syndicates, even the runners) have to take what they can get. But they also watch their magical assets like a hawk, playing one off another so as to keep some semblance of control. Corps may have to put up with them, but they don't have to trust these mavericks.

The second point to keep in mind is that the Awakened live in a world mere mundanes can't understand, and they perceive things of which mundanes remain blissfully unaware. They've seen things ordinary people wouldn't believe. Trying to order one's life according to the rules magicians follow is a rapid one-way trip to the nuthouse. It's a world that only another Awakened can even begin to comprehend, so they seek out each other's company to commiserate and make sense of it all.

METATYPE

Awakened characters can be of any metatype, and characters of any metatype can follow any magical tradition. Despite what certain racists may say, magic doesn't discriminate (which may explain why they fear it so).

Generally speaking, dwarfs make good magicians all around, as their better-than-normal Willpower is useful in resisting Drain. Elves can be more charismatic than other races, a trait that lends itself well toward traditions favoring the Charisma attribute (such as shamanism). Orks and trolls make good adepts because of their higher Physical attributes, but they can just as easily become skilled (and tough) magicians.

ATTRIBUTES

Without a doubt, the most fundamental attribute for an Awakened character is Magic; without it, they can do nothing. However, other attributes are also important to an Awakened character. Next to Magic, Willpower is also crucial. Not only is it one of the two attributes used to resist Drain, it also plays a role in many tests a magician may face. Further, Willpower is useful for trying to resist certain magical effects and attacks. The other Mental attributes (Logic, Intuition, Charisma) may also be important, depending on the tradition chosen for the magician. For adepts and mystic adepts, certain Physical attributes may help in the use of certain adept powers.

SKILLS

Magicians rely primarily on the Conjuring and Sorcery skill groups and the component skills within both groups. Beginning players should purchase these skill groups as a whole, as their all-around usefulness will help new players understand how magic works in *Shadowrun*. More experienced players, on the other hand, may find that certain skills in the skill group are more useful to them or their character concept than others, so they may instead purchase skills individually so as to attain higher levels of expertise.

Of the skills in the Sorcery skill group, perhaps the one a magician will rely on more than others is Spellcasting, as it is the skill that actually makes things happen. Counterspelling is also important, as it allows a magician to actively defeat a spell cast by an opposing magician. Characters whose concept revolves around anti-magic defense may find Counterspelling more important than Spellcasting in this regard. Newcomers to *Shadowrun* might initially find Ritual Spellcasting the least useful, due to its lengthy casting time; however, over time it will prove its value, as Ritual Spellcasting allows magicians to cast a spell without having to see the target, thanks to material or symbolic links (see p. 29).

Within the Conjuring skill group, Summoning and Binding are the most useful, in that magicians can obtain help from a spirit. Though both accomplish the same end (spirit services), they do it in different manner: a magician can use Summoning on the fly for immediate help, but he has the spirit's aid for a limited time. Binding, on the other hand, is an arduous and demanding process, but if successful the magician has command over the spirit for an indefinite time period. Banishing is another skill in the Conjuring skill group that should not be overlooked, as it allows a magician to forcibly dismiss a bound or summoned spirit, either one in service to an enemy magician or one of the magician's own that has gone uncontrolled.

Assensing and Astral Combat are useful to those magicians interested in the astral plane. Assensing allows a magician to read auras and see things as they really are. Astral Combat is essential in fighting the various threats and dangers residing on the astral plane, and it also gives the magician a new approach to fighting magical foes in the material world.

Two new skills, Arcana and Enchanting, are also presented in *Street Magic* (see p. 24). Both deal with the creation of magical goods: spells and formulae in the case of Arcana, and foci, fetishes, and other ritual materials in the case of Enchanting.

Take note that unlike other magical skills, Arcana can also be used to a limited degree by non-magical characters, giving them an added role in the magical world.

QUALITIES

To be Awakened, a character must purchase the Adept, Magician, or Mystic Adept quality. Additional qualities that players may purchase to tailor their characters more to the players' conceptions also appear later in this chapter (see p. 24). The type of quality that a character takes affects the options available to the character, both initially in character creation and later through advancement.

Magicians

By and large, the Magician quality is the most versatile, as it gives the character access to both sorcery and conjuring, as well as unrestricted access to astral space. Magicians also receive the largest share of metamagic options. Magicians fit in very well with any magically related character concept.

The standard model for magicians is that of a "general practitioner," capable of doing everything. Covering all those options, however, takes time and energy; you can become master of everything, but it's not going to happen overnight.

There are ways to make a magician more of a specialist. The Aspected Magician quality featured in this book (p. 26) narrows the focus of a magician's practice, allowing him to concentrate on those magical skills or spell or spirit categories that really matter to him. Alternatively, a magician can choose to ignore undesired or unwanted magical skills. Since magical skills cannot be defaulted, a magician without them is effectively powerless in those areas. Not spending BPs in undesired areas leaves more BPs available to be spent in those that are desired.

Mystic Adepts

Mystic adepts possess the second most versatile of the three qualities. Like magicians, they also have access to sorcery and conjuring. Unlike magicians, however, they have no access to astral space, but instead they gain access to adept powers. (In fact, they can gain some limited astral accessibility, as they can purchase Astral Perception as an adept power, though they cannot project.)

As mystic adepts are a hybrid of both adepts and magicians, so too are their roles a hybrid of magician and adept roles. You can play mystic adepts as magicians more grounded in the material world, turning away from the astral in favor of mastery over the physical. Like magicians, mystic adepts are general practitioners of magic, but they can also specialize as magicians can, either by using the Aspected Magician quality or by ignoring magical skills that don't fit their concept.

Alternately, you can choose to play a mystic adept as an adept that is turned more towards the arcane. In this perspective, spellcraft supplements adept powers to allow mystic adepts to do things normal adepts can't. Furthermore, conjuring abilities combined with various animal empathy powers can make a mystic adept a frightening beastmaster, ordering both physical and astral creatures to do his will.

Adepts

Of the three qualities, adepts are the least versatile, as they cannot use sorcery or conjuring, and they cannot access astral space (unless they divert points into purchasing the Astral Perception power). This does not mean, however, that adepts are one-dimensional "magical street samurai" with no opportunity to specialize or diversify. Many adept abilities have nothing whatsoever to do with combat, allowing adepts to perform physical feats no normal person could. Some adept abilities are geared toward the social arena, allowing adepts to become mystical faces, capable of smooth-talking even the most recalcitrant opponent. And while adepts may not use magic directly, their powers are nevertheless still effective against magical threats, making them useful in a "ghost hunter" type of role.

MAGIC AND TECHNOLOGY

The Sixth World is often described as a place "where man meets magic *and* machine." Magic and technology are generally incompatible, but people have found ways to put them together in uneasy coexistence.

Cyberware

Awakened characters may possess as much cyberware or other implants as the player wants; the primary caution against this is that implants (whether synthetic cyberware or organic bioware) upset the delicate balance of body, mind, and spirit needed to manipulate mana. Nevertheless some Awakened characters choose to accept a little cyberware to help them out in their work or daily life. Datajacks and internal commlinks are especially common among wage mages, who work frequently with computer information systems, and some adepts let themselves be enticed by the lure of the unique combat boosts offered by cyberware.

The Matrix

Awakened characters use computers and interact with the Matrix, just like any other character. Plenty of Awakened characters even dabble a little in hacking on the side. Very few, however, learn the in-depth programming and design skills necessary for a first-rate hacker. Doing so consumes time that could be spent honing magical talent. Conversely, time and effort spent perfecting one's magecraft is time and effort *not* spent improving one's codeslinging.

Regardless of magical tradition or training, no magical abilities work directly on augmented reality (AR) or virtual reality (VR) objects. The virtuality of the Matrix offers no substance on which a character can use magic; magicians cannot cast spells, summon spirits, or perform any other magical task while fully immersed in virtual reality. Adept powers don't work directly against virtual reality objects either (though it should be noted that powers such as Improved Ability that affect the adept himself, rather than things external to the adept, are still effective). Awakened characters cannot astrally perceive while in virtual reality, and magicians attempting to project while still immersed must make an Intuition + Willpower (3) Test to leave their bodies.

In augmented reality, where physical and virtual objects coexist side-by-side, magicians don't have it as bad. Magicians can function in augmented reality and make full use of their magical abilities—just not against augmented reality objects. AR objects can, however, block line of sight or provide sensory distractions that may throw off a magician's concentration or timing.

Note that it is impossible to perceive both augmented reality *and* astral space simultaneously. As noted on p. 191 of *SR4A*, astrally perceiving characters are not viewing physical objects, but rather reflections of physical objects on the astral plane. These reflections, however, lack detail, as some of them do not translate over into astral space. Unfortunately, augmented reality is one of those things lost in the translation into the astral plane.

In either augmented or virtual reality, magicians may have access to sensor systems (such as a drone's sensors). As with the rest of the Matrix, sensors offer no help to magicians in their craft. A magician cannot use magic against characters that she sees via a remote sensor feed. She must be able to see the target with her own eyes (as well as visual enhancements paid with Essence), not the artificial surrogate of sensors. Unlike cyber-implant sensors (like cybereyes), remote sensor feeds cost no Essence, so they have no link for the magician to channel mana.

Karma

Magic places significant demands on player characters' Karma. While other characters save up Karma, spend it to buy skills, or maybe raise an Attribute or two, the Awakened use Karma for *everything*. They burn Karma in the core rules learning new spells, bonding foci, and initiating. This book gives them even more ways to lavish it on conjuring more powerful spirits, casting more potent magic, and mastering more arcane metamagic. The reason for this is that a character progresses in the magical arts through dedication, experience, and luck—in other words, Karma. Those who spend Karma on non-magical affairs fall behind the curve fairly quickly, making themselves less effective magicians or adepts.

NEW AWAKENED SKILLS

The following descriptions provide a brief overview of the new skills introduced in this book. For information on skills in general, consult the *Skills* chapter in *SR4A*, beginning on p. 118.

ARCANA (LOGIC)

Arcana governs the practical aspects of a tradition's magical theory and the application of magic in creative new ways. Characters use the Arcana skill to develop new spell and magical foci formulae from scratch (rather than learning someone else's tricks) and to produce all types of spirit formulae. Initiates may also use Arcana to decipher the symbolism and meaning of visions induced by the Divining metamagic (see p. 56).

Note that mundanes as well as Awakened can learn Arcana. Though they can't put their formulations into practice, non-magical characters can design formulae just as well as magicians—in fact, some of the best spell formulators in the Sixth World are mundanes or burnouts with no magical ability.
Default: No
Skill Group: None
Specializations: Spell Design (by spell category), Focus Design (by focus type), Ally Spirit Formula, Free Spirit Formula

ENCHANTING (MAGIC)

Enchanting comprises the techniques needed to harness the latent magical potency in natural materials and the artificing of magical foci used to assist magic performance. It also includes the creation and preparation of spirit vessels and the evaluation of magical goods. See *Enchanting 101*, p. 79.

Only characters with the Adept, Magician, or Mystic Adept qualities and a Magic attribute of 1 or more may use this skill.
Default: No
Skill Group: None
Specializations: Artificing, Alchemy, Vessel Preparation

NEW AWAKENED QUALITIES

Listed below are some new qualities that are available to Awakened characters if the gamemaster approves. For more information on qualities in general, consult the *Qualities* section, p. 90, *SR4A*. Unless otherwise specified, a character must possess the Adept, Magician, or Mystic Adept qualities to obtain any of these.

POSITIVE QUALITIES

The following positive qualities are available to Awakened characters.

Astral Sight
Cost: 5 BP

Astral Sight grants mundane characters the ability to perceive into the astral plane. This quality is not available to characters who possess the Adept, Latent Awakening, Magician, Mystic Adept, or Technomancer qualities. This quality may only be taken during character creation and cannot be obtained using Karma.

Characters taking this quality acquire a Magic attribute of 1 that may *not* be increased during character creation or raised with Karma. This Magic point is, however, subject to normal rules for the impact of Essence loss on Magic. Characters with Astral Sight may perceive into the astral plane just like magicians (see p. 191, *SR4A*) and may also learn the Assensing and Astral Combat skills. They are unable to use any other aspect of magical talent besides astral perception, so they cannot learn or use Sorcery, Conjuring, or Enchanting. Characters with this quality may undergo initiation for the purposes of learning metamagics related to astral assensing or combat, such as Flexible Signature, Masking, Psychometry, and Sensing (see *Metamagic*, p. 52). Characters may bond with weapon foci, but bonus dice from these foci only apply during astral combat.

Latent Awakening

Cost: 5 BP

A character who takes the Latent Awakening quality starts the game as a mundane but may Awaken later and become magically active. At the start of the game, the character does not possess a Magic attribute and may not invest BPs in magical skills, spells, or bound spirits. The character may not have the Adept, Astral Sight, Magician, Mystic Adept, or Spell/Spirit Knack quality.

At some point during gameplay, the gamemaster may decide that the character Awakens. This decision is completely in the gamemaster's hands, and should be based entirely on creating a good story—and if the player is surprised, even better. Keep in mind that this is a chance for the player to roleplay the process of becoming magical—it should be a slow path filled with confusion, fear, and the sudden awareness of an entirely new world. It should *not* be viewed as a get-badass-quick power boost. The character is not likely to understand how to use or control his powers at first, and may need to seek the guidance of others.

When the gamemaster decides the character has Awakened, the character immediately gains a Magic attribute of 1. If the character has an Essence lower than 6 (due to implants or other causes), he still starts with a Magic of 1, but his maximum Magic attribute is adjusted according to the Essence loss. If the character's Essence is less than 1, he has lost any chance to be Awakened.

The gamemaster also chooses either the Adept, Astral Sight, Magician, Mystic Adept, or Spell/Spirit Knack quality, and immediately applies it to the character. This quality defines how the character has Awakened. The gamemaster should not, however, tell the player which quality the character has gained until the character figures it out for himself. This quality does not come free, of course. The character must pay for the quality with Karma, at a cost of (the quality's BP Cost – 5) x 2. For example, the Mystic Adept quality would cost 10 Karma (10 BP – 5 = 5, x 2). If the character does not have Karma available at that time, the gamemaster immediately collects it from any Karma rewards he earns until the debt is paid off.

The gamemaster may also choose one spell, adept power, or spirit type (as appropriate for the character's tradition) for the character to start with. It is highly possible that this is the magical power that character expresses when he Awakens. Keep in mind that many Awakenings occur as a result of stress—losing a loved one, being attacked, and so on. The character will not know how to cast this spell, conjure this spirit, or use that power until he has had proper training, of course—it is merely an accidental expression of the character's Talent, controlled entirely by the gamemaster. The gamemaster can, in fact, treat the character as if he has the Cursed quality (p. 26) for a limited period (and without the bonus BP), until he gets his magic under control.

If the gamemaster allows it, the character may also acquire other Magic-required qualities when he Awakens, such as the Mentor Spirit quality. The gamemaster chooses which qualities (positive or negative) to apply. These qualities must also be paid for—simply add the BP cost of all qualities together before subtracting 5 and multiplying by 2 for the Karma cost, as noted above.

Once the character has Awakened, he may learn and improve the Magic attribute, magical skills, spells, and other magical abilities normally, as dictated by his type of Awakening.

Spell/Spirit Knack

Cost: 5 BP

Characters with spell or spirit knacks have an *extremely* limited magical ability: the ability to cast only *one* spell, or summon *one* spirit. This quality may not be taken by characters who also possess the Adept, Latent Awakening, Magician, Mystic Adept, or Technomancer quality. This quality may only be taken during character creation and cannot be obtained using Karma.

When a character takes this quality, he gains a Magic attribute of 1 that may *not* be increased at character creation or raised with Karma. It is, however, subject to normal rules for the impact of Essence loss on Magic. The player must declare whether this knack is a spell knack or a spirit knack, and the one specific spell or spirit the character can affect. The character uses either the Sorcery or Conjuring skills (as appropriate) as normal, and either skill group or sub-skills are learned and improved as normal. Note, however, that Counterspelling and Banishing are also limited by the character's knack and will not affect other spells or spirits. Characters with knacks may initiate, but considering how rare knacks are to begin with, a knack initiate is practically unheard of. Characters with knacks cannot interact with astral space (unless the character also has the Astral Sight quality, though this is discouraged).

A character may only take the Knack quality *once*. Lenient gamemasters may consider allowing a character to possess both one *spell* knack and one *spirit* knack, but this is generally not recommended.

Spirit Pact

Cost: Spirit's Edge x 5 BP

The Awakened character has entered into a pact with a free spirit, which uses part of its spiritual essence to augment the character's magical power, stave off Drain, sustain the character's life, and so on. The specific nature of the pact should be discussed with the gamemaster and is subject to his approval. The cost of this quality depends on the Edge of the free spirit that has made the pact. For more information on spirit pacts, see p. 108.

NEGATIVE QUALITIES

The following negative qualities are available to Awakened characters, providing bonus BPs for assisting character creation.

Aspected Magician

Bonus: 5 to 10 BP

An aspected magician is focused in his power, able to perform fine in some categories of magic, yet much worse in everything else. This quality is only available to characters who possess the Magician or Mystic Adept qualities.

When a character takes this quality, the player must declare how his magic is aspected. When a character is performing magic that is not favored by his aspect, he suffers a –4 dice pool modifier. There should be an equally fair chance of an aspect occurring as not occurring.

Note that this quality may not be taken with the Incompetent quality (p. 95, *SR4A*) for any magic skills not covered by the character's aspect. It is also recommended that characters who also have the Mentor Spirit quality (p. 92, *SR4A*) only be allowed to choose an aspect that fits with their mentor spirit's advantages and disadvantages.

Listed below are several examples of aspected magic:

Conjuror Aspect (5 BP): The magician is aspected towards spirits. The magician uses the Conjuring skill group and its component skills, but he receives a –4 dice pool modifier to Sorcery, Assensing, Astral Combat, and Enchanting (and to Arcana for anything but ally design).

Sorcerer Aspect (5 BP): The magician's magic is aspected towards spellcraft. The magician can use the Sorcery skill group and its component skills normally, but he receives a –4 dice pool modifier to Conjuring, Assensing, Astral Combat, and Enchanting (and to Arcana for anything but spell design).

Spell/Spirit Aspect (10 BP): The magician is aspected towards a specific spell category/spirit correspondence of the tradition he follows. The character can cast spells or conjure spirits of that category normally, but suffers a –4 dice pool modifier for all other spell/spirit correspondences, as well as Assensing, Astral Combat, and Enchanting (and to Arcana for anything other than that spell/spirit correspondence).

Astral Aspect (10 BP): The magician can use Assensing and Astral Combat as normal, but he receives a –4 dice pool modifier for Sorcery, Conjuring, Enchanting, and Arcana.

Enchanter Aspect (10 BP): The magician can use Enchanting and Arcana as normal, but he receives a –4 dice pool modifier for Sorcery, Conjuring, Assensing, and Astral Combat.

Cursed

Bonus: 5 BP per rating (max rating 4)

Cursed characters seem to have a love-hate relationship with magic. Though they are Awakened, magic has a way of turning against them—spells go wrong, spirits get upset, wards collapse, and adept powers fizzle. For every 5 BP gained with this quality, reduce the number of 1s necessary to get a glitch (p. 62, *SR4A*) whenever that character is using magic. For example, a dice pool of 6 and the Cursed quality at rating 2 would trigger a glitch if a single 1 is rolled on the test. The gamemaster may also require the character to make a test for operations that would otherwise succeed automatically (such as passing through a ward the character created himself), simply to see whether or not a glitch occurs.

When describing the effects of a Curse-induced glitch, gamemasters should play up the oddity of the magical mishap. A magician summoning a water spirit might suddenly find his clothes on fire, or an adept with Improved Reflexes might suddenly find that his shoelaces are inexplicably tied together. Note that Cursed is a Negative quality—its effects should be hindering to the character (and entertaining to others). The Cursed quality should not be seen as an "offensive ability" where the character can cause wards to collapse by touching them. The character is the one Cursed—if he's hoping for one effect, the opposite should occur.

Focus Addiction

Bonus: 5 to 30 BP

Focus Addiction is a variant of the regular Addiction quality (p. 93, *SR4A*). A magician or adept who relies too much

on the power granted by foci eventually forms a mental and spiritual dependence on them, even to the point of becoming magically impotent when they are dormant or missing.

Note that if a character has a focus addiction, this assumes that the character has *already* bonded to at least one focus. Players should keep this in mind, as the gamemaster may require the player to spend BPs on buying and bonding foci. Buying and bonding foci isn't necessarily *required*, however; it's theoretically possible that a starting character could be addicted to foci he once had in the past, but is no longer presently bonded to, for whatever reason (players will likely need a good reason if they're going to convince the gamemaster). Of course, if this is the case, then the character begins play under the effects of withdrawal.

Mild (5 BP): At this level of addiction, few magicians recognize they have a problem. Mild focus addicts keep their foci active more often and use them regardless of whether they need the extra power or not. Some magicians begin to experience a euphoric psychosomatic "crackle" as they tap into foci. The addict suffers a –2 dice pool modifier to Focus Addiction Tests, Drain Tests, and to resist using foci.

Moderate (10 BP): The addiction at this level is marked— the magician refuses to take off or turn off foci under any circumstances, and many become obsessed with gaining more foci to supplement their abilities. Magicians at this level of addiction may become inebriated with power after magical activities, and while recovering from Drain often exhibit mood swings and slurred speech. The addict suffers a –4 dice pool modifier to Focus Addiction Tests, Drain Tests, and to resist using foci.

Severe (20 BP): Magicians at this level of addiction are out of control, constantly using their magical abilities to tap into the foci. Many addicts begin to neglect their physical bodies in a blasphemous parody of ascetic principles. The inebriation experienced in earlier addiction gives way to momentary relief from the aching loss of not using foci. Some addicts turn to drugs or BTLs to compensate for when they are too drained to use magic. The addict suffers a –6 dice pool modifier to Focus Addiction Tests, Drain Tests, and to resist using foci.

Burnout (30 BP): This is the same as a Severe addiction, except the addict has been in this state for some time and is experiencing the tell-tale signs of habitual use on his aura. Using foci at this level of addiction is physically painful for the addict, but even this comes as welcome relief from the hell the character's body has become. Reduce the character's maximum Magic attribute by 1. If the character does not kick the habit soon, he will continue to lose Magic at a rate determined by the gamemaster until he burns out.

Geas
Bonus: 10 BP

Geas (plural *geasa*) means "bond" in old Gaelic. In *Shadowrun*, a geas is a restriction an Awakened character voluntarily imposes on his own magical power. Perhaps he could never fully embrace the radical world paradigm of the Awakened, and the geas is a symbolic gesture to establish one last tie to reality. Or perhaps he may have suffered a traumatic loss of power, and he made up the geas to reassure himself that he's still got the touch. Regardless of the reason, if an Awakened character cannot fulfill the terms of the geas, then he finds it harder to manipulate magic, effectively becoming less powerful.

When the character takes this quality, he must declare what type of restriction his geas imposes. A geas must be something that affects *all* of an Awakened character's magical abilities and should not duplicate an existing limitation. If the geas consists of a special action, the character must have performed it within the past 24 hours to fulfill the geas. Likewise, if the geas consists of avoiding an action, then it is broken for 24 hours after the character performs the act. (This type of action must be ordinary and normally necessary in the character's life; avoiding a special circumstance that occurs infrequently with no hardship to the character isn't much of a limitation.) A character may take the Geas quality multiple times, each time specifying a different condition.

If a character breaks the terms of his geas, then his Magic attribute is effectively reduced by 1 point until the geas is again fulfilled. If a character has taken multiple geasa, breaking one geas breaks *all* of them, and the Magic loss is equal to the total of *all* geasa taken. If breaking geasa reduces the character's Magic to zero or less, the character temporarily loses the ability to use *any* magic and effectively becomes mundane. An adept whose Magic is reduced by not fulfilling a geas must choose 1 full Power Point worth of adept powers per geas; these powers will not function if any of the geasa are not fulfilled and the adept's Magic is reduced. Mystic adepts must also specify if Magic loss from breaking a geas affects their magic skills or adept powers.

Awakened characters crippled by broken geasa are in a dangerous position, as there is a real chance that such a loss could become permanent. If a character suffers a crisis of confidence while a geas is broken, Magic losses from geasa become permanent (see *Acquiring Geasa During Play*, p. 30).

If the gamemaster allows it, geasa may be worked off with effort and karma in the same way as other Negative qualities (see p. 271, *SR4A*).

Listed below are some common examples of geasa that characters can impose on themselves:

Condition Geas: You must specify a personal condition to do magic. For example, you must be astrally perceiving, unwounded, sitting in the lotus position, drunk, and so on. When you're not in this condition, the geas is broken.

Fasting Geas: If the character eats, drinks, or accepts any nourishment other than water, this geas is broken for the next 24 hours.

Gesture Geas: This geas requires the character to gesture visibly and freely to work magic. (This does not require the character to spend an additional action; it's part and parcel of the appropriate Magical Skill Test.) If the character is tied up, cuffed, paralyzed, or otherwise unable to move hands and arms, the geas is broken. A variation of this geas is dancing, which also requires the character to be able to move his legs and body.

Incantation Geas: The character has to speak, chant, or sing in a loud voice to make magic. If the character is gagged,

has lost his voice, or otherwise cannot speak clearly and audibly, the geas is broken.

Location Geas: You specify a location where your magic works. Most urban types, for example, choose the city. In any other area, the geas is broken.

Mentor's Geas: This geas restricts Awakened characters who follow a mentor spirit to performing only magic that provides a dice advantage. For example, a magician following Dog could only cast Detection spells and summon spirits of man while fulfilling the geas. Doing any other magic breaks the geas. Only magicians with the Mentor Spirit quality may take this geas.

Ritual Geas: The character must have performed a specific action within the past 24 hours to fulfill this geas. For example, the character must have bathed in natural spring water, prayed towards Mecca, had sexual intercourse with a partner, or whatever. If this action hasn't been performed, the geas is broken.

Talisman Geas: The character must use a specific fetish, called a *talisman*, to perform magic (see p. 81 for rules on creating talismans). To qualify as a talisman, an item must have at least three distinct characteristics describing it (for example, "a quartz crystal set in a silver medallion, hung on a gold chain"). If the character isn't prominently holding or wearing the talisman, the geas is broken. If it is lost, confiscated, or destroyed, the character must retrieve it or get another one very similar to the original. In some cases, a talisman may be irreplaceable, such as the locket from a deceased loved one, and *must* be retrieved. If an irreplaceable talisman is destroyed, then the character suffers permanent Magic loss, as detailed below, and the geas is eliminated.

Time Geas: You specify a time when the character's magic works. If your character uses magic at any other time, the geas is broken. The time can be day or night, a single season of the year, or a specially designated time period of observance (summer, for example). Similarly, you can specify a certain time when the geas is broken (for example, the Sabbath, Lent, or Ramadan).

ADVANCED MAGIC RULES

The rules below describe additional situations and variables that may affect a character's use of magic.

MATERIAL LINKS

During ritual spellcasting (p. 184, *SR4A*), instead of using an astral spotter, the ritual team may opt to use a *material link* to target the spell. This is particularly useful when sending a spotter may be impossible or impractical (for example, when the spotter doesn't know where the target is, or when security measures prevent the spotter from getting into a position to assense the target).

The material link is an integral part of the target that is in the ritual team's possession. If the target is an inanimate object, the material link forms an integral, essential part of its structure. For example, you can target a building using a brick from one of its walls. However, you can't use a picture that used to hang inside the building, as the picture is not an integral part of the building.

If the target is a living being, the material link is a tissue sample. Tissue samples have a limited duration as a material link, however, as decomposition eventually renders the sample useless. The amount of time available varies, depending on the size of the sample and external conditions; a bloodstain from a combat scene may only be useful for a few hours, while a severed finger may be useful for several days. Decomposition can be slowed or stalled by refrigeration or a Preserve spell; chemical preservation, however, destroys the sample's ritual viability.

The process of ritual spellcasting destroys the material link. If a spellcasting ritual is interrupted and has to be aborted, the material link is destroyed. In that case, the ritual team must either obtain another link or use a spotter.

Ritual groups may also combine material links (and *sympathetic links* below) with astral spotters to astrally track a target when its location is unknown. While the ritual team is casting a spell (using the material link), an astral spotter may track the target's location per the rules on p. 184, *SR4A*. The ritual need not be completed, just maintained long enough to allow the tracker to locate the target.

SYMPATHETIC LINKS

Initiates with the Sympathetic Linking metamagic (p. 58) can use a sympathetic link to target a ritual spell, if neither a material link nor a spotter is available. A sympathetic link is an object that isn't an integral part of the target but has the target's aura imprinted onto it, from special sentiment (a wedding band), frequent use (the target's trusty Predator), or recent use (the soyburger wrapper the target tossed in the trash five minutes ago). Sympathetic links are divided into three categories: favored objects, oft-handled objects, and recently handled objects.

Favored Objects denote items—clothing, jewelry, toys, mementos, etc.—which the target frequently wears or carries on his person and have significant emotional value to him. A dead lover's locket, a scrap of a childhood security blanket tucked into a pocket, and similar objects fit into this category.

Oft-Handled Objects include frequently worn clothing (a daily-worn company uniform), a familiar weapon (a katana used since training days), a favorite pen, and other such objects. These items tend not to have as deep an emotional attachment to the target as a Favored Object, but they are used often and have been in his possession for some time.

Recently Handled Objects have the least amount of attachment to a target. A coffee cup used at breakfast, an office toy, or a fast-food wrapper—items that have been in the target's possession for a minimum of five minutes—all fit under this category. These objects have limited effectiveness, however; they can only be used for a number of minutes equal to twice the target's Essence. If the ritual begins before this amount of time runs out, the link remains effective for the duration of the ritual. If the ritual is interrupted, the link is similarly lost. Also, the object in question may not be a Favored or Oft-Handled Object for someone else besides the target; not only will the Linking Test fail for the intended target, but the gamemaster may decide that the ritual group inadvertently succeeds in targeting someone else!

Since sympathetic links do not have as strong a connection to the target as material links, they make ritual spellcasting harder to perform. If the ritual team is using a sympathetic link, apply a modifier to the Ritual Spellcasting Test based on the link type, as noted on the Sympathetic Link Modifiers table (p. 27). This modifier applies to all teamwork tests, as well as the leader's final Spellcasting Test.

Symbolic Links

If an initiate with Sympathetic Linking metamagic can't find a sympathetic link, he may instead create a symbolic link: a picture, sculpture, or doll bearing symbolic likeness to the target. The most notorious example of a symbolic link is the infamous voodoo doll seen in many horror simflicks. Though symbolic links can work in cases a material link, sympathetic link, or astral spotter won't, they are more difficult to use.

To create a symbolic link, make an Intuition + Artisan Test with a threshold determined by the Symbolic Link Creation table (p. 27) and an interval of 1 day. The creator's Initiate Grade serves as a dice pool bonus to this test. Additional modifiers from the Build/Repair Table (p. 138, *SR4A*) may apply, as determined by the gamemaster.

Once an adequate symbolic link has been created, it can be used for ritual spellcasting. Symbolic links inflict a hefty –6 modifier to the Ritual Spellcasting Test. If the creator of the symbolic link is not a participant in the ritual sorcery, an additional –2 modifier applies.

SYMPATHETIC LINK MODIFIERS

Sympathetic Link	Dice Pool Modifier
Favored Object	–2
Oft-Handled Object	–4
Recently Handled Object	–6

SYMBOLIC LINK CREATION

Condition	Threshold
Creator has assessed the target	4
Creator has met the target	12
Creator is personally unfamiliar with the target	16

Symbolic Link Foci: To make a more potent representation, such as the voodoo dolls used by some houngans, a character may enchant the representation into a symbolic link focus. A symbolic link focus adds dice to the Ritual Spellcasting Test equal to its rating (effectively counteracting the symbolic link modifier). See *Artificing*, p. 82 for more information on creating symbolic link foci.

OPTIONAL RULE: ACQUIRING GEASA DURING PLAY

Though the Awakened have access to power beyond their wildest imaginations, their grip on that power is tenuous at best. During the course of their shadow careers, Awakened characters may encounter traumatic situations that shake their grip on their Talent. If such trauma shatters the character's fragile faith in his magic, he will resort to geasa to glue it back together.

Whenever an Awakened character suffers a critical glitch when using his magic, the character must make a Willpower + Magic (3) Test; if the test fails, then the character has suffered a crisis of confidence. The character suffers a –1 Magic attribute penalty, as if he had broken a geas, until the end of the adventure or some other convenient stopping point for the character to sit down and figure out what his geas will be. Once the character has identified a geas and adopted it, his Magic attribute returns to normal.

It is recommended that this rule only be applied when a character critically glitches on an action of significant consequence—something major enough to trigger a crisis of confidence. For example, the character should be trying to do something major (summon a powerful free spirit), should be under major pressure (the character is literally under the gun), or should have something personally at stake (everything he holds dear is on the line). If the character critically glitched on something inconsequential (summoning a watcher), this rule should not apply (unless the critical glitch is at the end of a string of failures to complete minor tasks …).

Jackyl and his team are on a shadowrun against Mitsuhama when a giant fire elemental bound to a Mitsuhama wage mage attacks them. Jackyl attempts to banish the elemental, but something goes wrong in the process, and he fails his Banishing Test. The gamemaster rules that Jackyl has suffered a crisis of confidence. Jackyl makes a Willpower + Magic (3) Test but only gets 2 hits, so he must take a geas.

As Jackyl stumbles through the ritual, he feels a little bit of the spark inside him slip away, as the mojo that would have snuffed out the elemental fizzles instead. His Magic attribute decreases by 1 and remains that way until after the run, when Jackyl has a chance to sit down and think about what happened. Shaken by his failure, he invents a little chant (an Incantation geas) that will help him concentrate the next time.

Way of the Burnout

Sometimes, a trauma will shatter an Awakened's confidence beyond his geas's ability to repair it. His magical ability snuffs out, potentially rendering the magician a mundane. These poor souls are referred to as burnouts; their faith in magic a charred husk smoldering in cynicism, despair, and misery.

If a character has already broken a geas (thus invoking a reduced Magic attribute) and suffers another crisis of confidence while in this state, Magic losses from broken geasa become permanent. Any geasa that the character had acquired disappear. Magic lost this way also reduces the character's maximum Magic rating.

Jackyl is on another run, this time against Renraku. The plan goes to hell, however, and the Red Samurai capture Jackyl as he's separated from the other shadowrunners. Realizing that he's a magician, the Renraku guards put a magemask over his head, preventing him from speaking his chant (thus breaking his Incantation geas.)

Jackyl has to get out of there and soon, because he made several enemies inside Renraku in the past. Chant or no chant, the only way he's going to do that is use a spell to break his bonds. He tries to cast the spell, but suffers a critical glitch instead. The gamemaster rules that Jackyl has suffered another crisis of confidence.

The Magic loss from breaking his Incantation geas is now permanent. Jackyl reaches deep inside him for the magic to break his bonds … only to find nothing there. Jackyl slumps dejectedly in one corner of his cell, his only hope now that his friends find him before his enemies do.

TWEAKING THE RULES

Every gamemaster has the option of altering the rules to fit more snugly with your group's personal style of play. Here are a few suggestions you can consider to tailor *Shadowrun's* magic rules closer to your own personal preferences.

Healing Drain

Normally Drain cannot be healed by magical means, only by complete rest or mundane medical attention. For a less gritty campaign, allow damage from Drain to be healed or alleviated by magical means.

Conjuring Drain

Dealing with spirits in *SR4* is an unpredictable and dangerous business, and Summoning, Binding, and Banishing Drain reflects this. For games where more predictable results are desired, an alternate Drain Value of half the Spirit's Force + its hits on the Resistance Test can be used. This results in both fewer cases of no Drain and fewer cases of incapacitating Drain.

Arcana

Rather than linking Arcana to Logic, you could link it to the magician's Drain attribute, as appropriate to his tradition. This would reflect that tradition's approach towards formula. Non-magicians using Arcana would utilize the Drain attribute appropriate to the tradition whose style they are using.

Enchanting

Instead of making Enchanting a single skill, you might consider it a skill group on par with Conjuring and Sorcery. This elevates its importance, though it tends to discourage characters from investing as much into Enchanting due to its increased cost.
The component skills and their specializations would be broken down as follows:
- **Artificing (Magic):** Fetishes, Foci, Ritual Materials, Unique Enchantments
- **Alchemy (Magic/Intuition):** Orichalcum, Radicals, Reagents (Animal, Herbal, Metal, or Mineral), Refining
- **Vessel Preparation (Magic):** Living Vessels, Inanimate Vessels, Homunculi Creation

Geasa

If a gamemaster wants to make geasa less of a threat, she can reduce the threshold of the Willpower + Magic Test to 2. Alternately, if gamemasters want to increase the threat of geasa, they can raise the threshold to 4, require the test whenever a standard glitch is made, or skip the glitch criteria altogether, ruling that a crisis of confidence occurs whenever the character fails in some major magical task (gamemaster's discretion, though this should be agreed on by the group before play). Another option is to make geasa more frequent for characters with high Magic attributes (6+), as the shock of failure could be even more jolting to a powerful magician or adept.

Adepts and Geasa

For a more adept-driven game, gamemasters may allow adepts to voluntarily take a geas for a specific adept power; in return, the Power Point cost for that power is reduced by 25 percent (round normally). In this case, breaking the geasa only affects that power; the adepts remaining geasa-limited powers are unaffected.

Spirit Edge

For those groups that think spirits are powerful enough as is, a spirit's Edge is only equal to half its Force rating, rounded down, instead of its Force, as specified on pp. 302-303 of *SR4A*.

Alternatively, spirits can be treated as grunts in service of their conjuror. As such, they do not have an innate Edge Attribute, but rather draw from a group Edge Pool equal to the conjuror's Conjuring or Binding skill level (as appropriate).

Magic Loss

Unlike in previous editions, magicians don't lose Magic from grievous wounds or by abusing certain drugs, like stim patches. For a more gritty campaign, gamemasters can reintroduce Magic loss under any or all of the circumstances below:
- The character glitches while resisting Physical damage.
- The character commits a glitch while under the influence of a stim patch.
- Another character providing medical treatment glitches during the Success Test.

A character may voluntarily take a geas to prevent Magic Loss from occurring in these situations.

More Common Knacks

For a more potent version of the Spell/Spirit Knack quality (p. 26), the gamemaster can allow the character with the knack to improve his Magic attribute with BP and Karma, as normal. This allows the character to create a more potent knack effect–however, it also allows a character with cyber- or bioware to effectively use this knack. Gamemasters should take care in allowing this–a street samurai who can toss a killer fireball may be too unbalancing. The gamemaster could also considering restricting Magic to a maximum of 3, or increase the BP Cost of the quality (perhaps 5 x max Magic).

Expert Aspected Magician

Rather than treating the Aspected Magician quality (p. 26) solely as a limitation, aspected magicians can be treated as ones who *excel* in one area at the expense of others. In this case, aspected magicians receive a +2 dice pool modifier when exercising magic according to their aspect, but suffer a heftier –6 dice pool modifier for all other uses of magic.

Ritual Magic

Normally only characters from the same tradition may participate in ritual magic teams, and all participants must know the spell. Campaigns desiring more inclusive and multi-tradition rituals may relax the restriction in either of the following ways:
- Magicians of any tradition may participate in ritual magic, but they must all know the spell.
- Not all magicians participating must know the spell, but all magicians must belong to the same tradition.

...PATHS OF MAGIC...

More gunfire filtered down from the ground floor of the IOND chapterhouse. Magpie looked up. Stiletto stood over the two unconscious guards, watching the stairway and looking at him quizzically. The room was near dark, but he knew she could easily see the stupid grin on his face. He shrugged. He couldn't help himself, this was what did it for him. This was why he played the shadows. Forget the rewards, the challenges were where the fun was.

"Move your ass, Magpie, things are getting hot up here!" crackled Stone's voice over the link. "Jinx can't hold them off for much longer."

On cue, Shin piped in, her voice strained, "My kami are holding their guardian elementals, but not for long. Whatever you're doing, Magpie, make it quick!"

"Yeah, yeah, rock, hard place, I get it ... just keep them off my back. I told ya the Illuminates would be a tough nut." He toggled off the sound, turned his back on Stiletto's silent glare, and concentrated on the sigils and marks on the pedestal his prize rested on. With a plea to Crow, he closed his eyes and shifted his senses to the astral. The basement vault lit up.

The walls and floor were decked in the arcane symbols, sigils, and concentric circles of hermetic wards and quickenings he had broken. As expected, the pedestal too was shrouded in protective magics. He frowned and tried again to glean some meaning from the patterns, but they still didn't make sense. He didn't get the retentive need of hermetics to impose their will on mana, to wrap and bind magic into unnatural patterns with their formulations and symbols. It was just plain unnatural. He'd take his totem's songs of power and the bones and sands in his medicine bag any day.

Magpie sighed. The hard way it was. Not that it displeased him, Crow loved a good puzzle. He focused on the complex anchoring around the bejeweled box and began the dispelling.

Suddenly, Stiletto was moving. He looked up as a fiery elemental materialized from a smoldering brazier. Stiletto's throwing blades had no effect on the flames moving to engulf her.

"Like hell! Not when I'm this close!" Magpie's last word came out as a ragged screech and he felt feathers bristle on his neck, his hand curving into a claw. Crow cawed in his ear, the anger and the power welled up inside him before streaming at the elemental guardian. The spirit recoiled as if an invisible truck had slammed into it.

Magpie shook, his will warring with the spirit's. Almost of their own accord, his hands reached into his medicine bag and drew a carved figurine. He held it up and shunted his will through it, summoning his own spirit backup.

"Cheveyo, protect me," muttered the shaman, and suddenly the small room erupted with the sound of beating wings, a murder of ravens materializing from the darkness and setting upon the elemental, clawing savagely, smothering its flames with their powerful wings.

Stiletto turned to Magpie. The stupid smile was back.

Street Magic

THE MANY PARADIGMS OF MAGIC

Traditions and magical paradigms are the basic building blocks of magical practice in the twenty-first century. Established traditions embody elaborate collections of lore, complete with esoteric rituals and potent symbolism that allow a magician to better understand and direct his innate ability to manipulate mana and interact with spirits. Each is a conceptual lens through which a magician focuses his will, and each endeavors to provide a complete cosmological framework of concepts and mystic correspondences to describe the fundamental workings of the magic arts and the spirit world.

THE PRACTICE OF MAGIC

The art of magic is inherently subjective, and amongst the Awakened of the Sixth World many different paradigms of magic co-exist. Nonetheless, since early on, Gifted individuals realized the latent power to be found in traditional mystical philosophies and arcane lore. Renaissance hermeticism, Native American shamanism, Japanese Shinto, Chinese Wuxing, and countless other sources of pre-Awakening mysticism were mined for answers to the emerging phenomena. The predominant modern traditions coalesced around these magical paradigms because, for the most part, they provided ready-made metaphysical beliefs, potent symbolism, rites, and spellcraft.

While a character's magical tradition in *Shadowrun* is very much a personal and cultural choice, the fact is that well-established traditions dominate the corporate and academic magical scenes. By the 2070s, the majority of magicians learn and practice magic based on such "mainstream" traditions, drawing on and adding to the knowledge of others who have walked the same path (or their writings in books and e-libraries). Each such tradition boasts tens of thousands of practitioners, all of whom subscribe to one paradigm developed over the years (or in some cases, centuries). The wide dissemination of these traditions makes it easier for practitioners to find instructors, formal education, formulae, appropriate magic materials, and, of course, like-minded magical groups—and helps the self-perpetuation of their dominance.

Magical development requires years of diligent study stressing the understanding of magic through the specific perspective of one's tradition. This makes the conceptual framework that constitutes the tradition's paradigm self-reinforcing. A mage trained to see hermetic formulae as the symbolic construct needed to mentally weave mana into a spellform will find it impossible to see magic as an animistic force of nature that must be cajoled to act the way the magician wants (as a shaman would). Such radically different approaches mean that a switch between traditions is almost unheard of. A magician would not only have to accept a possibly contradictory worldview, but he'd also have to relearn the basics of his craft from a fundamentally different approach.

Notable (and often inexplicable) exceptions exist, such as those magicians who walk toxic paths or are seduced by insect mentor spirits. Generally, such paradigm shifts are only believed possible as a symptom of an individual's insanity.

The Self-Taught Magician

For most magicians, well-established traditions represent the easiest path to realizing their Gift. These have the advantage of being supported by educational institutions, corporations, and organized magical societies; they are best-served in terms of magical resources; and they generally provide the foundations for magical groups to form around peer networks. Their greatest advantage, however, and possibly their greatest shortcoming, comes from representing a consensual, institutional, and well-documented view of magic, rather than an individual's personal views.

In *Shadowrun*'s dystopian world of unequal opportunities and social injustice, some Awakened characters never get the opportunity to follow formal studies, and some that do reject the dictates of formal education.

Since magic remains very much a personal and subjective experience, rooted in innate Talent, such magicians often find themselves walking self-devised paths of magic (consciously or not). Awakened characters who develop their own traditions—the mental and symbolic constructs necessary to effectively and predictably wield magic—are not uncommon, just exceptional. Without the guidance and support of peers, their path is often harder and development of their Talent more unpredictable. For instance, finding an initiatory group (see p. 68) may be much more difficult.

It is, however, possible to learn from instructors of similar traditions and beliefs—at the gamemaster's discretion, characters can incur anything from a –1 to –4 dice pool modifier on relevant Instruction Tests depending on his perception of similarities between the teacher's and the pupil's traditions.

It should be noted that in the sixty years since the Awakening, entire traditions have evolved from individuals mixing and matching elements of other belief systems and their own into not-always-coherent but still-functioning wholes. Though it is looked down upon by more conservative traditions, this is best epitomized by the modern tradition known as Chaos magic.

POSSESSION-BASED TRADITIONS

Some traditions believe in spirits that are invisible and intangible forces which project into the physical world through the power of Possession rather than Materialization. This understanding of the spirit world is part of the tradition's lore and integral to the magics used to summon and bind spirits. As such, all spirits conjured by magicians of a possession-based magical tradition replace the Materialization power in the spirits' statistics with Possession. Otherwise, all normal rules for summoned or bound spirits remain in effect. For more details on Possession, see p. 101.

FAITH, BELIEF, AND MAGIC

Given the way belief is entwined with the practice of magic, it is unsurprising that—even in the materialistic '70s—faith and religion, old and new, have a significant impact on the manner many of the Awakened perceive and practice magic. In the Sixth World, several traditions involve both formal magical systems and religious beliefs, and while

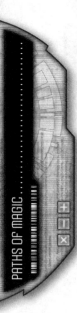

Shadowrun makes no pretense to perfectly represent or endorse any such belief, it recognizes that, in the fictional context of the setting, many such magical traditions exist and thrive. Considering that many religious beliefs include moral strictures and principles that inevitably clash with the vicious aspects of life in the shadows, a character following such a tradition is the perfect springboard for a host of stories and roleplaying opportunities.

Traditions that involve both religion and magic generally take one of three forms:

- Religious mystical traditions that perceive the divine (miracle) and the esoteric (magic) as separate, but allow a place in their theologies for magic use. In this case Talent might be seen as a sign that someone is touched by God, the gods, or the spirits, even when the practice of magic is not inherently pious or miraculous. Christian Theurgy, Qabbalah, Aztec, and Norse magic are examples of this approach.
- Faiths that view magic as a universal force, a natural part of life, and integral to their beliefs and cosmologies. This approach is common to neo-pagan beliefs and revivals (such as North American shamanism, Wicca, and Druidism), but many Eastern religions also have similar outlooks (Hinduism and Shinto to name but two). Mundane faithful sometimes, though not always, grant special deference to the Awakened, occasionally even according them clerical status.
- Sects in major faiths that consider magic a tool of evil. It is not unheard of for a magician from such a background to believe he does not use magic at all, but rather performs miracles. The absence of a true magical paradigm, spiritual cosmology, or common body of lore, however, makes these rarities "magical oddities" (see p. 45).

ALTERNATE MAGICAL TRADITIONS

The following section describes the best-established and most well-known magical traditions in the 2070s. This is by no means an exhaustive list of the myriad traditions that find their home in the Sixth World, just a representative sample of the most widespread traditions characters may encounter in mainstream society, the corporate world, and, inevitably, the shadows.

Gamemasters and players are encouraged to explore these and expand upon them with their own, keeping in mind that the more common the tradition is in the society providing the backdrop for his game, the easier it should be to find like-minded magical groups, appropriate magical supplies, and formulae.

THE ABORIGINAL TRADITION

Concept: In the Dreamtime, a *koradji* (an aboriginal shaman) can walk the songlines with the spirits that shaped the world and call upon them to reach into the world of today.
Combat: Beasts
Detection: Earth
Health: Plant
Illusion: Guidance
Manipulation: Air
Drain: Willpower + Charisma

The Dreamtime is the world of myth that stands out of place and time, where a koradji can meet the spirits whose footsteps created the Outback millions of years ago. The Aboriginal tradition is probably the oldest surviving tradition on Earth, passing down stories of the ancient Sky Heroes told by koradji tens of thousands of years in the past. It is tied closely to the land, which itself is a physical footprint of the actions of countless spirits. By communing with the land and entering the Dreamtime, the koradji can persuade these prehistoric spirits to change fate and the physical world.

Most Dreamtime spirits are primeval, taking the form of the animals whose movements created the mountains, deserts, and rivers. Some are humanoid, such as the Sky Heroes who came from the heavens and shaped Creation. All are truly ancient and endlessly wise, with patience that stretches across millennia. To the modern urban man, they would seem alien and strange, but to the koradji who still make the Outback their home, they are as fundamental as can be imagined. Sometimes a Dreamtime spirit will become especially interested in a koradji and will become his mentor spirit, though not all koradji have this relationship.

The Aboriginal tradition has not spread globally, but it has grown in strength in the Outback where the Dreamtime pierces into the physical world through raging mana storms. Nearly all koradji prefer to stay in their native lands, where they claim to keep a close eye on primal spirits who could destroy the world if freed from their prisons. Rarely, a koradji will venture out into the world to learn more about the spirits found elsewhere.

THE AZTEC TRADITION

Concept: By identifying and communing with the animal spirit that holds the other half of his soul, the *nahualli* (Aztec magician) is capable of performing magic and brokering deals with the spirits of the other world.
Combat: Guardian
Detection: Fire
Health: Plant
Illusion: Water
Manipulation: Beasts
Drain: Willpower + Charisma

Outsiders commonly miss the difference, but Aztec sorcery, though colored by it, is largely independent of Aztec religion. While many Aztec priests are also nahualli, there are at least as many nahualli who are unconcerned with appeasing the ancient gods. The traditional source of the nahualli's magic is not the gods, but the bond to his spirit animal twin. In Aztec belief, every person shares a portion of his soul with an animal spirit. Even the gods are bound by this state; the god Tezcatlipoca's animal twin is the jaguar, and the animal twin of Huitzilopochtli is the hummingbird. A nahualli has discovered his animal spirit twin and embraced it, gaining access to the spiritual world and the ability to evoke magical effects.

Every nahualli must possess a mentor spirit that represents their animal twin. Unlike some Amerindian shamans, this mentor spirit never represents a shared ideal but is seen as that nahualli's personal and individual spirit animal. Through the connection with the spirit animal, the nahualli can summon a variety of lesser spirits, which can manifest as animals,

humanoid minor divinities, and even as abstract phenomenon like blazes of fire or plumes of smoke.

Aztec magicians use elaborate ceremonial costumes for ritual magic, including feathered headdresses, and traditionally use an obsidian knife for blood sacrifices. Aztec magicians also use astrology for divining the future and determining auspicious days for their rituals.

There is a great misconception that Aztec rituals encourage the use of blood magic. While blood sometimes factors into offerings to Aztec spirits and gods during castings or summonings, the techniques of blood magic are unknown to most nahualli. Only secretive orders of the most powerful priests, backed by the nation of Aztlan and Aztechnology, have unlocked that twisted art.

BLACK MAGIC

Concept: A black magician's ultimate focus is a quest for personal power, regardless of whether this comes from mastery of the dark arts, secular powerbrokering, or pacts with the dark powers from beyond the mortal realm.
Combat: Fire
Detection: Water
Health: Earth
Illusion: Air
Manipulation: Man
Drain: Willpower + Charisma

Of the modern Western traditions, black magic suffers the worst reputation. Rather than subscribing to true evil, however, most black magic groups follow a credo which is part hedonist and part fascist—seeking self-serving advancement, emphasizing a will to power, and advocating freedom from the blinders and shackles imposed by "straight" society. This, coupled with their unsavory reputations fueled by persistent rumors of pacts with dark spirits, taints public and scholarly perception—not that such magicians care for mainstream opinion anyway.

Steeped in Christian, hermetic, and pagan symbolism, black magic is at times as rigid and disciplined as hermeticism and as ecstatic as shamanism. Various reversed Christian tropes (the Black Mass, inverted cross, and so on), and the pentagram are common symbolism. Hermetic and qabbalistic symbols are also given a darker twist and elaborate rituals are favored.

Black magic is the art of imposing one's will on the fabric of existence and the hidden energies and dominions of reality. Appropriate mentor spirit archetypes include Adversary, Dark King, the Horned Man, the Trickster, or the Seductress. Lesser spirits are seen as mischievous para-elemental entities and demons to be brought to heel under the black magician's iron grip. Conversely, black magicians are prone to striking spirit pacts with greater spirits and dark patrons. It is not uncommon for such magicians to become entangled in a web of pacts with various spirits in their quest for personal power—forcing them to tread carefully and be watchful of their allegiances.

Black magic is a minor tradition found throughout the Western world. Black magicians have a hard time finding acceptance in many corporations, given the public perception of their art, but have been known to pass themselves off as hermetic mages (many of their trappings and rituals are sufficiently similar) and to live on the fringes of hermetic society.

By the very nature of their beliefs and outlook, black magicians tread closer than most to the territory of the Twisted (p. 136). As such, they are particularly easy to use as the stereotypical human-sacrifice type of black magician and cultist in a game, though few black magic groups actually conform to such portrayals of their art.

THE BUDDHIST TRADITION

Concept: Magic springs from personal self-development along the path towards enlightenment, as revealed to the student by the master and as a method to understand the true nature of existence.
Combat: Air
Detection: Guidance
Health: Earth
Illusion: Fire
Manipulation: Water
Drain: Willpower + Intuition

The Buddhist magical tradition largely stems from one sect of Buddhism, Vajrayana or Tantric Buddhism. The other main Buddhist sects do not teach specific techniques related to sorcery and summoning and instead see magic as simply another part of reality that must be overcome to find enlightenment. In fact, many magicians who follow the Wuxing or Shinto traditions also consider themselves followers of Buddhism. Vajrayana Buddhism, however, expands upon its tantric methods to include magical knowledge as both evidence of approaching enlightenment and a method to reach it. Buddhist *yogis* (or female *yoginis*) must find a master to teach them the proper incantations and meditations to advance in their magical experience and in their journey towards enlightenment. In Vajrayana Buddhism, it is forbidden to learn spells simply from formulae; the techniques can only be properly taught from a master to a student.

Buddhist magical techniques include ritual incantations called *mantras,* methods of mind-and-body meditation called *yoga,* and representational diagrams of the universe called *mandalas.* Spirits often take the form of Buddhist divinities and guardian spirits, especially the Bodhisattva, enlightened beings who have decided to remain on Earth out of compassion for those still seeking enlightenment. Many Buddhist yogis have an abstract mentor spirit they call a *yidam,* an enlightened being (such as a Bodhisattva) that the yogi meditates on as an ideal of the state they wish to attain.

Vajrayana Buddhism was originally common to Tibet, and, though the nation is now largely sealed off from the world, it is presumed to still be common there. It can also be found in communities throughout Asia, from India to Japan, and has spread through popular teaching into North America, especially along the western coast.

CHAOS MAGIC

Concept: Magic is all about hacking the hidden operating system of the world. The signs and language used are means of rewriting the "machine code" that underlies reality. Ultimately, one's tradition is merely a mental tool to focus one's will to bring change in conformity—and like any good tool, it can be amply customized.
Combat: Fire
Detection: Air
Health: Earth
Illusion: Man
Manipulation: Water
Drain: Willpower + Logic

Chaos magic began as an occult movement designed to distill a "pure" magical system, devoid of dogma or credo, from the many different paths of power offered by myriad traditions, a system that would frame any belief system and transcend them all. The result was a highly eclectic and postmodern style, incorporating many symbols and ideas from different cultures and belief systems.

Chaos magic is a unique hybrid that seeks the inherent power and underlying potential of the symbols and trappings used by other traditions. *Chaos mages* usually favor a methodical quasi-hermetic foundation to their personal styles and beliefs, though their practice incorporates symbols and concepts from many different sources and often interacts with different mentor spirits and totems on astral quests.

By nature, this magic system is a hodgepodge of styles and trappings that drinks from numerous sources. A chaos ritual circle might include qabbalistic, runic, and even shamanic design elements, and their lodges range from hermetic-style libraries to stone circles to cavernous basements decked in elaborate Aboriginal drawings. Chaos magic's popularity among young magicians has come to influence even the hermetic paradigm, prompting the development of the Unified Magical Theory.

While it aspires to be universal, chaos magic shows clear signs of its hermetic heritage in regard to its understanding of the spirit world. Chaos mages subscribe to the belief that spirits are manifestations of the basic universal elements spontaneously drawn from the fabric of astral space by the magician's own will (hence their myriad guises). These entities can be summoned, controlled, and bound through the appropriate preparations and thaumaturgic rituals.

Chaos mages are the unabashed technophiles of the Awakened community, and commonly use technology in their magic to complement traditional ritual materials and resources: AROs to represent formulae, mediaplayers for music, holographic symbols for warding, digital storage for their mystical libraries, and so on.

CHRISTIAN THEURGY

Concept: Combining Renaissance hermeticism with Christian qabbalism and Gnostic cosmology, *theurgists* are those gifted by God with the ability to wield the natural energies of magic, and they devote their skills to the service of the congregations of the faith.
Combat: Fire
Detection: Water
Health: Air
Illusion: Earth
Manipulation: Guidance
Drain: Willpower + Charisma

To most Christians, magic is a powerful force created by God and bestowed upon mankind, as is any other force of nature. While some Christians still harbor doubts, the landmark *Imago Dei* encyclical redefined Catholic doctrine and led the way to similar edicts from other branches of Christianity. Most modern Christians believe the practice of magic is *not* divine, and consequently not a form of miracle (which remains a tell-tale sign of sainthood)—an understanding that often stigmatizes those who believe their power is divinely inspired. Hence the evolution of theurgy, a quasi-hermetic Christian tradition, laden with the faith's symbolism and doctrine, with roots in a mystical heritage that encompasses first-century Gnostic works, the writings of scholars such as St. Thomas Aquinas, and the arcane lore of centuries, carefully collected in the Church's libraries.

Though all major Christian theologies acknowledge magic is neither inherently good nor evil, and spirits are elemental manifestations of God's Creation, Awakened clergy carefully regulate magic use according to the tenets and strictures of the faith. Most ritual sorcery and conjuration is performed on consecrated ground in the church or monastery that serves as a theurgist's lodge—under the watchful eyes of their peers and superiors. Communing with spirits is discouraged as it brings up nebulous issues of doctrine and faith. Those theurgists granted special dispensation may summon spirits in the form of *angels* associated with the Archangels and their domains: Michael (fire), Gabriel (water), Raphael (air), Uriel (earth) and *seraphim* at the service of the Holy Spirit (man's immortal soul).

Theurgy's trappings and symbols are those of the Christian faith: the Bible, prayer, the cross or crucifix, the rosary, and holy water. God, Christ, the Holy Spirit, the various saints, and archangels are often invoked in healing, warding, and protective magic.

In most congregations theurgy is only enforced among clerical magicians; secular believers are free to follow or disregard the guidelines set down by each church at their own peril. The Roman Catholic order of magician-priests known as the Order of St. Sylvester is the most public organization of theurgists, but others exist, such as the secretive New Knights Templar and

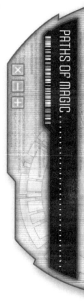

the obscure Vigilia Evangelica, the Westphalian theurgists in Germany, and the Orthodox Exarchs in Eastern Europe.

Note that while followers of some "revivalist" and liberal Christian theologies *believe* they work miracles and their practices have quasi-shamanistic aspects, for the purpose of these rules, those who espouse such beliefs are considered "magical oddities" (p. 45) rather than theurgists.

THE DRUIDIC TRADITION

Concept: Enlightenment comes to the *druid* through powers of the self, refined by the secrets of initiation and devotion. The druid—priest, mystic, and wise philosopher—is charged with the custody of the mystic bond between the sacred spirit of the land and its people.
Combat: Beast
Detection: Water
Health: Plant
Illusion: Air
Manipulation: Earth
Drain: Willpower + Intuition

Modern Druidism is a religion and a magic system that descends from the tradition of the Celtic priesthood, though its heritage may actually predate the Celts. In the Sixth World, three branches of Druidism aspire to the essence of that ancient heritage: nature-worshiping Celtic druids, wild druids, and hermetic English druids.

Celtic druids are by far the most common and have revived ancient Celtic culture wholesale—at least what could be reconstructed since the Celtic tradition was oral and few records exist. These druids revere the land, and their sacred duty is to consecrate the bond between the land and its people. They follow a modern pantheistic belief wherein the deities of the Celtic pantheon are seen as avatars of primordial nature and the gods and heroes of Celtic myth serve as their mentor spirits (see p. 183).

Wild druids follow a deeply primeval, totemic tradition that predates Celtic influence. Their magic is visceral and shamanistic, and they worship animistic elemental powers (through mentor spirits such as Oak, Sea, Sun, and Moon Maiden). Wild druids are rare and shun modern society, favoring deeper immersion in nature.

English druids borrow the esoteric correspondences, potent symbology and trappings of Druidism, but are actually a sub-school of hermeticism that seeks to separate the ideal of the druid as wise philosopher, scholar, and scientist from Celtic mysticism.

All druids invoke spirits of particular places and landmarks when conjuring, and they believe the spirits of nature to which they pay tribute are aspects of the greater spirit of the land. English druids believe these are simply para-elementals molded by the nature of the places they are drawn through.

Four annual festivals hold immense ritual significance to all branches of Druidism: Imbolc, Beltane, Lugnasad, and Samhain. Druidic circles reserve great rituals and initiation rites for these sacred dates. Circles are the backbone of druidic society, though mundane believers sometimes participate as a token of the druid's bond to his community. During ritual work, druids use robes of white and gray with elaborate brooches and torques to denote rank and initiation. Plants such as holly, mistletoe, and oak are potent holy symbols, as is the traditional golden sickle.

Druidic lodges are often located in places of natural beauty and vary from monolithic stone circles and natural caves to hidden glades and burial mounds. A number of ancient sites and stone circles are located on natural power sites and ley nexi.

The Druidic traditions are most widespread in the British Isles, Tir Na nOg, France and parts of central Europe.

THE HINDU TRADITION

Concept: The divine and the magical that permeate all existence are one and the same, but only the enlightened on the path of transcendence on the Wheel of Life may learn to control such forces through ritual devotion, karmic purity, and asceticism.
Combat: Beast
Detection: Water
Health: Plant
Illusion: Air
Manipulation: Earth
Drain: Willpower + Logic

Both religion and magical tradition, the Hindu paradigm believes the *atman* (soul) exists in a constant cycle of death and rebirth governed by the causal relationship of karma. Karma is neither good nor evil, but the natural cosmic order. Those who follow a selfish path and forsake their *joti* (vocation) will reincarnate as lesser beings. Those who embrace the dictates of their *varna* (caste) in their current life reincarnate as higher beings. Escape from the cycle of reincarnation comes through rebirth and eventual *moksha*, transcendence to a higher level of consciousness.

The Hindu tradition is embodied in two different paths that share the same cosmology, rituals, and religious observances. They differ, however, in their distinct approaches to personal enlightenment. The first is the highly ritualized priestly magic of the *brahmin* high-born caste, which espouses transcendence through religious devotion and observances along with strictly regimented behavior. The second is the path of the ascetic, the *saddhu* (feminine: *saddhvi*), where the path to transcendence comes by communion with the divine through selfless devotion, meditation, yogic practices, and the renunciation of worldly attachments. While the path of the brahmin focuses primarily on magicians, the path of the saddhu also embraces adepts and mystic adepts. Both paths use mantras, yoga, and ecstatic rituals in their magic. Music, dance, and sound in general play a vital role in all forms of Hindu magic. Sanskrit and complex mandalas are widely used in spellcasting, while Hindu prayers are common for conjuration. The sounds of certain words are believed to distill the natural vibration of the *braman* (the universal spirit). Combined, these divine syllables form mantras that are essential to most rituals and spellcasting.

To Hindus, spirits known as *ashuras* inhabit all places and may be dealt with through appropriate prayer and offerings. When manifest, ashuras often take either animal or humanoid forms—though the latter often have extra limbs, oddly colored skin, or animal features. Their elemental asso-

ciation is often a subtle clue to their true nature; a fire spirit may dance in a halo of flames, while a plant spirit may emerge from a sacred banyan tree.

Though Hinduism is a polytheistic tradition with thousands of gods, each saddhu traditionally embraces one god above the others as his particular patron. Vishnu, Shiva, Ganesha, Devi/Shakti and their avatars are common mentor spirits among saddhus and brahmin alike. Nearly any mentor archetype might be appropriate for one of the manifold avatars and emanations each deity possesses (such as Krishna, Rama, or Kali-Durga).

The Hindu tradition is most commonly found in the Indian subcontinent, but the high educational standards of the brahmin caste has led to its discreet spread throughout corporate culture.

THE ISLAMIC TRADITION

Concept: Inspired by ancient Arabic and Persian traditions and the ecstatic Sufi mysticism, Islamic magicians argue the prohibitions in *al-Qu'ran* distinguish between black magic (strictly forbidden) and mystical philosophy (*al-hikmah*), one of the natural sciences, devoted to understanding the unseen forces that Allah has placed in the world.
Combat: Guardian
Detection: Earth
Health: Plant
Illusion: Air
Manipulation: Fire
Drain: Willpower + Logic

More so than magicians of any other faith, Muslim mages—be they philosophical alchemists or Islamist mujahedin—strictly adhere to the tenets of their faith as a sign of their devotion to Allah (and to forestall fundamentalist persecution). Most believe they are touched by Allah, but some do not even perceive their talent as magical. In all instances, women are strictly forbidden from practicing magic.

Despite mainstream Islam's abhorrence of things magical, Muslims born with the Gift find some grudging acceptance as Sufi and Moorish-inspired alchemists, scholars, mystics (mostly in moderate Islamic countries and the West), or as *mujahedin* (holy warriors) utterly devoted to the defense of the Faith (many of whom ironically do not recognize what they do as magic).

Islamic mages are skilled in the meta-formulae and equations governing the natural philosophy of magic and make excellent researchers and academics. Many are trained in carefully supervised madrassas (Islamic schools) that serve as both mosque and magical lodge. Islamic mages use incantations in Arabic and evocative verses from the Qu'ran for sortileges, and elaborate mathematical and geometrical devices for conjuration and warding—the latter often expressed in complex arabesques and talismanic squares (*wafq*).

Islam considers interaction with spirits of any type to be a perilous undertaking, and as such Islamic magicians never adopt Mentor spirits. Given the proper precautions, however, Islamic mages may summon various *djinn* and *ifrit*. These "creatures of smokeless fire" tend to manifest in more humanoid shapes than other elemental spirits, some beautiful, others quite hideous. Passages from the Qu'ran are also often used as protective invocation against spirits.

Mystics of the dwindling Sufi sub-tradition are less tightly controlled and more tolerant of dealing with spirits. In Sufi magic, poetic incantations, music, ecstatic dance, and flowing cursive script are also common.

Islamic magicians can be found throughout the Islamic world from Morocco to Indonesia, but tend to congregate in more moderate nations. The strong religious strictures on Islamic magic has kept it from becoming widespread in corporate circles—except in the field of alchemy, where Islamic magicians' talents are renowned. The pan-sectarian monastic order known as *Jamil Islamyah* trains budding magicians and adepts in the strictures of Islamic law and acceptable magic use, though it enforces strict separation between Awakened and secular Islamic society.

THE NORSE TRADITION

Concept: Norse magicians believe the Old Gods once again watch over Midgard. *Ásatru,* the old faith of the Norse, has seen a popular comeback and with it the revival of its visceral and pagan magic. Norse magic embraces the cult of the *Aesir* (the Norse gods), *galdor* (the lore of runes), *gannr* (the weaving of spells) and *seidr* (the lore of visions and communing with spirits).
Combat: Guardian
Detection: Water
Health: Fire
Illusion: Air
Manipulation: Beast
Drain: Willpower + Charisma

A rich and multifaceted magical system, Ásatru received a remarkable boost in Scandinavia following the Awakening and remains a popular tradition in the Northern Europe and the Baltic region—despite the damage done in by the apocalyptic actions of the extremist Ásatru cult known as Winternight in 2064.

Norse cosmology is pantheistic, and all Ásatru magicians show some degree of devotion to the Norse pantheon or to one particular *Ás* (singular of Aesir). Popular sects include the cults of Odin, Thor, Freya, and the Vanir (see p. 184).

In many Ásatru cults, the Awakened fulfill the role of *gode* (priest) or *gydje* (priestess of clerics). While all share the Ásatru paradigm of magic, not all Norse magicians become priests. A *ganner* is a spellweaver. A *seidman* uses ecstatic trances to perform magic and summon spirits. A *runemaster* uses futhark runes (carved, spoken, and chanted) to enhance the potency of his magic. Of particular note are *berserkers* or *bear sarks* who adopt totemic animal mentors (such as Bear, Stag); most are adepts, though mystic adepts or magicians are not unknown. *Bear sarks* often manifest shamanic masks when in frenzies, and their abilities closely parallel those of their mentors.

Norse magicians believe they deal with the denizens of the other Realms of the World Tree. Those that can cross to *Midgard* are the fire giants of Muspellheim (fire spirits), the dark fae of Niffellheim (spirits of water), the dwarves of Nidavellir (earth spirits), the storm spirits of Thrudheim (air spirits), and

the Valkyrie (guardian spirits). Some are intractable and treacherous, disliking metahumans, and most require tribute before performing services.

Both Awakened and mundane Ásatru gather for great ceremonies known as *blots* and *sumbles*. These are traditionally held on Midsummer's or Midwinter's Day and the spring or autumn equinoxes. Common ritual elements include trances, shaking or dancing, libations of mead or blood, and torches. Blots are also often marked by ritual animal sacrifice.

THE PATH OF THE WHEEL

Concept: *Draesis ti Heron,* the "Wheel of Life" or "Wheel of Existence," is the metaphysical representation of the great cycles of existence that lie at the heart of an ancient spiritual tradition.
Combat: Earth
Detection: Guidance
Health: Air
Illusion: Water
Manipulation: Fire
Drain: Willpower + Charisma

Path magic is a rigidly stratified tradition hailing from the Elven nation of Tir na nÓg (the country formerly known as Ireland). It purportedly harkens back to a mythical age before recorded history when the enlightened spirits of the *Tuatha De Danaan,* the "Children of the Goddess Danu," came to Tír na nÓg. At its heart lies the metaphysical Wheel of Life, the *Draesis ti Heron,* a belief in the transmigration of the spirit from one life to the next, a journey towards greater spiritual understanding and magical Awakening.

According to path doctrine, enlightened spirits follow a curriculum in life, intended to move them further along the *Mes ti Draesis,* the five great paths that form the Great Journey of the Wheel of Life. Each represents a lifelong vocation associated with an Order of Tir society, an element of nature, and a province of Tír na nÓg. Each path also aligns with one of five metaphysical archetypes known as Passions, typically represented by appropriate mentor spirits.

The five paths are: The Path of the Warrior (for a mentor spirit, use the Wise Warrior archetype), also known as the Order of Cu Chulainn; the Path of the Steward (use the Great Mother mentor archetype) or the Order of Etain; the Path of the Bard (use the Fire Bringer mentor archetype) or the Order of Brigid; the Path of the Druid (for mentor archetype, combine the description of Owl with Moon Maiden's advantages and disadvantages) or the Order of Ogma; and finally the Path of the Rígh (use Sky King) or the High Order of the Sun, Moon, and Stars (reserved only for the Tir elite and believed to possess exclusive metamagics able to replicate all the advantages of the lesser paths).

Spirits are seen as incorporeal forces and *fae,* spiritual embodiments of the true elements of nature. Much like other nature-revering beliefs, path magic is respectful and cautious in dealing with such entities.

Though its rites and rituals are closely guarded secrets, path magic involves many Celtic stylings, tropes, and trappings, and in fact many parallels exist between druidic and Celtic myths and the beliefs surrounding the *Draesis ti Heron.*

Vaguely fascist and with clear racial supremacist leanings, path magic and doctrine is practiced by the elven nobility of Tir na nÓg, the Danaan families. It is taught almost exclusively to Tir elves, and only they are allowed to initiate into its higher mysteries. It is practically unknown outside the island nation, practiced only by a few Tir outcasts and pariahs.

THE QABBALISTIC TRADITION

Concept: the ancestral Hebrew paradigm of mystical and divine correspondences describes a *qabbalist's* initiatory roadmap to self-illumination through understanding of the Sephiroths, the 10 dominions and emanations that form the mystical Tree of Life.
Combat: Air
Detection: Earth
Health: Fire
Illusion: Water
Manipulation: Task
Drain: Willpower + Logic
Note: Qabbalistic magic is a Possession tradition

Grounded in both scripture of the Torah and the seminal works known as the *Zohar,* the *Sefer Yetzirah,* and the *Sefer ha-Bahir,* qabbalism is arguably one of the most ancient mystical traditions practiced in the Sixth World. Through the ages many other traditions, not least of which are hermeticism and theurgy, have adapted the qabbalistic psychocosm (model of the universe) and incorporated aspects into their own paradigms.

The qabbalah is a complex system of occult or esoteric philosophy, describing the influence and correspondences of the ten Sephiroths in the material and spiritual worlds and how to harness that power. The mystical potency and significance of the 22 letters of the ancient Hebrew alphabet, their numerical correspondences, and the *true names* they describe play an important role in qabbalistic magic. Ancient Hebrew is therefore often used in spellcraft and in the intricate formulae, equations, and diagrams at the heart of qabbalistic magic. Spells are often spoken in ancient Hebrew, numerical equations are used in diagrams and symbols on foci, and numerology and astrology are important elements in various rites.

To modern qabbalists, spirits are *elohim,* emanations of the various Sephiroth embodying their esoteric aspects of there dominions (angels, though not in a Christian sense). As ephemeral spiritual entities, *elohim* do not manifest in the physical kingdom, but instead temporarily wear the flesh of humans or homunculi (such as traditional clay golems) when they must interact with the physical world at the qabbalist's request. The ten Sephiroths embody archetypical aspects of enlightenment and self-knowledge and are sometimes used as mentor spirits.

In the Sixth World, the distinct approaches to qabbalistic magic can be simplified to two main schools: magicians who subscribe to an almost secular understanding of qabbalistic practices lore, and qabbalists of ultra-orthodox Hebrew sects who believe they follow their own undiluted teachings. The former are often thought to be a sub-school of hermeticism and are quite widespread, featuring prominently in some academic circles. The latter are found almost exclusively in Orthodox Jewish enclaves and in Israel, rarely if ever interacting directly with gentiles.

THE SHINTO TRADITION

Concept: Shinto magic originates in the relationship between the practitioner and the *kami*, spirits that invest every aspect of the world. It primarily concerns itself with ensuring that the practitioner acts in harmony with the kami spirits, with magic being a natural extension of this harmony.
Combat: Air
Detection: Water
Health: Plant
Illusion: Beasts
Manipulation: Man
Drain: Willpower + Charisma

Easily the most influential shamanic tradition in Asia, Shinto shares many similarities with Amerindian shamanism, though the two are distinct traditions. Unlike Amerindian traditions, Shinto *kannushi* (typically *miko* if female) do not follow the ideals of a particular totem, but instead try to reach a state of harmony with the collective body of *kami* spirits that inhabit all things. Respect for nature is a key concept of Shinto tradition, as is the idea of remaining physically and spiritually "clean" through careful attention to proper rituals. The kami are honored at hundreds of thousands of shrines that range in size and shape, though most include the iconic *torii* gate. Honoring the kami is necessary, since the kannushi typically ask many favors of them, including the use of magic.

Kami spirits come in all varieties, from elemental spirits to the ghosts of ancestors to strange and wonderful animals. They are so numerous that they are commonly referred to as the "Eight Million Kami." Some are kindly and helpful, while others are mischievous or selfish. Shinto kannushi use many ritual tools in their magic, including *haraigushi,* a wand covered in paper streamers used to purify an area, and *ofuda,* paper prayer strips used for good luck or to deal with malicious spirits.

Shinto is the state religion of the modern Imperial Japan, which makes it the most common tradition found in that nation. It has spread wherever the Japanese Imperial State reaches, and the young Emperor has encouraged the Shinto tradition by making its practitioners an integral part of the rebuilding of Japan. And unlike most other shamanic traditions, Shinto is even found in the ranks of corporations, especially the Japanacorps.

TRADITIONAL OR HEDGE WITCHCRAFT

Concept: *Hedge witches* weave magic the way they always have, through subtle incantations, hexes, poxes, and potions, in accordance with half-forgotten lore of the natural world and ancient women's mysteries known as the *Old Ways*.
Combat: Earth
Detection: Water
Health: Plant
Illusion: Air
Manipulation: Task
Drain: Willpower + Intuition
Note: Hedge Witchcraft is a Possession tradition.

Traditional hex-casters and wise women, the practitioners of this venerable tradition are known diversely as *weise frauen, sorcières, streghe, brujas, bruxas,* or *hedge witches* depending on their country of origin. Witches tend to be secretive about their craft and are often confused with Wiccans. Most hedge witches, however, conform better to fairytale images of hex-casting women than to neo-pagans. Another departure from Wicca is that traditional witchcraft is exclusive to women and the tradition is oral, passed down from witch to apprentice across generations. Exceptions are only made when a witch lacks a female heir and the line risks being lost.

Witches are notorious for pillaging Christian, pagan, and hermetic symbolism and practices and mismatching them with traditional practices such as hexcraft, charms, the evil eye, dowsing, cartomancy, and spirit pacts. In fact, traditional witchcraft eschews any form of religious definition, and hedge witches are wary of mentor spirits.

To witches, the inhabitants of the world of spirits include the disembodied souls of the deceased (good and evil), mischievous *fey*, and the animistic powers of animals and plants. Dealing with these entities is an art fraught with dangers, one that witches are normally discouraged from pursuing. Most witches believe their very souls are placed at risk when dealing with spirits since these manifest in the material world through possession. Nonetheless, hedge witches have developed potions and concoctions that may be ingested to facilitate possession by an amenable spirit.

Cauldrons, wands, herbs, candles, concoctions, and potions are a few of the common staples of a hedge witch's magical style, though many variations exist. Hedge witches—seers, herbalists, crones, and midwives—can still be found plying their trade in the rural areas and the backstreets of Old World villages and sprawls from Lisbon to Vladivostok. In North America some are still found among ethnic communities.

Traditional witchcraft can also be used as a template for numerous minor traditions focused on women's mysteries and witchcraft around the globe. For instance Romany (gypsy) magic and Shakti/Devi (ecstatic Hindu goddess worship) have enough similarities with the template above that it can be used as a guideline.

THE VOODOO TRADITION

Concept: A profoundly mystic religion where those touched by the great *loa* as their *serviteurs* (servants) on earth learn to deal and court the favor of the *invisibles*, the subtle inhabitants of the spirit world, and through them unlock the higher mysteries and the gates to the mystic realm of Guinee.
Combat: Guardian
Detection: Water
Health: Man
Illusion: Guidance
Manipulation: Task
Drain: Willpower + Charisma
Note: Voodoo is a Possession tradition

Voodoo is the tradition of those that follow the spirits known as *loa* (both singular and plural). It descends from the African tribal lore brought across the Atlantic by black slaves, mixed with Native American mysticism and elements borrowed from Catholicism in the melting pot of the Americas.

Voodoo takes many forms: *Voudoun* is the tradition as it is practiced in Haiti and New Orleans, *Santeria* and *Orishá* are its names in Hispanic areas, and in Amazonia it is practiced as *Candomblé*. Male practitioners of Voudoun are referred to as *houngans*, female as *mambos*. In Santeria, a practitioner is known as a *santero* (feminine: *santera*), in Amazonian Candomblé s/he is a *mãe/pai de santo*. The tradition as presented here is meant as a guideline for the various traditions descended from the African Diaspora.

A Voodoo magician's power is intimately linked to *les invisibles* (ethereal and intangible entities believed to be spirits of nature and the deceased), and magicians are seen by the mundane faithful as handpicked by the loa. While all the loa are worthy of devotion, each magician is believed to have been chosen at birth by a patron loa, known as his *mait-tete* (literally "master of the head"). To walk the path of the loa, the magician must seek to emulate his mentor's demeanor and behavior as closely as possible or suffer the patron's wrath.

The major loa go by various names but are most commonly known as Agwe, Azaca, Damballah, Erzulie, Ghede, Legba, Obatata, Shango, and Ogoun (see p. 184). The key to interacting with loa and the lesser spirits of their courts is tribute and respect for their powers. They must be courted and flattered, not commanded, in order to garner favor and service.

A distinctive aspect of voodoo traditions is that of calling forth the *invisibles* to possess the body of the summoner or even mundane *serviteurs* (literally "servants"). These spirit-ridden individuals gain great power at the cost of conscious control over their actions. Houngans use lodges known as *hounfours* (or a *casa de santo* in Santeria). This is most often a circular hut built around a *poteau-mitain* (center post), which represents the cosmic axis or crossroads. During important rituals, hounfours are decorated with *vevers*, evocative images of the loa drawn in flour or cornmeal on the floor. Dancing, chanting, and drumming play a major role in Voodoo ritual. Typical fetishes and foci are made from seashells, bone, and feather telesma. Ritual blood-letting and *gris-gris*, unique telesma (often in the shape of sealed jars or pots), are used in conjuring.

THE WICCAN TRADITION

Concept: The "Craft of the Wise" teaches how to live in harmony with nature and harnesses the Earth's natural energies and animistic spirits through Wiccan workings. The craft is also a belief built on the feminine/masculine duality of the natural world in the form of the God and Goddess.
Combat: Fire
Detection: Water
Health: Plant
Illusion: Air
Manipulation: Earth
Drain: Willpower + Intuition (Goddess Wicca)/Logic (Gardnerian Wicca)

Though inspired by ancient nature worship, neo-pagan Wicca owes as much to nineteenth century spirituality and modern New Age philosophy as to ancestral traditions. Wiccans believe in a unique blend of nature worship, fertility cult, and modern mysticism, the essence of which lies in the belief in their personal relationship with the powerful energies and spirits of nature, and communion with the spiritual figures of the Goddess (most commonly using the Mentor archetypes for Great Mother or Moon Maiden) and the God (usually Horned Man or Wise Warrior).

Wicca is not monolithic and instead groups several diverse sub-traditions or *lineages*. The two most popular branches of

Wicca are the Gardnerian lineage, which integrates the religious observances and tenets of Wicca with a distinctly hermetic style, and the revitalized nature rites of witches following the cult of the Goddess. Minor lineages include Celtic Wicca, feminist "Dianic" Wicca, and the "Eclectics" (who, not unlike Chaos mages, combine various styles into their Wiccan rites). Urban Wiccans are sometimes known as *street witches*.

Wiccans, depending on their lineage, see spirits as animistic forces coalesced from Gaia's own energies on the astral plane, as fickle entities channeling elemental forces, or as the fae of legend. In all cases, spirits are dealt with care, and small offerings are often made as a sign of respect and goodwill during summonings.

Wiccans of all lineages, Awakened and mundane, traditionally gather in covens and circles. To focus their workings and sortileges, witches use a number of common foci and ritual trappings: the traditional athame (ritual dagger), a boline, a pentacle, a ritual sword, wand, and the cup. Candles, staffs, cauldrons, and brooms are also quite common. A hermetic aspect of Wicca's heritage is the *Book of Shadows,* which functions as a grimoire and the focal point of a coven's lodge. Witches commonly perform ritual magic according to the cycles of the moon.

In the Sixth World, Wicca is widespread in North America, Britain, and Northern Europe with numerous followers, Awakened and mundane alike, coming from all walks of life, from corporate suits to radical eco-activists.

THE WUXING TRADITION

Concept: The manipulation of *qi*—or vital life energy—through ritual and technique to produce magical effects.
Combat: Fire
Detection: Earth
Health: Plant
Illusion: Water
Manipulation: Guidance
Drain: Willpower + Logic

This Chinese magical tradition ties mana to the concept of *qi*, an energy that moves through the universe and the bodies of every being in it. *Qi* can have varying characteristics that influence how it manifests in the physical and spiritual worlds, and *wujen* (practitioners of Wuxing) can manipulate these characteristics to produce sorcery. *Qi* has five states of being, represented by the five Chinese elements of Fire, Earth, Wood, Water, and Metal, and it is also influenced by the two poles of passivity and activity, yin and yang. Like Western hermetic mages, wujen often use complex rituals and formulae to change the state of *qi* to what they desire, but they are also known to use techniques of meditation, geomancy, and martial arts.

Even the Wuxing approach to spirits is logical and orderly, with wujen requesting the aid of heavenly beings who are themselves arranged in a celestial bureaucracy. The primary duty of these spirits is recording the actions and fates of mortals, and most see the inevitable summonings from wujen as annoying distractions. When manifest, most have visual clues that tie them to their element, but they tend to appear humanoid or in the shape of Eastern dragons or mythical creatures. It is also common for wujen to summon the spirits of their own ancestors and consult their wisdom or petition their aid. The adoption of mentor spirits is rare among wujen, but there are some who follow in the paths of the Jade Emperor or Monkey (use the Dark King and Trickster archetypes, respectively).

The Wuxing tradition is native to the Chinese states, though it has traveled with Chinese immigration to communities around the globe. Many Asian corporations employ wujen in their magical personnel, and Western corporations are starting to turn to wujen to fill their own ranks. It is important to consider that Wuxing is a magical tradition but not a religion; many wujen also follow the tenets of Buddhism, Daoism, or even Christianity.

THE ZOROASTRIAN TRADITION

Concept: Magic, to the Zoroastrian *magus,* is part of the struggle between ultimate good and evil, an otherworldly force bound up in the fate of humanity that can be harnessed through complex symbology and purity of spirit.
Combat: Guardian
Detection: Fire
Health: Earth
Illusion: Water
Manipulation: Man
Drain: Willpower + Logic

Zoroaster, the ancient prophet of Zoroastrianism, revealed to his followers in ancient Persia that mankind's place in the cosmos was as the tipping point in the conflict between the ultimate good of the One God Ahura Mazda and the ultimate evil of the god Ahriman. Humanity possessed the free will to decide between good and evil and the capability to harness power through knowledge. The Zoroastrian religion encourages mankind to work for good and teaches how to access the great mystical power of the cosmos through astrology, symbology, and knowledge of angelic and demonic beings called the *ahuras* and *daevas* respectively. The Zoroastrian tradition is sometimes called "hermeticism with a purpose" because Western hermeticism borrowed many of the techniques and symbols of Zoroastrianism, but Zoroastrian magi dedicate them to the cataclysmic battle between good and evil.

Zoroastrian magi regularly deal with ancient Near Eastern angels and demons in their pursuit of knowledge, and they realize that they constantly walk a line between salvation and damnation. The spirits often challenge the magi who summon them with difficult questions of morality, to test where they stand or to tempt them into darkness. Many magi learn powerful symbols to protect themselves from the influences of the demonic daevas. It is extremely rare for a Zoroastrian magus to take a mentor spirit, as it often signifies that his devotions lie somewhere other than Ahura Mazda.

While Zoroastrianism never truly died out, it experienced a true resurgence in the past decades. Backlash against the fundamentalism of the Euro Wars brought new converts to Zoroastrian communities in Iran, and the Parsis of India have gained a great deal of influence since the Awakening. The tradition has also caught on in traditionally hermetic circles, such as universities and corporations, providing a familiar technique but also a strong reason to pursue knowledge.

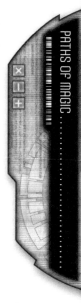

PATHS OF THE ADEPT

Unlike magicians and mystic adepts who require the mental construct of a tradition to channel and manipulate mana, adepts dispense with such esoteric crutches. Instead each follows a unique personal focus to their own somatic magical development known as an adept's *way*.

A way embodies the outlook and archetypical focus for magic that drive almost every adept character. It is the path an adept, consciously or subconsciously, follows toward an idealized self-image, and it defines the manner in which the adept's abilities express by channeling his magic in specific directions. For instance, a follower of the Artist's way is far less likely to develop destructive abilities given his gifts and outlook are naturally oriented towards creation, while an adept of the Speaker's way will naturally develop communication-oriented abilities, as opposed to combat ones. Adepts who have yet to find their personal way, and those that have found they lack that singular drive (sometimes called the "Lost"), inevitably find it harder to develop their gifts.

It should be noted that while ways are inherently personal, many cultures believe these mystical life paths are interwoven with other cultural mores and beliefs to the point of being inseparable. These cultural variants are not uncommon and find myriad expressions across the globe from Nordic *bear sarks* to New Zealand *whale-riders* to Islamic *mujahedin*.

Unlike many magical traditions that provide a common body of lore to practitioners, each way is unique and personal. Adepts often find it useful in developing their abilities, however, to associate and seek instruction from others who share similar ways and development focuses.

Below are some of the most common and popular adept ways to be found in the Sixth World. This list is a small and archetypical sample of common ways and is by no means exhaustive. Many other ways exist, of course, such as the Artist's way (using magic to enhance the adept's devotion to a style of art, from dancing to katas to vehicle mechanics) or the Spirit way (harmony with the astral world and its denizens, for adepts with astral sight).

THE ATHLETE'S WAY

Some adepts channel their mystical abilities towards an ideal physical perfection. Like the champions of old, their focus in life is the attainment of physical excellence, to excel at their sport, to reach their limits and overcome them—a passion fueled by the power of their magic. Followers of the Athlete's way focus on developing the somatic aspects of their potential. Their gifts are often less obvious than the flashy expressions of power of other adepts, instead expanding their natural attributes, skill, and endurance to prodigious levels.

Sixty years after the Awakening, the acceptance of things magical is still the main obstacle to an athlete adept's integration. Their ability at their chosen sport might be an adept's primary focus in life, but prejudice prevents all too many from participating in competitive sports. Many consider adept powers to be magical "cheats," and only a handful of professional sports, many of which also allow cybernetics, allow adepts to compete in regular leagues. Many disillusioned Athlete's way adepts, deprived of their dream of glory, find a home in the shadows, where they make for excellent intrusion specialists, sharpshooters, and even fighters.

THE WARRIOR'S WAY

The Warrior's way is the image of adepts popularized by the media, though in fact warrior adepts come in all shapes and sizes, from berserkers to tribal warriors to Buddhist monks. Warrior adepts are defined by an innate talent for conflict and violence; their sole common denominator is an aggressive personality and a focus on using their aptitude for violence to enhance their combat prowess. This focus does not make all warrior adepts bloodthirsty maniacs or urban predators; while a street brawler finds an outlet for his natural aggressiveness and thrives on violence for its own sake, a modern *ronin* follows a code and sees the way of the warrior as a path to personal development and martial excellence.

What separates an adept pit fighter from a kickboxer isn't so much his ability but his outlook; an athlete strives to excel in his field, while a warrior lives for the rush of the fight—and their power expressions reflect this. Warrior adepts range from masters of the martial arts to swordsmen, from Zen archers to those who have an uncanny facility for modern firearms. Many warrior adepts find applications for their talents in military or security service, while others use their abilities as soldiers-for-hire, mercenaries, or street fighters.

THE INVISIBLE WAY

Followers of the Invisible way—sometimes known as the Silent way—focus their magical powers on becoming masters of stealth and subterfuge. The polar opposite of warriors, these adepts shun direct confrontation, focusing instead on gaining the uncanny ability to act and move without drawing attention to themselves. Their magical potential is channeled toward making them shadows and phantoms, moving unseen, unheard, and unidentifiable. Some can walk through a crowd without being noticed, or stalk across snow or sand leaving no trace of their passing.

Their Gift makes them exceptionally skilled at sleight-of-hand, furtiveness, and deception, slipping out of sight and mind. Most are also able climbers and gymnasts, able to infiltrate their way into the most secure of places with no one the wiser. The most dangerous and lethal walk the path of the silent assassin, becoming as deadly as any Warrior adept. Some of the most accomplished cat burglars, spies, hunters, and stalkers of the Sixth World follow the Invisible way.

THE SHAMANIC WAY

More common among tribal cultures but increasingly seen among urban tribes, the shamanic adept—also called a follower of the Animal way—follows a totem spirit in a manner similar to a shaman. However, not only do shamanic adepts believe they are soul bonded to a particular mentor spirit, but such adepts perceive their totem (normally an animal) as an idealized model to emulate, something from which to draw power.

Shamanic adepts try to embody the qualities and abilities of their totem animal, seeing this as a path in itself. The adept's own powers are often seen as gifts of the mentor spirit, and as such mimic enhanced versions of the totem's natural abilities. Some go so far as to take geasa on their abilities in keeping with the mentor spirit's personality and behavior. There are even those that have been known to exhibit shamanic mask (p. 181, *SR4A*) when calling on their powers.

Various Asian martial arts boast "animal-like" abilities and techniques, though their approach to totemic power is entirely different. Adepts trained in these traditions distill the animal's natural savagery through Zen techniques until they are at one with the beast and channel its abilities.

THE SPEAKER'S WAY

Adepts of the Speaker's way represent one of the most surprising manifestations of somatic magical potential. Social adepts, as they are sometimes known, strive to become the epitome of the metahuman social animal, the aleph of every group and social network. A social adept's development focuses on boosting her personal magnetism and her social skills. A bewildering variety of powers are put to use, making them masters of the subtleties of human communication and interaction.

A typical speaker adept's repertoire of magical gifts allows her to entice you with a silver tongue, placing her voice at just the perfect pitch to convey a thrill, mimic body language to put you at ease, or simply fast-talk you into believing just about anything. Individuals' ethics and morals vary as widely as their abilities; some put those abilities at the service of their fellow man, others use them to swindle him out of his hard-earned nuyen.

Social adepts have no difficulty finding their niche in the shadows as faces, fixers, info brokers, and con men, or working for the Man as negotiators, middlemen, and Mr. Johnsons.

MAGICAL ODDITIES

Just as there are many ways of interpreting magic as practiced by magicians, there are many individuals who simply refuse to recognize their gifts or abilities as magic. These individuals credit their powers to mental abilities or miracles, and some even exhibit magical abilities as a result of madness.

PSIONICS

Though most people in the Sixth World eventually came to accept the existence of magic following the Awakening, this was neither a simple nor quick process. For most of humanity, understanding of the nature of magic has come slowly, through trial and error as much as intuitive discovery and scholarly research.

Initially, many scientific minds considered the changes in their world to be a result of extreme genetic mutation, or the influences of the collective unconscious, or even psionic manipulation of electromagnetic energies. While some investigators delved into the newly discovered power of ancient beliefs, others pursued the parapsychological hypothesis that magic was simply latent psionic ability expression. Funded by governments, militaries, and corporations, research institutes were established, only to fall on hard times as the ruling scientific paradigm moved on embracing thaumaturgy as a science. Some of these, like the Psionic Studies Institute in New Jersey (UCAS) and the Markov Foundation in Murmansk (Russia), still linger.

These days, psionics is considered a quaint and outdated paradigm by the wider magical community; a flawed understanding of magic being gradually eroded by its own inability to explain many of the everyday realities and accept the fundamental conventions of modern thaumaturgy. Nonetheless, die-hard psionics persist, denouncing so-called "magical traditions" and their esoteric teachings as superstitious hocus-pocus clouding the truth—that all "magic" is actually an expression of the power of the metahuman mind and will.

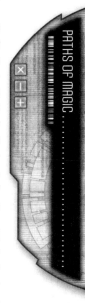

MIRACLES

Some magicians believe their magic is based on the power of their faith and an intimate bond to the divine. This is superficially similar to the shamanic practice of magic, with its belief that shamans are gifted people with the calling to bridge the worlds of man and spirits. While shamanism believes each shaman is empowered by a totemic patron, a mentor spirit, it still separates—as do most magical traditions—the working of magic from divine intervention. The former is seen as a metahuman gift, the latter as the domain of the god or gods.

Miracle workers, on the other hand, do not see their powers as their own, but as actual miracles, the doings of higher powers, and not "magic" at all. Their spells take the form of prayers, and the spirits they summon often appear as figures from their religious beliefs (e.g. angels, demons, devas, kami, ascended masters, or even alien spirit guides). Religious trappings and rituals are used as geasa, fetishes, and foci but are rarely recognized as magical.

Some self-proclaimed miracle workers even believe the practice of magic is evil, at the same time claiming that their powers come from another, higher, source. These individuals denounce the workings of magic while wielding powerful abilities of their own.

Shadowrun makes no judgments about the value of any individual religious belief. For the purposes of post-Awakening magic, all beliefs are equally significant. It is not the religious dogma itself that matters as much as the individual's belief in that dogma, turning it into an effective magical tool. There are no "better" or "correct" religions, magically speaking.

MADNESS

The experience of Awakening and dealing with forces mundanes cannot experience or understand has been known to seriously unbalance an individual's mind, leading many Awakened across the fine line dividing magical insight and madness. Even some of those who overcome the challenge and learn to wield magic see their sanity slowly eroded by the sheer power at their fingertips.

The magical style of an insane magician or adept could be virtually anything imaginable (and might include a few unimaginable things as well). Strange spirits out of a madman's personal delusions can appear, and a mad shaman may follow a mentor spirit embodying some strange entity from the depths of a twisted personal mythology. Madness can lead to insight, and those who have gone over the edge are often dangerously powerful. Player characters cannot choose to follow these paths—the journey to insanity cannot commence with a rational choice.

For more information on the twisted paths followed by such Awakened, see *Magical Threats*, p. 134.

BUILDING A MAGICAL TRADITION

The magical traditions presented in *Street Magic* and *SR4A* represent only the most well-established and predominant paradigms of magic in the Sixth World, and hence the most commonly found in both mainstream society and the shadows. Numerous others exist, and a potentially infinite number are possible. Given the subjective nature of magic use, different and contradictory beliefs not only co-exist but cannot be objectively disproved.

Enterprising gamemasters and players interested in exploring other magical traditions beyond those presented in official material may use the Creating a Tradition rules on p. 180, *SR4A*, to develop their own. The following section is intended to provide a step-by-step walkthrough of magical tradition creation.

STEP 1: CONCEPT

The first and most important step in the creation process is defining the concept. A magical tradition is seldom built on a single idea or isolated concept, but instead relies on an intricate set of beliefs, theories, and symbols. While some magicians may believe themselves to be the mystical love child of the Toaster God or a super-powered product of government experimentation, these should not qualify as traditions unless the character is slightly insane. This is because such concepts make no attempt to provide the character with the tools and mental constructs needed to wield and understand the forces of magic. One reason why many *Shadowrun* traditions extrapolate from real world mystical systems is that such traditions provide a coherent framework of concepts and beliefs that defines, amongst other things:

- a fundamental metaphysics that outlines the ultimate nature of magic and the world;
- a cosmology of the spiritual world and an understanding of the nature of spirits; and
- a set of rituals, symbols, and tools that allow the magician to wield magic reliably and safely.

> *Oliver is creating an Asian magician to play in his gamemaster's Pacific Rim-based campaign. Being a bit of a buff on Korean culture and having just read an interesting article on the renewed popularity of shamanism there, he decides it would be interesting to have his character be a mudang (Korean shaman). Rather than developing a tradition from scratch, he decides to convert the local shamanistic belief.*
>
> *Step 1 is to define the concept behind the tradition. A little research reveals Korean shamanism has many concepts in common with shamanism, Wuxing, and Shinto. It also reveals that Korean shamanism believes spirits interact with the physical world primarily through possession. The mudang is a mediator between the world of the living and the world of spirits and the dead, and his Gift is often (though not always) hereditary. Oliver comes up with:*
>
> **Concept:** *A mudang (Korean shaman) believes her Talent is either inherited through her lineage or a gift from the omnipresent spirit world. Hers is the Gift to channel the spirits of the dead, of nature, and of the small gods, and through them harness the chi (life energies) of the Earth itself.*

STEPS 2: SPIRITS

Spirits and their magical associations are one of the harder elements to devise when designing a new tradition. This is partially because *Shadowrun* abstracts spirits into 10 basic types (Air, Beast, Earth, Fire, Guardian, Guidance, Man, Plant, Task, and Water), and occasionally finding correspondences with traditional lore can be difficult. Obviously, when devising a tradition from scratch this is less of a problem, but if trying to adapt an existing historic or fictional mystic system this may cause difficulty. If some research (your local library and the internet may provide more sources than you expect) doesn't yield suggestions, then it's advisable to use a similar published tradition and its associations as a guideline.

Research will often also provide useful roleplaying cues and ideas that can be added to the tradition's description.

Moving on to Step 2, Oliver has to decide the type of spirits the mudang summons and what their magical correspondences are. His sources aren't very precise but indicate Korean shamanism has elements in common with both Wuxing and Shinto. Though it sees spirits much as Shinto sees kami (as minor divinities and nature spirits), and it has a strong element of ancestor worship, Oliver decides some of the associations and abilities these spirits are believed to exhibit are closer to a wujen's understanding. So he decides to use the Wuxing tradition template (p. 43) with a minor tweak (replacing wood with air, which, as the fourth element, plays an important role in Korean symbolism). The result is:

Combat: *Fire*
Detection: *Earth*
Health: *Air*
Illusion: *Water*
Manipulation: *Guidance*

STEP 3: DRAIN

Once the core concept is thought out, the Drain attribute used by a tradition is often self-evident. A tradition with a practical, scientific, and planned approach to magic suggests Logic as the secondary Drain attribute; for a tradition with a spontaneous, ecstatic, or artistic approach, Intuition would likely be better; finally, one which focuses principally on dealing, interacting, and wooing spirit forces should call on Charisma.

In Step 3, Oliver defines how a mudang resists Drain. Looking over his notes it seems obvious that a mudang's talent depends on courting the good will of the spirits. A natural sensitivity to protocol and social interactions would be essential for the role of mediator between the spirit world and metahumanity. Consequently Oliver decides on:
Drain: *Willpower + Charisma*

STEP 4: ROUNDING OUT

Just as important as the previous steps is defining the tradition's rituals, trappings, symbols, and practices, both in the interest of providing a solid foundation for roleplaying and rounding out the description of the tradition's overall paradigm with regards to magic and spirits, and how it interacts (if at all) with mundane society.

Oliver returns to his references and decides that the spirits mudangs summon should have the Possession power rather than Materialization power, so he adds:
Note: *Korean Shamanism is a Possession tradition*

Having completed the basic template, Oliver sets about describing the tradition's beliefs, practices, and symbols for roleplaying purposes, resorting once again to his notes, a little online searching, and a little creative extrapolation.

Description and Customs: *The Awakening did little to change Koreans' faith in magic and spirits, because they had never ceased believing in them. Korean tradition dictates that mudangs, hereditary or spirit-touched shamans, are go-betweens bridging the celestial world and material plane. Theirs is the sacred calling to maintain the delicate balance between the two with the help of cheonsa (good spirits). Mudangs appease tensions and punish transgressions; some are even charged with the eradication of ak-ma (evil spirits) at large in the Sixth World.*

All mudangs focus primarily on spirit lore in order to calm, banish, or petition the services of the nature spirits, local divinities, and ghosts that permeate our world. While some mudangs chose a patron spirit, most avoid showing preferences and do not take mentor spirits. Sorcery and spells are gifts from spirit patrons or helpful incantations taught by their metahuman tutor—or spirit mother—who in turn was instructed by the spirits. A mudang's magic is dominated by spontaneity, but rituals known as gut are a significant part of the mudang's responsibilities.

Traditionally, Korean shamans are female, though a few male practitioners are slowly popping up among the new generation. Another sign of the times is the inclusion of many technological elements in a mudang's rites and paraphernalia, paralleling Korean culture's fascination with both tradition and technology. Minor implants are quite common, and AR is often used for both decorative and ritual purposes, combining with traditional materials and trappings such as fans, bells, blades, modern musical instruments, and so on. Mudangs are universally respected among Koreans, both at home and in communities abroad (such as those found in California, Seattle, New York, Chile, etc.).

All Oliver needs now is his gamemaster's approval and he's ready to build his mudang.

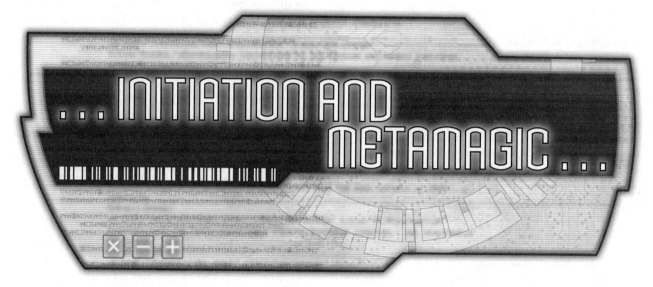

...INITIATION AND METAMAGIC...

The rain fell like black, bloated bullets from the loaded clouds, flooding the rooftops with the relentless drum and sizzle of a million soft impacts. The night roared as thunder rolled in off the Gulf and the sharp tang of ozone whipped in on a warm gust, mingling with the miasma of sprawl air.

Lord Shango was abroad, and, as was proper, Johnny Vendredi walked into the night to meet his mait-tête. His Maman had taught him well, and Johnny had been ready; it had been grueling, but he had found his way back to his poteau-mitain with his prize. His task was almost complete.

The houngan walked out of his hounfour into the fury of the summer storm, stripped to the waist and wearing only his patron's white. He was oblivious to the acid tingling of the rain on his bare skin, just as he ignored the dozens of small cuts and burns that covered his back and torso.

Muffled drumming floated from inside the rooftop shack, beating a counterpoint to the blood in his ears. The candles danced in the wind. His knife gleamed savagely in his hand as new lightning flitted down. His other hand held tight to the gris-gris jar.

Lightning slashed from the warring clouds on the horizon, the city's holograms dull by comparison.

He spread his arms and knelt on the half-flooded rooftop to honor his mait-tête, bowing his head and repeating the prayer three times, just as he had been taught. Then he raised his eyes to the sky. The stormclouds above looked lit from within, lightning frozen in place, the outlines of a face he remembered from as dreams as far back as he could remember. Lightning danced and the face seemed to smile.

"Shango, Lord of Lightning and Storms, hear me! I have walked to the Land Beneath the Sea and back. I am reborn to the world and seek your blessing. I have proven myself and returned with honor. Accept this gift as proof of my worth."

The gris-gris tingled with barely restrained power in his hand. Johnny spoke softly to the presence within. "Remember. My challenge was righteous and my victory just. There is no dishonor, great warrior. Tell your father. Do right by me, sogbo, I release you of my own free will!"

The houngan lifted his magical blade over his head and plunged it into the leather lid. Blue-white lightning burst free, coursed up the blade, flickered brilliantly for a moment, and fled up into the sky.

The voice that sounded in Johnny's ears roared like a tropical gale, "You show promise child. You have done well. I accept your gift with pleasure. What do you wish of me in return?"

"Nothing but your blessing, my lord," smiled Vendredi despite his weariness.

"That is a good answer, child," laughed the lightning, "So it shall be!"

Lighting crackled down to the rooftop, through the knife and into Vendredi. He felt the power of Shango course savagely through him. Then, as suddenly as it had begun, it was over. Vendredi opened his eyes and the world was changed. Even without his Sight he could sense the power in the storm, the magic thrumming electric over the sprawl, the comforting emanations of his hounfour behind him.

"I am not worthy, lord."

"No you are not, child. Not yet." And the thunder was gone.

Street Magic

INITIATION

After the chaos of the Awakening subsided, metahumanity took its first concerted steps in exploring the magical arts. Students immersed themselves in studies of the Art, exploring and testing their abilities. Some focused on refining and exploring the ability to spellcast and conjure, while others fathomed the nature of magic, gaining new insight and greater knowledge of the Talent. As comprehension of the underlying pillars of magic evolved, new arts developed, new techniques were discovered, and new dimensions of power revealed. Mastery of magic's higher mysteries and understanding of the secrets of initiation increased.

BEYOND THE DOORS OF PERCEPTION

In *Shadowrun,* initiation is the name given to the process of spiritual advancement and self-discovery that sharpens an Awakened character's innate sensitivity to magic and allows them to tap hitherto unknown aspects of their Talent. Initiates discover how to expand their Magic beyond its natural limits, wield metamagics (see p. 52), and unlock the metaplanes of astral space (see p. 130).

Like most paths of character improvement, initiation has a Karma cost. Usually a certain amount of time and preparation should elapse between the character acquiring the necessary Karma and performing an initiation, though the gamemaster has the final say on when a character may initiate. Basic rules regarding initiation and metamagic abilities can be found on p. 198, *SR4A*.

Note that while an initiate's grade is intended to be an abstract representation of a character's advancement on the path of enlightenment and control over her Gift, in most traditions it corresponds to a certain measure of professional accomplishment and prestige and affords some recognition among peers and magical society at large.

The following rules are intended to provide additional options and depth to the process and rituals of initiation.

GROUP INITIATION

While a character may initiate on her own (see p. 198, *SR4A*), she may also do so as a member of a magical group (see *Magical Groups,* p. 62). Initiates often band together with other like-minded souls in magical groups, societies, or circles, which facilitate initiation (by reducing Karma cost) in addition to offering material rewards. In fact, many magical groups are primarily initiatory by nature.

Nonetheless, not everyone is cut out to belong to a magical group, and an appropriate group may be hard to find. Other groups may be too selective in their membership or require members to abide by restrictive strictures. Inevitably, some characters will prefer to initiate on their own.

COST OF INITIATION

Initiation base cost:	10 + (Grade x 3)
Group initiation:	Base cost – 20% (round up)*
Initiatory ordeal:	Base cost – 20% (round up)*

* These may be combined for a net initiation cost of Base cost – 40% (round up)

THE INITIATION RITE

By definition, initiation is a milestone in a character's magical and spiritual progress. Be it a personal epiphany, a moment of spiritual transfiguration, or a ceremonial rite of passage, initiation is always a major step in a magician's development, one that is not undertaken lightly and one that demands spiritual, mental, and sometimes physical preparation. Most established magical traditions and many adept ways recognize initiation as an important element in understanding the mysteries and boast appropriate initiatory rites and rituals. Accordingly, initiations are often reserved for auspicious moments or mystically significant dates.

The character's chosen path and its beliefs (see *Paths of Magic,* p. 32) are a good starting point for ideas, but gamemasters should feel free to develop their own and allow players to come up with appropriate rites of passage. A shaman may perform a vision quest in the tribal sweat lodge; an aboriginal *koradji* may go on a walkabout; Aztec *nahualli* may need to bond with her animal twin in the wild; a hermetic mage may have to study diligently; a qabbalist may need to perform intricate purification rituals; or a shamanic adept may need to best her totem animal in combat. Rites vary enormously depending on tradition-specific beliefs and cultural mores.

Except for the basic time and effort required to undergo ordeals (below) or learn new metamagical techniques, the gamemaster is free to adjust the time spent and the initiation rite involved to suit the character and the flavor of his campaign. If the player desires, the initiation rite may include an initiatory ordeal. Ordeals are specific tests of will and ability to which the character willingly submits in order to prove herself worthy of initiation.

It is quite common for a character's mentor spirit to play an important role in the rite, the ordeal, or in both, though exactly what that role is should be tailored to the particular character, her tradition, the initiation rite she is undertaking and the nature of the ordeal she chooses. While the group's style of gaming may determine how much attention is devoted to initiation rites, the unique roleplaying and story opportunities these pose should not be overlooked.

INITIATORY ORDEALS

Characters wishing to initiate may undertake an ordeal—a task that tests the candidate's determination and ability, such as a trial by combat, a grueling aesthetic regime, or the crafting of a complex magical thesis. Undergoing an ordeal during initiation reduces the normal Karma cost of initiation by 20 percent (rounded up). Only one ordeal is possible per initiation, and the character must choose the ordeal before undergoing the initiation rite. She cannot "get an ordeal out of the way" ahead of time, with the exception of a deed (see below). If the character

passes the ordeal, she gains a new grade. If the character fails the ordeal, she must try again until she succeeds.

Karma Expenditure: If a character fails an ordeal, she does not need to repay the initiation Karma cost when attempting that ordeal again for the same initiation grade.

Metaplanar Quest

To successfully perform the metaplanar quest ordeal, the character must project to the metaplanes (see *Metaplanes,* p. 128) and overcome the relevant challenges. Characters unable to astrally project cannot undertake a metaplanar quest unless they gain access to the Astral Gateway power of a free spirit or great form guidance spirit (p. 57).

Before attempting a quest (see *Metaplanar Quests,* p. 130), the character must prepare by steeling herself through ritual and meditation, a process that requires a Magic + Drain attribute + initiate grade (12, 1 hour) Extended Test. There is no penalty for briefly interrupting the preparation process, but the process is demanding and leaves no time for any activities other than the most ordinary tasks.

The gamemaster should tailor the quest to be appropriately evocative of the initiate's tradition and beliefs. The quest itself works best as a metaphor for the difficult path towards enlightenment. If a character fails the quest, she may, if able, attempt the quest again until successful.

Asceticism

An ascetic ordeal involves giving up the creature comforts of modern life and devoting oneself exclusively to physically and mentally challenging activities for an extended period of time. The latter are designed to bring the inner spiritual self in tune with its physical and mental aspects, and may include rigorous fasting, strenuous exercises, ritual combat, prolonged devotional rites, walkabouts, living off the land, and other taxing endeavors.

A character must abandon her normal lifestyle and adopt a Street lifestyle for a period of at least 28 days (one lunar month). During this period she must strictly conform to an ascetic regime appropriate to her magical tradition and culture (subject to gamemaster approval), declining all but the most basic of comforts (such as food and clothing). The gamemaster may require Survival Tests (p. 137, *SR4A*) to determine how well she gets by. If the character manages to strictly adhere to the regimen for the full duration, the ordeal is successful. Asceticism may not be taken on two consecutive initiation rites.

Deed

A deed ordeal requires a character to perform some difficult task with a goal appropriate to her personal beliefs, tradition, mentor spirit, magical group (if she belongs to one), or moral code (if she has one).

Before the character commits to a deed ordeal, the gamemaster and player should agree on an appropriate task and introduce it through roleplaying. Such a task may develop into a run in its own right—though the run must be personally relevant and appropriate to the character undertaking it. As a general guideline, the Karma award for the run should be comparable to the Karma cost of the grade the character seeks. If the gamemaster approves the run as a deed, successfully accomplishing the goal of the run means the ordeal is accomplished.

Potential deeds include defeating some kind of magical threat (see *Magical Threats,* p. 134), overcoming or dealing with a free spirit (see *Free Spirits,* p. 106), experiencing a test of magic ability, communing with great spirits, going on a metaplanar quest for some greater end (other than as an ordeal), or some other experience that widens the character's knowledge of magic.

At the gamemaster's discretion, a character may carry out a deed before she is ready to initiate to another grade, essentially "saving" a deed and using it as an ordeal for her next initiation. A deed must be used for the character's next initiation, however, and cannot be saved beyond that grade.

Familiar

This ordeal requires the character to summon an ally spirit (see *Ally Spirits,* p. 103). It is only available to magicians able to summon ally spirits and then only to those who design their own ally spirit formula. The initiating character need not have taken the requisite Ally Conjuration metamagic (see p. 53) beforehand and may take it as the metamagic technique gained during the initiation she is currently undergoing.

Geas

To fulfill this ordeal, the character voluntarily accepts a geas limiting her magic ability. Choose a geas from the options available on p. 27, or create your own with the gamemaster's approval. A geas taken as an ordeal can never be removed.

Meditation

The character must spend time in daily meditation, trying to consciously bring the physical, mental, and astral aspects of her being into perfect balance. To achieve this, the character must succeed in two Extended Tests:
- A Body + Willpower (Charisma x Strength, 1 day) Test.
- A Logic + Agility (Intuition x Reaction, 1 day) Test.

To successfully complete the ordeal, the Extended Tests must both be completed in (desired grade x 4) days. Unless both tests are successful, the character must begin the meditative cycle over again. This ordeal is particularly demanding and leaves no time for any activities other than the most ordinary tasks. Environmental distractions must also be kept to a minimum: apply a –2 dice pool modifier if the character's lifestyle is Squatter or lower, or if the character is unable to meditate in peaceful seclusion. Do not apply this penalty if the character is living in the wilderness during this ordeal *and* has a Survival skill rating of 3 or more.

Oath

The oath ordeal, in which the character swears an oath to obey a given magical group's rules and strictures, is only available to members of such groups (see *Magical Groups,* p 62). Even if a character swears several oaths in her career, only the first qualifies as an ordeal.

Sacrifice

Common in many ancient and primitive traditions, a sacrifice ordeal calls on the magician to permanently sacrifice a part of her body (such as an eye, ear, hand, genitalia, etc.) or visibly scar part of her body. Such sacrifices may never be replaced or hidden through surgery.

The character undergoing this ordeal permanently gives up 1 point from an appropriate attribute (such as Charisma or Intuition for an eye, or Agility for a hand). This is a reduction to the character's natural attribute rating; augmented ratings (from cyberware, spells, or adept powers) cannot be sacrificed as part of this ordeal. The character's natural maximum rating (see p. 81, *SR4A*) for the attribute is also permanently reduced by 1. The character cannot sacrifice a point from an attribute that has a rating of 1. If this ordeal is taken multiple times, the character must reduce a different Physical attribute before she can reduce a previously reduced attribute again.

Suffering

To perform this ordeal, the magician must voluntarily subject herself to a test of extreme physical and mental hardship, such as being hung from a tree for nine days, suffering crucifixion, stepping through an astral gateway to some nightmare metaplane, or enduring ritual torture. In all cases, the ordeal should be horrific and test the limits of the magician's willpower and stamina.

The gamemaster may choose either to detail the ordeal through roleplaying or to circumvent such potentially disturbing matters by asking for a Willpower + Logic (2) Test *and* a Body + Strength (2) Test. Success in both is required to complete the ordeal.

The initiate emerges from the ordeal wiser and strengthened but also marked by her trials. She gains 10 BP worth of Negative qualities (p. 93, *SR4A*), chosen by the gamemaster.

Thesis/Masterpiece

This ordeal requires the Awakened character to formulate a thesis or create a masterpiece work of art that represents the sum of her magical knowledge and spiritual insight at that point in time. A thesis must possess a hard-copy (not digital) physical form, but otherwise is eminently personal and colored by the character's tradition and approach to magic.

To produce a thesis or masterpiece, a Logic + Arcana (8 + desired initiate grade, 1 week) Extended Test is required. Alternately, the gamemaster may allow an Intuition + relevant Artisan skill (8 + desired initiate grade, 1 week) Extended Test if appropriate.

By its very nature, a thesis or masterpiece provides a potent material link (see p. 28) to the author, and initiates are ever watchful of such creations. For this reason, initiates are typically reluctant to make more than one copy of their thesis or masterpiece. If *all* copies of a thesis or masterpiece are destroyed, however, the author suffers a crisis of faith at such a momentous loss and must choose to either take on a geas (see p. 27) or reduce her initiate grade by 1. Consequently most initiates risk making at least one backup copy.

Note that some magical groups require this ordeal. In this case, the thesis is often the second ordeal the group demands (oath being the first), and the members' theses or masterpieces are kept on file as loyalty insurance.

METAMAGIC

One of the rewards of initiation is access to metamagic techniques. Metamagic represent an individual's growing mastery over the core aspects of her Gift. Metamagic techniques enhance a character's ability to wield magic on a fundamental level, expanding her innate ability to use mana in unique new ways as well as diversifying her sorcery and conjuring abilities.

OPTIONAL RULE: LEARNING METAMAGIC

If the gamemaster approves, Awakened characters can learn metamagic techniques through other methods, in addition to the one they acquire at each grade of initiation. It costs 15 Karma to learn a metamagic technique outside of initiation. The maximum number of metamagic techniques that may be learned is equal to the character's Magic + initiation grade.

Metamagic via Metaplanar Quests

A character may learn a metamagic technique by performing a metaplanar quest (see p. 130). The initiate must successfully complete the quest and pay the requisite Karma cost to learn the new metamagic.

Metamagic via Metahuman Tutor

A character may learn metamagic from any Awakened metahuman who knows the technique. The teacher must be of the same tradition as the character (or close enough, subject to gamemaster approval). To learn the metamagic, the student must make an Extended Intuition + Magic (12, 1 day) Test. The teacher can make an Instruction test (p. 134, *SR4A*) to add dice to the learning test. There are no tutorsofts for metamagic.

Metamagic via Spirit Tutor

A character may learn metamagic from any free spirit that knows the technique. In this case, the Karma is actually paid directly to the spirit. See *Free Spirits*, p. 106. To learn the technique, the student must make an Extended Intuition + Magic (8, 1 day) Test.

Metamagic via Research

Characters may also research published metamagic techniques and attempt to learn them on their own, though this is more difficult. The gamemaster determines if such techniques are even available through public channels—or what the cost is through private channels. Learning via research requires an Extended Arcana + Intuition (16, 1 month) Test, representing the effort to locate reference material and absorb the knowledge.

NEW METAMAGIC

The following section expands the list of metamagic techniques available to initiates in the Sixth World (see also

pp. 198, *SR4A*). While most are accessible to any initiate, some advanced techniques require the magician to first master a basic metamagic before being able to unlock the advanced form (see *Advanced Metamagic,* p. 58).

Not all of the techniques introduced below are appropriate for adept characters. Adepts may learn Divining, Psychometry, and Sensing, as well as the exclusive metamagics of Adept Centering, Attunement (Animal and Item), Cognition, and Somatic Control, which are available only to adepts and mystical adepts.

Some singular metamagics are normally only available to followers of the Twisted paths, toxic magicians and insect shamans; these can be found in the *Magical Threats* chapter (p. 134). Gamemasters are advised to consider very carefully before allowing these to be made available to player characters since their implications may prove difficult to roleplay and unbalance the game.

Adept Centering (Adepts Only)

Adept Centering is a variation of Centering (p. 198, *SR4A*) available only to adepts and mystic adepts that allows an initiate to reduce negative dice pool modifiers to Physical and Combat skills by her initiate grade—as long as she can physically perform her chosen method of centering.

Ally Conjuration

For a magician to be able to summon the unique spirits known as allies (p. 103), she must first take the Ally Conjuration metamagic and possess a ready ally spirit formula. This metamagic grants her the power to mold and enhance a bound spirit she already possesses according to the "blueprint" of the ally spirit formula—thereby granting it remarkable new abilities and often modifying its original personality (often subconsciously grafting on an aspect of her own, especially when combined with the Familiar ordeal). For more details, consult p. 103.

Attunement (Animal) (Adepts Only)

This metamagic allows an adept or mystic adept to bond with a mundane, non-sapient animal. The process will not work if the animal is coerced, so the adept must first befriend the critter. This requires an Intuition + Charisma (12, 1 week) Extended Test. The magical aura of a prepared vessel interferes with Attunement, and consequently it is not possible to attune an animal vessel.

Once a rapport is established, the adept must perform a ritual bonding, spending Karma equal to the animal's Essence. The gamemaster and player should tailor this rite to the character's background, tradition, or way (p. 32). A shamanic adept, for example, might need to best a wild animal in combat to become the alpha.

A bonded animal gains the power of Sense Link (see p. 54).

Attunement metamagic applies only to one specific type of type of animal (e.g., Attunement (Lynx)). If an adept wants to attune a different critter, she must learn the technique again. A character may only attune a number of individual

SENSE LINK

Type: M • Action: Simple • Range: Adept's Magic x 10 meters • Duration: Always

An adept may experience the world through the senses of an animal bonded with Attunement metamagic (p. 54). The animal and adept remain in a low-level telepathic link as long as the animal is within range. The animal does not "talk" via this link, but it may emote and transmit sensory information. The adept may also issue simple, low-level telepathic commands to the animal through this mystic link. Commands do not automatically succeed—especially if the command puts the animal in danger. The gamemaster may call for an Intuition + Charisma or other appropriate test to ensure obedience.

The adept may experience any one of the animal's senses (or switch to another) with a Simple Action. The animal remains in control of its own actions and senses—the adept is merely along for the ride. The adept cannot make the animal focus on anything, and none of the adept's augmented senses (including astral sight) will work through the animal. Note that a dual-natured animal's astral sight is considered a separate sense from regular physical sight.

The Sense Link's range is (initiate's Magic x 10) meters. If the animal goes beyond this range, contact is lost. If the animal is hurt while this power is in use, the link channels the pain back to the adept who resists an equal DV of Stun damage with Willpower + Magic.

A NOTE ON ATTUNING ANIMALS

The description of the Attunement (Animal) power assumes the animal is of a "normal" size (between cat and horse size). At the gamemaster's discretion, the adept may be able to bond to a homogenous group of smaller animals (rats, sparrows, cockroaches, etc.) as if they were a single animal, requiring a single ritual and Karma expenditure. The adept may use Sense Link with any animal from the group (but only one at a time).

Likewise, if the adept wishes to attune to a much larger animal (elephant, rhino, whale, etc.), the gamemaster may wish to increase the threshold for any animal handling tests, as well as the bonding Karma cost appropriately.

Note that critters with the Sapience power can never be attuned.

animals equal to her initiate grade, and she may not receive benefits from more than one attuned animal in a single action. Attunement may be voluntarily severed at any moment (invested Karma is lost) and is automatically canceled if the animal dies. Attuned animals may be used as a material link (see p. 28) to the adept.

Attunement (Item) (Adepts Only)

This metamagic allows an adept or mystic adept preternatural intuitive understanding and control of a mundane vehicle, weapon, or piece of gear—to the point that using it feels like an extension of her own body and as natural as her innate abilities.

The adept must first familiarize herself with the mundane object to be attuned. The familiarization process involves a thorough acquaintance with the item's function, specifications, and limitations. This involves an appropriate Logic + Technical skill (12, 1 week) Extended Test; for example, Armorer skill would be required for a katana or gun, or Automotive Mechanic skill for a bike. Alternately, the adept may instead elect to build the item herself from scratch, following the normal rules for building/repairing items (p. 138, *SR4A*).

After successful familiarization, the adept must perform an appropriate bonding ritual. The gamemaster and player should tailor this rite to the character's background, tradition, or way (p. 32). A *mujahidin,* for example, might consecrate her blade to the glory of Allah. The Karma cost to bond to typical items can be found on the Item Attunement table, though gamemasters should feel free to use this as a guideline and extrapolate on a case by case basis.

Attunement (Item) provides a dice pool modifier to any skill tests involving use, control, or handling of the item equal to half the character's initiate grade (rounded up). Attunement, however, provides no bonus when the item is controlled through an electronic interface (be it digital, VR, AR, or DNI), nor does it work on the complex magical auras of foci, prepared vessels, or enchanted items. Attunement also provides no bonus to Active Magical skills.

Attunement metamagic applies only to one specific type of object (e.g., Attunement (Bike)). If an adept wants to attune a different item, she must learn the technique again. The adept may only attune a number of individual items equal to her initiate grade, and she may not receive benefits from more than one attuned item in a single action. Attunement may be voluntarily severed at any moment (invested Karma is lost) and is automatically canceled if the object is destroyed. Attuned items may be used as a material link (see p. 28) to the adept.

Channeling

Channeling is a metamagic power developed by possession tradition magicians to enhance their control of spirits, using the magician's body as a vessel. Through Channeling, a magician who was willingly possessed can find a balance between the two minds (the spirit's and her own) occupying her body and achieve greater control. The Channeling magician can use her own skills and has fine motor control over her body while enjoying the enhancing benefits of the Possession power (see p. 101). Control is still shared, however, and the magician is unable to tap the possessing spirit's powers without expending a service. Additionally, the vessel resists any mana spells or powers with the lowest Mental attribute of the two minds (whichever is lower, the spirit's or the magician's). Otherwise, resolve the effects and duration of Possession normally (see p. 101).

Cleansing

This technique allows an initiate to use Counterspelling to disperse emotionally charged mana and disrupt residual imprints on ambient mana (much in the way she would disrupt a spell). This technique can be used to curb the effects of background count of a domain (p. 117) and to eliminate emotional psychoactive traces and tell-tale astral signatures.

The character must be on-site and astrally perceiving or projecting to cleanse. She makes a Magic + Counterspelling Test (apply initiate grade as a dice pool bonus and background count modifiers as appropriate) with a threshold equal to the current background count divided by 2 (rounded up, minimum of 1). Each net hit temporarily reduces the background count by 1. Cleansing takes 1 Complex Action per point of background count cleansed.

If the effective background count is reduced to zero, or if no background count exists, a separate Magic + Counterspelling Test may be made with a single Complex Action to erase all astral traces and signatures. The threshold for this test equals the highest Force of the astral signatures present.

An area's natural background count will reassert itself (minus temporary traces) after (Initiate grade) hours. For cleansing of background count to be permanent, the cause or phenomenon behind it must first be removed. Cleansing the astral space in a toxic waste dump is futile until the waste itself is removed. Cleansing also proves ineffective on well-established and powerful background counts (such as those at Hiroshima, Stonehenge, or even an old community church). Whether a particular background can be cleansed or not is left to the individual gamemaster.

BASIC METAMAGIC TECHNIQUES

Adept Centering	p. 53
Ally Conjuration	p. 53
Attunement (Animal)	p. 53
Attunement (Item)	p. 54
Centering	p. 198, *SR4A*
Channeling	p. 54
Cleansing	p. 55
Cognition	p. 55
Divining	p. 56
Flexible Signature	p. 198, *SR4A*
Geomancy	p. 56
Great Ritual	p. 57
Invoking	p. 57
Masking	p. 198, *SR4A*
Psychometry	p. 57
Quickening	p. 198, *SR4A*
Sensing	p. 58
Shielding	p. 198, *SR4A*
Somatic Control	p. 58
Sympathetic Linking	p. 58

ADVANCED METAMAGIC TECHNIQUES (PREREQUISITE)

Absorption (Shielding)	p. 59
Anchoring (Quickening)	p. 59
Empower Animal (Attunement (Animal))	p. 60
Extended Masking (Masking)	p. 60
Filtering (Cleansing)	p. 61
Flux (Masking)	p. 61
Infusion (Adept Centering)	p. 61
Reflection (Shielding)	p. 61

Cognition (Adepts Only)

The Cognition technique used by adepts and mystic adepts allows an initiate to better comprehend, manipulate, and adapt to her environment. Cognition allows the initiate to focus and divert her mental, perceptual, and intellectual faculties at will.

To use this metamagic, the adept takes a Complex Action to make a Magic + Logic (2) Test; initiate grade is added as a dice pool modifier. Each net hit means an adept may temporarily shift one point from one Mental attribute to another. The change requires 2 full Combat Turns per point to take effect and lasts for (Magic) minutes. Such temporary changes may not exceed a character's augmented attribute maximums, and no attribute may be reduced below 1. Attribute changes (both positive and negative) affect all related dice pools.

After the effect wears off, the intense focus and concentration results in fatigue, drowsiness, and exhaustion, represented by Drain.

ITEM ATTUNEMENT TABLE

Gear	Karma Cost
Simple non-mechanical, handcrafted items:	
blades, traditional musical instruments	5
Modern crafted, mechanical items:	
katana, mechanical lockpick kit, mechanic's toolkit	6
Basic mechanical production line products:	
basic gun, basic dirt bike	8
Tech-intensive products and electronics:	
smartgun, car, racing bike	9
High-tech items and advanced electronics:	
monofilament whip, thunderbird, commlink	10

DIVINATION TABLE

Divination question was	Threshold
Vague (Are my old enemies catching up to me?)	1
General (Will I get hurt if I go on this next shadowrun?)	2
Specific (Will Mr. Johnson take a bribe from Yakashima?)	3
Very specific (Is Mr. Johnson picking up his bribe this evening?)	4

The adept using Cognition must resist a cumulative 3 DV of Stun damage for each attribute point shifted with Willpower + Body (e.g., shifting 3 points between Mental attributes would cause 9 DV Drain)

Divining

Divining allows the initiate to peer beyond the mists of time and see some of what the fate has in store for a specific subject. To use Divining, the initiate must first be able to assense the subject (be it an entity, a place, or an object), or possess a viable material link (p. 28). The initiate enters a mild trance state that reveals glimpses and flashes of what the future may hold—almost always couched in enigmatic symbolism and metaphor appropriate to the diviner's magical paradigm and cosmology. The diviner then uses her Arcana skill (representing her skill at translating her tradition's symbols and imagery from the abstract to the physical) to interpret the information retrieved using a fortune-telling technique appropriate to her tradition (options include astrology, dowsing, omens, dreaming, palmistry, cartomancy, sortilege, etc.).

Mechanically, with the subject or a suitable link at hand, the diviner declares her intent to use Divining and enters a mild trance (–2 dice pool modifier to all actions). She may then ask one question about an event in the subject's future—divination is only useful in answering questions about events, not personal details or histories. The diviner *always* receives some vision or sign, though its meaning might be unclear. She must then make an Arcana + Logic Test (initiate grade provides a dice pool modifier) to decrypt the true meaning of her visions, with a threshold determined by the Divination Table. Subsequent divinations on the same subject matter increase the threshold by +1 per attempt until the gamemaster deems that something significant about the situation or subject has changed.

The diviner's net hits measure how useful the answer is. A glitch means the vision is misinterpreted and misleading information conveyed. One net hit means a cryptic reply containing an underlying truth. Two net hits, the answer is mildly helpful. Three or more net hits achieve approximately the level of detail the diviner desired. In some cases it may be advisable for the gamemaster to roll the Divining Test for the character secretly so as not to give away undesired information based on the number of hits. Regardless of the number of hits achieved, the gamemaster should adjust the answer to be as specific or vague as suits the story and to maintain drama. Alternately, groups comfortable with the option may choose to do away with dice rolling completely and allow the gamemaster to tailor the divinatory vision entirely to suit the story.

Gamemasters should allow leeway for characters to receive hints and probabilities rather than hard facts. The gamemaster can enhance the flavor of this power by having characters experience divinatory "visions" and "omens" at unexpected, and perhaps inopportune, times. To ward off potential abuse, gamemasters may also want to occasionally introduce apparently contradictory or misleading information in divination.

Geomancy

An initiate who learns this power is known as a *geomancer* and learns how to subtly affect and manipulate the natural flow of mana, particularly the energy that pools around mana lines (also known as dragon lines, ley lines, or song lines) and power sites (p. 120). This allows the gradual aspecting (p. 118) of ambient background count towards the geomancer's particular style of magic. A site which is aspected towards a given type of magic is known as a *domain*. Rather than hindering all magic use, domains facilitate magic that is in sync with their aspect.

To use Geomancy to imprint the ambient mana flow, follow the rules for Ritual Spellcasting (p. 184, *SR4A*). The geomancer can do this alone or aided by a group, in which case she must be ritual leader. Treat the geomantic ritual as if she were casting a spell with a Force equal to twice the site's natural background count and with a threshold equal to twice the site's background count. At the end of each ritual, participants suffer Drain equal to (Force) DV.

This ritual must successfully be completed once each lunar month (28 days) for a number of months in a row equal to the site's background count for the aspecting to become permanent. Until that time, the background count retains its original aspect. Failing the ritual does not undo the work done (though a critical glitch might), but that month simply does not count towards achieving the goal—it merely maintains the process. If someone else attempts to aspect the site in the same month, however, only the geomancers who score the most net hits that month count as succeeding in the ritual, all others fail.

To ensure that the imprinted mana does not dissipate between rituals, and to maintain an aspect once changed, it is necessary to ensure the site itself observes the geomantic lore of the initiate's tradition. If the site does not already correspond to such criteria (an ancient stone circle would correspond to the Druidic tradition's criteria, but not a wujen's *feng shui*), the site may need to be "re-sculpted." This may require altering the immediate landscape, constructing a building from scratch, rearranging the furniture, performing regular religious observances, or offering sacrifices to local spirits. The nature and extent of each tradition's criteria are left to the gamemaster to define as appropriate to the situation. At the gamemaster's discretion, failing to comply with geomantic lore may apply a negative dice pool modifier to future geomantic rituals.

Magpie's group of urban shamans has staked out the basement of a condemned building in the Barrens that hides a minor power site (Rating 2 Background Count). Magpie and the other members of his group rearrange the space, clearing out the trash and decking out the basement in shamanic paraphernalia, before they gather for a geomantic ritual to aspect the site. They perform their first ritual (suffering a –2 modifier to their Magic attributes due to background count), achieving the threshold of 4 (twice the background count), and suffering a Drain of 4S. The next month they attempt another ritual (still suffering the full –2 Magic modifier) but fail to reach the threshold this time. The process is not interrupted, however, merely postponed, so they try again the following month. On their third ritual they beat the threshold again, fully aspecting the site to their magic.

Great Ritual

This technique allows an initiate to enhance the scope of Ritual Spellcasting. When involved in Ritual Spellcasting, the initiate who knows this technique may opt to not actively participate in the casting (adding no dice), but to function instead as a conduit for excess magic, effectively adding her Magic rating to the maximum size of the Ritual Spellcasting group *and* the maximum Force of the spell being cast (p. 184, *SR4A*). An initiate using this technique during Ritual Spellcasting may not serve as ritual team leader.

While she doesn't contribute dice to the ritual, the character is still an active member of the casting group and suffers Drain identical to any other participant.

Invoking

Initiates with the Invoking metamagic learn to enhance their bound spirits into *great form* spirits. An initiate must declare she intends to use Invoking when performing a binding (or rebinding) ritual (see *Binding*, p. 188, *SR4A*). The Drain from that binding ritual is increased by 50 percent (round up). If the ritual succeeds, the initiate immediate takes a Complex Action and makes an Invoking Test, rolling Magic + Binding. The bound spirit's Force is added as a dice pool bonus. The hits scored on the Invoking Test determine how successfully the initiate transforms the spirit into a great form spirit and expands its natural abilities, as noted on the Invoking Test table. If the Invoking Test fails, the spirit is still bound, but is not great form. If a great form spirit is re-bound, it does not need to be invoked again, but the Drain of re-binding is increased by 50 percent (round up). Note that only bound spirits may be invoked; watcher spirits cannot be great form.

Psychometry

This power refines an initiate's assensing ability, allowing her to extract and interpret lingering emotions, astral signatures, and sometimes even residual sensory impressions that are left behind on objects, places, or people. Due to the psychoactive nature of the astral environment, the more recent the impression, the greater the likelihood of retrieving useful insight.

INVOKING TEST

Hits	Result
0–1	The Invoking fails.
2	The spirit grows visibly bigger and more powerful (+1 Reach) when materialized, and the bond to its summoner is reinforced—the spirit gains a +1 dice pool modifier to resist Banishing attempts per hit on the Invoking Test.
3	The spirit gains access to an additional power from its list of Optional Powers, exactly as if it had a Force 3 higher than it actually has.
4	Any of the spirit's powers with a range of LOS may be used with a range of LOS (A). In addition, the spirit's Engulf power (if any) may also be used with a range of LOS (A) if desired. Unlike normal area effects, the spirit may voluntarily choose not to affect any number of targets within the target area.
5	The spirit gains a unique great form power appropriate to its type; see *Great Form Powers,* below.
6+	Each net hit over 5 adds 1 point to each of the great form spirit's materialized or possession Physical attributes (up to the augmented maximum).

GREAT FORM POWERS

Particularly powerful great form spirits gain a unique power appropriate to their type:
Air: Storm (see p. 103)
Beasts: Paralyzing Howl (p. 296, *SR4A*)
Earth: Quake (p. 102)
Fire: Storm (p. 103)
Guardian: Endowment (p. 99)
Guidance: Astral Gateway (p. 98)
Man: Compulsion (p. 293, *SR4A*)
Plant: Regeneration (p. 296, *SR4A*)
Task: Endowment (p. 99)
Water: Storm (p. 103)

Psychometry requires the initiate to come into physical contact with the subject and examine the astral patterns around with an Intuition + Assensing Test (add the initiate grade as a dice pool modifier). The Psychometry Table (p. 58) lists both applicable modifiers and the amount of information imparted, as determined by the net hits. When multiple impressions exist, the initiate reads different information from each set of impressions simultaneously.

The gamemaster should tailor this information to be as dramatic, vague, or specific as suits the story. The gamemaster also determines the form the psychometric feedback takes (visual, auditory, emotional, somatic, etc.) and the duration of the reading. If appropriate, apply a +3 dice pool modifier to an initiate's actions while in the grip of a particularly long or intense psychometric experience.

PSYCHOMETRY TABLE

Situation	Modifiers
Time since impression	
Less than 1 day	+0
Less than 1 week	–2
Less than 1 month	–4
Less than 1 year	–6
Less than 1 decade	–8
Each additional decade	–2
Subject has a strong connection to element depicted in the impression (wedding ring, beloved toy, etc.)	+2
Initiate has a strong connection to subject in the impression (friend, childhood home, etc.)	+2
Impression of violence or powerful emotions	+3
Impression of violent death	+4
Subject is a bonded focus	+(Rating)*
Subject is a place	–2
Chaotic or noisy surroundings (difficult to concentrate)	–1
Subject carries more than one significant impression	–1 for each
Astral signature(s) relating to impression has been erased	–1
Cleansing metamagic has been used to remove impressions	–6
Each subsequent attempt to read the same object	–2

* Modifier only applies to impressions related to the person to whom the focus is bonded. Stacked foci only grant the highest rating as a bonus.

Net Hits	Information Gained
0	None.
1	Flashes of insight, superficial and disjointed impressions.
2	Longer and deeper insights, though visions are still disjointed.
3	Greater detail, multiple sensory feedback, more coherence.
4+	Lengthy sequences, multiple senses, coherent visions, significant information.

Sensing

Sensing expands the initiate's assensing ability to an intuitive level. The character can sense fluctuations and elements of mana and astral topography in the vicinity without requiring active astral perception or projection, or even line of sight. Sensing will detect mana ebbs and surges, mana storms, astral rifts and shallows, voids, alchera, background count and other aspects of the astral terrain and mana field—it will not detect astral forms, spells, mana barriers, spirits, or foci. Sensing is an area-effect ability centered on the initiate. The greater the magnitude of the mana/astral phenomena and the nearer their location, the easier it is for the initiate to detect them.

Sensing requires the character to concentrate for a Complex Action and make a Magic + Intuition Test. Add initiate grade as a dice pool bonus. The power's base range is initiate grade x 500 meters; multiply a phenomena's rating by this base distance to determine how far away it can be detected. A mana storm detected from several kilometers away must be a big one! Use the Detection Spell Results table (p. 206, SR4A) to determine the results. Gamemasters may also choose to give the character a chance to sense some unusual nearby change even when they are not actively using Sensing; in this case the gamemaster should make the test in secret so as not to give anything away.

Somatic Control (Adepts Only)

Similar to Cognition, Somatic Control may only be used by an adept or mystic adept. This power extends the adept's conscious control over her own body, allowing her to overcome natural physical limitations and to magically redistribute her body's resources and energy. Somatic Control is used to exchange points between Physical attributes, enhancing some while reducing others.

To use this metamagic, the adept takes a Complex Action to roll a Magic + Body (2) Test, adding her initiate grade as a dice pool bonus. Each net hit allows one point to be temporarily shifted from one Physical attribute to another, raising one and reducing another. The change requires 2 full Combat Turns per point to take effect and lasts for (Magic) minutes. Such temporary changes may not exceed a character's augmented attribute maximums, and no attribute may be reduced below 1. Attribute changes (both positive and negative) affect all related dice pools.

When the effect ends, the gross physiological manipulation involved produces cramps, sprains, and fatigue, causing Drain. The adept suffers a cumulative 3 DV of Stun damage for each attribute point shifted (so shifting 3 points inflicts 9 DV), resisted with Willpower + Body.

Sympathetic Linking

This metamagic allows an initiate to unlock the secret of creating sympathetic links for the purpose of ritual magic and astral tracking (see *Sympathetic Links*, p. 29). The initiate also learns how to use the symbolic likeness of a subject, often in the form of drawings, sculptures, or dolls, to establish an astral connection to the individual or thing (see *Symbolic Links*, p. 29).

ADVANCED METAMAGIC

Advanced metamagic techniques require that the initiate first master a basic metamagic before being able to unlock its advanced form. All advanced metamagics note their prerequi-

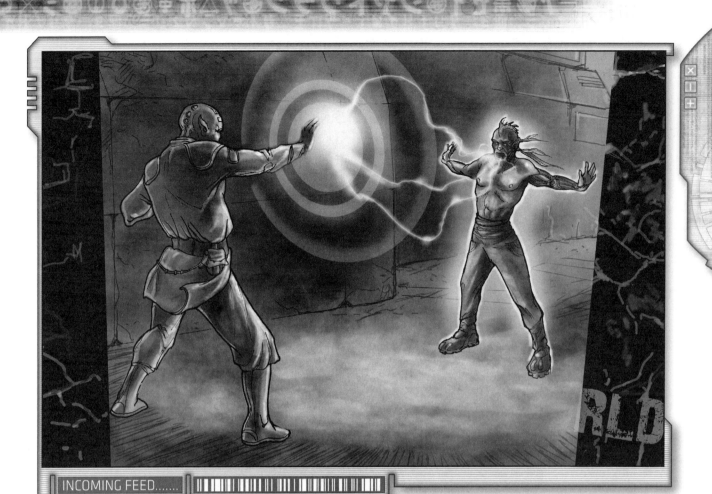

site in their respective descriptions. At the gamemaster's discretion, advanced metamagics may only be learned from a select few magical organizations or powerful free spirits that are already acquainted with them.

Absorption
Prerequisite: Shielding (p. 198, SR4A)

This advanced Shielding technique allows an initiate to siphon some of the mana away from a spell used against her. To use this metamagic, the character performs the usual Spell Resistance Test (p. 183, SR4A) using Counterspelling, and adding the initiate grade as a dice pool modifier. Regardless of whether the spell is fully resisted or not, each hit on the character's Spell Resistance Test allows her to absorb one Force point as one point of temporary "mana charge" (up to the spell's Force). This mana charge may be retained in the absorbing character's aura for (initiate grade) turns. Each point of mana charge may be used to reduce the Drain DV from casting a spell by 1, at which point it is used up. The maximum mana charge a magician can retain is equal to her Magic attribute. Each point of absorbed charge above this level dissipates, but not before causing an automatic 1 DV of Physical damage (such damage is cumulative: absorbing 3 points above the character's Magic causes 3 DV). If the mana charge is not fully expended in the time limit, the initiate must resist Drain with a DV equal to the remaining mana charge (if the mana charge exceeds the character's Magic, this Drain is Physical). Unused mana charge is then lost. A character cannot absorb mana from a spell she has cast herself or reflected with Reflecting metamagic.

Anchoring
Prerequisite: Quickening (p. 198, SR4A)

This advanced version of the Quickening metamagic allows an initiate to use her Sorcery skills to add a temporary construct of magical energies known as an *anchor* around a spell, keeping it from discharging until a pre-determined trigger condition is met. Trigger conditions must be defined before the spell is cast so they are "programmed" into the anchor (see *Anchoring Trigger Conditions*, p. 60). Unlike Quickening, Anchoring may be used on instant, sustained, and permanent spells.

To create an anchor, the initiate first chooses which spell to anchor and then what trigger condition(s) she wishes to include. Once a trigger or triggers are defined, the spell is cast as normal (the number of hits achieved should be recorded for later reference). The initiate must then resist Drain for the spell *twice*—once for casting the spell, and once for creating the anchoring construct. If the spell has a variable Drain (such as Heal), the caster must choose a Drain Value to cast it at; if that DV later proves to not be enough for the situation when the spell is released, then it simply fails.

The spellcaster then pays 1 Karma for every point of the anchored spell's Force to "prep the anchor." Anchored spells should be considered the same as quickened spells (p.198, SR4A) for the purpose of determining interaction with mana

ANCHORING TRIGGER CONDITIONS

Both anchors and anchoring foci (p. 84) can have pre-set trigger conditions that collapse the anchor construct and release the pre-cast spell. Though an anchor is reactive by nature, it has no sensory awareness of its own. It cannot be triggered by external environmental conditions or circumstances that do not interact with it in some way. For example, an anchor construct can't discharge its spell when it "hears" the word "attack," nor will it go off if someone specific walks into the room—unless it is linked to a spell designed to detect that individual.

Triggers must be chosen when an anchor or anchoring focus is created. It is possible to build multiple triggers into an anchor if so desired. Triggers may be set so that they only activate if another trigger condition is met (e.g, a contact trigger only activates when a Detection spell is activated first, so the anchor is safe to touch until the Detection spell gets a hit).

Possible trigger conditions include:

Background Count Trigger

The anchor is triggered if the background count of the area is modified in any way: raised, lowered, or undergoes a change of aspect (see *Background Count*, p. 117). At the gamemaster's discretion, any use of magic in the area may create minor and temporary background fluctuations enough to trigger the construct.

Contact Trigger

The anchor is triggered when either any living aura, a specific aura (previously assensed by the caster), or simply the "wrong" aura (not the spellcaster's) comes into direct physical or astral contact with the anchor (whether construct or foci). Note that dormant anchored spells are invisible on the physical plane, and take up "space" equal to the size of the caster.

Detection Spell Trigger

This trigger requires the creator to cast a Detection spell immediately after the initial anchoring. This second spell must in turn be quickened (see p. 198, *SR4A*) and linked to the anchor or anchoring foci by paying the trigger cost. If the quickened Detection spell detects whatever it is designed to attack, it immediately triggers the anchor. The Detection spell also functions as a means of targeting the spell about to be discharged.

Timing Trigger

The anchor is deliberately designed to "unravel" over a specific period of time, eventually collapsing and discharging the spell within. Such anchors may be programmed to collapse at any time from 1 Combat Turn to a maximum of (anchored spell Force) months. The exact time must be defined when the anchor is created.

barriers, astral combat, and dispelling attempts. Anchored spells remain linked to the spellcaster's aura and may be used for astral tracking (p. 183, *SR4A*) or as a sympathetic link (p. 29).

When the pre-determined trigger condition is met, the anchor construct collapses and the spell discharges as if it had just been cast (refer to the hits registered during the casting for the purposes of determining effects). The spellcaster suffers no Drain when the spell discharges. Once the anchor collapses and the spell inside is released, the effect ends and all Karma is lost. Sustained spells will remain sustained in the same manner as a quickened spell. Permanent spells will remain sustained until the effects become permanent, and then deactivate.

Unless the anchor has a linked Detection spell, it can only target someone or something in direct physical or astral contact with it. If a Detection spell served as the trigger, it can aim the anchored spell at any valid target it detects within range.

An anchor may be activated or deactivated at any time with a mental command from the construct's creator. This has no range limitation and does not count as a trigger condition.

An initiate may only have a number of anchors active at any time equal to her initiate grade. Anchoring is required to fashion anchoring foci formula (see p. 84).

Empower Animal (Adepts Only)

Prerequisite: Attunement (Animal) (p. 53)

This technique allows the initiate adept or mystic adept to temporarily lend one of her adept powers to an attuned animal companion through the mystic bond. The first time a power is transferred in this manner, the adept must pay Karma equal to its Power Point cost x 3 (round up). Thereafter, empowering the animal has no cost.

To empower an animal requires a Complex Action, and the adept and animal companion must be within the Sense Link power's range. Only one power may be transferred at a time, and it is unavailable to the adept while the companion uses it. The adept may empower more than one attuned companion, though a power can never be transferred to more than one animal at a time.

The amount of Power Points transferred at one time may never exceed the adept's initiate grade (note that this may mean an initiate will not be able to initially empower an animal with some of her more costly powers). If the animal does not possess an appropriate skill required to use the power, it instinctively taps the adept's own natural (unmodified) skill rating for any relevant test, but with a –2 dice pool modifier.

Extended Masking

Prerequisite: Masking (p. 198, *SR4A*)

This technique allows the initiate to extend her Masking metamagic to encompass her foci and any spells she may have

quickened, anchored, or may be sustaining. The masking initiate may disguise a number of auras (foci and spells), not counting her own, equal to her initiate grade. Each aura so masked must have a Force equal to or less than her Magic attribute. Masked foci and spells appear to astral observers as normal fluctuations in her magical aura.

To detect auras concealed with Extended Masking, a character need only make the usual Assensing + Intuition Opposed Test against the masking initiate's Intuition + Magic + initiate grade. As per the Masking rules in *SR4A* (p.198), if the character gets fewer hits than the masking magician, she sees only the false aura. If she gets more, she sees not only the illusory aura and the character's true aura, but also any masked foci or spells.

Filtering

Prerequisite: Cleansing (p. 55)

This advanced form of Cleansing allows an initiate to weave a construct of temporary disruptive energies around her person using her Counterspelling skill. This temporary astral construct, called a "weave," dissipates the normal warping effects of positive background count (and only background count) on ambient mana, effectively filtering it into a neutral state. The magician can then tap this "purified" mana to power her spellcasting, ignoring the usual interference of aspected background count (p. 117). This technique may be applied against the effects of domains and mana warps, but not mana ebbs or voids. The filtering effect is localized and normally not perceivable on the astral plane when used in an area saturated with background count.

To use Filtering, the character takes a Complex Action to perform a Magic + Counterspelling Test with a threshold equal to the local background count minus the character's initiate grade (minimum of 1). Note that background count does not affect the character's Magic for this test. Each net hit temporarily reduces the effective background count for the initiate by 1. The filter operates for (Magic) turns before becoming "clogged" and collapsing.

Abracadavre (initiate grade 2) is attempting to filter to facilitate spellcasting. He makes a Magic 4 + Counterspelling 4 Test (dice pool of 8) against a background count of 3. His threshold is 1 (background count 3 – initiate grade 2). He rolls 3 hits, which equals 2 net hits (3 – 1), effectively reducing the background count for him to 1 (3 – 2).

Flux

Prerequisite: Masking (p. 198, *SR4A*)

This metamagic extends the initiate's ability to manipulate her aura to the point where she is able to set it in constant flux for a limited time. While doing so makes her shifting aura stand out on the astral plane, it also allows the initiate to temporarily scramble the mystical links between herself and her bonded foci, attuned animals/items, summoned/bound spirits, mana barriers, active spells (sustained, quickened, or anchored), and potential ritual links (material, sympathetic, and symbolic). For as long as Flux is active, any attempt to use these links to astrally track or ritually target the initiate are "put on hold." Once Flux ends, tracking and targeting pick up where they left off.

The aura disruption caused by Flux can only be safely maintained for (Magic) hours per day. Excessive use of Flux beyond this allowance starts to permanently affect the initiate's links to bonded foci, spirits, mana barriers, and active spells. Beyond that period, there is a 50 percent chance that a link may be permanently disrupted: foci become unbonded, spirits are released, spells fail or can no longer be controlled, and so on. If the initiate continues to maintain Flux for another (Magic) hours that same day, all of those links are automatically broken. At the gamemaster's discretion, maintaining Flux even further may cause permanent damage to the initiate's aura, perhaps resulting in Magic loss or Negative qualities.

Infusion (Adepts Only)

Prerequisite: Adept Centering (p. 53)

Infusion allows an adept to boost her somatic powers at the cost of temporary burnout. To use Infusion, the adept must take a Complex Action to focus and supercharge her abilities.

For each point of initiate grade, the adept gains the capacity to temporarily channel a 0.5 Power Point "boost" that can be used to briefly enhance an existing power beyond its normal range. These enhanced powers can be used for (Magic) minutes, after which they fade. As the boost ends, the adept immediately suffers Drain equal to (Magic) DV to reflect fatigue from channeling excessive levels of mana. She resists this Stun damage with Willpower + Body. The adept also temporarily "burns out" a number of Power Points' worth of normal powers equal to the value of the boost. The burnout lasts for the same amount of time as the infusion was in effect. The gamemaster chooses what powers are temporarily burned out—the adept should not know a power is inaccessible until she tries to use it.

Reflecting

Prerequisite: Shielding (p. 198, *SR4A*)

Reflecting allows an initiate to deflect an incoming spell back at the original spellcaster. A character may use Reflecting anytime she resists a spell which targets her directly (regardless of whether it is area effect or personal) and of which she is aware. Regardless of success, attempting to reflect an incoming spell uses up the character's next available action as if she had used full defense as an interrupt action in normal combat (see p. 160, *SR4A*)—if the character has already used her next available action, she cannot reflect.

To use Reflecting, a character *must* be able to use Counterspelling during the normal Spell Resistance Test (p. 183, *SR4A*). As with Shielding, add initiate grade as a dice pool modifier. If the reflecting character achieves more hits than the caster's Spellcasting hits, she reflects the spell back at the caster. Spells are reflected at half their original Force (round up). The reflecting character's net hits are treated as Spellcasting hits as if she cast the spell. If the initiate successfully reflects the spell, all others protected by her Counterspelling are not affected by the spell. The reflected spell is always considered a single target spell against the original caster, even if the spell actually cast was an area-effect version.

... MAGICAL GROUPS ...

Valentine held tight to the overhead cornice while he hacked the sensor grid and deactivated the window alarm. He sliced the glass with his laser cutter and carefully lifted it clear. He had half an hour between shifts, as there was only a skeleton detail on duty—Winter Solstice was as big as Christmas in Britain these days. He pried open the window and slid through, landing sprightly on the Dunham Manor's ancient oak floor.

The opulent Edwardian drawing room was dark and empty, lit only by soft lights directed toward family portraits. He crossed to the door and cracked it open an inch. Sure enough, it opened onto the gallery overlooking the main dining hall. There it was. The sword gleamed in its wall mount, exactly where his Templar handler said it would be. He didn't know why the Lord Protector's Office wanted him to burgle a bigwig in the New Druidic Movement, but he knew better than to ask.

As he slipped into the gallery, he realized something was wrong. Too much light from below. Sinking into the darkness, Valentine dared a peek ... and his heart sank. The tables and chairs had been cleared to reveal a circle of brass and silver carved into the floor. Flickering torches lit the room. Eight robed and hooded figures stood around the circle, marked by insignia, torches, and staves. Druids. He should have known—after all, this was the Duke of Oxford's manor!

Valentine watched a young lad he recognized stepped forward—someone Valentine had seen often while deep in the political underground, before the fire had gone out of him and he became a pawn of the Templars. It was Thomas Bernal, errant heir to the Bernal family fortunes, now a political subversive.

The youth kneeled before one of the druids, offering his staff with both hands. The figure took the offering, drew the boy to his feet, and walked him to the glowing brazier at the circle's center. The druid drew a long, wicked *athame* with an ivory handle and handed it to the boy, reciting, "The Circle is threefold. The Circle is one with the Land, the spirit, and the flesh. The Circle is unity. Your strength, your blood, and the fire of your youth will bring greatness to our Circle."

Thomas Bernal took the dagger and sliced his own palm. "I pledge my strength to the Circle, my blood to the cause, and the fire of my youth to cleanse this land of the corruption that has tainted its soul. So pledge I."

The blood splashed into the brazier, sending green-blue flames flaring high. The lad's hand vanished into the blaze, and Valentine sucked in his breath. For a second he saw an incandescent figure in the flames, gone in a blink of an eye. The boy withdrew his hand, a Celtic swirl now burned in his palm.

The Circle broke into soft applause and moved to welcome their new member, while the Duke of Oxford pulled back his cowl—and turned his steel-gray eyes straight to where Valentine hid in the shadows. Valentine connected the dots ... he wasn't really expected to burgle anything. He'd been set up, deliberately brought in to see this affair. Now he had a message to take to his Templar masters and the Lord Protector—a warning that their false peace and martial law was about to crumble, that the underground had sympathizers at the heart of the Druidic Movement. Valentine just hoped they didn't shoot the messenger.

SOCIAL CIRCLES

Like other metahumans, magicians are social animals at heart, and the groups they form are the backbone of Awakened society. Magicians remain a rare breed, and, given the forces they deal with on a daily basis, it is no wonder that they seek out the camaraderie and understanding only the fellow Awakened can offer. Many gravitate towards magical groups early on. In tribal communities, the Gifted are often mentored by shamanic societies that tutor them and direct their talents to the service of the community; while in colleges and universities the "study circles" popular among many students of the art foster friendships that become the heart of full-blown hermetic groups in later life. Magical groups also represent an important social and career component for the typical wage mage. Most corps maintain several magical groups, providing them with financing and hard-to-acquire equipment and instruments in exchange for loyal service. Most megacorps also sponsor a handful of promising independent groups that serve as recruitment grounds or as conveniently unaffiliated magical assets (for security work, R&D, talislegging, etc).

Magical groups—be they orders, circles, lodges, temples, covens, or brotherhoods/sisterhoods—are the hubs of Awakened communities, allowing magicians to meet, share experiences and resources, practice magic, and find instruction. More than a social clique, true magical groups are devoted to furthering the art and aiding their members to develop their full potential. For the independent practitioner of magic, magical groups are more than just a social hub for like-minded individuals; they are a source of instruction, relatively inexpensive formulae and materials, and colleagues who can cooperate on projects and assist in initiation into the higher mysteries.

THE MAGICAL GROUP

While all magical groups are primarily devoted to furthering the Art, such groups invariably also have a driving agenda, magical and otherwise, that brings together Awakened souls under a common purpose. These organizations may be initiatory, conspiratorial, or devoted to particular goals or ideals, but each has its own focus. Depending on its purpose and direction, some groups are restricted to followers of a particular tradition, while others are much more liberal in their membership. Magical groups not only provide members with the fellowship of peers but also offer a means of pooling resources and materials, providing instruction, negotiating group deals with local suppliers, and potentially allowing sponsorship and patronage.

The decision to join (or form) such a group should never be taken lightly, since potential members need to be willing both to commit to the group's cause and ideals and to accept a mystical and often lifelong bond to the group (*The Group Bond*, p. 65). Among other things, this magical link allows the group to aid members in initiation and to bring different individuals into something greater than the sum of its parts. Magical groups with exceptionally large memberships usually divide into smaller subgroups, often called circles, lodges, ranks, or orders.

Of course, magical groups are not for everybody. Some of the Awakened are simply not comfortable with the demands such groups place on members, opting to walk their own path rather than dealing with the hassle of agendas, customs, and strictures.

PURPOSE

While a magical group's main reason for being is to promote the magical arts and to allow the exchange of members' experiences and resources, its *purpose* is what defines its focus and reflects its beliefs and agenda. This can range from an initiatory group established to pursue magical knowledge and support the development of the individual members, to a group dedicated to a social, political, economic, or religious cause.

Purpose varies greatly from group to group, and even among apparently similar groups. For instance, some initiatory groups are open organizations that welcome all seekers of enlightenment, while others are fiercely exclusive organizations that focus on the advancement of those who subscribe to their paradigm of reality. Some groups are devoted to a specific religious, social, or moral beliefs or magical traditions, with their magic linked to their spiritual code. Such groups use magic to pursue a specific belief and to teach or demonstrate that belief to the rest of the world. They might be altruistic organizations helping and protecting metahumanity, or they might as easily be fanatic cults using magic to force their beliefs on others.

Regardless of whether a group is a personality cult, a religious order, or an anarchist collective, its purpose defines its outlook, customs, and strictures. An order of Catholic theurgists might impose the customs and rules of the church and adopt strictures such as exclusive membership, fraternity, and belief (*Strictures*, p. 65). A secretive brotherhood that uses magic in the pursuit of power and wealth will adopt a veil of secrecy and seek to control their members using strictures such as oath, link, and obedience.

For the gamemaster, a group's purpose provides a guideline for integrating the group as a living and vibrant addition to the setting, as well as coloring the way members are roleplayed and perceived by other characters. Additionally, a group's purpose can provide a springboard for a multitude of roleplaying opportunities and story ideas.

CUSTOMS

Customs are the conventions, common practices, and rules dictated by a magical group's purpose and beliefs. While not magical in nature, customs are integral parts of a group's identity and are enforced on all members. They are also often integral to the group's organization and internal hierarchy.

Customs provide a group with unique roleplaying color or to round out its personality. Customs prevent a magical group from becoming a random set of numbers that players juggle to get cheap initiations, instead providing a framework for roleplaying, underlining the group's orientation and challenging the character's commitment. Depending on the group's purpose, they can be sensible or dogmatic, bigoted or enlightened. A group of nature-worshipping shamans, for example, will expect members to abide by customs supportive of conservationism, while a group of magicians backed by a local chapter of the Humanis Policlub will endorse racist

Street Magic

customs and a strong anti-meta creed. A group composed of top corporate wage mages will emphasize loyalty to the corp above all.

Prospective members should keep in mind that those who don't abide by the group's customs (or reject its purpose and agenda) will find acceptance and advancement difficult. Disobedience to or violation of a group's customs will get a member booted out as inevitably as breaking strictures.

Rank and Status

Depending on a magical group's purpose and customs, a member's status in the group may be decided by magical knowledge and initiatory grade, or these might be secondary considerations behind politics, social standing, and devotion to its central cause. Generally speaking, some level of recognition and respect is almost always accorded higher-grade initiates—though this might translate to an informal ranking if the group's purpose and beliefs dictates that "correct" behavior counts for more than grade or skill.

Ranking and hierarchies vary greatly and are defined as much by the group's size as its purpose. A large group might bow to the charismatic leadership of a relatively small inner circle, or it might be organized in highly structured ranks and circles of growing levels of authority and responsibility. A small group might forego formal hierarchy altogether, according deference simply based on seniority and experience.

Specific titles are often influenced by the dominant tradition in the group and its cultural context.

THE GROUP BOND

A true magical group is distinguished from a boys' club for magicians or a drinking society by the mystic bond that links its members to one another. This bond is essential for a magical group to realize its potential and function as an initiatory group. The bond also symbolizes the group's link to the fundamental forces of magic (see *Founding a Group* and *Joining a Group,* p. 69, for more details on establishing this bond).

The acceptance of certain strictures that are integral to the group's purpose and custom are critical to the bond and symbolic of the individual's commitment to the group. Consequently, violating these strictures destabilizes the individual's bond to the group and is apparent to other members of the group.

In practice, all group members are treated as sympathetic links (p. 29) to one another and may assist one another in initiation (*Group Benefits,* p. 67).

A member may permanently sever his bond to the group by successfully performing a ritual similar to the one used to join the group and paying 1 Karma.

Group Avatar

When the bond is first formed, the group may opt to entreat the patronage of a specific mentor spirit that is in sync with and symbolic of the group's beliefs and purpose. For example, the Bear Doctor Society reveres the Bear totem, while a group of Shinto practitioners might worship the powerful kami who they believe resides at a particular temple.

If successful, this mentor becomes the group's spirit *avatar*. While it provides no positive or negative modifiers to members, the spirit takes an active role in the group as a guide and counselor—as long as the group remains faithful to the avatar's purpose. The avatar may also aid members on metaplanar quests (*Metaplanar Quests,* p. 130).

STRICTURES

Similar to customs, magical groups have strictures, rules, and limitations on behavior and magic use that group members accept as symbols of their commitment. Unlike customs, however, strictures carry mystic significance and impact an individual's magical bond to the group. Strictures define what members can or cannot do. A member who breaks a stricture risks the group's collective magical bond (and potentially angers the group's avatar, if it has one)—and may lead to the guilty party's expulsion.

Violating Strictures

When a member violates a stricture, the gamemaster takes note. When the member applies for initiation or participates in ritual magic with the magical group, any such violations may cause problems. The group's magical link is attuned to the astral forms of members on a fundamental level, and the breaking of a stricture causes disturbances intuitively felt and immediately evident to other members when performing magic with the guilty party. The effect of breaking the stricture, however, may not be grave enough to disrupt the group's magical link.

If the violating member performs ritual magic with the group, the "bad vibes" resulting from the broken stricture echo over the link, disrupting the flow of mana and imposing a negative dice pool modifier to all participants in the ritual group equal to the number of strictures broken.

Overcoming Violations

To overcome the stigma of breaking a stricture, the magician must succeed in a Magic + Willpower Test when next attempting to initiate. The threshold for this test is the number of strictures broken. Since initiation brings with it greater understanding of the significance of such violations, the character's current initiate grade functions as a negative dice pool modifier. If the character passes the test, his lapses have not been severe enough to be dangerous. The tally of broken strictures is then erased; the initiation gives the character a clean slate. If the character fails the test, the group must expel him or have their magical bond broken. Most groups will expel an offending member outright, but some may be inclined to examine whether the member "did the wrong thing for the right reason." Such a group may decide to let an erring member remain in exchange for some appropriate quest or deed. At the gamemaster's discretion this penance may be sufficient to stabilize the group's magical link but should not wipe the character's slate clean. This is an excellent opportunity for good plot complications or new roleplaying twists.

Group Violations

Group strictures are taboos that can only be broken by the group as a whole. Strictures about membership, for example, can be violated only if the group accepts someone who does not fit the rule. If a group violates one of these strictures or decides to change their strictures, they break their magical bond; the group is no longer the same and must forge a new magical bond.

If the group loses its magical link, they must restore it before initiate members can benefit from group membership (*Founding a Group*, p. 69).

> *Magpie is a grade 3 initiate in a group of radical eco-shamans based in Puyallup, Seattle. The group has taken the strictures of secrecy and exclusive ritual. Magpie recently ran into a spot of trouble with some Mafia enforcers and threatened to call on his magical chummers to frighten off the mobsters, breaking the secrecy stricture. A recent run also involved some ritual sorcery and astral tracking. That's two violations.*
>
> *When Magpie petitions the group to initiate, his fellow shamans realize that he's broken some strictures, and Magpie must check whether his violations risk the group's magical bond. Magpie rolls Magic 5 + Willpower 5. The Test has a threshold of 2 (the number of broken strictures) and suffers from a –3 dice pool modifier (his initiate grade). Magpie rolls 7 dice but gets only 1 hit, failing the test.*
>
> *Magpie points out that he'd be in for some serious bodily harm if his threat hadn't made the mobsters back off, while the ritual work was performed to track down a toxic shaman. The group finds both arguments persuasive, but they have neither the time nor the Karma to rebuild their magical link right now. So, despite Magpie's best efforts, he's expelled before he permanently damages the group's bond.*

INDIVIDUAL STRICTURES

Individual strictures govern the actions of individual members of a group. Most groups have three or four such strictures.

Attendance

The group has regular meetings for group rituals, and attendance is mandatory. Most groups with an attendance stricture schedule meetings every one to three months, often on dates corresponding with a phase of the moon, the beginning of a season, or some other mystically significant time. Being out of touch is no excuse for breaking this stricture. It is the member's responsibility to inform the group where they can leave word of meeting schedules.

Belief

All members must adhere to a specific moral or philosophical belief. Any activity that violates the belief breaks

the stricture. The gamemaster is the final judge of whether a specific action, or lack of action, violates a belief, but keep in mind that in the real world, whole libraries have been written in arguments over doctrine or dogma.

Deed
All members must periodically perform an action for the benefit of the group or to show loyalty. Any type of deed may be required, such as an astral quest to gain magical knowledge for the group or a shadowrun to bring back telesma, exotic materials, or magical research.

Dues
Members must make a regular payment at a level determined by the group so that the group may maintain its holdings and services.

Exclusive Membership
Members of the group may not be members of any other magical group. If a member joins another group—that is, undergoes an initiation in that group—the stricture is broken. If a member of an exclusive group joins another exclusive group, he has committed a violation against both groups.

Exclusive Ritual
Members of the group may perform ritual spellcasting (p. 184, *SR4A*) only with other members of the group. If they perform ritual sorcery with anyone else, it violates the stricture.

Fraternity
Members of the group are expected to do whatever they can to assist other members upon request. Refusing to provide assistance within the member's ability is a violation of the fraternity stricture.

Geasa
Members of this group must take a geas (p. 27) reflecting some aspect of the group's purpose or beliefs.

Obedience
This stricture requires members to accept group commands. Most such groups have rank systems, with members expected to follow orders from those of higher rank (*Rank and Status*, p. 65). Failure to obey a superior in the group violates this stricture.

Service
Members must spend much of their time working on group-related matters. Members must spend 20 hours a week performing duties and services on behalf of the group. Failure to spend the requisite time counts as a violation of the stricture.

Secrecy
A secret group never admits its existence in public. Members never admit to membership. A secret group may decide to approach a potential recruit or reveal its existence for some pressing reason, but public exposure of the group is limited. If a member admits to being a member to an outsider or tells them about the group, the stricture is broken.

GROUP STRICTURES
Only the group as a whole can break a group stricture. If the group makes an exception to one of its group strictures, it automatically loses its magical link. A magical group may choose to have no group strictures at all.

Limited Membership
The group can only admit individuals of a particular gender, metatype, faith, and so on. This counts as one stricture even if it includes several limitations. For example, a Dianic coven is restricted to women who practice Wicca (i.e., witchcraft) as a religion.

Material Link
All members must give the group a material link (p. 28). This can be a small cell sample (a few drops of blood or a lock of hair) or a thesis (p. 52). Depending on the philosophy of the group, some groups return the link to a member who leaves the group; others keep it as a threat of ritual sorcery against former members who step out of line.

Oath
All members must, in their first initiation with the group, accept the oath ordeal (p. 51). If the initiate has never undergone this ordeal, it counts for reduced Karma cost on that initiation. If the initiate has previously sworn an oath, this oath does not count as an ordeal but still binds the initiate as specified in the rules. Effectively an oath means that a violation of the group's customs and beliefs also counts as a violation of this stricture.

GROUP BENEFITS
There are several benefits intrinsic to belonging to magical groups.

Group Initiation
Prospective initiate members may petition the group to aid them in initiating. Group initiation allows a 20 percent reduction (round up) in the normal Karma cost of initiation per the rules on p. 50 (and p. 198, *SR4A*). An appropriate initiation rite (p. 50) must be prepared in advance and must be attended by at least three other members. The number of members in a group equals the maximum grade one can achieve via group initiation.

Magical Instruction
The familiarity gained from regular interaction and close exchange of views provides members of a magical group with a +3 dice pool modifier on Instruction Tests involving Magical skills or techniques regardless of the magician's tradition.

Metaplanar Quests
The mystical bond linking group members allows them to accompany and aid one another on metaplanar quests (p. 130).

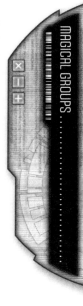

Members must project on the quest from the same physical location and must face the Dweller on the Threshold together before entering the metaplanes.

Ritual Magic

The magical bond formed between members of the same magical group allows them to transcend some of the usual barriers between magical traditions. Members can learn to perform ritual magic together and tap the common pool of power, regardless of their traditions. Articulating the workings and styles of different traditions, however, doubles the normal ritual time.

GROUP RESOURCES AND DUES

Groups usually boast resources available only to members. Resources are rated the same way as lifestyles (p. 267, SR4A) and are supported by membership dues and occasional one-time donations to obtain some specific resource. If the group has a patron, the patron usually picks up the tab for resources—generally in return for services of some sort—making dues minimal or nonexistent. Members pay a fair share of the cost of maintaining group resources, with dues generally equaling the member's share of the cost of maintaining the group's "lifestyle." For example, if a group with 10 members decides to maintain High resources, dues are 10 percent of 10,000 nuyen per month, or 1,000 nuyen per month.

Luxury Resources

The group has magnificent headquarters, possibly a spacious estate, with a residence, a ritual building, herb gardens, and so on. It also has other sites for use by members or can provide living accommodations (at Middle lifestyle but with some perks such as vehicles and entertainment budgets). The group possesses superb magical facilities, equivalent to those of a major corporation or university (1D6 + 10 rating magical lodges). Members can obtain ritual materials at a 40 percent discount.

High Resources

The group has a major headquarters and either has several lesser offices and ritual space elsewhere or can provide living accommodations for members at Middle lifestyle (but no car, entertainment budget, and so on). It has excellent facilities (1D6 + 6 rating magical lodges) and provides ritual materials to members at a 25 percent discount.

Middle Resources

The group owns or rents a nice space and possesses a decent set of working tools (1D6 + 3 rating magical lodges). Ritual materials are available to group members at a 10 percent discount.

Low Resources

The group rents headquarters space and can afford some simple working tools (1D3 + 1 rating magical lodges).

Squatter Resources

A group at this level has a cheap headquarters set up somewhere, probably in an abandoned area of the Barrens. At the very least this provides a private place for ritual work. Members must provide their own gear.

Street Resources

A group at this level maintains no material resources. Whenever the group needs to pay for something, the members must chip in.

PATRONS

A patron is an individual or organization that provides material backing in return for a group's magical assistance and services. In most cases the group's purpose is tied to the patron's own agenda. Sometimes though, the relationship is simply a mutually beneficial business agreement.

Patrons come in all shapes and sizes, from an eccentric millionaire with a fascination for unearthing arcane artifacts to corporations seeking to secure their assets or turn a profit. In fact, most megacorporations support magical groups and provide them with Luxury resources. In return, the corp gets the full-time services of the membership and reaps the formulae and goods they produce. Strictures and customs of such groups are based on loyalty to the corp. Most governments also support one or more magical groups. In some cases, this sponsorship comes in exchange for the good the group does in the community (as in the case of NAN-supported shamanic lodges or Hindu Brahmin temples), but other groups perform military and security duties for the state (such as the British Templars or Tir Na nOg's Order of Cu Chulainn). Security and intelligence organizations, both state and corporate, have sanctioned magical groups involved in intelligence gathering and covert operations, and several activist and radical movements are reputed to maintain magical groups as well. Even factions that oppose the use of magic may secretly do so in an attempt to fight fire with fire.

Patrons are a particularly useful tool to help gamemasters involve magical groups in the wider intrigues and workings of the Sixth World.

FINDING A GROUP

To join a group, the character must first track one down. With many large groups, this is quite easy: the Illuminates of the New Dawn, for example, advertise publicly and have noticeable lodges in major sprawls. If the character knows the name of a group or knows a member personally, he can probably find it just by asking—in which case the standard legwork rules (p. 286, SR4A) should suffice. If the character is looking for something less-advertised and that fits his particular needs, however—perhaps even a secret group—then use the following rules.

Finding a group requires an Etiquette + Charisma (12, 1 day) Extended Test. Each contact the character possesses who is Awakened, a talismonger, or a fixer who deals with the Awakened adds +1 dice pool modifier. At the gamemaster's discretion, other modifiers may apply (for example, a character who follows an esoteric tradition might suffer a hefty modifier). If the character succeeds, the gamemaster can cre-

ate a new group or use one of the sample groups in this chapter. If a character is searching for a magical group to join, the group he finds should fit his criteria.

JOINING A GROUP

After locating an appropriate magical group, a character may attempt to join. First, the character must convince the group to accept her application—depending on the group, this may simply be a matter of protocol, or it may require the character prove herself worthy, particularly if the group is devoted to a certain ideal, faith, or cause. Second, the character must also be willing to advance the first month's dues, though if the group is eager to have the character join, another member or members could potentially put up the money in her stead. Finally, the character must spend 5 Karma; this represents time spent preparing for membership, learning group rituals and other protocol. This Karma is expended whether the character succeeds in joining or not. If the character meets these requisites, she can join the group.

The magical group must then perform a ritual that bonds the applicant with the group. During the ritual the applicant must make an Arcana + Logic Success Test to bond with the group. The test has a threshold of 1 (+1 for every five members in the group). Note that large magical groups (such as the Illuminates of the New Dawn) are in fact associations of smaller groups, so only the local membership counts towards this threshold. If the character is already an initiate, she may add her initiate grade to the dice pool. Most magical groups frown upon applicants too dependent on geasa or suffering from focus addiction. Both are seen as signs of weakness and inability to control one's Talent. Characters with either Negative quality apply a –3 modifier to the dice pool.

A single net hit is enough to form the bond and admit the character to the group. If the test fails, the group cannot accept the applicant at the moment, and she may try again one month. If this second attempt fails, the group is simply unable to admit the character.

FOUNDING A GROUP

Rather than hunting down a magical group, characters may attempt to start their own. Starting a magical group requires two or more Awakened members who agree to the group's founding goal or purpose. Once a month, the members-to-be may attempt a ritual to form the group's magical bond—without which the group grants no magical benefits.

This ritual requires that all participants make an Arcana + Logic (number of members) Test using teamwork (p. 65, SR4A). If the character is already an initiate, his initiate grade adds to the dice pool. Apply dice pool modifiers as noted on the Group Founding Table (p. 69).

If all participants succeed in this test, the group bond is

GROUP FOUNDING TABLE

Situation	Dice Pool Modifier
If courting a mentor spirit avatar for the group:	–4
For each additional tradition the group admits:	–2
For each member previously initiated in a magical group:	–2
For each stricture the group adopts:	+1
For each additional 2 points of Karma spent:	+1
For each month of dedicated work by all members:*	+2

* The character may perform no other tasks except for the assorted preparations, studies, and meditations needed to attempt to establish a magical bond (along with anything required for basic survival).

established. They must now pay 5 Karma per character to make the bond permanent, granting members all the benefits of a full-fledged magical group.

CREATING A GROUP

Though players may very well found their own groups, a gamemaster will probably have need of one or more groups in the course of a campaign.

If the intent is to create a group for a player character to join, the gamemaster and the player should cooperate to build the group together using the elements in this chapter as a guideline. The player can outline the desired group, with the gamemaster reserving the right to add strictures, invent customs (which might not be the player's preference), and do pretty much anything that might lead to interesting subplots or dramatic tension.

If the gamemaster is interested in introducing a group or two for plot purposes, he should first sketch out a purpose and general description of the group, using that as a guideline to flesh out details relevant for the purpose the group serves in the campaign. For the best results it's advisable to round that out with further details on restrictions, customs and strictures, based on what the gamemaster feels is appropriate and interesting.

SAMPLE MAGICAL GROUPS

The following magical groups may be used as adversaries or groups for characters to join.

BEAR DOCTOR SOCIETY

Purpose: The Bear Doctor Society is a group of tribal shamans devoted to the medicinal magic at which Bear excels. The Society views itself as a custodian of the Salish people's spiritual and holistic well-being.

Members: 12

Strictures: Belief (see below), Fraternity, Limited Membership (Bear shamans), Oath (see below)

Resources/Dues: High. Members pay half normal dues; community pays the balance. Current dues are 625 nuyen per month. The society maintains a magical lodge 8 devoted to Bear, as well as a twenty-bed hospital with living quarters for members.

Patron: Salish tribe

Description and Customs: One of many shamanic societies that flourish throughout NAN territories, the Bear Doctor Society puts its collective healing talents at the service of the Salish community. The society keeps up with modern medical practice as well as traditional tribal healing methods, and most members are licensed doctors or otherwise skilled in the life sciences. The society is devoted to protecting life and forbids needless killing. The requirements of Bear are viewed as moral obligations, and Bear is the group's totemic mentor spirit.

This particular group is located on Council Island in Seattle, where Salish patients receive treatment free of charge, as do any patients who cannot pay. Some members served during the Salish-Tsimshian border conflict, returning traumatized by the horrors of war and the indiscriminate targeting of innocents by both sides. Disenchanted with the society's passive approach to its calling as holistic guardian of the Salish people, some members are pushing the society to cash in on the credibility it amassed over the decades to become more of a political force and truly heal Salish society. The impasse within the ranks is creating growing unease and troubling the Salish authorities who sponsor the group.

BENANDANTI XXV

Purpose: The goal of Benandanti XXV is to explore and fathom the mystical enigmas of the Sixth World and its Awakened inhabitants to better understand the underpinnings of magic.

Members: 25

Strictures: Deed (perform missions at the patron's request), Fraternity, Obedience, Material Link, Secrecy

Resources/Dues: Luxury, no dues (fully sponsored). The group's base of operations, the converted Clementium monastery in Prague, possesses lodging, various ritual buildings, enchanting shops and magical lodges for most widespread magical traditions (rating 9).

Patron: The great dragon Schwartzkopf

Description and Customs: It is rumored that the great dragon Schwartzkopf, professor of thaumaturgy at the prestigious Charles University in Prague, has been actively recruiting its brightest talents for years—though his purpose for this is the subject of intense speculation. A few select individuals may be invited to join the Benandanti XXV, sometimes known as the Travelers.

Inspired by a Dark Ages pagan cult known as the "Good Walkers," the modern Benandanti are a secret and multi-tradition group, fully sponsored by and loyal to Schwartzkopf and dedicated to exploring the great mysteries of the Awakening, searching for new paths to enlightenment and magical power.

Besides continuing magical instruction and initiatory support, members have access to one of the largest archives of modern arcane information in the world (Schwartzkopf's collections) and extensive magical resources. In return, some members operate as the dragon's eyes and ears in the Awakened community, while others chase down, investigate, and catalogue magical phenomena, strange magic, critters, and spirits on the great dragon's behalf. Schwartzkopf occasionally sets the group to specific tasks, but by and large members are encouraged to be proactive and follow their own nose—as long as all discoveries and records find their way to Schwartzkopf's great library.

While the group is based in Prague, members spend most of their time in the field working in teams of two or three individuals. The group's apparently insatiable appetite for magical knowledge often draws members to sites of unexplained magic events, strange spirit manifestations, and other types of magical weirdness.

BROTHERHOOD OF THE IRON CRESCENT

Purpose: The Brotherhood is a multi-tradition group established to provide initiation, instruction (both magical and military), and field support to Awakened mercenaries under contract with the mercenary outfit 10,000 Daggers.

Members: 50

Strictures: Limited Membership (10,000 Daggers mercs), Exclusive Membership, Material Link (for duration of tour of duty), Oath (loyalty)

Resources/Dues: High. Members pay full dues of 200 nuyen, though lodgings and facilities (including Rating 7 magical lodges for hermetics and Islamic magicians and Rating 6 lodges for several other traditions) are provided by the patron. The patron also provides magical supplies at 25 percent discount to members.

Patron: 10,000 Daggers (provides only discount on equipment and use of facilities)

Description and Customs: 10,000 Daggers has always capitalized on its metahuman talent to compensate for the lack of advanced technologies and gear at the disposal of competitors like MET2000 or Tsunami. Though best known for its elite commandos, scouts, and black ops units, 10,000 Daggers also possesses one of the best combat mage cadres in the biz. In the 2050s, several Awakened mercs, with the corp's blessing, founded the Brotherhood as a means to hone their magical and martial skills, research new battlefield magic, and train new recruits to operational levels.

The Brotherhood is based in Istanbul and has use of several of its patron's facilities on the outskirts of the central Tokapi palace district. Only mercs under long-term contracts with 10,000 Daggers are inducted, and the group is tight knit and has its own *esprit de corps,* despite members coming from diverse magical traditions. Though members spend most of their time in the field assigned to mundane tactical units, a core cadre is always present in the city state of Istanbul to provide basic training and initiatory support.

DEAD WARLOCKS

Purpose: The Dead Warlocks are poster children for the modern wizkid gangs, ferociously dedicated to increasing both the personal power of members and the gang's own clout in the Merseysprawl underworld.

Members: 13

Strictures: Deed (execute high-risk operations for the gang), Obedience, Exclusive Membership, Exclusive Ritual, Material Link

Resources/Dues: Low. Members contribute 25 nuyen.

The group possesses its own ritual space and a Rating 5 magical lodge in the warehouse behind *Perdido Station*, a nightclub it controls.

Description and Customs: The infamous wizkid gang known as the Dead Warlocks are notorious throughout the Merseysprawl. In the past three years the gang, led by Johnny Dee, a psychotic twenty-something chaos mage, has carved a significant slice out of the Merseysprawl crime scene. Currently ignored by authorities overstretched by maintaining martial law, Dee intends to become a major player in the British crime scene before he turns thirty—facing down Tongs, Yardies, and other local outfits. Accordingly, the Dead Warlocks delve into protection rackets, violent crime, and magical extortion. Organized like a minor syndicate, the group is motivated by ambition and greed. In truth, it's a front for Dee's quest for greater power.

The Warlocks accept any Awakened character into their ranks, and the group includes several self-taught magicians, chaos mages, hermetics, and even a black magician or two—applicants need only survive the harrowing initiation into the gang. The gang provides its members with an initiatory group and a ritual space, but other than that there are no particular benefits of membership except a small slice of the profits. Occasionally, however, Dee gifts a particularly successful member of the crew with magical items.

GLADIO

Purpose: Gladio is an example of adepts coming together in reaction to discrimination, in this case in professional sports, and it is both a unique magical group and a multi-million nuyen enterprise.

Members: 32

Strictures: Deed, Exclusive Membership, Limited Membership (registered UFC fighters/adepts), Service (work on Gladio's behalf)

Resources/Dues: Luxury. Dues are 5,000 nuyen and include UFC league membership.

Patron: Gladio Enterprises

Description and Customs: In 2059, an adept and former kickbox champion named James Royce brought together a number of adepts as an initiatory group for professional fighters, calling it Gladio. The group was initially intended to help hone an adept's abilities, and, almost like a union, to provide financial, legal, and material support to members.

Facing growing segregation in their various leagues, the members of Gladio began pooling resources, raising funds, and establishing themselves as a force to be reckoned with in pro sports. The group soon acquired the Ultimate Fighting Championship franchise and turned it into the premiere combat sport program in the world, broadcast in 120 countries through multi-million nuyen licensing and marketing deals. Plagued by trumped up charges of fight-fixing and corruption in the CAS and UCAS, Gladio denounced the persecution by the mundane sports promoters and relocated its offices from Atlanta to the free city of Caracas in South America—though members still travel to and fight in North America and across the world.

The magical group continues to exist as an organic part

of the Gladio organization. Application to the group is subject to a vetting process by a random panel of current members, and prospective members must be adepts and registered fighters in the UFC league. Only the five founding members possess shares of Gladio Enterprises, but all new Gladio members receive not only the benefits of a well-financed magical group, but also the media attention, marketing machine, and luxury lifestyle of stars of the ring. The nature of the sport, however, means the group sees a relatively high turnover, with members rarely staying for more than two or three seasons.

HERMETIC ORDER OF THE AURIC AURORA

Purpose: The Order of the Auric Aurora is devoted to the scholarly study of magic and the development of its members. The Order also actively opposes the abuse and harmful use of magic.

Members: 25 (broken into three ranks, known as circles)

Strictures: Fraternity, Limited Membership (mages only), Oath (uphold the Order's beliefs), Service (community service and teaching)

Resources/Dues: Middle. Dues currently 200 nuyen per month. The Order operates out of its leader's home, a sizable storefront near Pacific University in Seattle, where the group possesses a Rating 7 magical lodge and an enchanting shop. The basement serves as ritual space for the group. The ground floor is a small lore store, where members receive a 15 percent discount on magical goods.

Description and Customs: Similar to many minor hermetic circles the world over, the Order is a society of local mages dedicated to the study of the mystical arts and the initiation of its members into the higher mysteries of the hermetic path.

While favoring a circumspect and cerebral approach to magic, the group upholds the classic hermetic view that spiritual advancement demands ethical and moral discipline. Accordingly members not only abide by high ethical standards (though no formal stricture to this effect exists) but also proactively provide healing and magical assistance to the needy. The Order also runs classes in the rooms above the lore store for budding magical talents that haven't caught the eye of corporate recruiters or are uninterested in pursuing the career of a wage mage.

Despite its generally contemplative nature, the Order has been known to go out of its way to break up fledgling wizkid gangs and bring down Awakened conmen and racketeers causing problems in its area—they believe these to be the main cause of the suspicion and ill-repute many magicians still encounter.

ILLUMINATES OF THE NEW DAWN

Purpose The Illuminates of the New Dawn (IOND) is the world's largest public magical group, promoting members' development while lobbying for a progressive and magocratic political and social ideal.

Members 700 worldwide (10-20 per local chapter)

Strictures Belief (magocratic progressivism), Fraternity, Limited Membership (mages only), Magical Link, Oath (see below)

Resources/Dues Luxury. Dues are currently 200 nuyen per month, which is enough to sustain the group with money left over for the group's various special projects. Discounts on magical goods are sometimes available in lore stores belonging to other IOND members.

Description and Customs: The IOND is a powerful international organization based out of the Federal District of Columbia in the UCAS, where its Grand Lodge is located. Though a member's oath of service is to "elevate the science of magic above all else," the Illuminates are also political animals, devoted to a belief in the superiority of magic and magicians as a solution to many of the world's ills. The group's fundamental beliefs are laid out in the book "Legacy of the American Dream" by Dr. Rozilyn Hernandez, the current High Magus and a former presidential hopeful.

The Illuminates are fascinated by structure, and their own is very systematic. The Outer Order consists of a significant number of mundane supporters and the magical circles that operate in cities and territories around the world. Smaller circles answer to higher-level circles in larger cities. Each branch of the group is led by a Magus, normally a magician with significant social or economic clout. Magi are members of the Inner Order and Magus Council, which is in turn led by High Magus Hernandez in DeeCee. The Inner Order numbers around 700 members. Individual circles contain no more than a dozen members; some areas support more than one circle. Outer Order circles possess a chapterhouse with Rating 6 magical lodges and dedicated ritual spaces and ample accommodations. Inner Order circles normally possess small estates with dedicated buildings and various luxuries including Rating 8 magical lodges and enchanting shops.

JAMIL ISLAMYAH

Purpose: Jamil Islamyah is a brotherhood of Islamic magicians who are committed to redeeming their cursed birthright by putting their Talent and their lives at the service of the faith and the faithful as *mujahedin* (holy warriors).

Members: 250 worldwide, divided in groups of 5-8 individuals

Strictures: Attendance, Belief (Islam), Fraternity, Geasa (incant verses from the Qu'ran), Oath, Obedience, Service, Limited Membership (Islamic magicians and adepts)

Resources/Dues: Low, no dues (housing and equipment is always provided by the order). Each monastery possesses a carefully guarded Islamic magic library and a Rating 6 lodge.

Description and Customs: Even among the most anti-Awakened cultures, magical groups can be found. A perfect example is Jamil Islamyah, a pan-sectarian Islamic order that believes Islam must use the weapons of the infidels against them in order to ascend to its rightful place in the world. Risking the ire of conservative Islam, Jamil Islamyah calls out to those faithful stigmatized by their magical birthright—Islamic magicians and adepts alike—to prove their faith and devotion by applying their Talents to the greater glory of Allah and joining the order's monasteries.

The Awakened are trained and indoctrinated in one of the brotherhood's *madrassas* (schools). Each new class forms its own magic group, and each group of five to eight mujahedin is led by an *ulema* (teacher). These mixed groups of magicians and adepts almost never part, taking assignments together and returning to the monasteries to assume the role of instructors and ulemas when attrition takes its toll.

In recent years Jamil Islamyah has courted the favor of the Arabian Caliph, and its mujahedin can sometimes be seen supplementing Caliphate military units. Other groups are also charged with protecting preeminent Islamic individuals and communities across the globe—always returning to the isolation of the order's monasteries between missions.

MCT RESEARCH UNIT 13

Purpose: Mitsuhama's Research Unit 13 is an elite group of fiercely loyal magical specialists and troubleshooters. Unit 13 also doubles as an initiatory group for its members and a research tank for magical countermeasures to threats to the corporation.

Members: 10

Strictures: Exclusive Ritual, Limited Membership (MCT mages only), Link, Oath (protect and promote MCT interests), Obedience (to corporate superiors as well as to superiors within the Unit)

Resources/Dues: Luxury. No dues.

Patron: Mitsuhama Computer Technologies

Description and Customs: Funded heavily by MCT and composed of wage mages loyal to the company, Research Unit 13 is an elite corporate magical group. It is part of MCT's internal security operation and serves as a "SWAT team" when magic is used against the company. Unit 13 also carries out spot checks of site security, using control manipulations and mind probe spells to "validate" employee attitudes, and the group maintains astral observation of important suspects and members of R&D teams.

Members are expected to be loyal to MCT. As with many corporate groups, Unit 13 is riddled with office politics and scheming, making for a tense work environment. When members come up for initiation, they are expected to offer lavish gifts to their superiors. The going rate is cash or goods worth 1,000 nuyen times the superior's initiate grade. Unit 13 will use any means necessary to achieve a desired result. In the unit, success is the only measure of status. Failure is not acceptable, but even so it happens. According to rumor, a cell of Unit 13 magicians botched an important mission in Amazonia and went on the run. Though this allegedly happened more than five years ago, Unit 13 has taken upon itself, as a matter of honor, to locate and terminate the deserters.

MYSTIC CRUSADERS

Purpose: The Mystic Crusaders were created as the Atlantean Foundation's magical guardians. Well-trained and fanatical, the Crusaders guard the Foundation's secrets have access to many of its lore and artifacts.

Members: 33

Strictures: Belief, Fraternity, Exclusive Membership, Exclusive Ritual, Oath, Obedience, Service

Resources/Dues: High. No dues.

Patron: Atlantean Foundation

Description and Customs: Erroneously regarded as the Foundation's security arm and private taskforce, the Crusaders are in truth an order that follows a chivalric code laid out in an ancient mystic codex. Their alliance with the Atlantean Foundation is apparently motivated by mutual interests—though some suspect there is more to the loyalty they show the organization and its leader, Sheila Blatavska, than meets the eye.

Though the Crusaders count riggers, hackers, and men-at-arms in their number, the heart of the order is the magical circle that first deciphered the codex. The Inner Circle numbers 33 Awakened Crusaders, of various traditions and adept ways, and is based out of Atlanta. All Crusaders are dedicated to their internal code of honor, martial prowess, and the quest to unveil the secret history of the Sixth World.

Members are fanatically devoted to the group's goals and by extension to the Atlantean Foundation, for whom they guard digs, vaults, and important individuals, while also serving as a covert ops unit, snatching artifacts and relics of power from the clutches of the unworthy. Their code is harsh but honorable, and they are ruthless when dealing with those they deem dishonorable or untrustworthy (such as shadowrunners).

PATHFINDERS

Purpose: A tribal shamanic society, the Pathfinders were established specifically to study and deal with various volatile magical phenomena the Pueblo Corporate Council has encountered in the past decade.

Members: 21

Strictures: Deed, Exclusive Membership, Limited Membership (shamans only), Oath (defend the Pueblo nation), Service (monthly administrative duties)

Resources/Dues: High, no dues (fully sponsored). All Pathfinder branches possess Rating 8 magical lodges and are fully supplied with ritual materials. Members have 30 percent discounts on other magical goods acquired through government contractors.

Patron: Pueblo Corporate Council

Description and Customs: This shamanic society was founded in '67 with the express purpose of responding to any dangerous magical phenomena and potential magical threats Pueblo might face. The Pathfinders are far more than a magical strike team, though. Inspired by the tribal spirit dancers and hunter-shamans of Southwestern tribes, they hold the shamanic belief that only understanding the essence of a phenomenon can bring about balance, and that conflict is not always the solution. Investigation plays an important a role in their mission, and the group is equally divided between field agents and arcane researchers. Strangely, the group has fickle Coyote as a mentor spirit.

The Pathfinder's central lodge is located in Santa Fe, and the group is a fully funded and recognized part of the Pueblo Security Force. The group is active throughout the Pueblo nation, but it has chapters permanently assigned to the evolving situations in Los Angeles and the Mojave Desert. Rumor has it that the Pathfinders are also spearheading the investigation of the mysterious Anasazi ruins of Chaco Canyon.

The Pathfinders mission places them in constant danger, and the group is constantly recruiting new talent within the Pueblo and abroad.

THE RAT PACK

Purpose: The Rat Pack is a coven of urban shamans who believe they embody the last remaining wilderness and powers of the natural world among—or, to be specific, under—the glass and plasticrete canyons of the rebuilt corp enclave of New York.

Members: 14

Strictures: Exclusive Membership, Exclusive Ritual, Secrecy (outside the squatter community), Service.

Resources/Dues: Street. No real dues; members are expected to contribute with what they can from their smuggling profits.

Description and Customs: When New York was shattered and rebuilt following the Quake of 2005, many parts of the city and undercity were buried under cement and forgotten while the city became a prosperous corp enclave. Sometime during the teens, a trio of Rat shamans found their way down into the labyrinthine network of abandoned subway tunnels, sewers, and collapsed buildings below the city and, recognizing an opportunity, set up shop. The group they formed exists today at the heart of a small underground community that ekes out a living by smuggling and selling black market goods on the back streets and alleys of New York.

The Pack no longer numbers only Rat shamans, though it has Rat as a mentor spirit. It draws a variety of urban shamans and Awakened eccentrics from across the East Coast, using them to function as a multi-tradition initiatory group. Governed by its own code of conduct known as the Compact, the Pack serves as the unofficial leadership of the small squatter community that that secretly claims parts of New York's old underground and sewer system. The Pack inhabits the buried remains of a Broadway theatre and uses magic to ease the harsh lives of the squatters, performing curative magic, using spirits to guide people through their mazelike domain, and protecting them from the predators and other dangers that make the underworld warren their home.

SISTERHOOD OF ARIADNE

Purpose: A long-lasting urban Wiccan coven, the Sisterhood is linked to several social and environmental causes.

Members: 13

Strictures: Attendance (monthly full moon rituals), Belief (Wicca, protect the Earth, uphold rights of women, no harmful magic except to protect self or the Earth), Fraternity (Sorority), Limited Membership (female Wiccans only), Secrecy

Resources/Dues: Middle. Dues are 450 nuyen per month. The coven has a small farmhouse in Snohomish (Seattle) with enough privacy to do ritual work outdoors. The group buys magical supplies in bulk for the membership, getting a 20 percent discount. The house boasts a decent lodge (rating 6), and there is a ritual glade in the woods out back.

Description and Customs: The Sisterhood is a coven of witches, women who practice the neo-pagan religion Wicca. Wicca (as practiced by the Sisterhood) is a faith oriented toward the worship of the Earth or Nature. The figure of the Goddess (Moon Maiden) is evoked as the group's mentor spirit. Like many Wiccan covens, the group's mysticism and practices are a hybrid of shamanic and hermetic aspects, but its exclusively female membership dispense with hierarchies and ranks, differing only in seniority.

The Sisterhood is somewhat militant, believing that patriarchy (male rule of society) is responsible for most of the planet's ills. They believe matriarchy, rule by women, is a more natural and harmonious state. Male visitors are absolutely forbidden at rituals. The Sisterhood is also associated with several feminist and eco-activist movements, such as Mother Earth and TerraFirst! (the latter is suspected of "eco-terrorist" activities). When possible it opposes pollution and exploitation of the Earth, and the coven's more radical members may resort to magic to make their point if gentler means fail. Members often provide magical assistance on runs against corps attempting to pollute or exploit resources.

SONS OF THUNDER AND SEA

Purpose: The Sons are a small, tight-knit group of traditional ghost and demon hunter wujen (*wu ma*), whose lives have all been wrecked by spirits and who guard their community from rogue spirits.

Members: 5

Strictures: Deed, Fraternity, Limited Membership (magicians touched by spirits), Oath

Resources/Dues: Low. Members pay half normal dues; community pays the balance. Current dues are 200 nuyen per month. The group possesses no real base of operations but meets and operates out of a tea shop owned by the leader that possesses a Rating 6 wujen magical lodge and has a basement that can be converted to a ritual space if needed.

Description and Customs: The Sons of Thunder and Sea are all accomplished magicians who have seen their lives at one point or another ravaged by the direct or indirect actions of free spirits, specters, and demons. They have taken it upon themselves to stop such intrusions from the spirit world, existing to track down and deal with potentially harmful spirits. The unpredictability of the mana flows in some parts of Hong Kong has led to Hong Kong having an abnormally high population of free spirits and other astral entities, and the group has its job cut out for it.

Sometimes they form pacts with these spirits to ensure the spirits will do no harm to the locals. Sometimes they seek out spirit formulas in order to bind them. On occasion, they journey to the spirit's home plane to destroy it. To guard themselves from retribution, the Sons use enchanted demon masks that conceal their identities when on business, and they specialize in masking and changing their own auras through metamagics.

The Sons enjoy the support of their local community (the Yau Ma Tei neighborhood) because they ward off such evil spirits. But their methods are not entirely altruistic, as the Sons charge a protection fee from neighborhoods and businesses elsewhere—which has led some to suggest (out of earshot) that the Sons are becoming like the Triads of old and running a protection racket.

...MAGICAL GOODS...

The light of the holograms played across the surface of the mageblade. Lyran twisted the katana to catch the single vein of orichalcum running through it. On the astral, the sword gave off a dull red glow, like heated iron, and the magical alloy stood out like a streak of blue-white lightning.

The teahouse door slid open to reveal Lyran's hostess and clients. Lyran stood and bowed as three somber-faced Japanese men in black-on-black suits padded into the room on their very expensive silk socks and sat down. One of them carried a leather valise.

Lyran waited through the requisite formal greetings and pleasantries to offer the blade, hilt first, to her employer, but it was the bespectacled man to her left who took it. He would be the sword master, then. With painstaking care, the weapons scholar examined the anatomy and heft of the katana. Satisfied, he passed it to the man across the table. This Yakuza was the youngest of the group, and Lyran had already pegged him as the mage. His eyes rested for a long time on that thin vein of orichalcum before closing entirely. Finished, the mage handed the blade to the oyabun.

Shotozumi took the katana and caressed it with his own critical eye. A long fingernail traced the engravings on one side, and then flipped the blade with practiced ease.

"Would you be so kind as to indulge an old man and remind me of the terms of our contract?"

Lyran swallowed. "Ah ... honored Shotozumi-sama, you commissioned the construction of an enchanted blade in accordance with the ancient formula you provided, in return for one-point-five million nuyen worth of Mitsuhama corporate scrip."

"Indeed. A long sword of the shiho-zume-gitae style forged from a precise alloy, with a hilt carved from a dragon's tooth, decorated on one side by chrysanthemum blossoms." Here he paused.

"But as I recall, the instructions also called for a poem to be inscribed on the alternate side by the smith, to define the sword's power and spirit. Instead, I see a naked blade. Explain this, please."

Lyran licked her lips. "You will recall, most honored sir, from my earlier reports that I encountered significant difficulties in finding a smith of sufficient skill to craft the blade in the old style. In point of fact, it proved almost impossible; no one would risk your enemies' wrath. No smith that was living could forge the blade ... so I found a dead one."

Shotozumi's gaze was inscrutable. "Continue."

"Six years ago, Hiro Gassan, a descendant of the Imperial swordsmiths, arranged his own apparent death to cover his extraction. I managed to acquire his services to forge the blade. Gassan did inscribe a poem—but he did so on the tang, beneath the hilt."

Shotozumi looked satisfied. "Very well, then. The enchantment seems intact. Your reward."

Lyran accepted the valise of corporate scrip thankfully and left. She almost made it to her bike when a burst of dragonfire destroyed it. She looked up as the Eastern dragon flamed the teahouse.

Who knew the wizworm would be so mad about one little tooth?

THE INS AND OUTS OF TALISMONGERING

Posted By: Winterhawk

Talismongers are merchants who specialize in magical goods. Most cities can support only a handful of talismongers, while major metroplexes can support more than a dozen big chain lorestores and a smattering of Mom & Pop magic shops, as well as a sizable community of independent street dealers.

Good talismongers don't just sell spell formulae and foci; they are cornerstones of the local magical community, with extensive connections. Their clientele tend to be very protective. After all, where else are you going to get the gear you need if you can't make your own?

• That's not counting the talisleggers, unlicensed talismongers, and magicians who are capable of doing some enchanting but lack the desire or facilities to do so. Magic is big biz, and time is money—and enchanting always takes time.
• Lyran

• A talismonger is the magician's personal fixer. She can move your swag, find what you need, and put you in contact with anyone in the magical community. Need a formula? Looking for someone to teach you a spell? Trying to move that hot data from Pentagram's R&D host? Call your talismonger.
• Fatima

• Most legitimate talismongers won't buy or sell magical goods that they know to be hot. Talismongers who play the shadows, of course, will buy and sell almost anything, including Awakened drugs and illegal magical goods like combat spell formulae.
• Ethernaut

Creating magical goods requires gathering suitable reagents by hand in areas of untouched wilderness—areas often protected by native tribes or vicious paracritters—and individual talismongers may need to disappear for a couple months at a time to perform some bit of alchemy. Consequently, many talismongers—particularly the various chains like MageWerks and Pentacle—receive raw reagents and other small magical goods from megacorporate distributors.

• And what a racket that is. Aztechnology has a legion of semi-skilled, uneducated laborers doing backbreaking work without tools in some of the most dangerous areas of Latin America—all for a pittance while the corp rakes in the profit. All of the megas have similar set-ups. It's despicable.
• Ecotope

Chain stores usually aren't run by magicians, just mundane distributors for magic-savvy corporations. The top four distributors are Saeder-Krupp, Aztechnology, Mitsuhama, and Wuxing. Corporate talismongers almost never purchase goods from their customers—it's against corporate policy. Corporate talismongers, however, are more likely to stock the latest in magical theory and formulae.

• Most of the talismongers you deal with in the shadows are usually tied into one of the big syndicates, often one of the Triads, though both the Yakuza and Mafia have been getting in on the action these days. They typically have a wider selection than your average talismonger, but they see a high turnover in goods, and there's never any guarantee they'll have what you need in stock. They will also try and talk you into a loan to cover the focus you want to buy … and the first time you miss a payment, they own you.
• Jimmy No

Some talismongers specialize in specific categories of magical gear. The most common is the loremonger, or lore store. These folks buy and sell spell formulae, focus formulae, ally formulae, metamagical theses, and skillsofts on arcanoarcheology, mystical languages, parazoology, parageology, parapsychology, and magical theory. A couple of online lore stores operate in the Magicknet, but not many. Too often their wares end up pirated and traded around the Matrix.

• Talismongers may also specialize in whatever local traditions are most popular. Just good business, if you think about it, but a real pain in the ass if you're trying to pick something up away from home. You have any idea how hard it is to find a Voodoo gris-gris in Neo-Tokyo?
• Ethernaut

• The Magick Undernet is awash with active sharing of pirated magic formulae, but it also supports a thriving community dedicated to open source formulae. World-wide, dozens of magical groups create, modify, and release new spells, techniques, and theories for free, with the intent of furthering metahumanity's understanding of magic.
• Pistons

DOING BUSINESS

Posted By: Lyran

Picture yourself walking into a lorestore. A quaint little brick-and-mortar shop stuck into the concrete-coated sprawl you call home, maybe, or that bright new WeiseCrafters at the mall. Before you even darken the door, try and pick out the first layer of security: cameras, hidden sensors, maybe a physical security guard or drone. Then remember what you're not seeing: the wards, the guardian spirit, or the AR program querying your credit rating.

• Just because they've got one eye on the astral doesn't mean talismongers slack on IC.
• Pistons

Once you're inside, you pass through a section of tourist kitsch and maybe a rack of datasofts full of textbooks and horoscope programs. The décor is probably M-NeoPoMo (Magical Neo-Postmodern), with an AR overlay of hermetic symbols and complex Celtic scrollwork that shifts when you're not looking directly at it. Ignore the light show and the front-room crap—the owner probably orders it out of a catalogue anyway.

• Few talismongers get by on just selling magical goods. Sure, they make a bundle off every focus they sell, but they have to pay through the nose for security and special licenses to deal magical goods. That's why nine out of ten magic shops fill the front room with mundane gewgaws and worthless New Age texts. Talismongers make at least as much off gullible mundanes each year as they make off their magical clientele.
o Lyran

• Some people go seriously off the deep-end for the "magical lifestyle" and eat that stuff up. Magician-wannabes and poseurs, the lot of them.
o Ma'fan

• Yeah, they're poseurs, and God bless 'em—posing as a poseur can be an effective disguise if you need to stake out a lorestore. It's a great way to keep an eye out for local magicians, too.
o Mika

The local merchant keeps an eye on the good stuff (everything from telesma to spirit binding materials to actual foci). If it's a flesh-and-blood metahuman and not an AR salesprogram, you're probably staring at the manager or a certified talismonger. This is the person you talk to when you need to do business. Magical goods are kept under lock and key, and you will be watched by security at all times as you inspect the merchandise (assuming you have the appropriate licenses, natch).

• Formulae are handled a little differently: legal formulae are patented, and the merchant will give you a copy of the patent number to verify online. Illegal, homemade, or unpatented formulae are bought site unseen.
o Ethernaut

• Some outfits sell grimoires with a collection of formulae—some based on a theme, others not—instead of selling you the formulae one at a time. It's basically a scam to get you to shell out more cred.
o Lyran

Asking to make a large purchase—like a focus, or orichalcum—will probably earn you an invite into an office in the back. This is where you can talk shadow business, sell foci or other magical goods you've "acquired," and maybe even work a trade.

• A good talismonger will have a selection of foci on hand, and you can probably find what you're looking for, especially if you're not picky about telesma. Otherwise, the talismonger might take your "order" and a down payment (10-15 percent is typical). If you are willing to settle for what they have on hand, the talismonger will take the item out of the vault for you to inspect.
o Ethernaut

• Those vaults are a bitch to crack. Most are built from plasteel-reinforced ferroconcrete, and the electronic lock has so much IC on it penguins would feel at home—and then there's the wards or quickened spells.
o Ma'fan

• The sneaky bastards like to stick a watcher spirit inside it, too. Even if you crack the vault, the spirit sounds the alarm.
o Mika

Most talismongers don't keep their enchanting shop or most of their inventory on-site if possible, but there are exceptions. Some lorestores have an enchanting shop on the premises to rent out to customers; others don't want the hassle of transporting their magical goods any more than necessary. Renting an enchanting shop is a lot like renting a coffin at the motel, except the owner probably won't engage the self-clean function if you stay overtime—he'll have a spirit drag you out by the short and curlies instead.

• If you have a group of independent talismongers in the same area, they might form a consortium and go in on purchasing an enchanting shop they can share.
o Ethernaut

• Most of the lorestore chains don't make product on-site—instead they get their goods in heavily armored shipments from their megacorp distributor. Mom & Pop talismongers are often owned and run by one or more magicians, and they either order their magical goods wholesale or make their own, whichever is cheaper. Independents typically only make magical goods on commission, and few own their own enchanting shop.
o Axis Mundi

INSIDE THE ALCHEMIST'S LAB
Posted By: Ethernaut

Your typical enchanting shop is more than bubbling cauldrons and glassware (though they have those too)—it's an environment designed to facilitate the creation of magical goods. Enchanters make a special effort to ensure that the balance of magical forces in their lab is optimal for creating stable magical fields and for preserving the user's privacy. Magicians who don't set up permanent wards around their enchanting shop sometimes incorporate their mana lodge and provide astral barriers in that fashion. Corporate facilities, on the other hand, are fond of AR-inhibiting wallpaper and security measures to detract from corporate spies.

• "Balance of magical forces," huh? Sounds like feng shui.
o Ecotope

• In some cases, yes. Enchanting is easier on a place of power, whether natural or created through geomantic techniques.
o Winterhawk

Every enchanting shop includes some sort of furnace for smelting metals, heating crucibles, or performing assays, as well as a collection of more-or-less typical chemistry equipment for performing alchemical operations. A couple of

the tools have strictly arcane uses, like a silver-bladed knife, while others would just seem ridiculous to modern chemists, like an old-fashioned mortar and pestle. Modern enchanting shops also incorporate data terminals with calculation and conversion software, a small database of alchemical lore, and agents to assist in tracking equipment, managing cleaning drones, and directing fire suppression or chemical spill cleanup. Research to incorporate Sixth World technology into enchanting shops continues, but all enchanting shops contain some method of producing an actual flame and potable water.

> • I caught a glimpse of the specs for a Mitsuhama alchemy microlab last week. It includes a collapsible tank with engineered bacteria that break down organic waste to produce a methane-based gas for flame, and a microcistern that collects, filters, and distills water vapor from the surrounding atmosphere. I'm definitely saving up for one.
> • Winterhawk

Enchanting shops usually reflect the tradition of whatever magician put it together. A Catholic theurgist might have a lab containing the inscriptions from the gospels and the symbols and icons of various saints and archangels, while you'll see tribal artwork, a sacred bundle, and a totem mask in a Native American shaman's place.

GAME INFORMATION

The information in this section details the uses of the Enchanting skill, the creation of magical goods, the tools needed to design and create magical goods, foci, metamagic foci, and the creation of vessels.

ENCHANTING 101

Creating magical goods is a step-by-step process. This process has been summarized below for reference and convenience. Depending on the choices players and gamemasters make, some of these steps may lead to shadowruns the magician character will have to undertake, while others may be breezed through with a roll of the dice.

1) **Raw reagents** are the building blocks from which all magical goods are made (see *Getting the Goods,* p. 79). A player can either collect the raw reagents herself (see *Gathering,* p. 80) or buy them from a talismonger (see *Buying,* p. 81).
2) **Alchemy** is used to turn raw reagents into magical goods (see *Practical Alchemy,* p. 81), and also to process orichalcum (see *Orichalcum,* p. 81) and exotic reagents (p. 83).
3) **Focus Formulae** are the arcane blueprints used to create foci; a character can either buy one or research her own (see *The Focus Formula,* p. 82).
4) **Enchanting** a focus requires a focus formula and telesma (see *Telesma,* p. 83) before the player can make the Enchanting Test (see *Crafting Foci,* p. 84).

ENCHANTING TOOLS

Enchanting requires certain specialized gear for many of its operations.

> **OPTIONAL RULE: AID ENCHANTING**
> Bound spirits of the appropriate type may *Aid Enchanting* as one of their services. The spirit adds its Force to the magician's pool for the appropriate tests. The spirit must be present and bound throughout the duration of the test.
> **Air Spirits** aid tests to design foci.
> **Beast Spirits** aid tests to gather and refine animal reagents.
> **Earth Spirits** aid tests to gather and refine mineral reagents.
> **Fire Spirits** aid tests to gather and refine metal reagents.
> **Guardian Spirits** aid tests to enchant weapon foci and spell defense foci.
> **Guidance Spirits** aid tests to enchant vessels.
> **Plants Spirits** aid tests to gather and refine herbal reagents.
> **Task Spirits** aid tests to craft fetishes and talismans.
> **Water Spirits** aid tests to gather reagents near or under water.

A **talislegger kit** represents the bare minimum equipment necessary to gather reagents. Talislegger kits are cheap and relatively compact, able to fit in a small backpack. A talislegger kit can only be used to gather reagents.

Assaying kits fit inside a large backpack and contain all the equipment needed to gather and refine reagents, as well as fashion fetishes, talismans, or ritual materials.

An **enchanting shop** includes all the equipment necessary for making radical reagents and synthesizing orichalcum. A typical enchanting shop fits into a large van for transport but requires a basement or other reasonably large space to be set up. Individual magicians, small-time talismongers, and other prospective enchanters that can't afford their own enchanting shops can rent time or purchase one jointly. An enchanting shop can be used to refine or make radical reagents, synthesize orichalcum, and craft magical goods.

Recent years have seen an increasing number of high-tech **alchemy microlabs**. Rare and expensive, these alchemical laboratories are made of lightweight ceramics, smart plastics, and foamed metal, and when collapsed fit into the trunk of a large car. A microlab can be set up or taken down in only an hour in nearly any environment, deriving needed power from solar cells. Alchemy microlabs can be used to gather, refine, or make radical reagents, synthesize orichalcum, and craft magical goods.

GETTING THE GOODS

Magical goods are made from naturally occurring materials known as **reagents**. Reagents have a higher inherent concentration of mana than normal substances, but are otherwise identical to their mundane counterparts. There are four common types of reagents:

INCOMING FEED.......

Animal reagents are parts of normal and paranormal beasts, harvested after a specimen has been hunted in the wild and slain by hand or died of natural causes. Octopus ink, ivory, a grizzly bear skull, and eye of megasalamander are examples of this type of material.

Herbal reagents come from the kingdom of plants and fungi, and must be harvested from the wild, never cultivated. Mistletoe culled from deep forests with golden sickles, sea kelp from the Sargasso, and the sap of ancient, gnarled trees are examples of this type.

Metal reagents must be mined by hand tools from ore-bearing rocks and veins of pure metal; metallic sands and certain heavy clays may also be worked to gather the precious metal. Because modern refining processes would ruin the reagent for magical operations, metal reagents are worked by hand or smelted and worked in old-style blast furnaces. Bog iron, red gold, native silver, and copper ore are examples of metal reagents.

Mineral reagents are stones and crystals of various types, from raw diamonds to humble coal. Semiprecious and precious gems fall under the category of mineral reagents, and talismongers bargain with miners and jewelers for the uncut stones. Examples include fossils, geodes, amber, obsidian, and crude oil.

Most reagents gathered from the wild are **raw reagents**. By themselves, raw reagents have magical potential, but cannot be used to create magical goods. Magicians use alchemy to concentrate the mana within a reagent, creating a **refined reagent** that can be used in turn to create fetishes, talismans, and other magical goods. Skilled alchemists can purify refined reagents even further, and the products of their labors are bursting with magical potential. These **radical reagents** can facilitate some of the most powerful enchantments.

Under rare conditions, unharvested raw reagents are spontaneously transmuted in the wild into **natural refined reagents** and **natural radical reagents**.

Gathering

Before she can gather raw reagents, a character must first find a suitable spot of unspoiled wilderness—a virgin forest, an untouched cave, the bottom of the ocean, etc. Suitable sites are becoming rare in the Sixth World, and gaining access to them can be an adventure unto itself. Truly potent and primeval sites are often harsh and hostile environments, or protected enclaves fiercely guarded by eco-radicals, sentient paracritters, and the Awakened who have already claimed the reagent-rich area as their own.

Players must then specify the type of reagent they are looking for (animal, herbal, metal, or mineral) and make a Location Test (see the Location Tests table, p. 81). Characters who wish to search for a more specific reagent (deer antler, amber, copper ore, fossilized bone, etc.) receive a –2 dice pool modifier to the test. A successful Location Test indicates the character has found a single reagent.

For simplicity, gathering the reagent without damaging it requires about 30 minutes and a successful Gathering Test. The gamemaster may decide that harvesting the reagent takes more or less time depending on its accessibility (i.e., digging up a deep vein of gold may take significantly longer). Gathering reagents without a talislegger's kit or assayer's kit imposes a –2 dice pool modifier to the Gathering Test. In the case of animal reagents, a successful Location Test may only indicate the character has located a suitable critter or paracritter from which the reagent may be harvested. Most talismongers use traps to capture and/or sedate the animals to assure the reagent and the animal are undamaged, while talisleggers prefer the more expeditious method of killing the animal at a distance and then claiming their trophy. Some tribal cultures and traditions (and their focus formulae) insist that the reagent be taken from a live animal, or that the animal be slain by hand.

LOCATION TESTS

Goal	Test
Locating one raw reagent	Survival + Intuition (8, 1 hour) Extended Test
Locating one natural refined reagent	Survival + Intuition (16, 1 day) Extended Test
Locating one natural radical reagent	Survival + Intuition (12, 1 week) Extended Test

GATHERING TESTS

Goal	Test
Animal reagents	Zoology + Intuition Test
Herbal reagents	Botany + Intuition Test
Metal reagents	Metallurgy + Intuition Test
Mineral reagents	Geology + Intuition Test

Buying

Gaining access to a natural location and harvesting reagents can be a long, dangerous, and difficult process that is best left to professionals. Characters who don't have the time or inclination to get their own must purchase reagents, either directly from a talismonger or through their magical contacts.

Large corporations, government agencies, magical societies, and talismonger associations often have in-house talismongers with significant (10 to 20 percent) discounts for members and employees. Shadowrunners might bargain for access to in-house talismongers as part of their payment for a shadowrun or purchase some false ID and infiltrate the facility. Another option for magician characters is to join a magical society (see *Magical Groups*, p. 62)

PRACTICAL ALCHEMY

Alchemy is the art and science of tapping and harnessing magical potential. Enchanters specializing in alchemy concern themselves with the transmutation of base materials to those of magical potency. The bulk of magical goods are products of alchemy, and alchemy is a vital part of the magical economy of the Sixth World.

Refined and Radical Reagents

Raw reagents must be refined before they have any magical use. Raw reagents may be transformed into refined reagents with a successful Enchanting + Magic (number of reagents, 1 day) Extended Test.

To create radical reagents, the magician must tend a batch of refined reagents through a 28-day *circulation*. A batch may include a number of reagents of the same type (animal, herbal, metal, or mineral) up to the magician's Magic attribute. The magician must tend the circulation during this period and must check the circulation and make adjustments every 8 hours. At the end of the circulation, a successful Enchanting + Magic (2) Test transmutes a batch of refined reagents into a same number of radical reagents. Failure destroys the refined reagents.

Fetishes and Talismans

Crafting a fetish for use with a limited spell (see *Limited Spells*, p. 182, *SR4A*) requires a successful Enchanting + Magic (4, 1 hour) Extended Test and one refined or radical reagent. These reagents are consumed or incorporated into the finished product during the test. Fetishes are not attuned to any particular spell when created (see p. 182, *SR4A*).

A talisman (see *Geasa*, p. 27) is simply a type of fetish and is crafted in the same way, though enchanting it requires a radical reagent.

Ritual Materials

Conjuring materials (see *Binding*, p. 188, *SR4A*), ritual sorcery materials (see *Ritual Spellcasting*, p. 184, *SR4A*), and some magical lodge materials (see *Magical Lodges*, p.178, *SR4A*) are all examples of ritual materials. Crafting ritual materials requires a successful Enchanting + Magic (Force, 1 day) Extended Test and four refined or two radical reagents per point of Force. These reagents are consumed or incorporated into the finished product during the test.

Orichalcum

According to legend, the priest-kings of ancient Atlantis discovered orichalcum. Regardless of the truth of that claim, this orange-gold alloy is utterly absurd from any metallurgical point of view; only alchemy can create it. Scientific examination is difficult because spectroscopic analysis breaks orichalcum down into its component mundane metals. Orichalcum possesses many of the physical properties of gold, being dense and highly malleable. It alloys easily with iron, making it

> **FORM AND FUNCTION**
>
> Mechanics are all well and good, but what do magical goods actually *look* like? Magical goods can take many different forms, depending on the tradition of the enchanter and the reagents used in making them. The following are a selection of typical forms in which magical goods may appear; players and gamemasters are encouraged to come up with other forms that fit their characters and games.
>
> | Magical Good | Common Form |
> |---|---|
> | Raw reagents | A ragged foot encrusted with dried blood, a dirty tree limb scorched at one end with moldy bark, a crumbly rock with a large green vein running through it. |
> | Refined reagents | A clean three-toed claw, a piece of ash wood stripped of bark and sanded down, a rough ingot of copper, a stone that has been ground and cut into a geometric shape. |
> | Radical reagents | A shaped sliver of bone, a smooth shaft cut from the heartwood of an ash, a flawless pearl of pure copper, a polished stone displaying the veins running through it. |
> | Fetishes and Talismans | A ring carved from bone, wood, or soft stone; a calligraphic scroll of handmade paper; a bracelet of woven hair with seven knots. |
> | Ritual Materials | Multi-colored sands and paints used to inscribe mystic diagrams, candles made with certain herbs and mystic sigils, ceremonial wands and blades of wood or soft metal. |
> | Magical Lodges | A teepee or wigwam of carved wood and painted hide, a collection of books and artifacts bearing arcane symbols and scripts, a small Zen garden of smooth-polished stones with tools to tend it. |

preferred for weapon foci construction. *Aqua regia* dissolves orichalcum, but the magical metal can be reclaimed.

Creating orichalcum requires placing one unit each of radical copper, radical gold, radical mercury, and radical silver through a 28-day circulation. The magician must tend the circulation during this period and must check the circulation and make adjustments every 8 hours. A successful Enchanting + Magic (3) Test consumes the radicals and produces a number of units of orichalcum equal to the net hits scored in the Enchanting Test (to a maximum of 8). Failure consumes the radicals but only produces a worthless alchemical slag.

This test may not be rushed, and any interruption requires the magician to start again.

Just back from a successful talislegging trip into the wilds of the NAN, Lyran has 24 raw reagents that she wants to turn into magical goods. Lyran has Magic 2 and Enchanting (Alchemy) 2 (+2). Retiring to her enchanting shop, she sets to work refining the raw reagents. Her threshold for the test is 24, and she rolls 6 dice; in 12 days she has 24 hits and has transformed her raw reagents into refined reagents.

Lyran wants to use 20 of the refined reagents to create Force 5 conjuring materials. Her threshold for the test is 5, and she rolls 6 dice; in 3 days she has completed the conjuring materials and 20 of her refined reagents have been consumed.

The remaining reagents are a refined copper reagent, a refined silver reagent, a refined mercury reagent, and a refined gold reagent. Lyran puts the 4 reagents through an alchemical circulation to transform them into radical reagents. After 28 days of tending the circulation, Lyran rolls 6 dice and gets 4 hits. She now possesses 4 radical reagents, 1 each of copper, silver, gold, and mercury.

Combining the reagents in another circulation, Lyran attempts to create orichalcum. She spends another 28 days tending the circulation and makes her test. Lyran uses her Edge and rolls 8 dice, scoring 2 net hits. For her hard work, Lyran has been rewarded with 2 units of orichalcum.

ARTIFICING

Unlike other magical goods, a focus is powerful, reusable, and intimately tied to its owner. A focus represents a permanent and complex enchantment built up slowly from an arcane formula and finished with Karma. All foci follow the same basic creation process: first a focus formula is needed, then an appropriate telesma is selected, then the enchantment proper is created, and finally the finished foci is bonded. In many ways, artificing is the culmination of all enchanting.

The Focus Formula

Designing a focus requires a complex arcane recipe known as a focus formula. Focus formulae, like all magical formulae, are produced using the Arcana skill. They are too complex for metahuman magicians to memorize, and must be recorded in some fashion appropriate to the creator's magical tradition. Characters can buy formulae from lore stores and talismongers, but many choose to design their own in order to incorporate a specific item into the form of the focus.

All focus formulae specify the type of focus (spell, spirit, power, weapon, or metamagic), Force, form (wooden quarterstaff, gold ring, vibroknife, etc.), and tradition of the focus (hermetic, shamanic, etc.). If the formula is designed by a character it is always of the character's tradition. A focus formula does not dictate the telesma quality (mundane, handmade, virgin, or exotic) used to make it, but it may include various exotic reagents that must be used to create the focus. The formulae sold by talismongers typically use "traditional" forms in widespread magical traditions (wands, magical amulets, rune-carved swords, etc.)—another reason player characters commonly craft their own formulae.

Researching a focus formula is an Arcana + Magic (Force x Force, 1 day) Extended Test. Once complete, the focus formula may be used by any magician of that tradition to make that specific focus. A character can translate a focus formula from one tradition to another with an Arcana + Magic (Force, 1 day) Extended Test. Gamemasters may wish to enforce the limit on Extended Tests to preserve game balance.

Optional Rule: Exotic Reagent Requisites

The process of enchanting can be made more difficult or exciting by introducing exotic reagents as requirements to complete the enchantment. Exotic reagents include esoteric or unusual components such as those included on the Exotic Reagents Table, though gamemasters are encouraged to let their imaginations run wild when choosing such components. Requiring exotic reagents offers excellent possibilities for adventure hooks.

For every two glitches or critical glitch a character scores while researching a focus formula, an exotic reagent requirement is added to the focus formula. Gamemasters may choose a specific item they have in mind, or roll 2D6 and consult the Exotic Reagents Table. Exotic reagents do not count with other reagents when determining dice pool modifiers for the Enchantment Test.

Gathering exotic reagents should be an adventure in itself and should go beyond the limits of a simple Gathering Test. Characters may have to travel to distant lands, fight or bargain with powerful paracritters, or break into museums and megacorporate research labs to obtain exotic reagents.

Characters who choose not to fulfill the exotic reagent requirements for their focus may design a new focus formula and hope that they draw easier or fewer exotic reagent requirements the next time around.

Telesma

Before a character can attempt to create a focus, they need to acquire an item that matches the form defined in the chosen focus formula. An object being prepared for enchantment in this manner is known as a **telesma**. Obtaining telesma may be as simple or complex as the character chooses—if the formula calls for a knife, it may be no more difficult than buying a blade from the local Weapons World™ franchise.

Any inanimate object can serve as the telesma: a wooden wand, a jeweled charm, a weapon, a car, an oddly shaped stone,

EXOTIC REAGENTS TABLE

Die Roll	Material
2	A body part from a freshly killed dragon (natural animal radical).
3	A natural herbal radical from a remote corner of another continent.
4	A metal radical from an extraterrestrial source, such as a ferrous asteroid or meteorite.
5	1D6 x 10,000¥ worth of precious and semi-precious gem reagents.
6	A natural animal refined agent of blood from a living Awakened critter.
7	A lock of hair (or feather or scales) from an Awakened critter (natural animal refined reagent).
8	A mineral radical from an extraterrestrial source, such as a rock from Mars or the moon.
9	A unique radical (see *Unique Enchantments*, p. 87).
10	A bone or fossil from a dead Awakened critter or magician (natural refined animal or mineral reagent).
11	A natural mineral radical from a remote corner of another continent.
12	A sample of bodily fluid from a live dragon (natural animal radical). ("You want me to *what* in this cup?")

and so on. The more unprocessed and natural the object, or the more work a character performed to create it, the easier the telesma is to enchant. For this reason, enchanters with the technical or artistic skill to do so often create telesma themselves. Telesma are not reagents and do not follow the rules for gathering reagents. There are four types of telesma:

Mundane telesma are an items bought off-the-shelf, usually a highly processed item such as a monofilament chainsaw or a commlink.

Handmade telesma are shaped or put together by a magician in some way from, such as handmade jewelry or an amulet etched with diagrams. Firearms and other highly processed goods are generally difficult to manufacture in this fashion and are often less effective than their mass-manufactured counterparts.

Virgin telesma must be crafted from the raw, natural materials and shaped by the magician. A magician may shape a knife from a piece of flint, or weave a horsehair thong to hold a bird's skull as a form of amulet. Weapons made in this way are usually primitive and fragile.

Exotic telesma are crafted from exceptional and rare materials, particularly parts of innately magical paracritters. Examples of exotic telesma include an amulet carved from unicorn horn, a jacket made from the leathery hide of a dragon, or an obsidian mirror crafted from the heart of an ancient volcano.

Aspected Enchantments

An aspected enchantment is a limitation on when the owner may activate the focus, or how a focus may be used. Mechanically, a focus with an aspect enchantment has a geas that cannot be removed (see *Geas*, p. 27). The focus may only be activated when the conditions of the geas are fulfilled. A focus created with an aspected enchantment is easier to enchant (see *Crafting Foci*).

Aspected enchantments may be added into the focus formula, in which case any focus created with that formula bears the aspected enchantment (and is easier to enchant). Enchanters may also incorporate an aspected enchantment into a focus during the final stage of the enchanting process. A focus cannot have more than one aspected enchantment.

Common aspected enchantments include Time (example: a focus that only works at night), Incantation (example: a focus that only works while the user is chanting a prayer), and Ritual (example: a weapon focus that only works if the user performs a ritualized *kata* every day).

Crafting Foci

Once the enchanter has assembled the focus formula, the telesma, and any radical reagents or orichalcum she wishes to incorporate into the focus, she may attempt to enchant the item into a focus.

Crafting a focus is an Enchanting + Magic (16 + Object Resistance, 1 day) Extended Test. The enchantment must take place in a magical lodge of the appropriate tradition with a Force at least equal to the Force of the focus being enchanted.

The enchanter can gain a +1 positive modifier to her Enchanting Test by incorporating a number of units of radical reagents of the same type (animal, herbal, metal, or mineral) into the focus equal to the foci's Force. This modifier may be gained multiple times, each with a different type of reagent, to a maximum of 4 extra dice. In the case of telesma that meet multiple descriptors, only the highest dice pool modifier applies. Refer to the Enchanting Table for a full list of dice pool modifiers for this test.

After a successful Enchanting Test, the enchanter must pay 1 Karma to complete the enchantment. The focus is then ready to be bonded. The rules for bonding a focus can be found on page 199, *SR4A*.

ADVANCED FOCI

Beyond spell, spirit, power, and weapon foci are a diverse range of enchantments, designed to augment various applications of magical skill. As magical theory progresses, enchanting finds more advanced and specialized forms of foci for magicians to use. As with all types of foci, these may be bonded by any magician or mystic adept.

ENCHANTING TABLE

Focus Attribute	Dice Pool Modifier
Force of Focus	–Force
Mundane Telesma	–4
Handmade Telesma	+0
Virgin Telesma	+2
Exotic Telesma	+4
(Force) Radical Reagents of one type	+1 (cumulative per type)
Orichalcum, per unit	+2
Aspected Enchantment	+2

Stacked Foci

It is possible to combine two or more types of foci into a "stacked" focus. The effective Force of the focus is equal to the sum of the ratings of the different foci. A character requires a separate focus formula to create a stacked focus—she cannot simply use focus formulae for two or more different foci. The cost to bind a stacked focus is equal to the sum of the cost to bind the different focus types at the given Force.

Metamagic Enchantments

Initiates have pioneered new types of foci and materials to aid and expand their use of metamagic techniques. These metamagic enchantments are primarily useful to initiates, and are much more rare than other magical goods. A character researching a formula for a metamagic focus must know or collaborate with an initiate who knows the appropriate metamagic. Any enchanter possessing the correct focus formula may craft metamagic foci, whether they know the metamagic or not.

Anchoring foci combine aspects of sustaining foci (see *Sustaining Foci,* p. 199, *SR4A*) and metamagic anchors (see *Anchoring,* p. 59). Spells are cast into anchoring foci as if they were sustaining foci but are kept in a dormant state by the anchoring construct designed into the foci's form. The spellcaster must know Anchoring metamagic. When the focus leaves the magician to which it is bonded, the anchor construct and spell within draw energies from each other in a feedback loop, and the focus does not deactivate. Instead, it falls dormant until the trigger condition designed into the anchoring focus is fulfilled (see *Anchoring Triggers,* p. 60). Like other active foci, prepped anchoring foci are dual natured and active on the astral plane; mana barriers will block them.

Like anchored spells, anchoring foci can have one or more trigger conditions, such as the touch of a specific aura or the elapse of a certain amount of time. Once met, this condition instantly activates the spell. Anchoring foci may also be triggered or deactivated by the owner at any time, as long as she is in contact with the focus. Once activated, instant spells go off immediately. Anchoring foci will maintain sustained spells (and permanent spells until they become permanent) until deactivated or dispelled, or for (focus Force) hours.

Each anchoring focus is designed for a specific category of spell (Combat, Health, etc.). The combined Force of the spell cast into the anchor and any Detection spell triggers may not exceed the anchor focus's Force. Anchoring foci may be reused after the spell is triggered and discharged, but the owner must

re-cast the spell (different spells may be used, as long as they fit the category for which the focus was designed) and must re-set the trigger conditions (if any) to prep it again.

Centering foci add their Force to the magician's initiate grade when she uses Centering metamagic on a Drain Resistance Test.

Masking foci add their Force to the magician's initiate grade when making an Opposed Test to pierce her masking.

Quickening materials are a form of ritual material (see *Ritual Materials*, p. 81) that may be used with the Quickening metamagic (see *Quickening*, p. 198, *SR4A*). When quickening a spell to a living subject, an initiate may use quickening materials to bind the magic to the target's aura. Using quickening materials always creates a physical representation of the spell on the subject, normally a brand, tattoo, or ritual scar.

Quickened spells add extra dice equal to the additional Karma expended when quickening them to any tests to resist dispelling; quickening a spell with these materials allows the initiate to spend (Force x 2) additional Karma points to make the spell more difficult to defeat (normally, an initiate may only spend up to (Force) additional Karma points). The ritual re-quires a quantity of quickening materials equal in Force to the spell being quickened.

Shielding foci add their Force to the magician's initiate grade when she uses the Shielding metamagic on a Counterspelling Test.

Symbolic link foci enhance Symbolic Linking (p. 29) by adding their Force to the Extended Test to establishing the link to a particular ritual target (determined in the focus formula). The focus is usually a symbolic representation of the target.

FOCUS BONDING TABLE

Item	Karma Cost
Anchoring Focus	6 x Force
Centering Focus	6 x Force
Masking Focus	6 x Force
Shielding Focus	6 x Force
Symbolic Link Focus	1 x Force

Laura tells the gamemaster that her character Snowblood is going to create her own focus. Snowblood is a Salish shaman with Magic 3, Arcana 3, and Enchanting 3.

The first step is acquiring the focus formula. Laura decides Snowblood will research her own formula, and the gamemaster tells Laura that Snowblood has to pick out the type, force, and form of the focus—the formula will be shamanic, since Snowblood is a shaman. Laura decides she wants to create a Force 2 shielding focus in the form of a clay amulet. Laura rolls 6 dice (Magic + Arcana) and scores the needed 16 hits and 3 glitches in 5 rolls. Snowblood has completed the focus formula in 5 days, but the formula requires an exotic reagent. The gamemaster consults the Exotic Reagents Table and rolls 11 on 2 dice. After some consideration, he decides Snowblood's exotic reagent calls for mud (mineral reagent) from the banks of the ancient Euphrates River in the Middle East (a distant continent). Laura could roll again, but there's no guarantee her next focus formula would turn out any better. Looks like Snowblood is off to the Middle East.

After a harrowing journey, Snowblood arrives at a spot on the Euphrates that looks to have been untouched for centuries. Breaking out her assaying kit, she goes to work. Snowblood has Intuition 3 and Survival 4, and would normally roll 7 dice for the Location Test, but Laura decides she really wants to get out of here quickly and uses her Edge to speed things up. Rolling 10 dice, Snowblood locates the natural mineral radical she needs in 5 weeks, and she easily succeeds on the Gathering Test needed to harvest it.

Back at home, Snowblood shapes the clay she brought back into a small tablet around the mineral radical. With care, Snowblood uses a reed to press a cuneiform inscription on the soft clay and places the tablet in a kiln. Minutes later, Snowblood removes the tablet and loops a string through the hole at the top—her telesma is finished.

In her medicine lodge (Rating 4), Snowblood begins to enchant the tablet as a Force 2 shielding focus. The threshold for the test is 18, and Snowblood gains the dice pool modifier for using virgin telesma. Rolling 6 dice, Snowblood scores 18 hits over 7 days and pays 1 Karma to finalize the focus. Exhausted but triumphant, Snowblood undergoes the 4-hour long bonding ritual and pays 12 Karma. Slipping her new shielding focus around her neck, Snowblood lays down for a well-deserved rest.

VESSEL PREPARATION

Magicians of certain traditions practice the summoning and binding of spirits that cannot materialize but that can instead possess or inhibit a host (see *Spirits and Vessels*, p. 95) to affect the physical world. Enchanting is used to prepare a vessel—an enchanted being or object that may be possessed or inhibited more easily.

A spirit possessing or inhibiting a vessel can do anything the vessel can do normally. A car vessel can drive and play the radio, a toaster can make toast, and a dead body without legs can pull itself along by its arms. By the same token, a gun or magic lamp cannot move by itself. Spirits cannot perceive or use augmented reality or the Matrix, nor can they understand and use AR, cybernetic, or electronic controls or interfaces, including most cyberware. A spirit possessing or inhibiting a vessel is a dual-natured entity (see p. 294, *SR4A*), and, among other abilities, the possessed or inhibited vessel gains the power of immunity to normal weapons (see p. 295, *SR4A*).

Living Vessels

Preparing a vessel from a living metahuman or critter requires the subject to be either completely willing or helpless (physically bound, drugged, under a mind control spell, etc.). If the subject is unwilling (critters are always considered unwilling), the Essence or Magic rating of the subject (whichever is higher) acts as a negative dice pool modifier for the Enchanting Test.

Preparing a living vessel requires a successful Enchanting + Magic (vessel's Willpower, 1 day) Extended Test and two refined or one radical reagent. These reagents are consumed during the enchanting process. A possessed living vessel is under the control of the spirit and sees its Physical attributes enhanced by the possessing spirit's Force. For additional effects and details, see *Possession*, p. 101.

Inanimate Vessels

An inanimate vessel is a normal object enchanted to act as a vessel. Inanimate vessels can be more difficult to create than living vessels because they lack the connection to the astral that all living things have. Many magicians favor inanimate over living vessels, however, because of their hardiness and natural physical attributes.

To create an inanimate vessel, the magician must craft or obtain an appropriate object. This could be a statue, a skeleton, a weapon, or anything else. The form is inconsequential to the spirit. Preparing an inanimate vessel requires a successful Enchanting + Magic (Object Resistance x 3, 1 day) Extended Test and two refined or one radical reagent per 10 kilograms of the intended vessel. These reagents are consumed during the test.

Dead Vessels, sometimes known as zombies, are crafted from the corpses of dead critters and metahumans and are outlawed by most governments in the Sixth World. These vessels possess the same Physical attributes they did in life, minus 1 point from each attribute per week they have been dead, to a minimum of 1. The reagents used to enchant the vessel limit further decomposition, so prepared dead vessels lose 1 attribute point every month rather than every week. Cyberware and nanotech are mostly useless when not powered by a living body, but a dead vessel may retain armor and attribute bonuses from certain bioware implants and genetech (gamemaster's discretion).

Homunculus vessels are inanimate bodies specifically crafted for the magician as vessels and are constructed with hinges, pivots, wheels, and so on to be able to move in some fashion. Because its material form is non-living, a homunculus can be much more physically powerful and difficult to damage than a dead vessel. Due to structural requirements, a homunculus must mass at least (10 x Force) kilograms for the spirit to animate it, and the ritual to create a homunculus requires an additional radical reagent per 50 kilograms the homunculus masses.

Object vessels are any other type of inanimate object enchanted to act as a vessel. Many magicians prefer to enchant small, portable objects or weapons in this fashion. Some Awakened cults enchant their idols in this manner to cow their worshippers with the spirit's powers. At the gamemaster's discretion, large or complex vessels—particularly those with intricate mechanical parts or many components—may require the magician to enchant multiple components separately, rather than as a single Enchanting Test. An appropriate Technical Skill Test may also be required to reassemble the vessel.

Spirits possessing or inhibiting inanimate vessels won't be able to run around or throw a punch, but they may make full use of their powers. As they are dual-natured, they may also be used as weapons against astral forms (inflicting damage as appropriate to the object type, or spirit's Force ÷ 2, round up). For additional effects and details refer to p. 101.

Papa Dimanche is preparing his acolyte Pietro as a serviteur, a living vessel to hold the spirit servants of his patron loa: Ogoun, the Iron Warrior. Pietro is a believer and a willing subject. Papa Dimanche ritually paints Pietro with the distilled blood of a black cockerel (one unit of radical animal reagent) and rolls 10 dice, accumulating 4 hits in 2 hours. At the end of the enchanting process, Pietro is a living vessel.

Sample Vessels

The following are sample statistic blocks for various vessels (zombies and homunculi) and their construction costs. Gamemasters and players may use these as guidelines for constructing their own homunculi. F refers to the Force of the spirit possessing the vessel. The given stats already incorporate the attribute enhancements effected by the Possession power (see *Possession*, p. 101).

Plasteel Homunculus

Favored by magicians with fat cred ratings, plasteel homunculi are fully articulated statues of metallic polymers. Plasteel homunculi have occasionally been mistaken for anthroform robots. Constructing a plasteel homunculus requires (Force of vessel x 2,500¥) worth of plasteel ingots, an industrial mechanics shop, and a successful Industrial Mechanics (Force of vessel, 1 week) Extended Test in addition to the necessary reagents. Enchanting a plasteel homunculus requires a successful Enchanting + Magic (12, 1 day) Extended Test.

B	A	R	S	C	I	L	W	EDG	ESS	M	Init	IP
F+8	F–1	F–1	F+8	F	F	F	F	F	F	F	F	2

Movement: 10/25
Skills: As spirit
Powers: As spirit, plus Armor (8/8) and Natural Weapon (Fists: DV (F + 7)P, AP 0)

Stone Homunculus

Stone homunculi resemble normal statues, but the major joints are fitted with hinges that allow the homunculi limited mobility. Constructing a stone homunculus requires (Force x 1,000¥) worth of high-quality stone and a successful Artisan (Force of vessel, 1 week) Extended Test in addition to the necessary reagents. Enchanting a stone homunculus requires a successful Enchanting + Magic (6, 1 day) Extended Test.

B	A	R	S	C	I	L	W	EDG	ESS	M	Init	IP
F+6	F–3	F	F+6	F	F	F	F	F	F	F	F	2

Movement: 5/10
Skills: As spirit
Powers: As spirit, plus Armor (5/6) and Natural weapon (Fists: DV (F +5)P, AP 0)

Wicker Man

Primarily crafted by witches, a wicker man is a vaguely humanoid figure rudely crafted of wood, plants, and (occasionally) living sacrifices. Crafting a wicker man requires (Force x 100¥) worth of materials and a successful Artisan (Force of vessel, 1 day) Extended Test in addition to the necessary reagents. Enchanting a wicker man requires a successful Enchanting + Magic (3, 1 day) Extended Test.

B	A	R	S	C	I	L	W	EDG	ESS	M	Init	IP
F+2	F+1	F+1	F+2	F	F	F	F	F	F	F	F	2

Movement: 15/30
Skills: As spirit
Powers: As spirit
Weaknesses: Allergy (fire, severe)
Notes: A wicker man has +1 Reach.

Zombie

A zombie is a dead vessel possessed by a spirit. Many magicians favor zombies as cheap, eminently disposable muscle and physical labor. Constructing a zombie requires a fairly intact metahuman corpse in addition to the necessary reagents. Enchanting a zombie requires a successful Enchanting + Magic (3, 1 day) Test. C refers to the attributes of the dead body.

B	A	R	S	C	I	L	W	EDG	ESS	M	Init	IP
C*+F	C*+F	C*+F	C*+F	F	F	F	F	F	F	F	F	2

Movement: 10/25
Skills: As spirit
Powers: As spirit

*The physical attributes of dead vessels reduce over time (see *Dead Vessels*, p. 86). If reducing the attributes lowers the zombie's health track below its current damage, the vessel is destroyed.

UNIQUE ENCHANTMENTS

Enchanters can also use their skills to create unique enchantments, magical goods that bend and sometimes break the conventional rules of thaumaturgy. While this may appear game-breaking, there's no need for a unique enchantment to *do* anything in a direct magical sense. Probably the best use of any unique enchantment is to fulfill a requirement in an adventure.

A unique enchantment may grant its wielders cosmic power for the specific goal it was designed for, but it need not continue to grant that power. The power of the object is unique! If runners find a "Turn Spirit to Guacamole" focus, it may be an aspected enchantment that only works when the planets are in a particular alignment—which will happen again in just 127 years or so. Should the gamemaster allow player characters to develop unique enchantments of their own, it is advisable to use the standard magical goods creation rules above as a guideline, increasing the modifiers and thresholds as appropriate to reflect the singular nature of the enchantment.

Described below is a small sample of possible unique enchantments; many more exist. Unique enchantments fall outside the bonds of thaumaturgical theory, and gamemasters should feel free to create unique enchantments that fit their own campaigns.

> **MAGICAL COMPOUNDS IN YOUR CAMPAIGN**
>
> Gamemasters should think carefully before deciding what place magical compounds have in their campaigns. In a group with no magician characters, a magical compound can be an equalizer when encountering a magical threat. A group with several magicians might face opponents that use magical compounds against them.
>
> The magical compounds detailed here are only samples; gamemasters are encouraged to create their own magical compounds that fit their campaigns. When creating a new magical compound, the gamemaster must pick the critter power(s) the magical compound will grant, a fitting drawback for when the power wears off, and a suitably rare and exotic ingredient. The greater an advantage the critter power gives, the more devastating the drawback should be. As a rule of thumb, exotic ingredients should be located in remote and possibly dangerous locales. Alternately, the exotic ingredient may come from a paracritter that possesses a similar power to that imparted by the magical compound.

Magical Compounds

Magical compounds are unique enchantments created by magicians using alchemy. Mundanes cannot create magical compounds, even if they possess the correct formula and ingredients. Tribal medicine men and wise women have passed down the secrets to creating magical compounds as part of their tradition, while cutting-edge corporate alchemical researchers have discovered the formulae for others. Few are willing to part with their knowledge for any price. A character must possess a magical compound formula of a compatible tradition to create a magical compound. Each formula specifies at least one exotic reagent among the ingredients.

Only one dose of a magical compound may be created at a time. The magician brings together the ingredients in a special 28-day circulation, at the end of which she makes an Enchanting + Magic (4) Test. If successful, the magician has one dose of the magical compound; should the test fail or the circulation be interrupted, the ingredients are wasted.

Any character, Awakened or mundane, can benefit from a magical compound. Each magical compound has a shelf life of 1D6 weeks, after which the magical compound has no effect; certain corporate sorcerers are rumored to know spells that can sustain their effects indefinitely. Magical compounds are made to be ingested in different ways—some are elixirs or potions to be drunk, others are oils, pastes, and unguents to be spread over the body, and still others must be smoked, snorted, or sprinkled into an open wound. The method of ingestion is specified in the formula.

Sage
Duration: Essence + 1D6 hours, maximum 12 hours.
Effects: The mixture grants the critter power of Innate Spell (Detect Magic, Extended) and a +1 Perception increase.
Description: At the end of the duration, the character suffers 2 boxes of damage (unresisted) and a –2 Perception dice pool modifier for an equivalent duration.
Exotic Ingredient: A natural herbal radical of rare lichen from the North American tundra.

Spirit Strength
Duration: Essence + 1D6 hours, maximum 12 hours.
Effects: This compound grants the critter powers of Hardened Armor 5, Mystic Armor 5, and one enhanced sense of the gamemaster's choice.
Description: At the end of the duration, the character's natural Agility, Body, Reaction, and Strength attributes are reduced to 1 for an equivalent duration.
Exotic Ingredient: Three units of natural herbal radical teonanácatl mushrooms from Aztlan.

Witch's Moss
Duration: Essence + 1D6 hours, maximum 12 hours.
Effects: Grants the critter power Innate Spell (Petrify).
Description: At the end of the duration, the character's arms become crippled and useless for an equal duration. Apply a –6 dice modifier to any test involving the use of the character's arms.
Exotic Ingredient: A natural animal radical of barghest blood.

True Vessels

A true vessel is a person or object prepared as a vessel for a specific free spirit using the free spirit's spirit formula (see *True Names,* p. 107). A spirit might commission an enchanter to build such an item, encoding its true name into the instructions it gives the enchanter. A true vessel might also serve as a trap (to hold a free spirit like a genie in a bottle) or a shrine or statue where the spirit can survive loss of mana.

Unique Radicals

In the most forbidding places of the world, where nexi of mana lines overlap areas of raw elemental power, unique radical reagents might form. There are four known types of unique radicals, though others may exist. *Longlei* (dragon tears) are unique water radicals that most commonly resemble gems of unmelting ice. *Longqi* (dragon breath) are unique fire radicals that appear as small, pale, flames. *Longpi* (dragon skin) are unique earth radicals that resemble perfectly geometric shapes of metal, stone, or crystal. *Longfeng* (dragon wind) are unique air radicals that most commonly appear as thumb-sized clouds.

Handling or harvesting a unique radical requires an alchemy microlab. Exposure to a unique radical without these special tools causes 2P damage per combat phase. Unique radicals are volatile, and if combined cancel each other out—violently (4P damage per unique radical to everything within 1 meter). It is rumored that combining one of each of the known unique radicals in the proper fashion can create a unit of orichalcum.

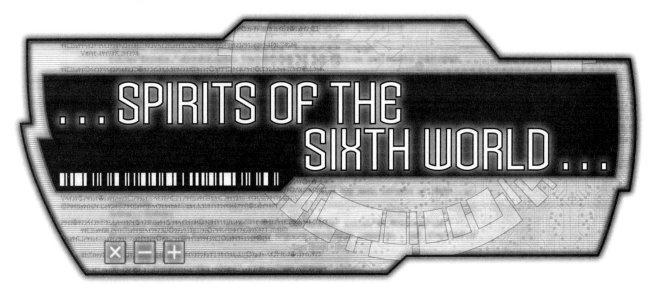
...SPIRITS OF THE SIXTH WORLD...

The cola wars had been going poorly for Jimmy No. Ever since he arrived in New Guinea on a mercenary contract, he'd been certain that he was on the losing side. Red forces had taken the Goroka Airport and he wasn't sure how he was going to get off the island. But plotting victory or escape would have to wait until tomorrow, Jimmy had been awake for nearly 36 hours of heavy spellcasting and sleep was long overdue.

Minute Men, the CAS-based special forces of a hostile cola giant, lit up the night sky with tracers trying to bring down the Wandjina attack drones the Blues had mobilized. The lights and noise were distracting, but Jimmy was weary enough that there was little doubt in his mind that he could sleep through it. Still, the obvious proximity of enemy forces gave him pause; if they found him asleep it could go poorly indeed.

Jimmy decided to chance using his magic one last time before dreamland claimed him, and began attuning himself with the five elements to summon the neak ta of the banyan trees under which he was going to sleep. He groggily opened himself to the metaplane of wood and felt his last reserves of strength nearly fail. The astral plane before him contorted itself into the tree-like form he had been looking for. The Drain almost felled him, but like a willow he bent rather than broke.

The neak ta rustled at him, and Jimmy knew that he could make just three requests before it would be finished with him and withdraw to the place from which it had come. With the darkness around him flaring incessantly to the rolling tide of battle, Jimmy's highest priority was protection from the coming storm during his sleep. He whispered softly, in some ways mimicking the patter of wind in leaves with his requests.

"I call on three protections. Protection from the dangers of the Earth, protection from the dangers of Magic, and lastly, I need protection from the anger of Men." Jimmy No looked to the neak ta and could feel its assent.

The spectral branches of the spirit canopied him, and Jimmy drifted to a deep and much-needed sleep. By dawn, the spirit would depart, but for now Jimmy was safe from both the scouts and the detection spells of the Minute Men, and that was as relaxing as it was going to get.

- I'm consistently amazed by how little mundane runners know about dealing with spirits. Urban legends and misconceptions abound, and both will get you dead quick on a run. What follows are some excerpts from what is probably the most unbiased and informative look at spirits in the world today, the *Manual of Practical Thaumaturgy* (23rd Edition, 2069). That means that it's only slightly better than nothing, of course—but that's still better than being flat wrong.
- Ethernaut

THE NATURE OF SPIRITS
Foreword on Practical Conjuration – Prof. Leonard Montenegro

What is a spirit? As of this writing, that is a thorny and unresolved question, quite possibly because there is no single and universal answer. Spirits take a multitude of corporeal forms, some of which resemble characters from folklore and mythology, while others claim to bear the semblance of normal people or creatures. Claims to normality on the part of spirits are intuitively absurd, and quite easily disproved by their lack of internal structures or organs, while claims of supernatural origin are undeniable in light of their ephemeral and archetypical appearances. Numerous competing theories and explanations on the origins and nature of spirits proliferate, espoused by renowned theorists and thaumaturgists, and in some cases, by the spirits themselves. While many of these competing paradigms are logically incongruous, few can actually be ruled out or debunked with the evidence at hand.

Our world boasts hundreds of recognized magical traditions, and with few exceptions practitioners from each are able to conjure forth a unique cadre of spirits which share many superficial characteristics. One of the few points of agreement is the generalized belief that spirits often come from a place, or group of places, that is likewise unique to their tradition. Due to the difficulties inherent in controlled studies of journeys to subjective ur-realities, colloquially known as the metaplanes, any such assertion remains unconfirmed. However many of these magical locations there actually are, most spirits appear to spend much of their time there even after they have been summoned. Some spirits appear ill-suited to make journeys back and forth, and spend almost all of their time in the physical world bound into vessels—which may be the primary reason for territorial conflict between groups of spirits and metahumans in some parts of the world (such as Chicago, Kinshasa, and Alice Springs).

ON THE INTELLECT OF SPIRITS

Whether the spirits are echoes of our own psyches or echoes of something greater, a magician calls and a spirit appears. Whether it is created or arrives at that time is something the magical community has not reached consensus on. Some spirits exhibit knowledge of concepts and conventions such as language, names, and popular culture that heavily imply or, some will undoubtedly say, prove, that these are creations of the magician's own mind. Paradoxical then are the documented instances where other spirits demonstrate knowledge and memories consistent with having independently existed in a particular location or even in another world altogether for much longer periods of time.

- The only rule regarding what you can expect from a spirit is that you can't expect anything. I've heard tales of spirits who could provide a detailed history of a specific location going back for decades, or who seem to be frustrated that they were pulled away from some project "back home," while other spirits seem to be newborn, with no knowledge of any existence before being conjured. To complicate matters, the spirits themselves are rarely forthcoming with information, and even if they know something there's no guarantee they'll share it or tell the truth.
- Ethernaut

- Heck, no one even knows if magicians are summoning different spirits each time or the same ones over and over—there's evidence for both (though for all we know, it may be the spirits "back home" share information with each other).
- Lyran

- There's strong evidence that much of a spirit's personality is influenced by the preconceived notions and general attitude of the summoner. Of course, there are exceptions to every rule …
- Icarus

One common anecdotal reference that underscores this conundrum are spirits conjured by magicians who have previously mistreated or disrespected other spirits. In numerous reported cases, new spirits summoned by these magicians were aware of these previous exchanges and responded accordingly—though admittedly there are no documented cases of spirits being able to cite specifics such as names, places, or words used.

Complicating the ongoing debate over the independent sapience of spirits is the fact that they have yet to be conclusively demonstrated to be alive in the classic sense. While a spirit can move, react to stimuli, and repair itself; evidence of spirit reproduction has been elusive. Further, it is not at all obvious what, if anything, a spirit "eats." As even the most generous legal codes require a being to be alive in order to have rights, spirits are not recognized as independent entities by many nations. The United Nations Accord on Sapient Species does not recognize spirits, despite the fact that several member nations possess spirits as heads of state.

So if they are alive, do spirits want anything? That has been the subject of intense debate since before they were generally recognized by scientific authorities. What theories have been produced are inadequate at best. For instance, while some seem to be naturally drawn to Earth, and particularly areas of intense background count, others seem to want nothing more than to escape it. Regardless, spirits certainly have things they don't want. Spirits object strenuously to expending their energies to power spell binding, most spirits resist (and perhaps resent) being bound to magicians, and many show an aversion to particularly intense astral auras.

ON THE FORMS OF SPIRITS

Spirits appear on initial inspection to incorporate a great diversity of materials into their corporeal forms, from water to bone, fire to plasteel. After decades of study, it appears that the

materialized forms of spirits are not actually composed of previously recognized substances. Indeed, the studies of Halthmer et al. demonstrate basic property equivalencies in the constituent structures present in earth elementals and the spirit of Mt. Rainier. The most commonly accepted interpretation of their data is that spirits are largely composed of some kind of common arcane material regardless of apparent structure—a recombinant protoplasm that replicates function, mass, texture and properties near enough as to provide no physical difference.

* In English, that means that a spirit is just as dangerous if it looks like a little girl with a lollipop as it is if it looks like a sword-wielding oni. A spirit can cut you in half just as well with a cardboard tube as with a katana.
* Sticks

* Unless that happens to be a katana that the spirit, y'know, picked up. Not all weapons wielded by spirits are part of the spirit's form.
* Haze

Substantial evidence exists that arcane properties and archetypical elemental oppositions also translate as properties of corporeal materialized forms. Spirits associated with water, such as water elementals, sylphs, and river spirits, exhibit hostile reactions to fire, and spirits tied to fire react similarly to water.

Another intriguing aspect of a spirit's corporeal form is its senses. Despite having no nervous systems, spirits react negatively to damage to their physical and astral forms—similar to how a physical creature displays pain. Spirits frequently object to being sent into positions where disruption is likely, and when directly questioned about the phenomenon, spirits have tended to describe disruption as an agonizing event more often than as simple dissipation. Likewise a spirit's sensory perception is very different from our own. Even when a spirit materializes into our world, it still exists primarily as an astral creature. When observing an object, a spirit sees the auras and shadows first and the physical characteristics second. Physical details metahumans characterize as obvious are frequently overlooked entirely by spirits. Interaction with technological display devices and simsense such as commlinks and simrigs is even more tenuous. The location of a spirit's visual ability is at the very least variable; and as there is no nervous system to connect to, the technical difficulties of making such an AR setup are far from trivial.

FREE SPIRITS

Sometimes conjured spirits become uncontrolled. These spirits usually vanish, but occasionally they stick around indefinitely pursuing inscrutable spirit activities. No one knows whether these spirits are acting out some distant echo of the mind of their original conjurer, or if they were simply independent entities all along. When a spirit begins acting on its own, it is called a *free spirit*.

Free spirits seem highly—if very specifically—motivated. Those so far encountered have tended to have personalities that were relatively uncomplicated, despite their alien nature. Almost like a character in a fairy story, a free spirit's behavior is often extremely predictable. Thaumaturgical research has identified the following six basic motivational matrices of free spirits, with most subjects falling quite squarely into one parapsychological profile:

Animae/Animi

Animae/Animi spirits identify strongly with metahumanity, and often help people in trouble. As their name suggests, these spirits tend to assume a specific gender. An animus spirit takes on male characteristics, and an anima spirit assumes female characteristics. Like most spirits (ignoring the few notable exceptions) their spiritual nature is normally unmistakable in materialized form. Taking on a metahuman appearance, both physically and astrally, they wander the Earth indulging their unbound curiosity about mankind's nature and society, and exploring metahuman behavior—to the point that a few case studies indicate amorous involvement with metahumans.

* Fair warning from direct experience: a spirit's idea of when you are "in trouble" is often not the same as yours. Further, their idea of help is often not what you would have picked for yourself.
* Haze

* A few years back, some free spirits went so far in their replication of human tropes as to make an anarchist artist commune. Genuine spirit art is hard to come by, but just trading in the fakes makes for a tidy profit.
* 2XL

* If I remember correctly it was in France, and I actually own a couple of those paintings. The real ones, I assure you. Honestly, they just look like someone tried to replicate an Edvard Munch with a dry brush. Similar to those computer renderings of composite landscapes: I like it, but is it Art?
* Mr. Bonds

Mimics

Like the animae/animi, mimics identify strongly with metahumanity. They are distinguished by a love of power, wealth, and the pleasures of the physical world. Mimics seem to be spirits enamored with human vices, which may be as innocent as an appreciation of gourmet food and drink, or as perverse as a taste for BTL chips or other human addictions. Mimics tend to form or join organizations to guarantee access to the resources they need, even going as far as to become involved in major criminal syndicates.

* How can a spirit become addicted to BTL chips? They don't have a nervous system, there's nothing for the trodes to connect to.
* Turbo Bunny

* Some spirits actually do have a nervous system, a spirit possessing or inhabiting a living (or recently deceased) creature for instance.
* Sticks

- Simply acting out the pantomime of human vice seems to be enough. I once sold a spirit 50 blank moodies on a dare. He sat down and went through the motions of chipping them all. Thanked me afterwards. Creepy.
- 2XL

Shadows

More menacing than tricksters, shadows enjoy causing human fear and suffering. Some enlist psychopathic metahumans to assist them. Theories put forth by occultists and paranaturalists postulate that these spirits are in some way addicted to the psychic energy of sapient beings in torment. Like trickster spirits, some shadows set up complicated situations for no reason the metahuman mind can fathom. Others simply revel in bloodletting, violence, and terrorism to feed their "habit."

Tricksters

Tricksters see the world as a big playground. They tend to interfere in human activities, often engineering complicated practical jokes for their own amusement. Some will ruthlessly destroy a person's reputation or career, or even drive a victim to suicide in pursuit of what they call "fun." Others may adopt more or less humane attitudes, acting like spiritual Robin Hoods, using their powers to take down arrogant businessmen and other "stuffed shirts" of metahuman society.

- It's not just human activities they mess with for entertainment. Some tricksters spend all day chasing pigeons in the park. If they don't directly interact with metahumans, they don't get much press.
- Arete

Vanguards

This tentative classification is primarily applied to the often-hostile denizens of the so-called "deep metaplanes." Vanguard spirits seem to see our world as a potential colony. This leads them to not only take up residence, but to actively encourage other similar spirits to cross to our world. Most vanguards are extremely selective about which spirits they bring in (for example, an insect spirit seeks to create a hive of insect spirits of its own type), while others seek to increase spiritual presence across the board. Tactics employed by vanguard spirits are equally varied, and range from encouraging metahumans to learn secrets of conjuring to subverting astral rifts for their own uses.

Wardens

Wardens seem motivated to protect the Earth from exploitation and the preservation of the environment. They rarely have much use for metahumans, though wardens have been known to form alliances with eco-activists and people who show a concern for nature in order to hold off resource-hungry corporations. More urbane wardens occasionally enlist deniable assets and other extreme measures to derail corporate plans for invasion of unspoiled environments.

- This is an example of the shamanic bias of the original author. While there are certainly warden spirits that behave in that fashion, let us not forget that there are also toxic wardens that help despoil the environment. A warden spirit is really just motivated to make or keep the world a specific way. Basically, it's trying to paint all of astral space one color. If you like that color, then maybe you can get along with them just fine.
- Ethernaut

WILD AND ABERRANT SPIRITS

Perhaps lending credence to the idea that spirits are autonomous entities, some spirits seem to exist independent of conjuration. Called *wild spirits*, their appearance and presence obeys no known paradigm or common rule, with the exception that they have not been summoned by metahuman means (as some will even attest to) and to a degree seem resistant to conjuring methods. Many (but not all) wild spirits hold an affinity to a particular domain, and are aspected to its local mana field. Many also adhere to the folklore and mythology of the local culture and traditions. Some theorists speculate that these spirits are natural inhabitants of these domains, and were born of the magical fluctuations at work there—and may have even been present here for centuries. Others suggest that these wild spirits are creations of the metahuman mind, that as mana is influenced by metahuman emotions and ideas, such spirits slowly form out of the disturbances. Indeed, you might be unknowingly helping a wild spirit to form right now.

A similar, but separate, classification of spirits is *aberrant spirits:* spirits that are simply inadequately understood by modern thaumaturgical theories. These rare spirits include unique entities that meet no known spirit categorizations, spirits whose presence in this world is fleeting and unexplained, and spirits only reported to come into being upon completion of certain legendary rituals (like the Great Ghost Dance or the Wild Hunt). Many of the spirit-like creatures commonly known as faeries are also considered aberrant, given their exhibition of unusual powers and free-willed existence.

In closing, let me quote Arthur White Eagle's caveat from the end of the famous 2035 UCLA Study of Magical Phenomenon: "If there is a single thing that our study has concluded beyond reasonable doubt, it is that we in the parascientific community are still dangerously in the dark when it comes to magical events in general and spirits in particular. Our categorization of spirits is as yet incomplete, and spirits which cleanly fit our classification system are outnumbered by aberrant spirits that do not. It would be wrong for future generations to cleave strongly to the categories and systems our team has developed, as it is almost certain that further exposition of the wild spirits will necessitate several overhauls of basic magical theory. Ours is an early step in a new discipline, and there is no guarantee that it has been in the right direction."

- Some aberrant spirits seem so disconnected from humanity as to doubt your existence. I had a discussion with a *vatch* that accused me of being a figment of its imagination. How they get into our world is anyone's guess, and I wouldn't hold my breath waiting for modern magical theory to explain them all. Even to-

day, every time we learn something new about magic, we find out two more things we don't understand.
• Ethernaut

NEW SPIRIT RULES

This section provides new rules and expanded definitions of spirit abilities.

ASTRAL MOVEMENT

Unless otherwise stated, spirits in astral form can move at the same speeds as an astrally projecting magician: 100 meters per Combat Turn while "walking," 5 kilometers per Combat Turn while "running." An astral spirit can reach any part of the world in no more than 3 hours and 21 minutes.

Metaplanar Travel

Each spirit has an affinity to one particular metaplane, called their native plane. A fire elemental, for example, is native to the hermetic metaplane of fire, a task loa is native to the metaplane of Guinee. Spirits can travel at will from physical or astral space to their native metaplane (and back again) with a Complex Action. Mana barriers cannot impede this movement.

Metaplanar Shortcut

Spirits that find their physical or astral movement impeded by a dual-natured mana barrier may take a quick trip to the metaplanes and back again to the other side of the barrier. This "shortcut" may only be taken if the spirit's conjurer is on the other side of the barrier (taking up one service) or if the spirit has been to the location on the other side before (a reason to never allow a spirit into your private sanctuary). Free spirits, who are not restricted to any conjurer's presence, often use this shortcut for near-instantaneous worldwide travel.

DISRUPTION

If a spirit in astral or materialized form suffers Physical or Stun damage sufficient to fill its damage track, the spirit is disrupted. A disrupted spirit returns to its native metaplane and cannot reappear on the astral or physical plane for 28 days minus its Force, with a minimum time of 24 hours. Spirits joined to vessels are only disrupted if they suffer sufficient Physical damage to kill them through damage overflow (see p. 253, *SR4A*). Watchers are never disrupted; knocking them out permanently destroys their fragile energies.

Disrupted spirits still count against a magician's limit of bound (and unbound) spirits, though a magician can release a spirit from its services even while it is disrupted. For unbound spirits, sunrise and sunset still count during its time on its metaplane, and a disrupted unbound spirit is unlikely to ever return unless the conjurer spends his time in an area where the sun rarely sets—such as Antarctica.

The only way to bring a disrupted spirit back from exile before its time is to make a metaplanar quest to the spirit's native plane (see *Metaplanar Quests*, p. 130). A possession spirit will need a prepared vessel before it can return, whether or not a metaplanar quest is performed.

LONG-TERM BINDING

A conjurer can semi-permanently assign a bound spirit to a service or set of services by paying Karma equal to its Force. Once bound with Karma, the spirit no longer counts against the magician's bound spirit limit and any remaining services are lost. The Karma-bound spirit will remain at its final service for a year and a day, unless banished or disrupted, in which case it will return to its duties after 28 days – Force (see *Disruption*). Corporations frequently bind spirits in this manner to guard and patrol their property.

SPIRIT COMBAT

Spirits are creatures of quicksilver and shadow and are nearly immune to physical attacks. They are also creatures of willforce and imagination, however, and can be disrupted by the sufficiently committed. A metahuman or other sentient creature can make an *attack of will* against a spirit, striving to harm it through sheer willpower rather than force of arms.

Attack of Will

An attack of will may only be conducted with a physical or astral melee attack—willpower simply doesn't work with ranged attacks. Sometimes you are better off trying to smack a spirit with a gun than attempting to shoot it. While an attack of will can damage a spirit in spite of its formidable resilience to non-magical attack, only the truly courageous, driven, or mad have enough force of personality to affect a spirit.

When in melee with a spirit, a character may elect to make an attack of will rather than a normal melee strike. The character rolls his Banishing + Willpower (or just Willpower) as his dice pool, and his base Damage Value is (Charisma)P regardless of whether he is attacking with a spanner, combat axe, or his bare hands. Reach modifiers (attacker's or spirit's) do not apply to this test. The attack of will bypasses the spirit's Immunity to Normal Weapons and is otherwise resolved as a normal melee attack (see p. 156, *SR4A*). This form of attack is only effective against spirits.

Spirit Forms and Combat

Spirits materialize in all manner of forms, including those equipped with weapons such as swords or claws. These "weapons" are (obviously) part of the spirit's materialized form, however, and do not provide any extra bonuses. A guardian spirit who materializes with a sword in hand, for example, does not gain any benefits of a sword's Reach, nor does the sword deal any more damage than the spirit's materialized fist. Note, however, that there is nothing that prevents a materialized spirit from picking up an actual weapon and using it to full effect (though most likely in an unskilled fashion).

SPIRIT SERVICES

A spirit's relationship with its conjurer may vary greatly depending upon how the magician has treated it and others of its kind. When a spirit owes services and a service is requested, however, the spirit must obey. A service can either be situational (such as "Help fight these Triad enforcers" or "Put out that fire") or power-related (such as "Sustain Concealment on me until I ask you to stop"). If a spirit is asked to perform a specific task, it will use any and all powers in its arsenal to complete that task, but will terminate those powers once the task is complete. If the spirit is asked to use a single power, it will continue to do so for as long as it is able to or until the conjurer asks it to cease.

Physical tasks require services only if they are especially dangerous, complicated, or require the spirit's powers or paranatural abilities to complete. A spirit is fully capable of performing the task "Please hand me a soda" without the expenditure of a service, though it may not be willing to if the spirit has a particularly strained relationship with the conjurer. Even complicated tasks can be broken down into a series of simple tasks that don't individually use up services at the gamemaster's discretion. This is especially important for characters who are possessed by their spirits, as they might conceivably be forced to manage their spirits' physical actions just to put on clothes or eat lunch.

Passive powers such as Astral Form, Energy Aura, or Materialization don't require the use of services, they are assumed to be included with any other service that requires their use. Since Guard is a physical power, it requires the spirit to be physical in order to activate it (though not to sustain it). Therefore, a spirit ordered to use Guard on someone would need to use Materialize or Possession before it could do so, and both actions would only require one service (though it might immediately go back to astral plane while sustaining the Guard effect, depending on what other services it was performing at the time).

Spirits, especially high Force spirits, are actually quite intelligent and have the same facilities of language as their conjurer—presumably through their mental link. As such, they are fully capable of understanding and carrying out a proactive service. "Set fire to anyone who comes through that door" is a perfectly acceptable service, though it will use up a service whether anyone trespasses or not.

SPIRITS AND EDGE

A spirit is generally under the control of the magician who conjured it, but to one degree or another it is still an independent entity. Even while bound and compelled to obey, a spirit has its own fate and its own free will—as such, a magician cannot compel a spirit to use (or not use) Edge on a given test. Spirits will likely use Edge to save themselves from disruption or banishment, or to assist with the completion of a goal important to the spirit or if completion of a service demands. Any use of Edge is at the discretion of the gamemaster.

Spirits can also use Edge to assist their resistance roll to the original summoning, but will generally not do so unless the discrepancy in power between them and an impudent conjurer is large or the conjurer has a history of mistreating spirits. And yes, spirits do know if a conjurer has mistreated other spirits. Whether the rumor mill in the metaplanes works really fast or spirits can somehow pick up the telltales in a conjurer's aura, the spirits know if a magician's been bad or good.

SPIRITS AND VESSELS

Certain spirits temporarily project into the physical world through the power of Possession (p. 101) rather than Materialization. Other spirits take up permanent residence within physical bodies via the Inhabitation power (p. 100). Both types of spirits take over physical hosts known as *vessels*. Possession may (and Inhabitation *must*) be facilitated by prior preparation of the vessel (see *Vessel Preparation*, p. 86). Possessed/inhabited vessels are dual natured (p. 294, *SR4A*), active on the physical and astral planes simultaneously. Only one spirit may occupy a vessel at a time.

The body of a magician or mystic adept is considered a prepared vessel for any spirit he conjures, no special preparation needed. Likewise, an astrally projecting character's empty body counts as an available vessel, whether it has been specially prepared or not.

Regardless of how a spirit has entered a vessel, the spirit's mind has control of the body and the host's mind (and abilities) is either temporarily subdued (via Possession) or destroyed (via Inhabitation)—with two exceptions. A conjurer whose body is possessed by a spirit he summoned can retain some control by issuing mental commands to the spirit (in a manner similar to a hacker/rigger and a subscribed drone). In this case, the conjurer is aware of the spirit's actions (he still perceives through his body), but he has only indirect control rather than direct motor control. Similarly, an initiate conjurer can use Channeling metamagic (p. 54) to exercise even more control when a spirit he summoned has possessed his body.

Optional Rule: Corps Cadavres and Living Dolls

The watchers of possession traditions are able to interact with the physical world to a much greater degree than the watchers summoned by other traditions. These watchers have the power of Possession (p. 101) and the skills of Perception 1 and Artisan 1. A dead body possessed by a watcher is called a corps cadavre. A homunculi possessed by a watcher is called a living doll. A watcher's physical movement is 10/25.

SPOTTING SPIRITS

The spiritual nature of any materialized spirit form is unmistakable. Even if the spirit materializes looking like a toaster or a Lone Star officer, any sentient observer will have no difficulty understanding that they are observing something unnatural. Spirits that are possessing or inhabiting a vessel (see *Possession*, p. 101, or *Inhabitation*, p. 100) are harder to spot, though powerful spirits tend to be quite noticeable. To notice a spirit possessing/inhabiting a vessel, an observer must make a Perception Test and beat a threshold of 6 – the spirit's Force. Success not only notices the possessing/inhabiting spirit, but also delivers some clues as to what the spirit "really looks like." A character who perceives someone possessed by a loa of Agwe, for example, will detect distinctive traits of the god of the sea. At the gamemaster's discretion, the use of the spirit's powers may create an effect like a shamanic mask, adding a +2 dice pool modifier to the Perception Test.

SPIRIT APPEARANCE

Just what does a spirit *look* like anyway? If it's in astral form and you're a physical observer, the answer is easy: it's invisible unless manifesting, in which case its presence may be marked only by a barely discernible discoloration in the air. If the spirit is possessed into a body, the answer is equally simple: the spirit looks just like the vessel, modified by its basic spiritual presence and whatever powers it has (most of which are invisible until used, but powers like natural weaponry and energy aura are quite dramatic).

While a materialized spirit can't be mistaken for a material creature or object, it can look like almost anything, depending upon the tradition responsible for its conjuration (though a particular spirit will have only one materialized form—it will not change forms). Considering that literally hundreds of magical traditions are practiced worldwide, the sky's the limit. If you're stuck coming up with a snazzy and distinctive look to represent a particular spirit in your game, here are some examples:

Air: A spirit of the sky might appear as a flock of crows or butterflies with iridescent wings. An air elemental may materialize as a tornado, a chaotic dust-devil, or a beautiful woman made of clouds. An ifreet of the air could appear as a swirling maelstrom of smoke, whereas an Aboriginal Sky Hero might take the form of a terribly wise platypus.

Beasts: Many spirits of beasts appear as a giant animal or mythic creature. Others appear as chimeric mixtures of animal parts. Nothing limits a beast spirit to appear as a single animal, or even to appear as an animal at all. A beast spirit could just as easily appear to a Hindu magician as a swarm of rats sent by Vahana or to a Druidic magician as a stag.

Earth: An earth elemental can be made of dirt or stone, metal or wood. Spirits of the land represent the solidness and vibrancy of the land, and may appear as any year-round terrain feature, such as a roving hillock or animated pile of stones. Voracious trees, flowing mudpools, and the faeries known as knockers can just as easily stand in for a spirit of the earth.

Fire: All fire spirits have an energy aura, meaning that they are bathed in energies both visible and deadly. Though details of their forms are almost always obscured by the infernos, lightning storms, or smoke surrounding them, an individual fire elemental might have a bird, a serpent, or even a simple sphere in the middle. A fire elemental is often human shaped, a spirit

Continued on page 97

Spirits that are inhabiting a vessel with the Inhabitation power are more difficult to spot. Hybrid-form merges require a Perception + Intuition (5) Test to detect the spirit's presence, though the body's warped physical features are visibly apparent unless disguised. Flesh-form merges cannot be detected physically. Both hybrid-form and flesh-form spirits are dual natured and easily detectable with assensing.

Assensing and Spirits

If a character gains 5+ net hits on an Assensing Test, they can determine how many spirits a subject has bound, even if those spirits are on remote services or on standby in the metaplanes. If both conjurer and spirit are observed, the fact that the one was conjured by/bound to the other is determinable with just 2 net hits.

NEW SPIRITS

The *Shadowrun, Fourth Edition,* rules present information on some of the spirits it is possible to conjure in the Sixth World. *Street Magic* introduces four new categories of spirit that are conjured by traditions such as the followers of Wuxing or Voodoo (see *Paths of Magic,* p. 32). Unless otherwise stated, spirits follow the general rules for conjuring and astral forms found on p. 186, SR4A.

Guardian Spirits

Whether a stalking angel of death or a mighty loa, a guardian spirit is a fearless and capable warrior and defender.

B	A	R	S	C	I	L	W	EDG	ESS	M	Init	IP
F+1	F+2	F+3	F+2	F	F	F	F	F	F	F	(Fx2)+1	2

Astral INIT/IP: F x 2, 3
Movement: 15/40

Skills: Assensing, Astral Combat, Blades, Clubs, Counterspelling, Dodge, Exotic Ranged Weapon, Perception, Unarmed Combat
Powers: Astral Form, Fear, Guard, Magical Guard, Materialization, Movement, Sapience
Optional Powers: Animal Control, Concealment, Elemental Attack, Natural Weaponry (DV = Force), Psychokinesis, Skill (a guardian spirit may be given an additional Combat skill instead of an optional power)

Guidance Spirits

Oracles, dream guides, and even ancestral spirits—guidance spirits embody knowledge and omens, and are trusted (if confusing) advisors.

B	A	R	S	C	I	L	W	EDG	ESS	M	Init	IP
F+3	F−1	F+2	F+1	F	F	F	F	F	F	F	Fx2	2

Astral INIT/IP: Fx2, 3
Movement: 10/25
Skills: Arcana, Assensing, Astral Combat, Counterspelling, Dodge, Perception, Unarmed Combat
Powers: Astral Form, Confusion, Divining, Guard, Magical Guard, Materialization, Sapience, Search, Shadow Cloak
Optional Powers: Engulf, Enhanced Senses (Hearing, Low-Light Vision, Thermographic Vision, or Smell), Fear, Influence

SPIRIT APPEARANCE (CONT.)

of the fiery firmament is often a bird, and a Buddhist fire spirit is often a snake that spreads falsehood.

Guardian: Guardian spirits are often mighty warriors, but also appear as stalking deaths or avenging angels. Spirits of conflict and protection, they take on forms meant to frighten or reassure. Whether an Islamic ifreet or a Norse valkyrie, guardian spirits are almost always armed, or at least ready to fight.

Guidance: An Aboriginal dreamguide could appear almost exactly like a metahuman or as a spirit animal. Its spiritual nature will always be immediately obvious, even if an observer could not describe why. An ancestor spirit might appear as a beloved great-grandfather or as a particularly wise animal. A wujen may summon a dragon for advice, while a Christian theurgist would pray for the appearance of an intervening angel.

Man: While some spirits of man appear as actual metahumans, they are not going to be confused with a Lone Star officer or hotel receptionist. Many spirits of man appear as items associated with humanity, such as street signs, trashcans, or household appliances. Others appear as animals associated with metahumanity, either by behavior (monkeys, coyote) or by proximity (dogs, goldfish).

Plant: A wujen conjures spirits of plants as wood spirits that take the form of anthropomorphized versions of especially auspicious trees such as banyans. A Celtic druid conjures a plant spirit as a dryad. Other traditions view them as spirits of cultivated or wild plants exclusively. A Shinto priest calls forth a great tree kami, while a Khmer wujen summons the neak ta of a particularly fortunate plant.

Task: Many traditions perceive these spirits as smiths, carpenters, or other workers. A houngan conjures a work loa such as Mounanchou, greatly favored for being practical and earthly compared to other loa. Qabbalists place task spirits in golems to perform heavy labor and aid with otherwise tiring alchemical processes. Other traditions see task spirits as anything from esteemed consultants to lowly servants.

Water: A water spirit can plausibly be anything from a mermaid to a dogman made of water to a constantly cresting wave. The association with water is a constant. A water elemental is a humanoid actually composed of water, while a spirit of the Mississippi might take the semblance of a riverboat gambler or an alligator.

Plant Spirits

Representing a single flower, a centennial tree, or the entire forest, spirits of plants are patient and persistent entities embodying the power and resistance of the green kingdom.

B	A	R	S	C	I	L	W	EDG	ESS	M	Init	IP
F+3	F–1	F+2	F+4	F	F	F	F	F	F	F	Fx2	2

Astral INIT/IP: Fx2, 3
Movement: 5/15
Skills: Assensing, Astral Combat, Counterspelling, Dodge, Perception, Unarmed Combat
Powers: Astral Form, Concealment, Engulf, Fear, Guard, Magical Guard, Materialization, Sapience, Silence
Optional Powers: Accident, Confusion, Movement, Noxious Breath, Search

Task Spirits

Brownies and workers, spirits of task are skilled craftsmen.

B	A	R	S	C	I	L	W	EDG	ESS	M	Init	IP
F	F	F+2	F+2	F	F	F	F	F	F	F	Fx2	2

Astral INIT/IP: Fx2, 3
Movement: 10/25
Skills: Artisan, Assensing, Astral Combat, Dodge, Perception, Unarmed Combat
Powers: Accident, Astral Form, Binding, Materialization, Movement, Sapience, Search
Optional Powers: Concealment, Enhanced Senses (Hearing, Low-Light Vision, Thermographic Vision, or Smell), Influence, Psychokinesis, Skill (a task spirit may be given an additional Technical or Physical skill instead of an optional power)

NEW SPIRIT POWERS

The powers listed here are in addition to the normal critter and spirit powers found on pp. 292–298, *SR4A*.

Astral Gateway

Type: M • Action: Complex • Range: LOS (A) • Duration: Sustained

The spirit can open an astral rift (p. 116), forcing all physical objects within the area to be dual natured, as well as allowing even mundanes to astrally project. The astral rift can connect to any metaplane the spirit can visit itself (so while a fire elemental can probably open a rift to the Plane of Fire, it probably can't open a rift to The Hive).

Aura Masking

Type: M • Action: Free • Range: Self • Duration: Sustained

This power functions as both the initiate powers Masking (p. 198, *SR4A*) and Extended Masking (p. 60). The spirit uses its Edge in place of initiate grade. The spirit can also hide the use of any of its powers on itself within the masked aura. Only characters who pierce the masking can see the spirit's use of spirit powers on itself. A spirit can always attempt to appear as another form of astral creature (even if not capable of astral projection), but masking itself as mundane would be entirely pointless unless it is joined to a physical body or has the realistic form power.

Banishing Resistance

Type: M • Action: Auto • Range: Self • Duration: Special

For purposes of resisting banishment (see *Banishing*, p. 188, *SR4A*), treat the spirit as if it has a number of services equal to its Edge that refresh every sunrise and sunset—these are cumulative with any services the spirit may actually owe a conjurer.

Desire Reflection

Type: M • Action: Complex • Range: LOS • Duration: Sustained

Desire Reflection enables the spirit or critter to discover the greatest desire of a single target within its line of site and evoke a full-sensory illusion keyed to the desire in the target's mind. Certain spirits make use of this power to draw in potential new victims. The spirit itself can appear as a harmless or pleasing aspect of the illusion at will. To use this power the critter must succeed in an Opposed Test pitting its Magic + Intuition against the target's Willpower + Intuition. If it scores more net hits, the victim is deceived by the illusion. Otherwise the power fails to affect the victim.

Left to their own devices, victims indulge themselves as if their secret desire were coming true. If the victim is attacked, injured, or slapped in the face, he may make another Opposed Test to resist the illusion (similar to resisting Mental Manipulations, see p. 210, *SR4A*). Each hit reduces the spirit's net hits on the original Opposed Test. If these hits are reduced to 0, the victim can break free of the illusion. Those who fail are lost and entranced, caught between illusion and reality.

Divining

Type: M • Action: Special • Range: Special • Duration: Special

This power functions like Divining metamagic (p. 56), though the spirit uses Magic + Intuition rather than Arcana to divine meaning.

Endowment

Type: M • Action: Complex • Range: Touch • Duration: Sustained

The spirit grants the use of one of its powers to the subject. The spirit does not lose the use of the power while the subject gains it, and the spirit can grant a power to a number of subjects equal to twice its Magic. No character may gain more than one power from a spirit in this way at a time.

Energy Drain

Type: M • Action: Complex • Range: Touch or LOS • Duration: Permanent

The Energy Drain power is used by a number of dangerous critters and spirits in different ways. Each version of this power is slightly different, depending on the entity using it. All versions entail the creature using this power to suck life energy from a victim, in the form of Karma, Force, Magic, or Essence. The Essence Drain used by vampires (p. 301, *SR4A*) is a variant of this power. For some creatures (blood spirits, shedim, mantid spirits), this power is Touch range, meaning a resisting victim must somehow be subdued first or drained unwittingly (as FAB does). For other beings (shadow spirits), this power merely requires line of sight, allowing the critter to feed off its victims from afar.

INHABITATION MERGES

True Form

When a spirit inhabitation results in a *true form*, the vessel is destroyed or consumed during the merge and cannot be recovered. The spirit takes form on the astral plane and gains the powers of Astral Form and Materialization (see pp. 293 and 296, *SR4A*). A true form spirit bares no resemblance to the original host vessel and has the skills, attributes, and knowledge of the spirit alone. A true form spirit can persist in the astral plane and/or physical world indefinitely without needing ties to a conjurer or a spirit formula. Once disrupted, however, the spirit requires a new vessel to inhabit before it can return.

Hybrid Form

A *hybrid form* is a hybridization of the vessel and the spirit into a single dual natured entity (p. 294, *SR4A*). A hybrid form merge enhances the host's Physical attributes by the spirit's Force. The spirit retains the host's natural abilities though it only has few of the host's memories and none of its skills (the spirit retains its own skills of course). A hybrid form spirit has Immunity to Normal Weapons (p. 295 *SR4A*), but loses the ability to assume an Astral Form (p. 293, *SR4A*). The inhabited body exhibits signs of the spirit's takeover, as the merger physically warps the vessel with visible telltales of the spirit's own nature (see *Spotting Spirits*, p. 95). The spirit is under no obligation to return to its metaplane of origin if/when its services are banished away and will simply persist as an uncontrolled spirit indefinitely. Unlike possession spirits, hybrid form merges can operate a direct neural interface and the host's cyberware (if any) continues to function for the spirit.

Flesh Form

A spirit which attains a good merge with its vessel becomes a near perfect *flesh form*. The combined entity retains all of the memories, abilities, and skills (both Active and Knowledge) of the host, and its appearance is virtually indistinguishable from that of the original vessel. A flesh form spirit is a dual-natured creature (p. 294, *SR4A*), has Immunity to Normal Weapons (p. 295, *SR4A*), any of the vessel's natural and augmented abilities, and also gains the powers of Realistic Form (p. 102) and Aura Masking (p. 98).

Draining a point of Karma, Force, Magic, or Essence requires a Willpower + Magic (10 – target's Essence/Force, 1 minute) Extended Test (for some critters, the interval may differ, as specifically noted). If the critter is disturbed or interrupted before this test ends, the point is not drained. If the Extended Test is completed, the critter drains one point of the specified energy, adding to its own. (In some cases, the energy is converted to an appropriate rating point at a 1:1 ratio, as noted; for example, blood spirits convert drained Essence to Force.) Some critters (FAB, mantid spirits), used the drained energy to reproduce, as noted in their individual descriptions. Drained points are permanently lost.

Living victims find this process draining at best, extremely painful at worst. Victims suffer 1 box of damage for each point drained. Depending on the critter, this may be Stun damage (shadow spirits, FAB) or Physical damage (blood spirits, shedim). Victims who take Physical damage appear drained, withered, and hollow, and are sometimes marked permanently (white hair, hair loss, wrinkles, premature aging, or other strange markings).

If a character's Magic is reduced to 0, he burns out and becomes mundane. If a critter's Magic is reduced to 0, it dies. If a spirit, sustained/anchored/quickened spell, focus, or mana barrier's Force is reduced to 0, it is destroyed. If a victim's Essence is reduced to 0, he dies.

Engulf

Type: P • Action: Complex • Range: Touch • Duration: Sustained

The Engulf power is just as usable by a spirit joined to a vessel as it is by a spirit materializing a body of its own. Spirits need not drag their victims inside their body, as engulfing materials can appear next to the spirit. As Engulf is a sustained power, a spirit is capable of leaving the vicinity or even line of sight of the victim while the Engulf continues. The Engulf power inflicts damage as noted on p. 294, *SR4A*, modified as appropriate to the spirit type below:

Guidance: The victim is wracked by nightmares, visions, and madness, suffering Stun damage. The damage is resisted with Willpower instead of Body, and armor is ignored.

Plant: The victim is entwined in vines, branches, or thorns, suffering Stun damage.

Inhabitation

Type: P • Action: Auto • Range: Self • Duration: Special

While most spirits live on the astral plane, able to affect the physical world only transiently through materialization or the possession of vessels, a spirit with Inhabitation exists on the physical plane continuously. An inhabiting spirit permanently *merges* with a prepared vessel, and cannot be separated with Banishing or even by the spirit's choice. An inhabiting spirit is not disrupted until the vessel is killed from Physical damage overflow (see p. 253, *SR4A*). If the vessel inhabited by the spirit was living, the spirit gains complete control over the body and some access to its memories (see below). During merging, the vessel's original spirit (if present) is consumed and for all intents and purposes that character is essentially lost (though, as always, gamemasters may decide otherwise if appropriate to their stories).

In order to inhabit a vessel, a spirit must have the assistance of a magician of an appropriate tradition who must prepare the intended vessel in advance (see *Vessel Preparation*, p. 86) within a magical lodge with a Force equal or higher than the spirit's. Once the vessel has been enchanted, the spirit may use the Inhabitation power upon it immediately. The process of inhabitation takes a number of days equal to the spirit's Force. At the end of that period, the spirit makes an Opposed Test pitting its Force x 2 against the host's Willpower + Intuition. The spirit's conjurer (if any) may influence the result by adding her Binding skill to either dice pool as desired. If the spirit is attempting to inhabit an inanimate vessel, the spirit rolls Force x 2 versus the vessel's Object Resistance threshold (p. 183, *SR4A*). To determine the results, compare the net hits with the Inhabitation table and check the *Inhabitation Merges* sidebar (p. 100). If the vessel rolls a critical glitch, the result is always a true form. If the spirit gets a critical glitch, the merging is unsuccessful and the vessel is immune to future inhabitation attempts by that spirit.

The period of inhabitation is trying for both vessel and spirit. If the vessel is removed from the lodge before completion, both the spirit and host will die (gamemaster's discretion). At the end of the inhabitation period, the spirit takes full control over the host as determined by who won the Opposed Test and to what degree. For more details, see *Spirits and Vessels*, p. 95.

INHABITATION TABLE

Net Hits	Result
2+ net hits for the spirit	True Form. The host's body is consumed.
Less than 2 net hits for host or spirit	Hybrid Form. A combination of the host's body and spirit is produced.
2+ net hits for vessel	Flesh Form. The host's body remains unchanged, inhabited by the spirit.

QUAKE TABLE

While the effects of an individual quake are highly dependent upon the conditions of surrounding soil, the quality of engineering, and the preparedness of the surrounding citizenry, the following vague guidelines can be used:

Hits	Effects
1	Motion detectors useless for the duration; sleeping people awaken.
2	Top-heavy objects fall; unlatched doors and windows swing open or shut.
3	Furniture shifts; objects fall off shelves in bulk; drivers of land vehicles must make Vehicle Tests.
4	Ordinary buildings damaged; doors jam; mine fields detonate.
5	Furniture overturns; windows break; entire area considered difficult ground.
6	Freestanding fences, walls, and trees sag or fall over; gas lines are unsafe.
7	Roadways become impassable; some buildings collapse.
8	Many buildings collapse, crevasses appear in pavement and open ground.

Magical Guard

Type: M • Action: Free • Range: LOS • Duration: Instant

A critter with the Magical Guard power can use the Counterspelling skill and provide spell defense and dispel spells the same as a magician can (p. 185, *SR4A*).

Mind Link

Type: M • Action: Simple • Range: LOS • Duration: Sustained

A critter with the Mind Link power can open and maintain telepathic mental communication with another sapient creature. The spirit can maintain a number of mental links at one time equal to its Magic attribute. If multiple sapients are engaged via Mind Link with the same spirit, they may communicate freely with each other as well as the original spirit.

Possession

Type: P • Action: Complex • Range: Touch • Duration: Special

Some spirits lack the ability to materialize, so they must possess vessels in order to interact with the physical plane. Each possession attempt requires a Complex Action in which the spirit touches the vessel's aura and then accesses the physical plane and attempts to possess a vessel so that it may stay there. The spirit makes an Opposed Test pitting its Force x 2 against the vessel's Intuition + Willpower Test (for living vessels). For inanimate vessels, the spirit makes a Force x 2 (vessel's Object Resistance) Test. Apply a +6 dice pool bonus to the spirit if the vessel has been previously prepared (see *Vessel Preparation,* p. 86). If the test fails, the spirit is immediately forced back into the astral plane. If the test succeeds, the possession takes hold: the vessel and the critter are considered a single dual-natured entity for the duration. For the detailed effects of Possession, refer to the *Possession and Vessels* sidebar (p. 102).

A possessing spirit may be ejected from the vessel into the astral plane with a normal Banishing Test (p. 188, *SR4A*). If the possession fails or the spirit is banished, the critter may not attempt to possess that vessel again until the sun next rises or sets. For more details, see *Spirits and Vessels*, p. 95.

POSSESSION AND VESSELS

When a spirit possesses a vessel, the combined being that results is dual-natured, has Immunity to Normal Weapons (p. 295, *SR4A*), and boasts all of the spirit's powers and skills. Occasionally a possessing spirit's nature manifests through the vessel in an effect similar to a shamanic mask (p. 181, *SR4A*).

Living Vessels

If the vessel is a living creature, the spirit's Force is added to the vessel's Physical attributes. While possessed, the spirit's Mental and Special attributes are used (which means that a possessed technomancer cannot access Resonance), with Initiative recalculated as normal (use the spirit's normal Initiative Passes). The spirit is in full physical control of the vessel, but does not have access to the host's knowledge, skills, or experience. The mind of the vessel remains in whatever state it was when possession began; if conscious, it becomes an impotent witness locked inside its own body for the duration.

Possessing spirits cannot perceive or operate AR or direct neural or cybernetic interfaces, and do not benefit from implants, cyberware, or nanoware that would require active control (i.e.: a spirit can benefit from a vessel's bone lacing or eye replacement, but cannot activate vision enhancements or a datajack).

Dead or Inanimate Vessels

If the vessel is inanimate or dead, the spirit's Force is added to any appropriate Physical ratings (at the gamemaster's discretion). For instance, a corpse's attributes would be appropriate, as would a jar's Barrier rating, or a vehicle's Body, Armor, and Speed—though not it's Handling. The spirit does not enhance any tech- or software-based statistics such as an object's Device rating or a vehicle's Pilot software. While the spirit may use all of its powers on the physical plane through such a vessel, it may only animate it to perform actions the vessel could otherwise mechanically perform. For instance, a possessed gun would be able to fire or eject a clip, but would be unable to move by itself or access its smartgun functions. Likewise, a possessed bright-red SAAB Fury would be able to drive itself, but not access GridLink, use a Pilot program, or target weapons with sensors. As a rule of thumb, spirits can control mechanical functions, and not those which require complex electronic, DNI, or wireless controls. Ultimately,

Continued on page 103

Quake

Type: P • Action: Complex • Range: Special • Duration: Instant

The spirit can create earthquakes with potentially devastating effects in areas which are particularly vulnerable to them. The quake affects an area with a radius of (spirit's Force) kilometers, and the shaking persists intermittently for (Force) minutes. Areas especially vulnerable to earthquakes are usually not areas that receive them frequently, as people in those areas tend to build dwellings with earthquakes in mind. An earthquake that has little effect in the San Francisco might be very destructive were it in Istanbul. The spirit makes a Magic + Willpower Test and the number of hits represents the magnitude of the quake, as noted on the Quake Table (p. 101).

Realistic Form

Type: P • Action: Auto • Range: Self • Duration: Special

A spirit with Realistic Form can be mistaken for a normal physical creature or object when it materializes, or it appears unremarkable when joined to a vessel. A spirit that appears as a metahuman would have a heartbeat and a regular breathing rate. A spirit that appeared as an object mimics the object's normal functionality; for example, a toaster could be plugged into the wall to toast bread (though it would have no Matrix link, making it an antique toaster). The spirit is in no way disguised from the astral plane, but to physical observation appears to any senses to be a natural part of the physical world.

Note that spirits with the Materialization power normally only have one materialized form. Materializing spirits with this power can choose to appear using Realistic Form or their normal materialized form. A fire elemental can still appear as a column of angry flames, but might also be able to appear as a beautiful woman.

Shadow Cloak

Type: P • Action: Free • Range: Self • Duration: Sustained

This power allows a creature to envelop itself in utter darkness, making it appear to be a shadow. Though Shadow Cloak is useless in full daylight and redundant in complete darkness, a creature with this power can be difficult to detect in any other lightning conditions. Apply a –2 dice pool modifier to Perception Tests to detect the creature in Normal Light and a –4 dice pool modifier in Partial Light conditions. In Glare conditions, apply a +1 dice pool modifier to notice the creature.

Silence

Type: P • Action: Complex • Range: Special • Duration: Sustained

A creature with this power can surround itself with a sphere of silence with a radius equal to the creature's Magic in meters. Sounds originating from inside the area are muffled, and sound entering the area is harder to hear either by the creature or anyone else. Sound-based Perception Tests and the Damage Value of sound-based attacks are reduced by the spirit's Magic.

Storm

Type: P • Action: Complex • Range: Special • Duration: Special

A spirit with this power can send a massive and destructive elemental storm against an area. Icy rain, bolts of lightning, hurricane force winds, and worse strike the area with reckless abandon. The affected area's radius equals the spirit's Magic x 100 meters. The spirit makes a single Magic + Unarmed Combat Test, and all creatures and objects in the area are subject to Suppressive Fire (see p. 154, SR4A). The Storm's base Damage Value is the spirit's Force and it inflicts Physical damage.

ALLY SPIRITS

Initiates can learn to conjure powerful and unique *ally spirits* to create a servant or magical companion, similar to familiars and spirit companions of folklore. Allies are seen in different lights by different traditions: a Sioux shaman might call forth a spirit of beasts to inhabit a wolf companion, while a chaos mage might conjure a Jungian reflection of his idealized self. Since the way allies are viewed varies from tradition to tradition, the following rules are meant to be as generic as possible, leaving definitions up to individual characters and their traditions.

CONJURING AN ALLY

To create an ally, the initiate requires an appropriate ally spirit formula (see below), spirit binding materials equal to the Force of the ally, and must know the Ally Conjuration metamagic (p. 53). If the ally spirit has the Inhabitation power rather than Materialization, the conjurer must have a previously prepared vessel on hand (see *Vessel Preparation*, p. 86).

Ally Spirit Formula

Before conjuring an ally, the initiate must first prepare a unique spirit formula which shapes the ally spirit's essence and dictates its abilities and powers. There are two known means of acquiring an ally spirit formula:
- The conjurer may devise the formula from scratch by making a Logic + Arcana (Force x 5, 1 day) Extended Test. If you aren't too paranoid, it is conceivable to have another character design the formula for you.
- The formula may also be gained via a metaplanar quest (see p. 130).

The spirit formula must have a physical representation appropriate to the character's tradition (much like an initiate's thesis, p. 52). Copies of the formula may be made, but since a formula can be used to astrally track the ally or used as a sympathetic link (p. 29) to the ally for ritual magic, copies do not come without risk. On the other hand, if every copy of an ally's formula is destroyed, the ally is disrupted and cannot return until a new formula is created. If an ally ever goes free, its formula does not change.

Note that a spirit formula (either the original or a copy) must be worked into the vessel prepared for an ally spirit with the Inhabitation power.

Creating an Ally Spirit

The ally spirit's formula defines its unique essence, statistics, abilities, and powers. This formula also dictates how much Karma the conjurer must sacrifice during the binding ritual before the spirit is invested with these abilities. The following steps will help you calculate the ally spirit's Karma cost (as well as its forms, powers, and skills).

POSSESSION AND VESSELS (CONT.)

it's up to the gamemaster to rule what the spirit can control and what it can't.

The combined entity uses its enhanced attributes (or simply the spirit's if it lacks attributes) to calculate Initiative, and uses the spirit's normal Initiative Passes.

Possession and Services

Possession functions much like Materialization with regards to a spirit's owed services (see also *Spirit Services*, p. 94); meaning that once the spirit has completed its services it will return to the astral or metaplanes, abandoning the vessel (the vessel reverts to its state prior to possession, except for any damage incurred, which it retains). The spirit will also return to the astral at its summoner's command.

Roleplaying Possession

A magician possessed by a spirit he summoned is fully aware of what the spirit is doing, and is still able to give it commands and directions. In the interest of fairness, it is suggested gamemasters allow a player of a possessed magician to roleplay *the spirit* that they command and which is controlling their body. Gamemasters may want to consider extending this option to players whose characters are possessed by "friendly" spirits so that they are not relegated to the sidelines.

Damage

A possessed vessel's Physical damage track will generally increase (since its Body increases by the spirit's Force). If the spirit *or* the vessel has already sustained damage, that damage stays with them, though only the greater set of combined wound penalties apply during possession. Physical damage inflicted during possession is tracked as a single entity. If the spirit and vessel separate, both retain the full amount of damage they've taken while joined (cumulative with any previous damage). Keep in mind that when possession ends, the vessel's Body and Physical damage track will return to its normal levels—possibly aggravating the situation if the damage track decreases significantly.

Step 1: Choose Force—An ally spirit's base cost equals 8 Karma times its desired Force rating.

Step 2: Choose Form(s)—The ally spirit may either have the Materialization power (p. 296, *SR4A*) or the Inhabitation power (p. 100). Materializing allies start with one with base form they may materialize as (typically appropriate to the summoner's belief system). The ally spirit can have additional forms that it can

switch between at will (requiring a Complex Action) at the cost of 2 Karma each. Inhabiting allies must have a vessel prepared for them. Inhabiting allies may also have additional forms purchased for them, however these are only available if the Inhabitation results in a true form ally spirit (in which case the spirit's base form will still reflect the vessel's original form).

Step 3: Choose Powers—Each ally spirit automatically starts with the powers of Astral Form, Banishing Resistance, Realistic Form (p. 102), Sapience (p. 297, *SR4A*), and Sense Link (p. 55) for free. Each also receives one additional power per point of Force, chosen from any powers available to spirits the initiate may conjure. The initiate may give the ally extra powers available to spirits his tradition can conjure at a cost of 5 Karma each. If the magician chooses the Elemental Attack, Energy Aura, or Engulf powers, he must specify what form the power takes.

Step 4: Choose Skills—All ally spirits automatically start with the skills of Assensing, Astral Combat, Dodge, Perception, and Unarmed Combat at a rating equal to their Force. The conjurer may grant the spirit additional skills at a rating equal to Force from among those that he possesses or that the ally needs in order to use its powers or innate abilities (such as Exotic Ranged Weapon if it has the Noxious Breath power, or Counterspelling if it has the Magical Guard power) at a cost of 5 Karma each. Ally spirits may also be given the Flight skill (p. 292, *SR4A*), assuming it fits the spirit's form. Allies may never possess skills from the Conjuring skill group.

Step 5: Choose Spells—An ally spirit can be given any spell that the character knows at a cost of 3 Karma each. An ally spirit can also be taught spells that the character does not know at a cost of 5 Karma each (spell formulae are still required).

Conjuring Ritual

The conjuring ritual must be performed in a magical lodge with a Force equal or greater than the desired Force of the ally spirit. The initiate first summons the ally at the desired Force, following normal summoning rules (p. 188, *SR4*). Immediately after summoning, the ally spirit must be bound following the normal rules for binding (p. 188, *SR4*). Drain is calculated as if summoning and binding a normal spirit of equal Force.

If the binding is unsuccessful, the ally spirit never takes shape and its spirit formula is rendered useless. If the binding is successful, the initiate immediately pays Karma equal to the cost of the ally spirit (see *Creating an Ally Spirit,* above). The character must expend the predefined amount of Karma or the ritual fails. The initiate now has his very own unique ally spirit.

If the ally spirit has the Inhabitation power rather than Materialization, the conjurer must have a previously prepared vessel on hand (see *Vessel Preparation,* p. 86). Immediately after the ally spirit is bound, it must immediately use its Inhabitation power on the prepared vessel. As detailed under the Inhabitation power (p. 100), the conjurer may chose to influence the outcome of the Inhabitation Test. Inhabitation takes a number of days equal to the force of the spirit; the entire process is considered

Street Magic

part of the conjuring ritual and the magician must attend it continuously for the duration—prospective ally conjurers should be careful to provision themselves adequately.

ALLY SPIRIT ABILITIES

An ally spirit follows the standard rules for spirits with the following exceptions:

Aid Sorcery and Aid Study

An ally spirit may Aid Sorcery and Aid Study (see p. 187, *SR4A*) exactly as if it was a normal bound spirit. An ally spirit is considered to be appropriate for every spell category for this purpose, and does not count against the limit of one bound spirit aiding in the learning of a spell.

Attributes

An ally's attributes (both physical and astral) equal its Force; allies using the Inhabitation power follow the rules for *Inhabitation Merges,* p. 100, to determine physical attributes. An ally begins play with an Edge attribute equal to the conjuring character's Edge, rather than its Force as normal for spirits.

Loyalty

Ally spirits are substantially more loyal than ordinary bound spirits (in fact, such loyalty is hardwired in due to the spirit formula). An ally effectively serves a character until they are freed by their master's death (or potentially near-death). Unlike other spirits, bound or otherwise, an ally spirit might go out of its way to help the character and volunteer information it believes may be of assistance—though if the character is particularly cruel to the ally, it may eventually turn on him to the best of its ability. If necessary, consider ally spirits to have a Loyalty Rating of 6 (see p. 285, *SR4A*). For many magicians, the ally is more than a servant and is seen as an equal—or even a superior.

Magic Skill Use

Every ally spirit possesses the Magician quality (p. 91, *SR4A*) and can be designed with *any* Magical skills known to its summoner such as Arcana, Counterspelling, Enchanting, Ritual Spellcasting, and Spellcasting. Ally spirits, however, can never use skills from the Conjuration skill group. Ally spirits may not initiate. An ally inhabiting a vessel may not astrally project.

Native Plane

The native plane of the ally is specified by its spirit formula and is invariably a plane significant and appropriate to the magician's tradition and beliefs. The ally receives no special powers or abilities by virtue of its native plane, but a magician can destroy the spirit by making a metaplanar quest (p. 130) to that plane.

Open-Ended Service

An ally spirit's services are never exhausted. Ally spirits can be called upon to perform any service possible of an unbound or bound spirit (p. 188, *SR4A*) an unlimited number of times. Such services include Aid Sorcery and Aid Study (see above), Loaned Service, Resist Drain (see below), Spell Binding, and Spell Sustaining, among others.

Note that ally spirits do not count towards the initiate's limits on bound or unbound spirits.

Resist Drain

As a service, an ally spirit may take the Drain for a spell its summoner is casting in his stead. The ally's Magic attribute is used to determine if the Drain is Physical or not. Alternately, the character can buy an extra success on any Drain Resistance Test at the cost of the ally suffering one box of Physical Drain (no resistance test allowed). In either case, this is an agonizing process for the spirit, and if used frequently will encourage animosity in the ally.

Sense Link

Ally spirits have the power of Sense Link (see p. 54), which allow them to share sensory data with their conjurors at a limited range, just like adepts and attuned animals. The initiate may not target spells via this power.

ENHANCING AN ALLY

At a later time, an initiate may choose to modify an ally spirit's formula to grant the ally spirit additional forms, skills, powers, or spells. The character may also raise the ally's Force in this manner. Modifying the spirit formula requires a new Logic + Arcana (desired Force x 5, 1 day) Extended Test or another metaplanar quest.

After designing or acquiring the modified spirit formula, investing the spirit with new abilities requires a new binding ritual—sometimes called a Ritual of Change—in a magical lodge with a rating equal to or greater than the Force of the ally. Conjuring materials equal to the spirit's Force are also required and Karma must be spent on the relevant changes at the costs outlined above. Raising Force, however, is twice as expensive this way (1 point costs 16 Karma).

A new Inhabitation Test is not required for inhabiting ally spirits, though the conjurer can provide a new vessel and have the spirit merge with it instead (leaving the old vessel a discarded husk).

LOSING AN ALLY

Characters who are especially cruel or callous can lose the respect and friendship of their ally, just as they can anger any other contact or acquaintance. If the magician becomes over-dependent on his own ally spirit or regularly endangers it, the ally may become resentful and attempt to seek its own freedom. An ally can only attempt to break away during a rebinding ritual or if its master is incapacitated by Physical damage or Drain, and even then will only make the attempt if it feels that is has been wronged.

If the ally spirit attempts to break free, it must make an Opposed Test pitting its Force x 2 against the magician's Magic + Binding (the ally does not need to add dice to the master on this test). If the spirit wins, the ally goes free (see *Free Spirits*, p. 106). If the ally breaks free during a rebinding ritual, the ritual fails and the Karma remains unspent, but the conjuring materials and time are expended without effect. The magician also must resist a Drain Value of 2 x the number of hits the spirit achieved

on its test. If the magician is incapacitated by Drain, the spirit immediately goes free.

The enmity of an ally spirit is nothing to laugh about. While it is incapable of disobeying an order, and cannot directly harm its master, it is every bit as intelligent as its conjurer. For this reason, despite the gross difference in power between the conjurer and the spirit, most conjurers treat their allies very well. The ally spirits of threat magicians, on the other hand, often clash with their conjurers, possibly because the ally is just as selfish and power hungry as its maker.

FREE SPIRITS

The Sixth World is also inhabited by spirits that know no allegiance to any metahuman magician or that have broken free of their former masters. These entities are known collectively as *free spirits* and their agendas, interests, and personalities are no one's but their own.

As master of its own fate, a free spirit gains a number of advantages, but also finds its development limited. Free spirits are not native to the physical plane, and must rely on legitimate residents of the physical world for karmic handouts if they want to become firmly established. Ironically, a free spirit is in some ways even more dependent upon metahumanity than it was when it had a metahuman master.

BORN FREE

For most free spirits, the moment that spirit broke away from its metahuman master and became free is considered its "birth." Though wild spirits (p. 110) are also considered free spirits, how and when they were "born" (if at all) remains a mystery.

Whenever a spirit becomes uncontrolled, the gamemaster decides whether or not it becomes a free spirit, as fits the story. As a guideline, most bound spirits with a Force greater than 6 become free, whereas lesser spirits will simply fade away. Spirits with a long history of association with mankind and the natural world go free more often, though unbound spirits almost never go free.

To determine randomly if a spirit goes free, roll an Edge (3) Test for the spirit. Success means that the spirit is now free, with an Edge of 1. Every net hit increases the free spirit's initial Edge. If the test fails, the spirit simply returns to its native metaplane. Unbound spirits rarely go free and suffer a –4 dice pool penalty to the Edge Test. Spirits which have had especially memorable or frequent encounters with metahumanity receive a +2 dice pool bonus, and may even elect to burn a point of Edge to get even more.

New Powers

Every free spirit gains the Magician quality (p. 91, *SR4A*) and the Banishing Resistance power (p. 99) the moment they go free. Free spirits can learn and cast spells as a magician does, but are not bound by spirit correspondences of metahuman paradigms. Though a free spirit never needs spell formulae (learning the spell intuitively from observation of mana flow), it still needs to spend Karma and time to learn spells. The free spirit will likely need to learn the Spellcasting skill. Note that free spirits can never learn any skills from the Conjuring skill group, nor may a free spirit inhabiting a vessel astrally project unless it has the Astral Projection power (p. 109).

Additionally, when a spirit becomes free, it gains a number of new powers equal to its remaining Edge attribute. As spirits bind their fate more closely to the Earth, their powers increase, gaining a new power every time their Edge increases, or each time they initiate. These optional powers can come from the following:

- The spirit type's normal optional power list.
- One of these powers available to some spirits: Astral Gateway, Aura Masking, Divining, Essence Drain (free spirits do not actually lose Essence, but they can still use this power to siphon Essence away to fuel their attributes; see p. 294, *SR4A*), Materialization, Possession, or Realistic Form.
- Any of the metamagic techniques available to metahuman initiates may be taken as a free spirit power. Free spirits use Edge in place of initiate grade. It is possible that certain powerful free spirits may also command metamagics yet unknown to metahumanity, providing the gamemaster with a unique opportunity to introduce new metamagic into the game.
- A unique power available only to free spirits, chosen from those listed under *Free Spirit Powers*, p. 109.

Free Spirit Services

A free spirit does not normally owe services to anyone, but can, if it so desires, perform any service that can be asked of a bound spirit (see p. 188, *SR4A*). A free spirit can, however, be bound by its spirit formula (see below) and compelled to perform services, though it does not vanish to metaplanes once those services are complete (or if the master dies).

TRUE NAMES

A spirit's *true name* is a complex and abstract arcane formulation that represents the totality of the spirit's essence and nature, and which is believed to come into existence when a spirit becomes free. While the true name is an intricate and abstract description of forces and concepts foreign to metahuman minds, once it is identified, anyone with the Arcana skill can translate it into recognizable human symbols and terms in the form of a *spirit formula*. A spirit formula is a powerful magic instrument that grants anyone that possesses it the ability to command the spirit. For this reason, few free spirits are willing to tolerate the existence of multiple copies.

Learning the Spirit Formula

There are several methods of learning a free spirit's formula:

Firstly, it is widely believed that a representation of the true name is discreetly imprinted on an object, person, or possibly even place in the spirit's vicinity when it first breaks free. This is recognizable in the same manner as an astral signature—with 3 hits on an Assensing Test (though free spirits have been known to quickly but quietly relocate this physical representation to a safe place at the first opportunity). This true name may be translated into a spirit formula with an Arcana + Logic (spirit's Force x 5, 1 day) Extended Test. A bound spirit can assist in this task as part of an Aid Study service, whether it is of a similar type to the free spirit or not. The formula takes a form appropriate to the magician's tradition: a thaumaturgic formulation for a hermetic, a totemic statuette for a shaman, a complex mandala for a Buddhist magician, or a jade figurine for a Shinto, and so on.

Secondly, an initiate may attempt to learn the spirit's true name through a metaplanar quest (p. 130) to the spirit's home metaplane—which may be obvious or obscure. For example, it's easy to guess that the cyclonic conflagration that incinerated your new moped may be native to the Plane of Fire. Lacking such subtle clues as to an origin, the character must assense the spirit (requiring 2 net hits) or an astral signature the spirit has left (requiring 5 net hits). The gamemaster should ensure a metaplanar quest of this type is an appropriately harrowing and difficult experience. It may even require a spirit guide in order to reach the appropriate plane (e.g., if the metaplane in question is one unfamiliar to the magician, such as the Metaplane of Death). A successful quest etches the true name in the magician's mind's eye with such clarity that if he has the Arcana skill he is able to translate it into a spirit formula at any time thereafter.

Lastly, if a metaplanar quest is out of the question, a character who has very carefully observed the free spirit's aura (achieving 5+ net hits on the Assensing Test) can attempt to design a functional spirit formula from scratch. Doing so is time consuming and difficult, requiring an Arcana + Logic (spirit's Force x 10, 1 day) Extended Test. It is recommended that the gamemaster enforce the limit on the number of tests possible before failure.

Spirit Formula Copies

A spirit is instinctively aware of the location of all copies of its formula—where any of them are when they are created, moved, or destroyed—no matter how many astral barriers exist between the spirit and the formula. If a new copy is made, the spirit automatically becomes aware of its location.

FREE SPIRITS AND KARMA

Free spirits need Karma to grow in power, but are unable to earn it on their own. Short of stealing Karma with Energy Drain (see p. 99), they must receive it as a gift from sapient, physical beings native to Earth. Spirits cannot normally take a metahuman's life force, it must be given freely. When a character negotiates a deal with a free spirit, Karma is the usual payment, though some spirits have a taste for resources such as services, contacts, rare goods, unique enchantments, or even plain old material wealth. Karma is not the only thing free spirits want, but they value it above all else.

Feeding the Free Spirit

Giving Karma to a free spirit requires either a spirit pact (see p. 108) or a ritual involving the presence of the spirit's formula, putting spirits in quite a bind. While Karma is desperately needed, allowing metahumans to have their formula or enter a spirit pact leaves the spirit potentially vulnerable. It is in a spirit's best interest to make sure that every former donor is kept happy—or dead. Giving Karma through a ritual is a time consuming process, taking 1 hour per Karma point.

Using Karma

A free spirit can use Karma in several ways at normal character costs (see *Character Improvement*, p. 269, *SR4A*). Spirits normally have no racial maximums on their skills or attributes.
- It may raise its attributes separately (which all begin at the Force it had when it went free).
- It may raise or purchase additional skills.
- It may initiate as a magician does, though the process grants one additional free spirit power per grade rather than a metamagic technique.

- It may raise its Force by 1 point at a time at the cost of new Force rating x 10. Raising Force raises all of the spirit's attributes and powers that are based on Force.

BINDING A FREE SPIRIT

The powerful magic of the spirit's formula allows anyone—including mundanes—to summon a free spirit and, with a proper ritual, to bind it.

Summoning a Free Spirit

Summoning a free spirit with a spirit formula is a simple matter, and may be performed by anyone who has the free spirit's formula in hand. The summoner merely concentrates on the spirit formula and calls on the spirit it represents. The free spirit is forcefully drawn from wherever it was, no matter what it was doing, manifesting nearby nearly instantaneously in a puff of smoke and bad temper. The conjurer suffers no Drain. The summoning itself confers no services, but no roll is required, and no known magic can prevent it. Even a spirit currently possessing a vessel must appear if summoned through its formula in this manner (leaving the vessel behind). Free spirits inhabiting a vessel with the Inhabitation power, however, are resistant to this pull as their Essence is anchored to the physical plane. In that case, the inhabiting spirit is still forcefully drawn to appear before the summoner, but must use the best physical means at its disposal to get there. If the summoner moves, however, the summoning is broken and the inhabiting free spirit is no longer drawn.

The Binding Ritual

The free spirit is compelled by the power of the spirit formula to subject itself to a binding ritual and is unable to harm the summoner in possession of the formula until it is over. The ritual requires an Arcana + Logic (1) Test to prepare and ritual binding materials equal to the spirit's Force. The ritual takes a number of hours equal to the spirit's Force and may be performed anywhere (no magical lodge required). During the ritual, the would-be spirit master attempts to assert his will upon the free spirit, and at the end he makes an Opposed Test pitting his Willpower + Binding skill (if any) against the spirit's Force + Edge.

If the character wins, the free spirit is bound and owes a number of services equal to the victor's net hits. Such services are invariably one-off commands, uses of the free spirit's powers, or performing any service possible of an unbound or bound spirit. Exceptionally, this binding ritual produces no Drain.

Until a bound free spirit's services are used up, the spirit cannot directly harm its master—though given the opportunity it will conspire to put him in harm's way or ruin his life. The instant the free spirit is no longer indentured to the character, it can do anything it wants (which generally goes poorly for the mortal). The spirit can be rebound with its formula through a new binding ritual, of course. This can be done an unlimited number of times, but if the master glitches on the rebinding test, the free spirit will get 1 Combat Turn to do anything it wants before it is brought back under control. If the character gets a critical glitch on the rebinding, all services he is owed are forfeit and the spirit can do anything it wants.

SPIRIT PACTS

Free spirits with the Spirit Pact power can enter into pacts with voluntary sapient creatures, usually magicians, though each individual spirit can usually only offer one or two different varieties of pact. There is actually relatively little to be gained from shrewd negotiation with a spirit—a free spirit's first offer is often the only offer it can make. Ending a spirit pact without the death of one or both of the participants is usually not possible and is the stuff of epic magic and plot devices. Any time a character and a spirit have a pact, either party may be used as a sympathetic link (see p. 29) to other or to astrally track the other.

Possible Spirit Pacts

The gamemaster should consider game balance carefully before introducing any spirit pact into her game or allowing a character to take the Spirit Pact quality (see p. 26). The following are some examples of spirit pacts; gamemasters should also feel free to create their own.

Drain Pact: The spirit ties its own magical essence to the character, allowing him to use magic more easily. For as long as the pact is maintained, the magician gains a positive dice pool modifier on all Drain Resistance Tests equal to the spirit's Edge. Using magic in this way is addictive, however, and unlike most pacts the spirit can cut the magician off at any time. The spirit may demand Karma from the magician to continue supplying mana to the magician.

Dream Pact: The spirit gains control of the character's body while the character is asleep, always possessing the character the moment he closes his eyes. The character's body never sleeps, though he is rested when he awakes. The spirit gains Karma during the time it controls the character as if it were the character. The character regains control of his body when he awakens but has no recollection of events that may have transpired.

Formula Pact: The spirit infuses a copy of its spirit formula into the character, who then carries it with him for the rest of time. The character gains the power Immunity to Age (p. 295, *SR4A*), and the spirit cannot be affected by the use of any other copy of its formula for as long as the character lives. The character's aura is visibly tainted by the spirit's signature. The character himself may be used (or use himself) as the spirit's formula for any purposes.

Life Pact: The free spirit's life force is tied to that of the character. The character can maintain his own life by drawing on the life force of the spirit—but he loses Karma in the exchange. The character may spend a Complex Action to heal 2 boxes of Physical damage, but the spirit siphons away 1 point of Karma in return. The spirit does not need to be present, nor is the spirit inflicted with the damage.

Magic Pact: The spirit allows the magician use of its Magic in exchange for allowing the spirit to use his Edge. Once a day, the magician can enhance his Magic attribute by half the spirit's Magic attribute (round up) for (spirit's Force) Combat Turns. In turn, the spirit can spend the magician's Edge for any purpose at any time.

Power Pact: The spirit links its magical abilities to the character. The character may use one of the spirit's powers (except Astral Form, Materialization, Possession, or Inhabitation), and the spirit may cast one of the character's spells (if any). This pact only lasts 24 hours, but may be renewed an unlimited number of times provided that the spirit can be bribed sufficiently to want to do so.

BANISHING A FREE SPIRIT

A free spirit can be banished like any other spirit (see p. 188, *SR4A*), though all free spirits possess the power of Banishing Resistance (see p. 99). Since a free spirit is normally unbound to any magician, it lacks services to be banished away. Instead, its unspent Edge is reduced for each net hit the banisher achieves (bound free spirits add their unspent Edge and owed services together). A free spirit whose available Edge is reduced to 0 this way is temporarily disrupted and vanishes to its native metaplane. Of course, when its Edge replenishes it may return.

A spirit that is successfully banished or disrupted can be prevented from ever returning if the banisher immediately destroys a copy of its spirit formula and succeeds in an Opposed Test between his Willpower + Banishing (if any) and the spirit's Force + Edge. Unfortunately for the banisher, there's no way to tell if he succeeded or not, unless the free spirit later returns. The banishing attempt may be repeated, but another copy of the spirit formula is necessary.

FREE SPIRIT POWERS

The following powers are only available to free spirits.

Astral Projection

Type: M • Action: Complex • Range: Self • Duration: Special

The spirit can astrally project, just like a magician (see p. 192, *SR4A*). This power is only available to spirits with the Inhabitation power. A spirit which does not return to a body after (Force x 2) hours is disrupted.

Mutable Form

Type: P • Action: Auto • Range: Self • Duration: Special

Spirits normally materialize using the same form every time. A free spirit with Mutable Form can appear differently each time it materializes. The spirit's magical aura is unchanged. If the spirit also has the Realistic Form power (p. 102), add the spirit's Force to any Disguise Tests it makes to impersonate someone. This power is only available to spirits with the Materialization power.

Personal Domain

Type: M • Action: Auto • Range: LOS • Duration: Sustained

The spirit literally leaves its personal mark all over a portion of the astral plane up to 10,000 square meters per Force point. Over time, this area accumulates a background count aspected towards the tradition the spirit represents (see p. 117). The gamemaster determines how quickly the background accumulates, but the process should take months if not years, and the background count should not exceed the spirit's Force ÷ 2 (round up).

Regeneration

Type: P • Action: Auto • Range: Self • Duration: Always

This power is similar to the critter power of Regeneration (p. 296, *SR4A*), and applies only to the spirit's materialized, possessed, or inhabited form. Additionally, if the free spirit with

this power possesses or inhabits a vessel that used to be alive, the vessel will gradually regenerate back to its original living form. A wooden homunculus grows leaves and roots, for example, while a corpse regains the semblance of life.

Spirit Pact

Type: M • Action: Special • Range: Special • Duration: Special

The free spirit gains the ability to enter into one or more spirit pacts (see p. 108). The game master has final say as to which pacts a spirit can enter into.

GREATER POWERS

Greater powers are abilities of free spirits that are so dramatic, unusual, or powerful that they are easily capable of defining an encounter with the spirit all by themselves. Gamemasters are advised to make these powers rare, and even then to limit only one such power to any given free spirit. While it might seem cool to have a spirit individually capable of doing it all, in practice this runs the risk of the spirit feeling confusing rather than mysterious to the players.

Hidden Life

Type:P • Action: Complex • Range:Touch • Duration: Permanent

With this power, the spirit permanently places its life force in some creature, place, or object. As long as the hiding place remains safe, the spirit cannot be permanently banished or destroyed by any means. The spirit is able to return after a year and a day even if banished with its spirit formula, but a character holding the formula can attempt to call and command the spirit.

The hiding place gains the powers of Immunity to Normal Weapons (with a Magic equal to the spirit's), and Immunity to Age (p. 295, *SR4A*). If the hidden life holder is destroyed, the life force returns to the spirit, and the spirit is treated normally.

Energy Drain (Karma)

As described on p. 99, with a Range of Touch and causing Physical damage.

Vessel Trading

Type: P • Action: Complex • Range: Touch • Duration: Instant

The spirit can use its Possession power to not only take over a living vessel, but also to evict the victim's life force from it, either ejecting the victim out as an astrally projecting creature or putting the victim's life force in its old vessel. If the old vessel already contains a (previously subdued by possession) life force, the new victim may not be placed there, and is forced to astrally project instead. Follow the standard rules for the Possession power (p. 101). Victims placed into a vessel (living or inanimate) are not able to control it like a possessing spirit—they are trapped there and typically find the experience inexplicably horrifying. The only way they may escape is if a free spirit with this power switches them back, they are capable of astrally projecting and freeing themselves, or the vessel is exposed to an astral rift or entity with the astral gateway power. Victims trapped in an inanimate vessel or astral space will feel their life force ebbing away, and will die after (Magic or Essence) x 2 hours.

Wealth

Type: P • Action: Complex • Range: LOS • Duration: Special

A spirit with the Wealth power can produce precious metals, jewels, rare plants, and other items of great value to mortals. Where these items actually come from—perhaps they are magically created or transported from a metaplane—is a question no spirit has felt the need to answer. Once per month, the spirit may make a Magic + Edge Test. Every hit generates 10,000¥ worth of mineral alchemical reagents (normally precious metals or gems). These materials are permanent creations and indefinitely carry the spirit's astral signature. Market conditions may vary, and it may be very difficult to sell magical gems depending upon location.

The spirit can also generate a similar amount of *temporary* wealth every day, but these seemingly valuable items vanish the next time the sun rises or sets, or transform into non-valuable goods such as dirt or beans. For this reason, savvy businessmen are reticent about purchasing magical gold.

WILD SPIRITS

More than half a century after the Awakening, the world remains a mysterious and unpredictable place. One of the phenomena that underscores mankind's incomplete understanding of magic is the existence of the spontaneous, free-willed spirits known as "wild spirits." Legends and rumors abound on all continents and in all cultures of men-o-the-woods, faeries, daevas, manitoo, the Wild Hunt, and other eldritch entities. Wild spirits are established inhabitants of the Sixth World, though they are rare and not yet understood.

Wild spirits often do not conform to metahuman traditions of magic and defy easy categorization. While some wild spirits, particularly those linked to unspoiled wilderness, are openly hostile to mankind, most are simply indifferent to metahuman concerns. Some are drawn or are associated to particular locations and domains, while others are free-roaming. Many seem focused on a single task or goal (such as protecting a certain forest, or haunting an old mansion) appearing only to further their enigmatic calling, while a few appear to take a permanent interest in the physical world and metahumanity. All are particularly sensitive to the general emotional states that permeate the ambient mana (and create the background count). Areas attuned by great joy will usually draw friendly spirits, while negative emotional background count will bring fierce and angry spirits.

For game purposes, wild spirits are handled as free spirits, though their unique statistics, abilities, and personalities are left to the gamemaster. Though all have a Force and various powers, wild spirits can possess any form or any combination of powers the gamemaster deems appropriate and balanced.

Wild spirits are always uncontrolled and also exhibit a remarkable resistance to Conjuring. All possess the power of Banishing Resistance (p. 99). Even if banishment is successful, a wild spirit may not be subsequently summoned and controlled unless the conjurer possesses its spirit formula (assuming it has a spirit formula …).

...ASTRAL SPACE AND THE METAPLANES...

"Welcome to Eden, Corporal Warren."

Corporal Carter Warren sprung over the threshold of the airlock, his step boosted by a mix of tense excitement and Daedalus station's 0.8 Earth gravity. He had been briefed on Eden already, but the sight of it was nothing he could have been prepared for. Here at LaGrange Point 4, far from the Earth in a pod on a rapidly-spinning orbital space station, stretched a greenhouse full of exotic plants genetically tailored for this unique environment. Broad and flat leaves hung effortlessly in the lighter gravity, casting a green canopy over the entire area and almost making one forget they were in space.

"This way, sir" The other soldier interrupted Carter's gawking, as he probably had to do with most new visitors to Eden. Despite the beauty and amazement of this place, it served an extremely serious purpose. Every single plant here was carefully grown in order to maintain a weak, but stable, mana field throughout Eden. It was anemic in comparison with the thriving Gaiasphere, but it was an island of wonder in the vast, empty void beyond Earth.

Carter was escorted to a glade circled with ergonomic chairs that appeared to have been ordered from an obscure Scandinavian designer. Each one was hooked up to a discreet suite of medical monitoring equipment and in each one reclined an Ares Firewatch magician. One seat remained open for Carter.

"Sir, the focus is just past the circle, over there." The soldier-escort pointed beyond the reclining mages to a pedestal surrounded by ballistic glass. On the pedestal sat a bracelet in the shape of a serpent, an odd bit of unintentional humor here in Eden. The focus itself was unimportant to the mission—its value was in the astral link that tied it to its bonded magician. More importantly, the link itself was key because it would lead the Firewatch astral team exactly where they needed to go: to the queen insect spirit that Ares had marked for destruction on its home plane. "The astral link has been rerouted four times," the soldier explained. "The fourth and final metaplanar quest along the link will take you right into the Hive."

"Where we will take a slight detour." Carter noted the two specially-trained adepts flanking the focus and was grimly reminded that the link could be followed both ways. If the Firewatch team could follow the link into the Hive, theoretically something from the Hive could follow it back. If that happened, the adepts were here to slow down whatever came through long enough for Ares to jettison this entire pod into the void. Carter also noted that the magician linked to the focus was nowhere nearby; he or she was probably under heavy guard in some equally-secure Ares location somewhere. Given where they were standing now, that could be just about anywhere.

Corporal Warren sunk into the chair left for him while a medic wired him for observation. Before meditating in preparation for the metaplanar quest, he turned to the other soldier. "Oh, and soldier—" he grinned "—make sure you water the plants while I'm gone."

> **A QUICK ASIDE ABOUT MANA**
> Mana is the stuff of magic, the inexplicable energy that fuels magical effects. Though mana is most visible on the astral plane, where it provides a suffuse glow, mana is in fact present on the physical plane as well, though it is invisible. A spell cast on the physical plane does not draw mana from the astral, it uses mana from the physical side. Mana seems to flow freely between the physical and astral, however, so if an astral area is polluted by background count or aspected towards a particular type of magic, the physical mana in that area will be the same.

THE MIRROR WORLD

The astral plane is a dreamlike realm shaped by eddying flows of mana, the glow of life and the natural world, and the echoes of emotion.

ASTRAL TOPOGRAPHY

The terrain that makes up the astral plane is diverse, following rules unlike those that govern the physical universe. The different aspects of the astral plane are often divided into four categories, depending on their substantiality and whether they are natural reflections or constructed objects.

Shadows

Much of the astral plane's terrain is made up of insubstantial shadows, drab reflections of lifeless objects present in the physical world. The more mankind creates, the more the astral plane becomes cluttered with these colorless shadows. A shiny new sports car, when viewed from the astral, appears dull and grey and gives no resistance to astral forms passing through its minimal presence. The insubstantial nature of shadows means that astral forms cannot interact with them; they simply pass through them as if they were not there. While this makes travel in the astral plane easy (as astrally-projecting magicians can walk right through buildings), even the simplest physical task such as flipping through a book is impossible on the astral.

The physical details of real-world objects are not as distinct in their astral shadow counterparts. Features such as color, texture, smell, taste, sturdiness, text, and images are difficult to discern. Even if the book in the above example was already flipped open to the correct page by someone in the physical world, the text on the page is all but impossible to read on the astral. Partly, this is due to the nature of astral perception, which is more akin to a psychic sense than physical sight. Shadows, like many other terrain features on the astral, are influenced by the emotional charges of the physical objects they mirror. If the book were a significant tome whose words have had an emotional impact on many people, the text may have enough emotional resonance to be understood from the astral plane. Emotionally charged shadows are still insubstantial, but are visibly sharper than their less significant counterparts. Some may even bear impressions tied to the events that make them so important, which can be interpreted through assensing or Psychometry metamagic (p. 57).

Auras

Unlike the dull gray shadows of physical objects, the reflections of living and magical things glow brightly in the astral. Any living thing—microbe, plant, or animal—possesses an aura which can be seen to some degree on the astral plane. Though auras are as insubstantial as shadows, they are vivid and lively, reflecting the status of the plant or creature on the physical plane. Even the simplest plant's health can be read in its aura and for more complex creatures, even emotional states are visible. The more complex a living being, the more complex its corresponding aura. While collections of microbes may just cast a hazy glow in astral space, metahuman auras flicker and dance with layers of emotion and composition. Magic auras are equally complex; spells, physical mana barriers, and active adept and critter powers are alive with color. A skilled assenser can read volumes about a being or magical effect from the aura it casts onto the astral plane.

Auras are insubstantial and therefore offer no resistance to an astral form attempting to pass through them. The living being that corresponds to the aura, however, may sense when something or someone has passed through his aura (see *Astral Detection*, p. 193, SR4). While clothes and other non-living objects are often outshone by the brightness of the wearer's aura, intrusive non-living objects like cyberware leave shadowy gaps in auras. In addition, spells cast upon a person are visibly attached to an aura as long as they continue to be sustained. The auras of instant and permanent spells are no longer visible once the spell ends/is made permanent, though both of course leave an astral signature.

Astral Forms

Astral forms are active and substantial presences on the astral plane. Projecting magicians and spirits are free-roaming astral forms, but the astral forms of dual-natured beings (including those using astral perception) are tied to their physical world bodies. Astral forms are even brighter in the astral plane than auras, but most importantly, they are solid. An astral form cannot pass through another astral form.

It is important to remember that astral forms are not defined by physical laws. A projecting magician's physical body does not determine the characteristics of his astral form. Astral forms are idealized images formed of belief and emotion, and defined by mental or spiritual characteristics. No matter how strong a magician may be in the physical world, his astral form's strength is determined by his force of character and will.

Constructs

Constructs are a catch-all term for non-living astral entities that are substantial and active on the astral plane, such as active foci (which are dual natured). Mana barriers (such as wards) that are dual-natured or created on the astral are also considered constructs. Spells cast on the astral and similar magical effects, however, are not constructs; they remain insubstantial if highly visible auras.

Though the vast majority of constructs are man-made (or spirit-made), some constructs have been discovered whose origins are not yet totally understood. Astrally-projecting magicians have come across features in the astral terrain which are clearly not shadows and are entirely substantial, but appear to have been created though unknown means. Alchera (p. 115) are one such example.

Astral Visibility

The astral plane follows different universal laws than the physical world and even something as simple as visibility functions differently in astral space. Within the Gaiasphere—the astral space surrounding the Earth—the astral plane glows in a perpetual dawn cast upwards from the living Earth. This glow constitutes standard astral visibility, but alone it can offer advantages to those who can perceive the astral plane. While an urban alleyway may be pitch dark in the physical world, when one switches over to astral perception, the same alleyway glows dimly and allows for astral sight.

While this makes astral perception advantageous in some cases, it is not always a boon. Because illumination in the astral plane is also cast from the auras of living and magical things, what might be a normally visible scene in the physical world can be crowded with the cascading glow of many auras in astral space. With too many auras overlapping in one space, discerning one particular astral form, aura, or shadow can become very difficult.

The ideal conditions for astral visibility are high contrast: when a single aura stands out starkly against a backdrop of shadows, lit only by the soft glow of the Earth. Many factors may affect astral visibility, including the glare of too much life, the noise pollution of too many auras/astral forms, the clutter of obstructing shadows, the dimming of a low-mana area, or the swirling clouds of a high-mana area. These factors inflict modifiers on Assensing and Astral Combat Tests, as noted on the Astral Visibility table. Note that while these modifiers replace some physical world perception modifiers (such as the light level), other physical world modifiers still apply. If the perceiver is distracted, he will suffer a –2 dice pool modifier whether he is viewing physical space or astral space, for instance.

Determining cover works the same way on the astral plane as it does in the physical world (see p. 160, *SR4A*). Shadows of physical objects in the astral plane may be drab and insubstantial, but they are still opaque and can prevent targeting. Items that are transparent or mirrored in the real world (like a car window) simply impair visibility as astral shadows. Since there are no ranged weapons on the astral plane and spell targeting depends on seeing your target, hiding behind physical shadows works as well as hiding behind a vibrant aura.

ASTRAL VISIBILITY

Background Illumination	Modifier
Sterile (clean room, hospital)	+2
Barren (city streets)	+1
Developed (suburban area, desert)	0
Cultivated (park, light forest)	–1
Teeming (jungle, forest)	–2
Aura Noise	
Devoid (no living traffic)	+2
Sparse (scattered, occasional bystanders)	+1
Moderate (frequent presence of living creatures)	0
Steady (regular movement of living creatures)	–1
Crowded (packed with living creatures)	–2
Other Factors	
Shadow Clutter	–1 to –4
Background Count	Opposite of Rating*
Aerosol FAB cloud (p. 126)	–2

* For example, a Rating 7 mana warp confers a –7 visibility penalty, whereas a Rating –4 mana ebb confers a +4 visibility bonus.

Other Senses

It is important to remember that assensing is a psychic sense. Though it is often referred to and experienced in visual terms, it is not entirely the same as physical sight (which is why blind magicians and ghouls can assense without penalty). Assensing also picks up other sensory input that is sometimes experienced in a way commonly associated with taste, smell, hearing, and touch, but in other ways is quite different. The emotional content of what is perceived, as well as the living and magical energies, are much more relevant than the physical sensation. For example, a room may "taste" happy if numerous people have been rejoicing there, while a long-deserted building may "smell" like desolation and lifelessness, and the aura of a spell with "tingle" with energy and purpose. Though astral forms and constructs may be "touched," this is perceived as a flood of emotions and energies rather than a physical contact. Characters may converse and be heard in astral space, and language is still a communication barrier there, but an assensing character will be struck more by the emotive content rather than by the words themselves. It is also possible to eavesdrop on the noises, communications, and even smells of the physical world from the astral plane, but just like reading a physical book, the assensing character will perceive the emotional tone and impressions rather than the physical sensation.

THE LIVING EARTH

One constant in the astral plane that has caused much debate and speculation is the fact that Mother Earth is a dual-natured entity, possessing substance on both the physical and astral planes. Wherever the Earth has not been paved over or built upon, its astral form casts a dim luminescence up into the astral plane. Unlike the shadows of man-made objects and the auras of living beings, the Earth's astral form is solid under the

feet of spirits and projecting magicians. Possibly due to its sheer size, the Earth's astral form seems to be porous and other astral forms can press through the Earth's astral presence, but doing so takes considerable effort and carries great risk.

Pushing through the astral Earth is similar to pressing through an astral barrier (p. 194, *SR4A*) except that the Earth is an exceptionally thick barrier and does not possess a singular Force rating. In fact, the Earth's astral form is not as solid as most astral barriers and projecting magicians have often likened pressing through the astral Earth to pushing through dimly glowing molasses. The process for pressing through the astral Earth is handled as an Extended Magic + Charisma (meters, 30 minutes) Test. Any interruption in the test means the magician stops where he is. To continue on or go back to his body, he must start the test over again; no "tunnel" is created during the process that can be followed forward or back. Magicians that stop and linger mid-way or glitch during the Extended Test must immediately make a test to avoid getting lost (*Getting Lost,* below). If the magician rolls a critical glitch, his astral form is disrupted; he is sent immediately back to his physical body and is knocked unconscious (fill in the character's entire Stun Condition Monitor). It is important that the magician get where he is going and return to his body before he reaches the limits of his astral projection and dies, as covered under *Astral Projection,* p. 192, *SR4A*.

Getting Lost

Pressing through the claustrophobic, viscous mass of the astral Earth can be disorienting. To determine if a character loses his way in the Earth's embrace, roll an Intuition + Assensing (3) Test. Failure means the magician has gotten lost and must use astral tracking (p. 193, *SR4A*); add the number of meters the character has traveled through the earth so far as a threshold modifier.

> *Apollo is tasked with scouting an underground corporate lab before his team sneaks in. The main entrance to the underground lab is heavily warded and patrolled by spirits, so he decides to press through the astral earth surrounding the facility instead. Ten meters of earth separate Apollo's astral form and the lab, so he faces an Extended Magic + Charisma (10, 30 minutes) Test in order to reach the facility. After 30 minutes, Apollo makes the test with a dice pool of 9 (Magic 6 + Charisma 3) and he rolls 2, 3, 3, 3, 3, 4, 5, 6, 6—3 hits. On his second roll, after a full hour of pressing through the Earth, he rolls 1, 3, 4, 4, 5, 5, 5, 5, 6—5 hits. On his third roll he rolls 1, 2, 2, 2, 3, 4, 5, 5, 5—3 more hits and enough to reach his threshold after 90 minutes. Now Apollo is inside the astral space of the underground lab, but he still needs to make it back to his body, which means passing through 10 meters of astral earth again. Hopefully his return trip will go as quickly as his first, since he only has 6 hours to spend in the astral plane.*

ASTRAL PHENONEMA

While the vast majority of the astral terrain is made up of shadows, auras, astral forms, and constructs, there are exceptions to the rule which are coming to light as mankind explores more of the astral plane. These phenomena are not totally understood yet, but are believed to be produced when the barrier between the astral plane and the physical world weakens or frays. Nearly all of these phenomena fall under three categories: alchera, astral shallows, or astral rifts. Even if he cannot immediately see an astral phenomenon, a person passing through one may detect it as if sensing an astral form passing through his aura (see *Astral Detection,* p. 193, *SR4A*).

Alchera

Alchera is a term from the Arrernte Aborigines in Central Australia used to describe the Dreamtime, the co-existing past, present, and future world shaped by the spirits and gods. It has been adopted by the global magical community to describe unusually complex astral terrain features that occasionally appear on the physical plane. Sometimes alchera take the form of natural terrain such as lakes, rivers, or mountains. Other times they appear as seemingly man-made structures like buildings or bridges. Whatever form they take, they appear on the physical plane in one of three ways: manifestation, materialization, or displacement and typically appear only for short periods of time, often during the anniversary of a significant event or during a time of astrological importance (such as an equinox).

Manifest alchera appear on the physical plane as they do on the astral, but they are insubstantial and cannot be interacted with by physical beings (much like a manifesting spirit). They appear ghostly and hazy and are believed responsible for some sightings of haunted mansions, ghost ships, UFOs, and the like.

Materialized alchera actually become dual natured, and as such are solid to physical beings and can be interacted with. Materialized alchera cannot replace existing terrain or objects and only appear on otherwise unoccupied physical space. Despite their physical presence, materialized alchera often carry some otherworldly aspect to their nature, such as being cold to the touch or emitting a smoky haze or strange glow. If a character is caught within a materialized alchera when it materializes or de-materializes, he must make a Willpower + Intuition (3) Test or become disoriented, suffering –2 dice pool to all actions for 10 minutes. Getting caught in a (de-)materializing alchera is rarely dangerous; characters are shoved aside to avoid being trapped in materializing walls and placed upon the ground when terrain vanishes out from under them (though gamemasters may alter this to keep the characters on their toes …).

Displacement alchera are similar to materialized alchera, except they actually replace existing terrain, sending it to an unknown location for the duration of the alchera's appearance. Wherever the terrain is sent to, living creatures do not go with it—they are instead moved and disoriented, similar to being caught in a materializing alchera. Magical constructs placed upon the original terrain—such as sustained spells or wards—collapse when the original terrain is displaced, but otherwise the original terrain reappears when the alchera vanishes as if nothing ever happened to it. Displacement alchera, like materialized alchera, are dual natured and can be interacted with by physical beings.

ON LOCATION: *The Deep Lacuna (Alchera, Los Angeles)*

Here is a brain-twister for you: how do you flood a city that sits on high ground? The answer: you undermine it. The twin Californian earthquakes of 2069 were devastating, but it wasn't just the earthquakes that managed to sink large portions of the California coastline, including substantial sections of Los Angeles and San Diego. During the simultaneous earthquakes, traumatized witnesses reported seeing vast sections of Los Angeles collapse into massive sinkholes, which then flooded with water from the Pacific. The disease-ridden toxic stew that followed kept scientists and researchers from investigating the claims until recently, but what they have found in the past months is nothing less than amazing.

It appears that an unbelievably massive tunnel complex just *appeared* under parts of California during the earthquakes, especially in the coastal south. With no sign of the earth and subterranean utility works that used to occupy the space of the tunnels, it is believed that the entire underground honeycomb appeared in a fashion similar to the astral phenomenon of alchera, but so far the tunnels have shown no sign of disappearing. Additionally, the tunnels may be linked to the increasingly common appearance of other localized astral phenomena in Los Angeles since 2069.

The surviving locals refer to this tunnel network as the Deep Lacuna, *lacuna* being a Latin word for a gap or hollow and also the origin of the word lagoon, which many parts of today's California can now be considered. Most of the Deep Lacuna remains flooded by the Pacific Ocean, causing the inland lagoons that run through the Central Valley, Los Angeles, and San Diego. There are local stories, however, about dry tunnels or air pockets where the walls are covered in strange carved sigils and statuary. One infamous Los Angeles lagoon preacher claims to have found an ancient subterranean city in the Deep Lacuna, though he also rants about the precursors that lived there hiding from the wrath of God that scoured the Earth in an ancient time, so take it all with a grain or two of salt.

Magical scholars believe that alchera may be formed by emotional historical events or the consensual belief of many metahumans, but so far the appearance of alchera has been too haphazard for true experimentation. Stranger still, not all alchera are even permanent features on the astral landscape. These impermanent astral constructs do tend to linger on the astral plane before and after appearing on the physical, but they will fade from even the astral plane over time. Whether they completely dissipate or simply move somewhere else is unknown, but this observation has fed a competing theory that alchera originate from the metaplanes as they come into conjunction with the Gaiasphere.

Astral Shallows

Astral shallows are spaces where the barrier between physical and astral space becomes so thin that even mundane, physical beings can see into the astral plane. Astral shallows are temporary in nature, most lasting only for a few hours or days, but magicians remain baffled as to what produces them. When standing within the area affected by an astral shallow, a non-magical character may use astral perception (p. 191, *SR4A*), but is not considered dual-natured in the typical sense. While the character can see into the astral plane, he cannot affect or be affected by purely astral forms, unlike a normal astral perceiver. In an astral shallow, one may look but not touch. A magical character who can normally use astral perception and projection may do so within an astral shallow with only one difference: switching from normal to astral perception for these characters only requires a Free Action instead of the normal Simple Action.

Astral Rifts

Sometimes the barrier between planes becomes so thin and strained that it tears, allowing mundanes to actually project themselves to the spiritual realms. These areas are called astral rifts and though they are almost always short-lived phenomena, at least one, the Dunkelzahn Rift in Washington D.C., shows no signs of fading away. Some astral rifts, including the Dunkelzahn Rift, appear as tears in space, whereas others appear as nothing more than aurora-like ripples. No matter how they look, astral rifts function similarly.

Astral rifts are essentially bridges across multiple planes. Each astral rift is connected to a region of physical space and the corresponding region in astral space, or in some cases directly connect the physical plane to a particular metaplane, or both. The barrier between these locales has frayed to such an extent that even the non-Awakened can project into the corresponding astral locale or into the connected metaplane. Furthermore, crossing into the associated metaplane through an astral rift allows the astral traveler to bypass the Dweller on the Threshold (see *Metaplanar Quests*, p. 130). Using an astral rift to reach planes one normally cannot access, however, carries great danger. A non-Awakened being projecting through an astral rift or an uninitiated magician using an astral rift to reach a metaplane must use the astral rift to return to his body. If the rift closes or his physical body is removed from the astral rift's influence before he returns, he is cast adrift until his astral form dissipates and he perishes.

Since astral rifts are two-way bridges, spirits can and sometimes do use astral rifts to cross from the metaplanes into astral space. Unless the spirit uses its own Materialization, Possession, or Inhabitation powers, however, it cannot take on a physical form after emerging from an astral rift.

Deep Rifts: Some astral rifts display additional properties. Deep rifts seem to pull physical forms towards the astral or metaplanar worlds. Within a certain proximity of a deep rift

(which may range from a few meters radius to a few kilometers, and may vary over time), physical beings must succeed in a Willpower + Charisma (3) Test to avoid being forced into astral perception or astral projection, even if they do not usually possess these abilities. If a character fails a test against forced astral projection, they may find their astral form yanked into the astral plane or the connected metaplane.

THE NATURE OF MANA

The astral plane is eternal; it is a spiritual twin of the physical world that never leaves its side. But we know that before the Awakening, the astral plane was far more difficult to reach. A theory first proposed by magical scholars from Tir Tairngire claims that this change is due to the availability of mana. Mana is a form of energy unique to the spiritual worlds and governed by universal laws that do not apply to our physical world. It is believed that mana flows from the metaplanes, though whether it originates from all of them, a few of them, or one particular metaplane is unknown. From its source in the metaplanes, mana seeps into the physical and astral planes, seemingly attracted to the auras of living things and the emotional residue we create.

Magicians can interact with the free flows of mana on the physical and astral planes, channeling it through their own bodies and astral forms and shaping it into the effects commonly known as spells. The Awakened have learned that a greater availability of mana can make spellcasting easier, and they seek out pools of mana drawn to centers of emotional or spiritual significance. Some magicians have even learned to draw from the mana that pockets itself in the auras of the living, using their own blood or the blood of others to power their spells.

Mana is often treated as an unlimited resource by those who use it, but that may not be the case. Our own history shows us a recent time when our world lacked mana, when magicians, metahumans, and paranimals were nothing more than myths. Studies by magical researchers seem to indicate that the level of mana flowing into the astral plane rises and falls, though whether it is a natural cycle or one manipulated by our use of it remains unclear. Someday the mana may recede again and all the advancements of the Awakening will fail us. But perhaps that inevitability is less a worry than what a world might look like that had far greater access to mana than we do now.

BACKGROUND COUNT

Though mana does flow from the metaplanes, it does not circulate uniformly. It swirls and eddies around the Earth, rages down ancient ley lines, and pools in places of great tragedy and wonder. The varying availability of mana creates another layer of the astral topography, shaping areas where magic is strong and weak and giving form to mankind's history and mythology.

When magical scholars discuss the available ambient mana in a given area, they refer to it as *background count*. The simplest model for displaying the range of background count throughout the world is to align it along a horizontal scale. In the center of the scale is the zero point, the current standard ambient mana level that most magicians are familiar with. As the scale moves down, it represents less mana being available, a lower ambient mana level. At the lower end are *voids*, areas

> **ON LOCATION:** *The Watergate Rift (Astral Rift, Washington D.C.)*
>
> The Watergate Rift—perhaps the most infamous astral rift on the globe—sits on the exact spot of the great dragon Dunkelzahn's assassination on the inaugural night of his presidency, just outside the Watergate Hotel. It is a luminescent tear in space that hovers six meters over the still-cratered street, but you'll be hard-pressed to see it at all. The UCAS Army is responsible for observing and safeguarding the Watergate Rift and "for safety concerns" they have built a heavily-guarded warehouse-like enclosure around the rift itself.
>
> Throughout the last months of 2061, while Halley's Comet streaked through the sky, dozens of strange spirits poured through the Watergate Rift into our astral space, culminating with the arrival of the great dragon Ghostwalker as he tore his way out of the shimmering rift. Since the passing of Halley's Comet, activity at the Watergate Rift has calmed, though lately Army personnel and researchers stationed there have reported a periodic pulsing and throbbing from the rift, like the beating of a heart.
>
> It is believed that the Watergate Rift bridges into the deep metaplanes, but the exact destination is unknown. Some rumors indicate that Army magicians have entered the rift and returned to tell the tale, but if true, the military is staying silent about it. The physical bodies of twenty-six people who entered the rift either intentionally or accidentally remain comatose and are medically maintained at the nearby Army-controlled Riverside Hospital.
>
> … This article has been tagged by someone in your network.
> … Accessing tag.
> • Not quite. Twenty-five comatose patients are on life support at Riverside. The twenty-sixth, Tanya Reilly, was also the first person to be sucked into the rift shortly after it appeared. I have it on good authority that she awoke from her coma a few months ago, thrashing and ranting. She managed to carve four symbols into her own flesh with her fingernails and then passed away. The Army is keeping the whole thing under wraps as they try to decipher the symbols. I have heard that three of the symbols are similar to ancient cuneiform words for "birth," "death," and "transformation." The fourth is a complete mystery.
> • Elijah

empty of mana entirely, but before that you find *mana ebbs* where mana is available, though its scarcity makes it more difficult to draw upon. As the scale moves upwards, it indicates a higher than standard ambient level. In most cases this mani-

If background count reduces a character's Magic to attribute to 0 or less, he is rendered unable to use any magical abilities within the area. A background count-modified Magic attribute counts for all uses of magic, including dice pools and limitations imposed on the Force of spells or spirits. Additionally, the process of gathering and shaping mana is more difficult in areas with background count, so the absolute value of the background count is also added to the Force whenever a character resists magical Drain. Adepts that suffer a reduced Magic attribute temporarily lose powers as a result; the player must choose 1 Power Point worth of powers to be nullified for each point of Magic reduction. In the case of mystic adepts, the gamemaster determines whether the reduced Magic attribute deducts from his magician abilities or adept powers first, but the player gets to decide on which adept powers are temporarily lost. At the gamemaster's discretion, paranormal critters may also lose access to some of their critter powers as a result of a reduced Magic attribute.

Spirits, being creatures of living mana, are perhaps even more vulnerable to background count. A spirit's Force is reduced in the same manner as a character's Magic, thus affecting the spirit's attribute and spirit powers as well. A spirit is disrupted (*Disruption*, p. 94) if it's Force is reduced to 0 or less.

fests in *domains,* areas of emotional, natural or spiritual significance that cause a pooling of mana. In extreme situations, however, *mana warps* may result—places where chaotic and twisted mana floods into a region that has experienced great trauma or a natural power spike.

Background Count and Magic

Whether positive or negative, in game terms background count reduces a character's Magic attribute by its absolute value. In mana ebbs and voids, this represents the scarcity of available mana, making it more difficult to work magic. Though mana is readily available in domains and mana warps, the intensity of so much focused mana works against the magician in a similar way, tainting any attempts to use magic—unless the area is aspected towards his particular tradition (see *Aspect,* below). This means that areas with background counts of –2 and 2 affects a character's Magic the same; a character with Magic 4 would act with a modified Magic attribute of 2 in both areas.

Pre-existing wards, mana barriers, active foci, sustained spells, and quickened/anchored spells are similarly affected. Reduce their Force by the absolute value of the background count. If the Force is reduced to zero or less, wards and mana barriers will collapse, foci will deactivate, and spells will fizzle. The enchantment on a quickened/anchored spell or ward/mana barrier will repair itself once removed from the background count, returning to its regular Force.

Background count also affects astral visibility (see p. 114), which affects both assensing and astral combat.

Aspect

In areas of positive background count, the accumulated excess mana takes on a psychoactive charge, affecting how it is used for magical activities. This influence on the collected mana's utility is referred to as its *aspect*. Regions of aspected background count are called *domains*. The aspect of a domain usually adheres to a particular magical tradition (in fact, aspect may be manipulated with Geomancy metamagic, p. 56). A domain's aspect may work for or against an Awakened character, depending on whether that character's tradition meshes with that of the aspect.

If the character works magic in the same paradigm (or one that is sufficiently similar) as the domain's aspect, it is advantageous. In this case, the background count does not reduce Magic as described above. Instead, the Awakened character receives a dice pool bonus for any Magical skill tests and Drain Resistance Tests performed in the domain's area of influence equal to the background count (up to a limit equal to his Magic attribute).

If the character uses magic in a different or contrary paradigm than the domain's aspect, the flavor of the mana makes his efforts more difficult, and he suffers the standard Magic reduction described above.

MANA ANOMALIES

Beyond the simple scale of background count in an area, there are also rare and often temporary anomalies that can affect the use of mana by magicians. *Mana surges* are areas where the flow of mana shifts rapidly, sometimes draining out and sometimes flooding in, which causes fluctuations in spellcasting and summoning. *Mana storms* are regions where raw and chaotic mana actually leaks into the physical world, causing spontaneous elemental and illusory manifestations.

A person entering a mana anomaly may sense it, even if they are not astrally aware or even Awakened. Use the same test used for detecting an astral form passing through one's aura (see *Astral Detection*, p. 193, *SR4A*). Magicians with the Sensing metamagic (p. 58) are automatically aware of the change.

Voids

More than six decades after the Awakening, the presence of mana is taken for granted. But there are areas so deprived of mana that even when it is introduced, it loses cohesion and diffuses into the surroundings. These voids are exceptionally rare on Earth because typically the biosphere and the emotional content of metahumanity can easily support the gathering of mana. As you get farther from the Earth's astral form and the presence of living material, however, astral space becomes one vast void. At the upper mesosphere of Earth's atmosphere and beyond into deep space, the astral plane is a singular void with small pockets of weak mana located at orbital stations and lunar colonies.

Unfortunately, space is not the only place where voids can be found. There are persistent reports of voids (sometimes called *foveae*, or "blind spots") located in Earth's astral space. So far, these earthbound voids have been rare and found in certain areas that have suffered from massive contamination (the radioactive wasteland of the SOX and within the former Chicago Containment Zone) or heavy manipulation of local mana levels (the nation of Aztlan). The government of Aztlan has denied requests to study the astral space of their nation and areas of the SOX and Chicago remain dangerous for researchers, so the claims remain unverified. What could possibly cause voids of mana in Earth's astral space also remains a mystery. The exact astral appearance of a void is also unclear; while most magicians who have experienced them describe their environment as pitch dark, they also frequently suffer from hallucinations that make objective descriptions impossible.

Voids have background count ratings ranging from –7 to –12. The first effect of a void is that it renders most magicians unable to use magic, due to the absence of available mana; re-

> ### FLEXIBLE ASPECT
> At the gamemaster's discretion, aspect may be more fluid and more flexible than described here. Aspect could, for example, apply only to certain uses of magic (a domain that favors conjuring, for example) rather than tradition. Likewise, an aspect could be so broad as to encompass multiple traditions (embracing any paradigm that treats the Earth as sacred, for example, such as Druidism or Wicca). An aspect could also work in specific opposition to a tradition or activity (such as spellcasting), working as standard background count against that, but aspected for everything else. Finally, aspect could even be partially neutral—aspected for and/or against some traditions/activities, but treated as neutral (no background count) for everything else. After all, magic has a knack for being unpredictable, and it will keep your players guessing.

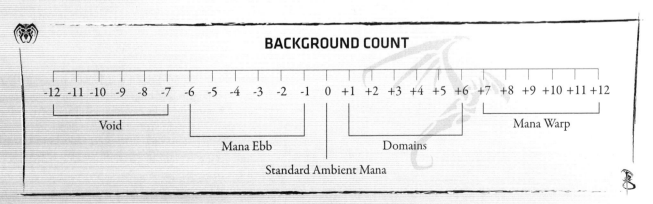

BACKGROUND COUNT

–12 –11 –10 –9 –8 –7 –6 –5 –4 –3 –2 –1 0 +1 +2 +3 +4 +5 +6 +7 +8 +9 +10 +11 +12

Void — Mana Ebb — Standard Ambient Mana — Domains — Mana Warp

ON LOCATION: Crater Lake (Rating –4 Mana Ebb, Tir Tairngire)

Nowadays it is hard to imagine that Crater Lake used to be one of Tir Tairngire's most beloved tourist attractions. The beauty of the region certainly lends itself to visitors, with tree-lined volcanic cliffs surrounding a placid lake sitting in an ancient volcanic caldera. Even though tourists enjoyed this tranquil and revered region for decades, however, it has been sealed off by the Tir military for over fifteen years. No explanation has been given, but it likely has something to do with the strange behavior of mana at Crater Lake.

Observers claim that for a handful of years before and after Crater Lake's military containment, the lake was a powerful domain rich with magical power. That changed in 2057, approximately at the time of Dunkelzahn's assassination and the declaration of a "state of emergency" within Tir Tairngire. Since that time, Crater Lake's magical power has leveled off and even moved in reverse, draining mana from the surrounding area. Today it is a deepening mana ebb, but if the Tir government knows why this is occurring, they are certainly not saying.

The shake-ups in Tir Tairngire's government have not succeeded in lifting the veil of secrecy from Crater Lake. Peace Force troops are still stationed there and still intent on keeping gawkers out. Despite this, "eyewitness accounts" describe huge geometric constructs floating above an island in Crater Lake called *Tesetelinestéa* (or "Skull of the Dragon" in Sperethiel). Other rumors have mentioned "crazed spirits" engaging the Tir soldiers, which seems puzzling, since most spirits try to avoid mana ebbs.

duce the character's Magic by the background count rating, as described under *Background Count and Magic*, p. 118.

If a character exposes himself to the astral plane (either by astrally perceiving or projecting) while in a void, he risks having his astral form torn apart as it dissipates into the surrounding emptiness—as would air in a vacuum. Each Combat Turn the character is astrally active, he suffers Physical damage with a Damage Value equal to the absolute value of the void's rating (so a –8 Rating void deals a DV of 8). Dual-natured or astrally-perceiving characters resist this damage with their Body attribute, while pure astral forms (such as projecting characters) resist with their Willpower attribute. If the character has any form of astral armor (such as the Mystic Armor critter power), it applies to this test. Characters experiencing this damage often suffer disorientation and terrible hallucinations, and the gamemaster may chose to apply Negative mental qualities to any character who has suffered astral exposure to a void.

Thomas is a Grade 5 initiate and magical researcher working for a Saeder-Krupp operation on the moon's surface. He has a Magic attribute of 11 and a Spellcasting skill of 6. The moon is lacking a substantial gaiasphere of its own, so the laboratory where he works is considered a Rating –9 Void. Thomas attempts to cast a Force 4 Phantasm spell. While this would be routine and simple on Earth, it pushes his limits here on the moon. Since the void reduces his Magic by its rating, his effective Magic here is only 2 (11 – 9). A Force 4 spell is the limit of his ability here (Magic x 2) and since the Force is higher than his effective Magic, the Drain is Physical. He rolls 8 dice on his Spellcasting Test (6 Spellcasting + 2 Magic) but he will have to resist a great deal of Drain just to pull off this small spell. The typical Drain for a Force 4 Phantasm spell is 4 ((Force ÷ 2) + 2) but here the void adds the absolute value of its rating to the Force of the spell for calculating Drain. Instead of facing a Drain Value of 4, Thomas has to face a Drain as if it was a Force 13 (4 + 9) spell, or a Drain Value of 8 ((13 ÷ 2) + 2). Even a simple illusion can be a difficult task for a trained initiate this far from Earth.

Mana Ebbs

While similar to voids in many ways, mana ebbs are far less severe. The reduced flow of mana within a mana ebb is restrictive but manageable, and enough mana is present to keep astral forms from losing cohesion. This means that astral forms and dual-natured creatures entering a mana ebb do not suffer damage, but attempting to shape mana into an effect within a mana ebb (such as spellcasting or conjuring) will be dampened (see *Background Count and Magic*, p. 118). Mana ebbs have background count ratings ranging from –1 to –6.

Astral space within a mana ebb tends to appear dimmer than it should. Auras and astral forms do not radiate as vividly as they do in standard astral space. Aside from the mana ebbs in the upper stratosphere and lower mesosphere, most mana ebbs are temporary anomalies. Dual-natured creatures and spirits are typically uncomfortable within a mana ebb, even though it doesn't cause them any harm directly.

Domains

A fascinating and important discovery about the nature of mana is that not only does it tend to pool and collect around areas of natural beauty and emotional or psychological significance, but its properties can actually be influenced by that outpouring of emotion. Depending on the events that caused the mana to pool in one region or flow along a certain path, that mana can be easier to use for some purposes and more difficult to use for others (see *Aspect*, p. 118).

By its nature, the background count in a domain is aspected. The cause for mana pooling or traveling along a domain is also the source of its aspect. For instance, the environmental and psychoactive blight of a toxic waste dump draws mana to collect around the site, becoming background count. The same blight "flavors" the mana, tainting its use by most magicians but favoring its use if the magician is a toxic shaman. Similarly, the strong religious significance of a druidic stone circle draws mana to collect around

the site, making it easier to use for druids but harder to use if one does not work their magic along a druidic paradigm.

Domains do not always fall in the shape of circular pools of mana, of course. Sometimes a domain takes on the shape of a line or river, a pathway along which mana flows from one destination to another. These lines crisscross the globe along routes of historical or mystical significance, known by different cultures as mana lines, ley lines, song lines, dragon lines, and countless other terms. In astral space, the bright eddies and swirling pools of mana make domains easily recognizable. Particularly powerful permanent domains are colloquially known in the Sixth World as power sites or mana nexi.

Domains have a background count rating ranging from +1 to +6, and affect magic as described under *Background Count and Magic*, p. 118. Domains, unlike voids and mana ebbs, can be influenced by metamagic techniques such as Cleansing (p. 55) and Geomancy (p. 56). Domains also remain permanent at least until the source of domain is removed (such as the toxic waste producing a toxic domain). Even then, many domains persist until formally cleansed, while others take decades to become neutral.

> *Vyk is about to learn that facing a toxic shaman on his own turf is a bad idea. The shaman, being chased by Vyk's team, has taken shelter in his own territory, a sludge field produced by the runoff from a local chemical company. The sludge field is a Rating 3 domain, its background count aspected to toxic magic. So now the toxic shaman gets a bonus of 3 dice on any Sorcery or Conjuring Tests made here, while Vyk will suffer a Magic reduction of 3 since Vyk's totem, Bear, is certainly not aligned with toxic magic.*

Mana Warps

Sometimes, obeying laws not yet understood, mana inexplicably flares and surges chaotically. Other times the emotional events that create domains are twisted and dark, such as the death-tinged domain at Auschwitz. Since the Awakening, some events have combined sudden and heart-wrenching emotion with massive manipulations of mana. When these rare conjunctions (natural or man-made) occur, mana can become trapped in a violent and maddening mass that is dangerous to draw from or travel through.

Mana warps have a background count rating between +7 and +12. Mana becomes caught within the warp and builds up as if under pressure, flooding out if a magician attempts to work magic in the area. This affects characters as described under *Background Count and Magic*, p. 118. Aspect does not apply in a mana warp—the turbulent flows shred apart any psychoactive imprints left upon the ambient mana.

Exposing oneself to the astral plane within a mana warp is as dangerous as attempting to tap its power. Dual-natured beings and astral forms are buffeted by painful, roiling mana that flays their soul and drives them mad. Mana warps cause damage to dual-natured beings and astral forms in the same manner as voids (see *Voids*, p. 119). Within the astral space of a mana warp, one can only experience madness and senseless chaos. The gamemaster may apply Negative mental qualities to any character that has been exposed to a mana warp in astral space.

DOMAIN EXAMPLES

Rating 1: These domains include areas where the emotional impact was significant but brief or areas that are of minor spiritual or magical significance. Examples include the scene of a violent crime or passionate love affair, a bar frequented regularly by the Awakened, or a rural church that is important to its small town residents.

Rating 2: These domains are generated by the emotional impact of a great number of people or by a steady emotional, spiritual or magical influence over a long period of time. The sold-out concert of a legendary musician could qualify, as could a maximum security prison or enchanter's workshop.

Rating 3: These domains are created by a significant event in the recent past (usually within the last century). The event may be long over, but the area still reflects the event in some way. Examples include the site of a major battle or the ruined land from an environmental accident. An important cathedral or monastery where a great spiritual event occurred also qualifies.

Rating 4: These domains were not only the site of a significant event, but also still experience that event or something similar on an irregular basis. A battlefield that is honored with an emotional yearly consecration, for example, or a public park that once witnessed a massive and brutal riot and is still occasionally hosts political demonstrations.

Rating 5: These domains experienced a significant event, and the conditions that created it still exist (a meltdown area still scarred by radiation, or a major battlefield that still sees regular fighting). Sites of great emotional, spiritual, or magical significance that aren't tied to a specific event but have generated significance over time also qualify, such as Arlington National Cemetery or Stonehenge.

Rating 6: These domains were created by historic events of epic scope that have significance to most of humanity. The blast sites of Hiroshima and Nagasaki are Rating 6 domains, as is the former Nazi death camp of Auschwitz and the Native American "Re-Education Center" at Abilene.

Mana Surges

In some areas of the world, the flows of mana are strained by overuse, frequent manipulation, or even unpredictable natural tides. With mana constantly pulled this way and that, attempts to manipulate mana may end up with more or less mana

ON LOCATION: Cermak Blast Zone (Rating 7 Mana Warp, Chicago)

The Cermak Blast Zone is perhaps the starkest reminder of the traumatic struggle between metahumanity and insect spirits waged within the Chicago Containment Zone. It is here that a tactical nuclear warhead was detonated in a desperate attempt to stop thousands of insect spirits from completing a powerful magical ritual to invest their captive hosts. The blast site itself, however, is smaller than it should be. The effects seem to have been somehow *contained*, since the damage and radiation was intensely focused at the site of the explosion but drop off substantially after a radius of just a few hundred meters.

Even more devastating than the physical site of the explosion is the chaos left in the astral plane. Twisted streamers of warped mana swirl around the blast zone emanating feelings of nausea and pain. Visitors to the Cermak Blast Zone have claimed to be able to see insectoid faces or screaming metahuman faces in the clouds of darkened mana, but those stories cannot be confirmed. Spirits and dual-natured paracritters react violently to the Cermak Blast Zone and will typically avoid getting closer than half a kilometer from the center. Even the clouds of magic-draining FAB III bacteria in Chicago are seemingly unable to feed from the mana warp here and are instead destroyed by it if they get too close.

Perhaps the most frightening truth about the Cermak Blast Zone is that dozens, if not hundreds, of insect spirits are trapped in torpor in the hive below the blast zone. They were knocked into a perpetual sleep by the nuclear blast but can be awakened if magic is performed near the site. If they are awakened, they must first pass through the damaging mana warp to escape the hive, which has made the few insect spirits to escape maddened and even more violent than usual.

---

than intended. Unlike mana ebbs and domains, mana surges are unpredictable in their manifestation; even their effects may not prove consistent while a magician is within their area of influence.

When a magician uses any of the Sorcery or Conjuring skills within the area of a mana surge, roll 1D6 and consult the Mana Surge Table. In cases where the Force of the spellcasting or conjuration effort increases or decreases, be sure to adjust the results and the Drain. Increases in Force are limited by the magician's Magic attribute x 2.

MANA SURGE TABLE

1D6 Result	Effect
1	Glitch
2	Reduce Force by 1D6
3–4	No Effect
5	Increase Force by 1D6
6	Witches' Mark

If a 1 is rolled, the spell or summoning is altered as if the magician had suffered a glitch. Spells may take on unexpected cosmetic differences or quirks (see p. 184, *SR4A*) while a conjuration attempt may result in a particularly anti-social or odd spirit (see p. 188, *SR4A*). If a 6 is rolled, the magician has temporarily earned what the magical community calls a "witches' mark." The spell or summoning fails completely and something absolutely unexpected happens around the magician. Frogs may rain from the sky, auras may flicker visibly in physical space around the magician, paranormal vermin may suddenly be attracted to the magician, etc. The gamemaster is encouraged to be creative.

Mana Storms

Mana storms are violent and unpredictable disturbances that seemingly roam at random and leave swathes of magical destruction or chaos in their wake. Mana storms whip up the mana on both the physical and astral planes simultaneously, often creating spontaneous elemental and illusory effects. With the exceptions of the Maya Cloud around Tibet and the mana storms around Sydney, Australia, mana storms are typically sudden and short-lived events, lasting mere hours before fading away.

Mana storms originate inside a domain or mana warp, and as they travel they carry those effects with them. A mana storm that spins off of a Rating 4 domain becomes a moving Rating 4 domain with the same aspect as its source. On the astral plane, a mana storm appears as swirling cloud system of glowing mana, crackling with energy, often tinged with the emotional signature of the domain or mana warp that birthed it. In the physical world, a mana storm appears similar to violent weather patterns like thunderstorms, hurricanes, or tornadoes, though it also carries with it strange magical effects.

Within a mana storm's physical manifestation, spontaneous elemental and illusory formations are common. The storm literally spins off magical spells, almost always elemental (such as Lightning Bolt or Acid Stream) or illusory (like Trid Phantasm or Chaotic World). These spells are cast with a Spellcasting Test using the mana storm's rating x 2 at a Force equal to the mana storm's rating. Sustainable spells can be sustained indefinitely by a mana storm as long as the storm lasts, since there is more than enough mana to feed the effect.

In addition to the obvious danger of spontaneous magical effects, mana storms carry with them real weather effects in the physical world, often spawned and fed by the elemental magic churning inside them. Rain, hail, blizzards, wind storms, and sand storms are common additional effects of passing mana storms.

ASTRAL SECURITY

The Sixth World is an increasingly dangerous place and the astral plane is no exception. Since the very first days of the Awakening, magical defenses and security have been a priority in

thaumaturgical research, and in this particular field humanity has progressed in leaps and bounds.

WARDS

Wards (see p. 194, *SR4A*) are the astral equivalent of the oldest form of security: the wall. Since they are relatively easy to build and maintain, wards have become the foundation of astral security everywhere. Many corporations have staff magicians who construct and maintain their wards, though independent firms and freelance ward designers are common alternatives. Though wards are versatile approaches to astral security, there are important limitations that must be considered.

The Shape of a Ward

Though wards are limited by the standard 50 cubic meters times the Magic attribute of the creator, the shape of a ward can vary and must be determined at the time of the ward's creation. A variety of basic three-dimensional geometric shapes are possible, such as globes, domes, cubes, rectangles, trapezoids, ovoids, and more. Experiments with complex three-dimensional shapes have proven unstable, however, with the ward collapsing at the completion of the ritual. Experimental astral security designers and astral artists have had to rely on combinations of multiple simple wards to create complex astral constructions.

A ward must also extend at least one meter in every direction from the physical anchor that it is attached to (see below), which prevents ward shapes that are very tiny or very thin in any dimension.

The Physical Anchor

All wards must be anchored to a physical, non-living object. Only an object that casts a shadow onto the astral plane can qualify; living objects with auras or astral forms cannot be used as the anchor for a ward. Because the Earth has an astral form, it cannot be used as an anchor for a ward, which is why many magicians who secure outdoor sites use rock formations or other markers. The created ward may share part of its structure with the physical anchor (such as a ward placed on a physical wall), but it does not have to. If the physical anchor does not make up part of the ward's structure, however, it must at least be present inside the ward. A warded stone, for instance, must sit within the warded area. The physical anchor of a ward must be marked in some way (often with painted symbols, rune carvings, etc.), making them identifiable as a physical ward anchor both in physical and astral space with a Perception or Assensing Test.

Minor damage to the physical anchor will not destroy the ward, but if the physical anchor is utterly destroyed, the ward will collapse. For instance, putting physical holes into a warded wall will not cause the associated ward to collapse, but bringing down the entire wall will. Similarly, chipping a piece off of a warded stone will not collapse its associated ward, but breaking the stone in half would.

Remaining Stationary

Wards are not portable astral objects. The warding ritual creates an astral link between the shadow of the physical anchor and the space being warded. If the physical anchor moves more than a few centimeters from its location at the time of the warding ritual, the entire ward collapses. Ward

ON LOCATION: The Maya Cloud (Rating 8 Mana Storm, Tibet)

Enveloping the entire mountain nation of Tibet is the largest mana anomaly on Earth: the Maya Cloud. It has effectively sealed off Tibet from the rest of the world since the Awakening, foiling nearly all attempts to travel in and out of the secluded Himalayan nation. Magical scholars regularly debate whether the Maya Cloud was created by the Tibetans through a massive magical ritual similar to the Great Ghost Dance or whether it appeared spontaneously during the Awakening. A few have even speculated that the Maya Cloud was created far earlier and merely reappeared when magic returned to the world.

On the physical plane, the Maya Cloud appears as a massive, ever-churning blizzard, a wall of white that stretches as far as the eye can see among the peaks and valleys of the Himalayas. On the astral plane, the Maya Cloud is a swirling miasma of mana that totally obscures astral sight and carries an emotional signature heavy with feelings of betrayal, loneliness, and fear. The twisting eddies of mana within the storm frequently spin themselves into spontaneous spell effects, often elemental effects or illusions inflicted upon those attempting to travel through the Cloud. Though the Maya Cloud itself is painful and dangerous to spirits and many paracritters, unusually high numbers of both linger around the borders of the storm, adding to the dangers of traveling to Tibet. In fact, the Cloud seems to make the spirits more hostile, or perhaps it just attracts more hostile spirits.

The Maya Cloud is only a few kilometers thick around the Tibetan borders, though the mountainous terrain and harsh conditions make for a long and harrowing journey through the mana storm. Electronic equipment does not stand up well under these conditions and the effects of the Maya Cloud further confuse or impede electronic signals, making most communication through the Cloud impossible. Some hardy travelers claim that the Maya Cloud has been steadily weakening since the Awakening, but it is certainly far from weak.

… This article has been tagged by someone in your network.
… Accessing tag.
» There exist five magical Tibetan seals that allow the bearer to pass through the Maya Cloud without suffering from the mana storm (though you still need to contend with the mountainous terrain, cold, and high altitude). Dunkelzahn used to own one, the Seal of the Green Gloves, but these days all five are in the hands of an order of Tibetan monks known as the Sect of the Lotus Throne. They use the seals to travel outside Tibet and keep their nation in contact with the rest of the world.
» Am-mut

designers must carefully choose their physical anchors; choosing an object that must be moved obviously makes a poor choice.

Wards are Exclusive

Wards cannot be layered or overlap in the same area of astral space. Magicians seeking redundant astral security measures will often put a series of wards in place, much like a gauntlet an intruder would have to pass through, but they cannot place multiple wards on the same space in an effort to make intrusion exponentially more difficult. Attempting to place a new ward where it would intersect with another ward results in the new ward simply failing.

Fooling Wards

Sometimes a magician just has to get through a ward. Attacking it or pressing through it are viable options (see p. 194, *SR4A*), but both alert the ward's creator to the action, which the magician may want to avoid. The most covert way of bypassing a ward is to take advantage of the fact that every ward allows its creator to pass through it freely. If an intruding magician's aura mimics an aura approved to freely move through the ward, the intruding magician may pass harmlessly through without alerting anyone to the action.

Only magicians with the Masking metamagic technique (p. 198, *SR4A*) or spirits with the Aura Masking power (p. 98) may attempt to synchronize their aura with a ward in such a way. In order to synchronize one's aura so it mimics a ward's creator, the synchronizing magician or spirit must be able to see the creator's aura to use as a reference. One way to do this is to track the astral link present between a ward and its creator (see *Astral Tracking*, p. 193, *SR4A*). Then an Opposed Test is made between the initiate's Intuition + Magic + initiate grade and the ward's Force x 2. If the intruding magician succeeds, the ward no longer inhibits them. If the ward wins, it continues to inhibit the intruding magician, but does not alert its creator until the intruding magician tries to force his way through by another method.

If tracking the ward's creator through the astral plane isn't an option (the creator is behind another barrier, the intruding magician doesn't want to risk being spotted, etc.), the intruding magician can instead use a material, sympathetic, or symbolic link for the synchronization process (see *Material Links*, p. 28). Any dice pool penalties incurred by using those links in ritual sorcery also penalize the Opposed Test for fooling the ward.

Spirits and Wards

As astral beings, spirits are capable of creating wards and will do so for a magician at the cost of a service. Further warding rituals to extend the duration of a ward count as additional services and attempts to breach the ward notify the spirit that created the ward, not the magician who conjured the spirit (though many spirits will convey the information to their master). If a spirit's terms of service are expended and it returns to its home metaplane, any wards it created will continue to function until their duration ends. The spirit is no longer bound to inform the magician if the ward is breached when its service is up, however, and most will not bother.

If a spirit has the Aura Masking power (p. 98), it is capable of creating masking wards (below).

WARDS WITH A TWIST

A basic ward is essentially just a visible wall that alerts its creator when it is attacked. It does the job well enough, as long as the job is simply to be a barrier to intruders. Astral security experts, however, have researched and developed advanced wards that can do more than just be a simple barrier. Creating these advanced wards is more difficult than creating a basic ward, but their existence allows for more flexibility when designing astral security schemes.

Creating an advanced ward uses the same test as creating a basic ward (see *Wards,* p. 194, *SR4A*) but has a threshold of 3. Net hits over the required threshold apply to the duration of the ward, as per standard ward creation rules. In some cases, an advanced ward may have further limitations, such as size restrictions or the requirement that the creator knows a certain metamagic technique for their construction. These limitations, where applicable, are included in the description for the advanced wards.

Alarm Ward

Alarm wards are designed to be as unobtrusive as possible and simply alert its creator when an intruding spell or astral form has passed through it. Instead of being solid and opaque like a typical astral barrier, alarm wards are specially camouflaged to blend into the local astral space. In order to notice an alarm ward before passing through it, the observer must make an Assensing + Intuition (3) Test. Note that because alarm wards still require a marked physical anchor, the alarm ward designer must be careful to choose an anchor which isn't immediately noticeable to the intruder.

Alarm wards are intentionally diffuse astral constructs and as such allow just about any astral form (Force 1 or greater) to easily press through them without a required test. Doing so will alert the ward's creator, however, which is the intended purpose of an alarm ward. Though alarm wards are difficult to spot before passing through them, it is not as difficult to realize you have just walked through one. Use the standard test for noticing that an astral form has passed through your aura (see *Astral Detection,* p. 193, *SR4A*).

Attacking an alarm ward notifies its creator just as well as passing through it, so the best way to foil an alarm ward is to synchronize your aura to it (see *Fooling Wards,* p. 124). Sometimes alarm wards are deliberately tripped by intruders to serve as a distraction from astral intrusion elsewhere.

Charged Ward

Unlike basic wards, charged wards actually fight back when attacked in astral combat. The ward designer must possess the Reflecting metamagic technique (p. 61). In most respects, a charged ward acts exactly like a basic ward, but when it is struck in astral combat, the astral form striking it must resist the ward's Force in Stun damage. This damage is resisted with Body (if the attacker is dual natured) or Willpower (if the attacker is an astral form) plus any astral armor the attacker has (such as the adept ability Mystic Armor), like a standard astral attack.

Charged wards will also reflect spells targeted at them. If the ward successfully resists the spell with its Force, it reflects the spell back at the caster at half the spell's original Force (round up). Net hits on the Spell Resistance Test are treated as net hits on the reflected spell's Spellcasting Test.

A charged ward may be "pressed through" like a standard ward (see p. 194, *SR4A*), but if the ward wins the Opposed Test, the intruder must resist the ward's Force + net hits in Stun damage. The safest way to deal with a charged ward is synchronize with it (see *Fooling Wards,* p. 124) and pass harmlessly through it. Unfortunately, charged wards are not easily distinguishable from basic wards; an Assensing + Intuition (3) Test is required to spot the difference.

Masking Ward

Though a masking ward acts as a mana barrier like a basic ward, its main purpose is to conceal magical activity on the astral plane. The ward designer must possess the metamagic technique of Masking (p. 198, *SR4A*). Similar to alarm wards, masking wards are transparent on the astral plane, but they also conceal any magical activity performed inside of them, making the magical activity appear mundane to an outside observer. Only magical effects (such as sorcery or conjuring) that have a Force lower than the Force of the masking ward may be masked this way.

Since the ward is transparent, noticing it requires an outside observer to either come into contact with it (since it is still a solid astral barrier) or make a successful Assensing + Intuition (3) Test. Being aware of the ward, however, does not mean you can see through the masking effect. Piercing the illusions of the masking ward requires an Opposed Test between your Assensing + Intuition and the ward's Force x 2. If the observer is successful, the ward's concealment does not work for that observer, but subsequent observers must make their own tests. Destroying the ward through astral combat will break the masking ward's concealment.

Polarized Ward

A basic ward is hazily opaque to anyone other than the ward's creator and those he has specifically approved. Polarized wards, however, are only opaque from either inside or outside the ward, much like mirrored glass. Aside from being transparent or opaque depending on viewing direction, polarized wards function as basic wards and block unauthorized spells and astral forms. Polarized wards are difficult to notice from the transparent side, however, and require an Assensing + Intuition (3) Test to see.

Trap Ward

Trap wards combine an alarm ward with a basic ward, using the alarm as a trigger that solidifies the astral barrier around the intruder *after* he has passed through. The ward designer must

ASTRAL PATROL MODIFIERS

Situation	Modifier
Patrol area is less than 2,000 square meters	+2
Patrol area is 2,001 to 5,000 square meters (roughly an acre)	+1
Patrol area is 5,001 to 10,000 square meters (roughly a city block)	+0
Patrol area is greater than 10,000 square meters	–1 per additional 10,000 square meters

possess the Anchoring metamagic technique (p. 59). Trap wards appear and function exactly like alarm wards (p. 125) until they are triggered. Once an intruder passes through the ward and sets off the alarm, the ward changes composition, transforming into a solid astral barrier. Though the trap ward can be destroyed in astral combat or pressed through like a basic ward (see *Passing through Barriers*, p. 194, *SR4A*), the intent is that it slows down the intruder long enough for security to respond to the alarm. Trap wards are only triggered by astral forms, not spells.

TOOLS OF THE TRADE

Besides wards, there are many natural and supernatural tools utilized for astral security. Some corporations raise and train dual-natured paranimals to patrol alongside skilled handlers as the creature's astral awareness expands the patrol's abilities. Barghests, hellhounds, and nagas are just some examples of Awakened animals that have been successfully trained and used for security purposes. Some criminal syndicates have also been known to turn to Awakened drugs and magical compounds for astral security, as these drugs allow mundane guards to perceive or even project into astral space. The associated risks involved with Awakened drug use prevent them from being regularly used as a solution for most mainstream security, but in businesses where human life is already of little value, the benefits outweigh the risks.

The two most common alternatives to wards, however, are patrolling spirits and the utilization of dual-natured plant-life. Bound spirits work tirelessly in service of their masters, making them desirable to corporations looking for simple solutions. Awakened plant-life can offer a variety of different security options and the plants themselves are far cheaper and easier to maintain than trained Awakened animals.

Astral Patrols

Corporations often make use of spirits as astral guards, patrolling a region of astral space and reporting or attacking intruders. Astral patrolling is considered a remote service (see *Remote Services*, p. 187, *SR4A*) because it typically takes the spirit outside the magician's immediate area. Reporting an intruder does not count as a separate service from patrolling, but attacking an intruder often does, meaning that unbound spirits typically cannot be ordered to attack intruders while patrolling. Though spirits typically patrol from the astral rather than the physical, they can be tasked to look for physical or astral intruders, or both.

As a spirit patrols a region of astral space, its chance to discover an intruder primarily revolves around an Assensing + Intuition Test with the appropriate astral visibility modifiers applied (see *Astral Visibility*, p. 114). If more than one spirit is patrolling the same area, treat the test as teamwork (p. 65, *SR4A*), or simply use the largest dice pool from the group and apply +1 die per additional spirit, up to +5. Modifiers from the Astral Patrol Modifiers table should also be applied, as appropriate.

Awakened Ivy

Awakened ivy is exactly what its name implies: a species of the typical ivy vine that is dual natured. Because it is dual natured, it has an active astral form and acts as a barrier to other dual-natured or astrally-projecting beings. To a dual-natured being, awakened ivy is little more than an annoyance. If the vines are physically moved out of the way, the ivy's astral form is moved also. Astrally-projecting beings that cannot materialize, however, have no way to move the physical vine out of the way, leaving them with only one option: astral combat. The astrally-projecting being can try to destroy the ivy's astral form as he would a normal astral barrier, but destroying the ivy's astral form will kill the ivy, causing it to rapidly and visibly wilt on the physical plane.

Awakened ivy is rated by Force, which usually corresponds to the ivy's density on a given surface. The higher the Force, the more expensive Awakened ivy is per square meter covered. If the Awakened ivy is supplied with steady nutrients, it can survive for decades, which makes it a cheap astral security option for the exteriors of many buildings.

Fluorescing Astral Bacteria (FAB)

FAB is a genetically engineered strain of bacteria with properties that affect astral forms. It was originally designed as a security measure, but certain breakthroughs (read: research accidents) led to the use of FAB as a weapon against astral beings as well. FAB comes in three strains, each with an increasing level of astral interaction.

FAB I is an engineered bacteria kept in aerosol dispensers. The bacteria is highly sensitive to the effect of an astral form passing through it, causing it to die and release a chemical that glows under ultraviolet light. When dispersed into the air, FAB I can reveal the presence of an astral form, which leaves a glowing silhouette of dead bacteria under UV light.

FAB II is dual natured. It provides a barrier to astral movement when placed in a nutrient suspension inside a physical container, like a wall. The bacterial colony has a Force rating that is used for astral barrier purposes. Airborne FAB

Street Magic

II has no effect on astral forms other than preventing the use of astral movement faster than 100 meters per Combat Turn and applying a –2 astral visibility dice pool modifier inside the FAB cloud. UV light can also reveal the passage of astral forms through the bacterial cloud as the FAB is displaced, leaving a dark "shadow" where the astral form is.

FAB III is a dual-natured mutant variant of FAB II that actively seeks out and feeds on magical energies and astral forms. It seeks out astrally active Awakened characters and critters, foci, and astral objects such as wards in order to latch onto them. FAB III travels in clouds. Each cloud has a Force rating measuring the cloud's strength and covers a spherical area with a radius in meters roughly equal to its rating. At any given time, the area of the cloud may be larger or smaller as the bacteria move around astral space and feed. When a cloud attaches itself to a target, it usually contracts into a smaller volume so that all of the bacteria in the cloud can be closer to the food source. On the physical plane, these clouds of bacteria are invisible and harmless, though they frequently attach themselves to Awakened characters who unwittingly act as carriers. FAB III clouds are visible on the astral plane as a faintly glowing cloud. Unless a character succeeds in an Assensing + Intuition (3) Test, however, he will mistake it for a harmless low-level background count.

A FAB III cloud moves slowly (1 meter per Combat Turn), so it is fairly easy to avoid if you know it's coming. If an astrally active target comes into contact with a FAB III cloud, the cloud will attach to it and begin to drain it of magical energy using its Energy Drain (Magic/Force) power (Touch range, 6 hour Extended Test interval, Stun damage, use Force x 2 for the Opposed Test; see p. 99). The cloud continues to drain its target until there is no more energy or it is killed.

When the cloud reaches Force 11, it splits. The Force 6 cloud continues draining its victim, while a new Force 5 cloud wanders off in search of new prey. A FAB III cloud will always move toward the most potent (highest rating) target; characters who mask their auras (see *Masking*, p.198, *SR4A*) to appear as mundane are ignored.

A character infected with FAB III can simply stop being astrally active to hinder a cloud's feeding. Likewise, objects like foci can simply be deactivated. The target will still be a carrier, however, as the bacteria linger and wait for the target to become astrally active again. Dual-natured critters cannot cease being astrally active and so have no way to discourage a cloud of FAB III. FAB III does not seem to exist on the metaplanes, however, so a spirit can "disinfect" itself by returning to its home metaplane.

FAB III can be killed according to the standard rules in astral combat as well as by the Sterilize spell. The Cure Disease spell can also destroy it; treat FAB III as a disease with Power equal to its Force. If it is reduced to 0, the cloud is destroyed.

FAB III clouds with nothing to feed on begin to starve, losing one point of Force a week. They may feed off areas with positive background count, but they can only survive there for extended periods at a Force equal to the background count.

GloMoss

Native to Central Europe but now grown just about everywhere with hydroponics, glomoss is a dual-natured, hardy moss that is exceptionally sensitive to astral forms and concentrations of mana on the astral plane. Whenever it senses these disturbances in the astral plane, the physical moss displays a bioluminescent pale green glow. Because of this feature, glomoss is often used in conjunction with cameras or photoreceptor sensors as a cheap astral security system. Due to its sensitivity, however, glomoss can result in many false positives triggered by authorized spellcasting, patrolling spirits, and temporary background count. Glomoss is rated by Force, which typically corresponds to its density in a given area. Treat glomoss as if it has the Magic Sense adept power (p. 178), using Force in place of Magic.

Guardian Vines

Guardian vines are a nastier relative of the Awakened ivy, originally found in its native habitat of Amazonia but since bred locally in many regions of the world. Unlike Awakened ivy, however, the astral form of a guardian vine can move independently of its physical form like an astrally-projecting magician, though the vine's astral form always remains rooted to its physical form and can only move a few meters in astral space. Guardian vines actively defend themselves from predators, using both their physical vines and astral vines to trap and ensnare those who come in contact with them.

Both in physical and astral combat, guardian vines attempt to constrict their opponent, using Subduing combat (see p. 161, *SR4A*). Typically a vine will attempt to maintain a grapple and inflict Stun damage until its opponent is knocked unconscious or disrupted. Guardian vines, like Awakened ivy, are rated by Force, which usually reflects a greater density of the vine on the surface it is growing on.

Black Guardian Vines: The rare black vines are a variant form of guardian vines that possess the Energy Drain (Force/Magic) power (Touch range, Stun damage; see p. 99). These vines can apply the Energy Drain ability while maintaining a grappling hold (instead of inflicting Stun damage or improving their hold), siphoning off an opponent's Magic or Force to increase its own growth.

Haven Lily

The haven lily is native to the deserts of North and South America, but can thrive in any dry and well-lit conditions. This dual-natured white lily plant displays the unique ability to create mana ebbs, possibly as a defense mechanism to deter dual-natured creatures (which are uncomfortable in mana ebbs). Corporations have since adapted the use of this plant to engineer the creation of mana ebbs in areas where they would like to limit or restrict the use of magic.

The rating of the mana ebb created by haven lilies depends on the concentration of lilies in the area, but never exceeds Rating 3. Haven lilies are dual natured and can be attacked and easily destroyed on the astral plane. Thinning out a group of haven lilies will lower the rating of the associated mana ebb and killing all the lilies will return the background

METAPLANAR GAZETTEER: Crystalwell

On a far edge of the Pole of Elemental Air, where droplets of elemental water drift in on cold breezes and large snowflakes, floats a strange crystalline structure known as the Crystalwell. The rectangular crystal hangs in the empty air, with cold winds whipping around it. A traveler that journeys close can see pier-like crystals extending from the structure and doorways leading inside.

The Crystalwell is home to Sigh-on-an-Arctic-Wind, a powerful free air elemental, and her legion of lesser air elemental servants. From here she entertains herself by dabbling in the courts of air and water elementals, acting as a diplomat between the two elemental poles. She is a pragmatic and analytical spirit who can often cut through the tempers of more emotional elemental beings, making her an invaluable asset here on the border between planes. In fact, it is not uncommon to see some strange conveyance docked at the crystal piers, whether a vast airship or an inconceivably large flying whale, as spiritual parties seek Sigh-on-an-Artic-Wind's audience.

Hermetic mages who have angered entities from the Poles of Elemental Air or Water often travel to the Crystalwell in an attempt to come to a peaceful compromise. Some ambitious or foolish mages have come in an attempt to force Sigh-on-an-Artic-Wind to part with the considerable secrets she has on many entities in the two planes. Still other mages have found their way here by accident, perhaps after summoning one of the air elementals who typically lives here in service to its frosty mistress.

count to its natural state. Haven lilies cannot grow in areas of higher-than-normal ambient mana, such as domains or mana warps, nor can they grow in voids.

THE METAPLANES

Somewhere, outside the twin planes of the physical and astral, swirls a string of many worlds collectively called the metaplanes. It is within the metaplanes that spirits make their native homes and it is from the metaplanes that mana originates. Beyond that, they are virtually impossible to define. Some say the metaplanes are really just a single infinite expanse divvied up and shaped by spirits. Others say that they are countless separate worlds orbiting the physical and astral planes in a clockwork metaphysical dance. Still others say that the metaplanes have no true form at all and are simply a way of tapping into mankind's universal subconscious, which shifts in nature based on the perceiver. Perhaps the spirits that make the metaplanes their home know the answer, but whatever explanations they give are more deception than truth. Maybe even the spirits do not understand the nature of their homes; they do not care to debate the matter.

WORLDS BEYOND POSSIBILITY

The celestial mechanics of the metaplanes are largely beyond comprehension, but that does not stop some driven magical scholars from attempting to understand them. Some magicians claim that the metaplanes correspond to the types of spirits that exist. The native plane of a spirit of air would be, quite obviously to these theorists, a Metaplane of Air. It becomes very hard to prove or disprove this theory when no definitive map of the Metaplane of Air exists, nor do the descriptions of such a place match up from one magician to another. To complicate the matter further, many magicians claim their spirits come from places unique to their traditional outlook and no one can prove if those places are separate or part of a greater whole. A Chinese magician might track the home of one of his spirits of man to a heavenly city that houses the Celestial Bureaucracy. Is this heavenly city a separate metaplane or simply a region within a greater one? Who can really say? Perhaps the only thing magicians agree upon about the metaplanes is that they can bring you great power or a horrible death. Next to that, the details seem very academic.

Traveling to the Metaplanes

Journeying to the metaplanes is never something to be undertaken lightly. Only an initiate to the higher mysteries of magic can travel to the metaplanes without outside assistance (see *Initiate Powers,* p. 198, *SR4A*). Even then, the initiate must first face the Dweller on the Threshold, as detailed under *Metaplanar Quests,* p. 130. It is possible for mundanes and non-initiates to travel to the metaplanes, but only through the effort of some outside source, such as a spirit's Astral Gateway power (p. 98) or contact with an astral rift (p. 116). Certain Awakened drugs and magical compounds can also cause a mundane or non-initiate to enter the metaplanes, though their use is often dangerous and the user's destination is unpredictable.

Metaplanar Physics and Metaphor

A traveler to the metaplanes experiences each plane much like he experiences the physical world (rather than astral space). The look and feel of a metaplane may differ quite drastically from any place in the real world, however, and even the physical laws may be different. The ineffable nature of the metaplanes makes describing them difficult, but each place within the metaplanes can be described according to a specific *metaphor*. This metaphor governs the physical characteristics, environment, and laws of the place—including the form the character takes (see *Metaplanar Forms*). Metaphors often suit the spirits or the tradition that correspond to that particular metaplane, and may range from the simple (an underwater metaphor for the Plane of Water) to the bizarre (see the Crystalwell description, p. 128).

Street Magic

Metaplanar Forms

When a traveler has arrived in a metaplane, he takes on a metaplanar form, similar to an astral form (see *Astral Forms*, p. 191, *SR4A*). Damage inflicted upon a metaplanar form can be either Physical or Stun damage and the magician's earthbound body will feel and react to such damage. Similarly, damage inflicted on the earthbound body will affect the metaplanar form. If a magician is killed in the metaplanes, the earthbound body will go comatose, much like when a magician dies while astrally projecting (see *While You Were Out…*, p. 193, *SR4A*).

Unlike an astral form, however, the metaplanar form is based entirely on the metaplanar visitor's physical body—modified as necessary to fit the plane's metaphor. Physical attributes are used on the metaplanes, as are the standard rules for combat. In many cases, any cyberware or bioware the visitor possesses will also function in the metaplane, though it may appear differently, depending on the metaphor. For instance, if the metaplane were based on an Industrial Age society, cyberware may appear as steampunk pistons and clockwork gears. If the metaplane is naturalistic and wild, cyberware may appear as fetishes and charms worn by the visitor. If the metaphor of the metaplane supports the necessary technology, hacking and rigging may be possible (at the gamemaster's discretion). Astral perception is also typically possible on the metaplanes, but a metaplanar form can never astrally project as he is already outside his real body, no matter how real his metaplanar form may seem.

Unlike astral projection, a metaplanar visitor can maintain his metaplanar form indefinitely (unless he is in the deep metaplanes, see below); the traveler's body simply remains in a coma-like state until he returns. Time within a metaplane is subjective, however, so what may feel like weeks in a metaplane make only take a few minutes of real world time (and vice versa).

The Deep Metaplanes

Over the course of decades, initiates have visited the metaplanes countless times, journeying to the places where the spirits they conjure originate. Even differences in tradition do not bar an initiate from these planes; a hermetic mage may visit a metaplane that is home to many spirits of beasts as easily as he would visit the home metaplane of the fire elementals he conjures. Though teaching and belief may limit the spirits a magician can conjure, these metaplanes and the Earth share a link that allows spirits and magicians to travel between the worlds—but this is not so with all of the metaplanes.

Some metaplanes—collectively known as the deep metaplanes—are harder to reach and more dangerous to explore. Scholars are unsure what makes these metaplanes different, but many believe there is a link between the difficulty of reaching these metaplanes and the ambient mana level on Earth. An initiate may not simply choose to journey to a deep metaplane as he would a typical metaplane; he must be guided there. In most cases, this requires a spirit native to the particular deep metaplane to guide the initiate, but there are

METAPLANAR GAZETTEER: Emergence Lake

According to Navajo creation myth, the Navajo people ascended to the Earth from the depths of a primordial lake known as the Emergence Lake. Around the shore of this lake grow massive stalks of all the four sacred plants: corn, squash, beans, and tobacco, and the nearby Rain People carry the clouds that blanket the region with life-giving water.

The wise Najavo shamans who have managed to reach the Emergence Lake through vision quests have found it to be exactly as the legend describes. A massive, bottomless lake stretches as far as the eye can see, its shoreline worn into a path by the journeying feet of thousands of Navajo ancestors. Along the path stretch the stalks of the sacred plants, reaching up to the clouds born on the heads of the Rain People, giant spirits of the air who circle the Lake perpetually. The Rain People will be reluctant to talk to the visiting shaman as they are already burdened by their important rain-giving task, but the spirits of water who swim in the Emergence Lake are much more cooperative. Also, if a shaman wanders the lake-side path long enough, he is bound to come across spirits of man, ancient Navajo ancestors who have returned to the Lake that birthed their people.

rare cases where an astral rift may open to a deep metaplane or an astral construct or link may point the way.

The spirits that are native to these deep metaplanes are themselves strange and alien, different in many ways from the typical spirits that magicians deal with. These extraplanar denizens are known to include insect spirits and shedim, among other strange creatures (see *Extraplanar Menaces*, p. 148), but no one knows how many more beings may live in these metaplanar depths. Encounters with these spirits have often been disastrous, but fortunately for metahumanity it is just as difficult for these spirits to travel to Earth as it is for magicians to travel to them.

When these spirits enter the astral space around Earth, they suffer from Evanescence, a steady degradation of their astral forms (see *Evanescence*, p. 148). Similarly, if a magician finds his way to the deep metaplanes, his own metaplanar form begins to degrade. Every hour the magician spends in a deep metaplane, his Magic attribute is temporarily reduced by 1 (returning at the same rate once he leaves the deep metaplanes). If his Magic is reduced to 0, his metaplanar form is traumatically torn from the deep metaplane and forced suddenly back to his body. Many magicians disrupted in this way take on psychological traumas related to the deep metaplane they visited. The gamemaster may inflict Negative mental qualities upon a character who suffers this disruption. A magician disrupted while visiting the home of insect spirits, for example, may develop a severe phobia of insects. If there are methods for magicians to avoid this degradation of their metaplanar forms in the deep metaplanes, the techniques are not widely known and are probably quite difficult and unpleasant.

METAPLANAR QUESTS

The metaplanes are a source of undeniable power and knowledge to the initiated. As the homelands of spirits and the wellspring of mana, it goes without saying that magicians find the secrets held within the metaplanes to be an irresistible lure. When an initiate seeks something in the metaplanes, he must undertake a metaplanar quest to find it. These quests are never taken lightly, for at the very least, they broaden not only the magician's understanding of the universe, but also of the depths of his own soul. Some magicians never recover from what they find there.

Preparing a Metaplanar Quest

Initiates must prepare themselves for the metaphysically taxing act of journeying to the metaplanes. The specifics of this preparation vary from one tradition to another; some require a period of spiritual cleansing while others require meditation. Whatever the nature of the preparation, the magician must make a Magic + Drain attribute + initiate grade (12, 1 hour) Extended Test. Brief interruptions in the preparation do not invalidate the ritual, but the initiate cannot undertake other complex tasks during this period.

Since a magician's soul is away from his body during a metaplanar quest, many initiates also take certain precautions before journeying to the metaplanes. It is not uncommon for a magician to construct a ward around his body to protect it from astral beings or to leave his physical body under the watchful gaze of friends or trusted allies. Corporate magicians typically confine themselves to competent, magically-minded healthcare.

Once the initiate has completed the preparation ritual and feels his body is sufficiently protected, he simply needs to astrally project and choose to enter the metaplanes. When he does, the first step is facing the Dweller on the Threshold.

The Dweller on the Threshold

Crossing the barrier into the metaplanes is a challenging metaphysical feat, and the first obstacle an initiate must face comes from within. Before an initiate can access the knowledge and power of the worlds beyond the astral plane, he must first face his own secrets, weaknesses, and fears. Some believe this is the universe's test of the magician's will and wisdom. Others theorize that the magician's subconscious creates this step; that his own doubts manifest to hold him back. Whatever the truth, the Dweller on the Threshold takes the form of some deeply personal challenge the initiate must first overcome in order to enter the metaplanes on his quest. For example, a character may be forced to admit that he has an addiction or is responsible for something in his life gone bad, and must agree to take on the problem or other-

Street Magic

wise make amends (and if he fails, the Dweller will certainly remember the next time …).

The gamemaster is encouraged to make this step an exploration into the player's character. The Dweller on the Threshold manifests as some personal hindrance, whether it is a fear, a hidden secret, or a debilitating weakness. The initiate must literally face their own demons to move beyond this stage. The encounter with the Dweller on the Threshold is rarely fatal or even injurious, but it is harrowing and emotional.

If multiple initiates are on the same metaplanar quest, their experiences facing the Dweller on the Threshold often overlap. In these cases, the cooperating initiates can't help but learn the hidden shames and fears of their compatriots. The Dweller does not play favorites, however; each initiate present must face his own demons and the exposure of those demons before his allies. Many magicians find that the most difficult step of all, and it would not be surprising if that is why many of them go on metaplanar quests alone.

If the initiate cannot overcome or get past this experience, the metaplanar quest has failed and he returns to his physical body without achieving his goal. If the character satisfactorily faces down his fears and learns from them, the gamemaster should allow the initiate to continue on the metaplanar quest, leaving the Dweller on the Threshold behind and entering the intended metaplane.

Note that characters that enter the metaplanes through an astral rift or a spirit's astral gateway power do not have to face the Dweller on the Threshold. The reasons for this are unknown, but perhaps it is because their destination is not their own choice in these cases.

The Trials

The trials are the meat of a metaplanar quest: the challenges that an initiate faces within the metaplanes in order to accomplish his goal. In most cases, the trials will take place in a single metaplane that is central to the quest itself. For instance, if retrieving a disrupted spirit is the goal, the trials will take place in that spirit's home metaplane. The gamemaster should be creative in determining the adventures that take place during this phase of a metaplanar quest, but they should be connected to the goal in mind. An initiate seeking to hide an astral link within the Realm of Elemental Earth, for example, might have to undertake a daring spelunking expedition deep into endless and dark caves to find just the right hiding place.

Except for the simplest of metaplanar quests, the trials are usually a string of multiple scenes and challenges, much like a typical shadowrun. There is no hard and fast rule to determining how many scenes should be in a given trial, but a gamemaster can sometimes use the goal as a guide. If an initiate is undergoing a metaplanar quest to destroy a Force 6 free spirit, the trial could consist of six challenging scenes. More importantly, the difficulty of the trials should match the difficulty of the goal. Hiding an astral link for a weak focus shouldn't be a terribly dangerous affair, but hunting down a powerful spirit in its home turf with the intent of destroying it should be epic in scope.

> **METAPLANAR GAZETTEER:**
> *The Hive*
>
> The writhing, organic mass known as the Hive is believed to be the original home of the insect spirits, or perhaps just some metaplanar world that they have completely overrun. If there is any surface to this world, no visitor has ever seen it. Instead it seems to be an endless labyrinth of dark, humid tunnels humming with a constant, maddening buzz and crawling with insect spirits of all types. Countless Queen and Mother spirits have hives here, and they are all in perpetual war for space and resources—perhaps why they seem all too eager to travel to Earth.
>
> Few magicians who have traveled to the Hive survive very long. Hostile insect spirits will defend their branch of the Hive to the death and a visiting magician is seen as a hostile trespasser who threatens the Queen or Mother. Even if the magician manages to avoid the insect spirits, he will suffer from Evanescence as his metaplanar form slowly loses cohesiveness (see p. 148). There are dark rumors that a magician can stay in the Hive indefinitely if he undergoes a metamorphosis into an insect, but there are few who are willing to go to that extent.
>
> Most of the magicians visiting the Hive are Ares bug-hunters and their visits are noisy and violent attempts to utterly destroy Queen and Mother spirits. To get around the need of a native guide to take them to this deep metaplane, the Ares bug-hunters have redirected concealed astral links into the Hive that they can follow like a trail of breadcrumbs at a later date. Since these links can be followed in either direction, however, Ares keeps the origin and terminus of the link under close guard (both the linked magician and the item).

Fortunately for an initiate, he rarely has to undertake the trials alone. For details on how the other players can assist a magician during his metaplanar quest, see *Friends in High Places* (p. 132).

GOALS OF A METAPLANAR QUEST

There is no way to enumerate all the secrets that can be learned through a metaplanar quest. Magicians have traveled to the metaplanes seeking answers to every metaphysical question under the sun. While most return only with more questions, some have returned with a deeper understanding of the magical cosmos and the greater power that comes along with it. The gamemaster is encouraged to work with the players to unlock new motivations to quest in the metaplanes, but some examples are given below.

FRIENDS IN HIGH PLACES

Metaplanar quests are extremely personal journeys, but that does not mean they are solitary endeavors. Even Dante had Virgil for his trip through Hell, and similarly initiates can project spirit facsimiles of their closest companions into the metaplanes with them. These "spirit companions" function and behave exactly like the initiate's real world allies and the gamemaster is encouraged to allow the other players to control these companions during the metaplanar quest. In some cases, these companions might even be "dream forms" of his runner team if appropriate, though they may also be doubles of close relatives, lifelong buddies, pets, lost lovers, respected heroes, or even childhood imaginary friends. In addition to the obvious benefit of providing aid to the questing initiate, this allows other players to join in on the adventure without having to be initiates themselves. Gamemasters should, however, limit this to the initiate's usual teammates; this is not an opportunity for an initiate to bring along an army of allies.

It is important to remember that these projections are not the actual characters themselves. Damage taken by the projections is not reflected in the physical bodies of the actual companions. If the projected companion is knocked unconscious or killed during the metaplanar quest, he may no longer assist the initiate but the actual character suffers no penalty. In fact, the actual characters carry on their real lives as usual and will have no knowledge or memory of what their projected selves have experienced. As such, though the projected companions face no real risk, they also gain no rewards from the metaplanar quest. The goal of the quest is the initiate's alone to gain as is any Karma earned along the way.

These special conditions extend only to characters that are not actually present in the metaplanes but are reflected in a spiritual double. If mundanes or non-initiates enter the metaplanes through an astral rift or a spirit's astral gateway power, they function just like any other metaplanar visitor and are subject to all the dangers as well. Other initiates may come along on a metaplanar quest also and are there fully as metaplanar forms, subject to all the risks of metaplanar journeying. In the case where actual companions are along for the quest (whether they are initiates or mundanes who came through a rift or spirit gateway), they may benefit from Karma rewards given for the metaplanar quest.

There is one universal exception to an initiate's ability to project spirit companions: no spirit doubles may travel with an initiate into the deep metaplanes. These metaplanes are too far removed and too alien; the only way to exist within a deep metaplane is to travel there yourself.

Astral Concealment

Many things bear an astral link to a magician that can be used to track the magician through astral space. Spirits, foci, spells, and material links are all things that can lead right back to a magician. It is possible to divert these links through the metaplanes, concealing the link to the magician to all but the most determined pursuers. The initiate undertaking this type of metaplanar quest must be in contact with the item or being linked to him and a metaplanar version of the item travels with the initiate during the quest (if the magician is concealing a link to a spirit, the spirit accompanies the initiate during the quest).

Succeeding in this type of metaplanar quest conceals the astral link within the metaplane. Anyone who attempts to track the astral link (see *Astral Tracking,* p. 193, *SR4A*) can tell immediately that the link has been diverted into the metaplanes. If they want to continue tracking the link, they must go on a metaplanar quest at least as difficult as the initial quest used to conceal the link. In effect, they first trace the link to where it is hidden in the metaplanes and then can continue to track it back to its end.

A single link can be concealed more than once, requiring multiple astral quests to track the link to its original source. A single link, however, can only be redirected once for every two grades of initiation the linked magician has earned. If a link is redirected more than once, someone following the link on a metaplanar quest can go from one hidden location to the next without restarting a new metaplanar quest. In essence, they will face a new set of trials for the next hidden location but do not need to prepare separately or face the Dweller on the Threshold again.

Compelling a Spirit Pact

Free spirits can offer to engage in a variety of spirit pacts with magicians (see *Spirit Pacts,* p. 108). If the spirit does not offer up a pact or accept one through negotiation, a magician can also attempt to use the free spirit's formula to bind it and "negotiate" a spirit pact with it. Alternatively, an initiate who wishes to compel a spirit to grant a spirit pact without angering it through binding can instead attempt to do it a favor or hold it to an ancient agreement. If the initiate succeeds, the free spirit is bound by karma to offer a spirit pact as a reward.

The first step in this sort of metaplanar quest is to determine if there is a favor or ancient agreement that qualifies to compel the spirit and whether the spirit is capable of offering the type of pact the initiate seeks. If the spirit has been free for some time, it may be possible to research its past for clues. In this case, the initiate must make an Academic Knowledge (16, 1 week) Extended Test using a Knowledge skill deemed appropriate by the gamemaster for such occult research. If the spirit was only recently freed or the initiate isn't an expert on occult lore, his alternative is to try to talk to the spirit and attempt to get the information out of it. This method requires proper roleplaying and/or an Opposed Negotiation Test (see *Using Charisma-Linked Skills,* p. 130, *SR4A*). If the test succeeds, the spirit will tell the initiate whether it can offer the pact desired and what the initiate has to do in the metaplanes to receive the offer.

The difficulty of this metaplanar quest should vary depending on how powerful the spirit is and how powerful the pact is. Binding your soul to an ancient and powerful spirit should require a legendary metaplanar quest.

Destroying a Spirit Utterly

Defeating a spirit in combat in the physical world or astral space only disrupts the spirit, sending it back to its home metaplane and barring it from returning for a length of time. If a magician wishes to absolutely destroy a spirit forever, in order to prevent it from ever returning, he must undertake a metaplanar quest to the spirit's home metaplane and defeat it there. This is far easier said than done, since most powerful spirits have carefully guarded homes and lesser spirit servants to protect them. In some cases, the spirit's native plane may not be obvious, in which case the magician must first study the spirit and try to discern from where it originates (see *Learning the Spirit Formula,* p. 107). If the magician succeeds, he need not worry about the spirit ever returning again—but if he fails, he has likely made a powerful enemy.

Initiation Ordeal

An initiate may use a metaplanar quest as a method for reducing the Karma cost of initiation (see *Initiatory Ordeals,* p. 50). The difficulty of the metaplanar quest should depend on the initiate grade being sought, but even a Grade 1 initiatory ordeal quest should not be easy. The nature of the quest should be based upon the magician's tradition and the philosophy of his magical group.

Learning a Metamagic Technique

In addition to learning a metamagic technique at each grade of initiation, an initiate may undertake a metaplanar quest in order to learn further techniques (see p. 52). Like an initiation ordeal metaplanar quest, this type of metaplanar quest should take on a metaphor appropriate to the magician's tradition and magical group. At the successful completion of the metaplanar quest, the initiate must pay 15 Karma in order to complete his mastery of the new metamagic technique. No matter how many metaplanar quests of this nature an initiate performs, he may never know more metamagic techniques than his Magic attribute + initiate grade.

Retrieving a Disrupted Spirit

Normally, when a spirit is disrupted, it cannot return to the physical world or astral space for 28 days minus its Force. If an initiate wishes that spirit to return before that exile is up, he can journey to its native metaplane and release the spirit from its banishment. The state of a spirit during this time varies from one spirit to another, but something is always preventing it from re-entering the world. Some spirits become befuddled and confused while others lock themselves away in their homes. Sometimes a powerful spirit takes advantage of a recently disrupted spirit's vulnerable state and binds it into a short-term slavery. During the metaplanar quest, it is up the initiate to discover what state the disrupted spirit is in and free it from that state. The more powerful the disrupted spirit, the harder this task should be. If the initiate is successful, the spirit may be summoned back to the Gaiasphere as if it had not suffered disruption at all.

Seeking a Spirit Formula

By traveling to the native metaplane of a free spirit and undertaking this type of metaplanar quest, an initiate can discover a free spirit's spirit formula and use it to gain considerable influence over the spirit (see *True Names,* p. 107). Much like the metaplanar quest to destroy a spirit on its home plane, a spirit's formula is often very well protected and very difficult to discover. If the initiate is successful in this quest, he has seen the spirit's formula so clearly that he can reproduce it in the physical world. Depending on how the initiate uses this knowledge, he may make an enemy of the spirit in question. Even if the knowledge is used to the spirit's benefit, most spirits are notoriously nervous about magicians having access to such personal information.

This type of metaplanar quest can also be used to make the process of ally spirit creation easier (see *Conjuring an Ally,* p. 103). By successfully completing this type of metaplanar quest, the initiate is not required to make the Extended Test normally necessary for creating an ally spirit formula. In this case, the initiate creates his ally spirit's formula from the formula of a pre-existing spirit, so the quest to obtain this formula is as difficult as obtaining the spirit formula of a free spirit.

...MAGICAL THREATS...

All he'd ever wanted was to help. It was why Azaca had chosen him, why he'd labored through a degree in holistic thaumaturgy, why he worked as a paramedic and later a clinical healer despite the prejudice against his tradition. It was a calling.

The satisfaction he gained from helping others, though, was shadowed by the helplessness he felt when he failed. Telling a relative that he had been unable to save a loved one despite the power at his fingertips had always been devastating. He took every loss to heart, more so than most doctors he knew. He bottled up the feelings of impotence and defeat. The despair he experienced, though, never entirely overshadowed the joy. His successes were enough to keep his failures at bay.

One fateful night, that all changed. Victims of a car crash were brought into the ER. Most of the five people involved suffered minor injuries, except for one: Liana, his fiancé. There in the emergency room, both her life and the life of their unborn child slipped through his fingers. Caught broadside by a drunk driver, her ruined body was beyond recovery. He used all his talent, called on Azaca's gifts, poured all his will into the mending ... but it wasn't enough. He was on the verge of killing himself through channeling when the others on staff intervened, sedating him and dragging him away. He'd failed both of them. His magic had not been strong enough to bring them back. He couldn't forgive himself. That night, he bribed the duty officer at the mortuary and took his sweet Liana from the cold darkness to a safe place.

Obsessively, he delved into every scrap of arcane lore he could find on the spirits of the dead and the unliving. His friends tried to stop him. His experiments in reanimating corpses led to his dismissal from the hospital. Exploring the Petro rites led to disbarment for "unlawful magical practices." He persevered. Despite the sacrifices, it was worth it. His mait-tête understood. His was a holy quest, the restoration of the vital spark—the ka as the ancient Egyptians called it. The more he learned, however, the more despair set in ... until chance rekindled hope.

In Cairo, he was approached by an unfamiliar spirit. It offered to help him find the temple of Heqet and the tablets he desperately sought. Like a fool, he accepted the devil's bargain. He thought that if only he could hold her again, even for a short while, his resolve would be restored.

The ritual brought Liana back. She was flushed and alive and her breath was warm on his skin. That first night, they made tentative, awkward love. He opened his Sight to bask in the passion they had so often shared—and discovered the price had been too high. The mind that looked out from Liana's hazel eyes was not her own—it wasn't even human. In fact, it seethed with hatred for the living. He barely swallowed his revulsion.

That was two months ago. Now that the pieces were in place, it was time to get her back. The runners had gathered the appropriate paraphernalia. Now it was time to bring his bride home.

"A pleasure to see you again, Mr. Johnson." The one called Jimmy No bowed deeply. "What can we do for you this time?"

Street Magic

> **THE PERCEPTION OF EVIL**
>
> The dystopian nature of the Sixth World casts shadows in countless shades of grey. Judging whether an individual or deed is evil is a far more subjective exercise in *Shadowrun* than in most other settings. Where the line is drawn (if at all) is left to the individual gamemaster and his group.
>
> References to evil in the context of magical threats illustrate the general opinion of the man-on-the-street in the Sixth World as well as the Awakened community, as opposed to case-specific judgments. Shadowrunners, for instance, live at the murkier end of the grey area. Mainstream society views (and sometimes even glorifies) their actions as criminal, violent, and evil, particularly those who engage in premeditated acts of terror, destruction, and assassination. By the same measure, the machinations of insect spirits and shedim are considered evil by both society at large and those who live at its edges, though thaumaturgical scholars might argue that they are not evil so much as alien and inhuman in nature (and therefore beyond metahuman values and morality).

THINGS THAT GO BUMP IN THE NIGHT

The magicians, spirits and critters in this chapter are intended to provide a formidable selection of foes for any *Shadowrun* game. While some of these threats can be used as cannon fodder or a one-off opponent in the course of a single run, all have the potential to become the focal point of an entire campaign. The shadows of the Sixth World teem with Awakened menaces, both human and inhuman. In their line of work, shadowrunners inevitably find themselves either fighting back the darkness or serving as its unwitting pawns. As always, it is up to the gamemaster to pick and choose which are appropriate to the tone and feel of his campaign.

Dark powers are at large, both in the Sixth World and within the metahuman heart. Even those who work magic are not fully aware of the dangers that lurk and scheme in the darker corners of the world. Those who are speak of them only in whispers to avoid drawing their attention. Some believe that metahumanity has unleashed these dangers by venturing too far, too soon—unwittingly drawing the gaze of alien and hostile entities. Others claim that the true danger lies within: man's hubris and thirst for power unlocks the flood gates to all manner of corrupting influences, driving the Gifted down twisted or even toxic paths.

Whether entities from beyond metahuman ken or magicians consumed by madness, magical threats come in a multitude of natures and forms. Some are subtle manipulators who crave worldly power, while others are dark seducers tempting hearts and minds down sinister paths. Some thrive on the darkest of human emotions, existing to spread misery, pain, and suffering. Others are all-too-human psychotics feeding their own dark desires. Some menaces view mankind as cattle to be slaughtered or a disease that must be purged from the Earth; others yet may well represent the vanguard of a coming invasion. If there's anything metahumanity has learned in the past sixty years, it is that the Awakening is far from over. What unexpected menaces does the future still harbor? What if the chilling entities encountered so far have been just the prelude?

USING THREATS

Gamemasters should keep in mind that a magical threat is driven by unique motivations. These motivations are often less tangible and more complex than the mundane accumulation of power, influence, and wealth—especially in the case of spirits—but no less dangerous or interesting.

Several of the threats described herein, such as shedim (p. 154) or insect spirits (p. 149), share unfathomably alien motivations. Hailing from distant metaplanes, their intellects can only be described as inhuman. It is no surprise that such entities do not share metahuman emotions, values and morality, nor do they respect life or metahuman conventions and ethics.

Comparatively, a metahuman threat such as a twisted magician is driven by much more human motives. Metahuman threats usually have a sociopathic desire for personal ascendancy, secular power, hedonistic pleasure, or some sadistic urge or simple insanity. Despite their warped magic and troubled minds, even toxic magicians follow a recognizable agenda. Their warped beliefs fuel all-too-human obsessions.

Threats often boast well-laid plans to achieve goals. They create webs of intrigue into which shadowrunners are easily drawn. When working for or against such threats, runners might never know who or what lies behind the scenes, instead interacting with Johnsons, henchmen, and grunts. Alternatively, they may come face to face with the menace, unveiling a secret evil that threatens to consume them.

Threats can be dangerous working alone, but that danger is nothing compared to what they can pose when acting in concert. The resources available to such menaces vary widely, and depend as much on their ultimate goals as on how consolidated their powerbase is. Fortunately for metahumanity, a handful of groups have "taken up the sword" against such groups. Some are sponsored by corporations, others by religious institutions. There are even loosely associated individuals seeking to take out these threats. These groups walk a fine line, however, since they are more exposed than most to the corrupting influence these evils pose.

THE DARK PATHS

Among the Awakened community, the term *twisted* is used to refer to those magicians and adepts who have crossed the fine line between magical insight and madness. Some Awakened are driven over the edge by fate, consumed by a personal crisis (loss, murder, desire for revenge). Others tap into powers that fuel (or feed off) latent sociopathic and even psychotic traits or simply crack under the strain of dealing with forces beyond human understanding. All have lost their grip on reality and found that madness can lead to insight, becoming uniquely powerful.

While the twisted may be victims of hubris or some dark craving, there are also those Awakened who consciously choose to deal with dark powers out of greed, ambition, or some more sinister urge. Some are driven to their path by circumstance, while others have been lead astray by malicious spirits. Magicians and adepts who give in to the temptations of arcane power that lie in wait for the overambitious and weak-willed are known as *corrupted*. Most corrupted are, at the very least, sociopaths and hence considered a subset of those who follow the twisted paths.

Shadowrun does not distinguish between the two paths in terms of rules or makes judgments about the nature of sanity, good, or evil. In the following material, the terms twisted magicians and twisted paths are used to refer to both. In either case, the Awakened are touched by the darkness within—as such, they provide particularly challenging and dangerous adversaries for those unlucky enough to cross swords with them.

THE DARKNESS WITHIN

Walking the dark paths always involves crossing a personal threshold; one of the few things such Awakened have in common is that their fall from grace rarely happens overnight. Lingering resentment, moral corruption, detachment, and fear are often accompanied by a slow discarding of principles, values, and friendships. Helplessness and impotence (e.g. an eco-shaman) in the face of an implacable and superior enemy (e.g. a polluting corporation) could also push someone over the edge. Even the most honorable and well-meaning causes can lead to extremism and terrorism—and ultimately betrayal of one's own conscience. As the saying goes, the road to hell is paved with good intentions.

A personal crisis, a broken heart, a psychotic break, or an act of passion can set even a "good" person down a twisted path to madness and revenge. It often takes several steps, however, before a person crosses the point of no return. The number of steps depends on the situation and the nature of the individual. Some people delude themselves into producing "legitimate" justifications for their amoral or ruthless deeds. Others have an amoral, corrupt, or sociopathic streak to begin with and freely give in to their personal demons and desires, welcoming freedom from the conventions of society and morality. It becomes easy to lose yourself in madness, embracing your inner darkness and turning it into power.

PATHS OF THE TWISTED AND CORRUPTED

Those who follow the twisted paths do not discard their traditions or mentor spirit—instead these become warped or corrupted beyond recognition, embracing magics and mentors considered evil and forbidden by other members of the tradition. While the normal and twisted paths of a magical tradition can be viewed as two sides of the same coin for simplicity, it is best to say such paths are viewed through a prism that distorts the tradition's core beliefs and meaning. A twisted magician can be anything from a raving lunatic, to a fanatic believer, to a quiet and unassuming professional. In fact, part of the reason twisted magicians are dangerous is that their magic can pass for that of a typical member of a tradition, concealing their true natures and agendas.

In game-terms, the twisted are like any other practitioner of a particular tradition and follow no unique rules. A twisted magician's perspective, however, is either distorted by the individual's unbalanced mind and delusions or focused on darker aspects of the tradition's lore. These are an integral, if often unspoken, part of most established traditions (for instance, Satanism figures in Christian Theurgy, the Petro path in Voodoo, and *daevas* in Zoroastrianism). Unfettered by the ethical mores of society and tainted in mind and spirit, such magicians have been known to indulge in blood magic or even darker arts.

The Dark Twin

When a twisted magician following a mentor spirit turns down his new path, he does not abandon his mentor spirit. Just as each tradition has its forbidden practices and lore, there is also a dark side to most totems and deities. Most magicians believe a mentor spirit's good and bad traits are in balance, but the sinister side of a mentor comes to the fore through the tinted prism of a twisted magician's perspective. He embraces his patron's dark reflection (e.g. Bear the berserker rather than Bear the protector). Though this reflects how animal totems and divinities are sometimes portrayed in legend and folklore, it is unverifiable whether the change is simply in the magician's head or if a change occurs in the mentor spirit itself. The twisted magician is seldom aware of this shift, but another magician following the same mentor would realize the difference if confronted with it.

Tainted Spirits

Since a spirit's form and behavior are at least partially dictated by their summoner's beliefs and tradition, a twisted magician's spirits can be the tell-tale of the taint upon his soul. Such spirits often embody negative aspects of the tradition's beliefs, ranging from unusually fierce nature spirits called forth by an avenger eco-shaman to the demonic appearance of spirits of man conjured by Goetian theurges or Faustian hermetics. This is also true with twisted magicians who follow possession traditions, whose summoned spirits often exhibit a fiercer and malevolent intelligence.

Spirits conjured by twisted magicians show a particular aversion to long-term binding. They can become dangerous and unpredictable if bound too long to a twisted magician.

In game terms, twisted spirits suffer no modifications to their normal statistics. Gamemasters are urged to use their appearance and personality to convey a different feel and attitude.

TWISTED AGENDAS

Given the madness that characterizes twisted magicians, the twisted paths are not normally available to player characters (see *Playing the Twisted*, p. 138). The following twisted agendas are presented as examples of the many options available to gamemasters in developing authentic and unique foes for their campaigns. Note that numerous secret societies, radical cells, and obscure cults exist in the Sixth World to draw like-minded twisted magicians together, some of which serve as magical groups.

PLAYING THE TWISTED

While many shadowrunners might qualify as borderline sociopaths and psychotics, roleplaying a truly demented individual with Awakened power at his fingertips is beyond the scope of the *Shadowrun* rules and the team nature of a typical game.

That said, allowing player characters to follow twisted paths may provide a unique challenge to gamemasters and players willing to explore mature and potentially disturbing characters and themes in their campaign. Roleplaying an "unbalanced" magician or a magician without conscience should never be taken lightly and should be approached with caution. Inexperienced gamemasters and groups not interested in allowing such a character into the fold are advised against this. If the group is comfortable with allowing a player to play a twisted magician, several issues should still be kept in mind:

Though not as deranged as toxic magicians, the twisted typically exhibit strong asocial tendencies, socio- or psychopathic behavior, and varying degrees of schizophrenia. Most twisted are contemptuous of and disaffected by society's rules, values, and morality, and do not balk at crimes such as murder, rape, or defilement. For example, blood magic is a ruthless practice that involves the cold-blooded murder of a living creature for fleeting empowerment. It is the kind of heinous act only a completely callous, unscrupulous, or highly-disturbed individual might commit. Despite some runner's reputations, such activities are not conducive to a long career and acceptance in the shadows.

Additionally, the twisted gain access to obscure arts and unique metamagic techniques that can be potentially unbalancing in a player's hands; gamemasters should consider carefully before allowing them into the game. If they are made available, they should remain rare. Finding an appropriate instructor should be a difficult, harrowing quest for the character.

Avengers

Avengers believe they see the truth of the world that others are too blind to realize. As magicians, avengers are attuned to the life energies of nature itself and are uniquely sensitive to man's depredation of the planet. The damage dealt to Earth's biosphere and astral space has touched them personally and spiritually, driving them to radical activism. Avengers see metahumanity and modern society as a cancer that will kill the planet if not sanitized. Misanthropic or sociopathic avengers don't shrink from eliminating those they blame for the damage—their life-affirming creed becomes the intolerant dogma that drives inquisitions and holy wars. Avengers often turn from eco-shamanism (or other nature-revering traditions such as Druidism, Wicca, or even Wuxing) to Deep Green direct action activism and even bioterrorism (particularly actions that might lead to population reduction). Some avengers find themselves attuned to particular environments, seeking not only to defend but to expand and promote that particular environment or domain at the expense of all others.

Zealots

Arcane extremism is not confined to environmentalism. Zealots often emerge from religious and racial bigotry common in certain cultures and magical traditions. Zealots are born both in the religious radicalism found in certain sects of Christianity, Islam, and other beliefs and their associated mystic traditions, along with militant political and racial extremism fanned by tribal genocide, supremacist movements, and radical activism. Often sociopaths, zealots are contemptuous not only of the enemies of their faith or ideology, but also of those who share their beliefs but don't have the spine to take action. Zealots fervently pursue some agenda within the boundaries of their religion or creed, fanatically devoting their magic to accomplish its objectives—even when this means breaking pillars of their faith or the laws of society. Violence, coercion, and terror are means to an end and used in the name of a "greater cause."

Faustian Mages

Often seen as a stereotypical corrupted path, Faustians embraces their inner darkness as the price they must pay for greater power and insight. A Faustian mage's conversion to the dark arts is most often premeditated and planned, their decision driven by cold logic.

Though Faustians specialize in dealing with powerful spirits and engaging in spirit pacts (hence their name), they never do so frivolously. Their intent is to hold the upper hand in any pact they enter—collecting every scrap of information about a free spirit and undertaking metaplanar quests (p. 130) to unearth its true name. To slake their perpetual thirst for power, knowledge, and control, Faustians also seek out forgotten lore in ancient tomes and folios, attempting to unearth secrets and artifacts better left untouched for the knowledge and power they might contain.

Path of Blood

Bloodletting and blood sacrifices have been integral to nearly all civilizations and religions at one point or another. These practices can still be found in many mystical traditions. The Path of Blood, however, delves beyond the symbolic potency of blood. Its followers believe that through ritual immolation and obscure metamagic, magicians can tap the life energies locked within to fuel powerful magic. Though the secrets of blood magic are best known among the twisted *nahualli* of the Aztec tradition, blood rites and human sacrifice are not restricted to Aztlaner mysticism. Voodoo, Druidism, Asatru, Qabbalism, and other traditions have been known to produce followers of the Path of Blood.

Path of the Dead

The Path of the Dead is walked by *bocor* (Petro houngans) and necromancers of various traditions. They are feared and reviled for their profane attitude toward death and the spirits of the dead. This contempt for the peace of the dead and the sanctity of the grave makes such practices forbidden and sacrilegious in many countries and cultures—though this does little to dissuade the path's followers. Besides accusations of ensnaring the souls of the recently departed, necromancers have been accused of being in league with shedim (see p. 154).

Traditionally, necromancy is the art of communing with the souls and spirits of the departed for counsel and guidance. In the Sixth World, those who harbor few reservations about disturbing the dead stand to gain much with the creation of zombie labor and guardians.

Some necromancers seem to be fascinated with the "spark of life" (the soul, essence, spirit, or ka), its nature, and the possibility of preserving it beyond the moment of death. Their studies and understanding of metahuman life force have proven crucial in techniques used for cybermantic rituals in megacorporate delta clinics.

Path of Maho/Demons

Translating literally to "evil spirit rites," *maho* is a synonym for the practice of dark arts in Japan. Though the maho tradition originates from the Shinto worship of the kami, the *maho tsukai* (magic bearer) is beholden to a pantheon of darker spirits, the *magatshui-no-kami* (dark kami) and Amatusu Mikaboshi, the God of Evil. Dark kami come in all varieties, from *onis* (demons) to *mononokes* (dark spirits) or malicious spirits like *tengu* and *kappa*.

Demonolatry is the counterpart to the Path of Maho in Western and Middle-Eastern cultures. Goetians, black magicians, and devil worshippers in Judeo-Christian-Islamic traditions (often reductively pigeonholed as Satanists) deify demons, following "dark twins" or devilish entities (such as variations of the Adversary or Seductress mentor spirit archetypes) as patrons and practicing dark rites in their name.

TWISTED ADEPTS

Adepts can fall from grace as easily as any other Awakened character. An adept's powers and abilities are fueled by their idealized self-image—there will always be those who look into themselves and find nothing but darkness. Since adepts look inward for their magic, they are particularly vulnerable to personal crisis, mental breakdowns, or psychotic breaks. Other adepts are driven by unquenchable ambition or the belief that their abilities place them beyond society's rules and shackles. They are willing to do anything to satisfy the twisted urges that burn in their breasts, even engaging in spirit pacts to tap "forbidden" powers and acquire unique abilities. In this manner, some twisted adepts have unlocked the blood magic techniques known as Cannibalize and Power Bleed (p. 140).

BLOOD MAGIC

Bloodletting and symbolic sacrifices play an important role in many mystical traditions including Voodoo, the Aztec and Asatru traditions, and some sects of Wicca, Druidism, Theurgy, and Orthodox Qabbalah. In the Sixth World, the term "blood magic" refers specifically to the practice and techniques involved in sacrificing someone's lifeblood and life energy to fuel magic. Blood magic is believed to have been learned from malicious spirits or ancient tomes. As a vicious sacrificial act, it is illegal in most nations, with the notable exception of Aztlan, though most of the sacrifices performed in public there have a religious rather than arcane connotation.

In *Shadowrun,* blood magic is represented by mastery of a number of obscure metamagic techniques whose mysteries are jealously guarded by secretive magical brotherhoods, malevolent spirits, and psychotic cults. It is strongly advised that twisted metamagics remain the province of NPCs. Player characters should not have access to these powers unless the gamemaster allows them to become twisted.

Sacrifice

This metamagic may only be learned with the aid of an instructor of the same tradition or a free spirit who knows and is willing to share the technique. It can never be learned through self-initiation.

An initiate using Sacrifice can reduce the Drain of any magical skill test by drawing on the life energies of a "donor." To do so, the initiate must inflict a physical wound on the willing or unwilling donor; for symbolic purposes, the damage must be inflicted with a melee weapon and must draw blood.

Sacrifice requires two Complex Actions completed consecutively. Taking any other action between the two required actions will negate the attempt. The initiate first performs a normal melee attack using the appropriate melee weapon skill. The target may attempt to parry, block, or dodge as normal. If the target is restrained or prone, appropriate melee modifiers apply (see p. 157, *SR4A*).

While any living creature can be used as a donor, the blood of sapient donors (metahumans and critters with the Sapience ability, such as sasquatches and dragons) is more potent. For each box of Physical Damage inflicted on a sapient donor, the Drain in the subsequent action is reduced by 1. For non-sentient critters, the DV is reduced by 1 for every 3 boxes of damage (possibly less if the donor is significantly smaller than an average human). Spirits can never be donors, even if they are currently possessing a living body. An initiate may use himself as a donor, drawing on his own life force to reduce the Drain of his spells. A blood magician can inflict any desired level of Physical damage on himself.

Sacrifice is the prerequisite for a number of advanced metamagic techniques.

Invoking Blood Spirits

Prerequisites: Sacrificing and Invoking (p. 57)

While Sacrifice is known to several twisted paths, few share the knowledge of invoking blood spirits. Blood spirits are primarily summoned by nahualli of the Aztech tradition and more rarely by blood magicians of other traditions.

To use this advanced metamagic, magicians must first master both Sacrifice and Invoking. A blood sacrifice (during

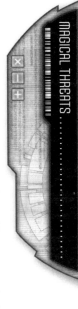

which the donor must be killed) is performed as part of a modified Invoking ritual. Rather than invoking an appropriate great form spirit from a bound spirit, the ritual transforms the bound spirit into a great form blood spirit. The death of the victim reduces the Drain of the Invoking ritual per the Sacrifice rules.

When the invocation is fueled by the sacrifice of a living entity, the essence of the donor is imprinted on the invoked spirit. Blood spirits tend to take the appearance of bloody and savage amalgams of the donor and the bound spirit type (e.g. a blood-soaked Aztec guardian spirit with the face and body of the donor from whom it was created). The violent nature of the sacrifice makes the invoked blood spirit aggressive and difficult to control. It will always turn on its summoner if it becomes free.

Aside from the abilities normally conferred by Invoking (see p. 57), blood spirits also automatically gain the following powers (see p. 99 and pp. 295–296, *SR4A*): Energy Drain (Essence), Fear, and Natural Weapon (DV = Force Physical damage, AP 0). They also acquire the weakness of Evanescence (p. 148). Essence drained by blood spirits is added to the spirit's Force at a 1:1 ratio. Blood spirits never gain unique powers through the Invoking Test.

A free blood spirit is a terrifying entity. It still must feed on Essence to survive, though free blood spirits only lose 1 point of Force per week rather than 1 point every sunrise or sunset. As with other free spirits, free blood spirits will engage in spirit pacts (see p. 108) to sustain themselves.

Cannibalize (Adepts Only)

Twisted adepts and mystic adepts may learn a unique version of the Sacrifice metamagic known as Cannibalize. The sacrifice and consumption of the donor's blood or flesh allows the adept to temporarily enhance his own abilities—literally feeding off the power of his enemies. Cannibalize functions just like Sacrifice (p. 139), except that instead of reducing Drain, the adept may add a temporary rating point to any one of his Physical attributes for every 3 boxes of Physical damage inflicted on a sapient victim or every 6 boxes inflicted on a non-sapient victim. Multiple rating points can be distributed among the adept's Physical attributes as he chooses, but temporarily augmented ratings may not exceed the character's augmented maximums. The enhancement lasts for (Magic x initiate grade) Combat Turns. If the adept immediately spends Karma equal to the total rating points gained, he may extend that duration to (Magic x initiate grade) days.

Power Bleed (Adepts Only)
Prerequisite: Cannibalize

This advanced metamagic requires knowledge of the Cannibalize technique. It allows the blood adept to siphon his victim's powers away along with life force, for the adept's own use. Power Bleed functions just like Cannibalize, except that for every 3 boxes of Physical damage dealt to the "donor," the blood adept may also siphon one adept or critter power from his victim (assuming the victim has any such powers).

Only one power at a time may be bled from a victim, and the victim remains able to use the power themselves. A power acquired this way lasts for (Magic x initiate grade) Combat Turns. The blood adept may extend this duration to (Magic x initiate grade) days by immediately spending 3 Karma points.

TOXIC MAGIC

Toxic magicians are Awakened characters whose sanity, outlook, and magic have become tainted by environmental blight or human desolation. Through either prolonged exposure to the abysses of modern society or some tragic, life-changing event, the minds of toxics become warped and poisoned.

Most normal paths of magic emphasize the harmony between the character and his environment, keeping the physical and astral in balance. Even the twisted tap the vibrant natural magic energies of the Gaiasphere. Toxic magicians, on the other hand, abandon their beliefs to embrace the foulest of hostile forces, reveling in the spiritual taint and sterility that is the anathema of natural order. They seek to impose their toxic beliefs on society and the world.

THE TOXIC PATH

Toxic magicians are often loners, driven by hatred of their species and themselves. Having left behind their former paradigms (and mentor spirits), they now follow the toxic path. They revel in blight and disaster, spreading various types of poison (not necessarily pollution) to feed their agenda. Some are gleefully insane, while others are methodical nihilists, deep ecologists, or neo-Darwinists. They all look forward to destroying life on Earth to one degree or another.

As the toxic magician's approach to magic transforms due to his personal insanity, he develops his own ways to practice magic. Toxic magicians still follow the basic rules of a tradition (see *Magical Associations and Drain,* p. 180, *SR4A*), but each toxic magician pursues his own personally-warped paradigm and concept—and thus follows a unique tradition that fits his agenda. This personal toxic tradition determines which five toxic spirits he can summon and which attribute is employed for Drain.

TOXIC AGENDAS

Having lost faith in their former tradition, toxics are consumed by the distorted ideals and corrupted philosophies that drive them. Though each toxic magician is unique in his beliefs, many ultimately share a common or similar agenda. The sample toxic agendas that follow are simply the most common encountered so far. Many more exist.

Poisoners

Most toxic magicians are *poisoners*. Poisoners believe they have been touched by the new elemental forces at loose in the world, and see themselves as the avatars of those forces. As rampant pollution slowly subsumes the natural world and evolutionary path, they see it as the key to greater power. To a poisoner, other magicians are wasting their time with obsolete traditions—particularly those that worship nature—as the entire world will soon be drowned in toxins.

Poisoners are heralds of a new order, which is why most poisoners are arrogant at best. They revel in their own accomplishments and power, more so than other toxics. Several eco-disasters of the last decade have been flagged as the handiwork of poisoners. Green regimes, eco-friendly organizations, Deep Green activists, and eco-terrorists abhor and actively persecute poisoners.

While poisoners represent a common toxic agenda, individual toxic magicians vary greatly in their particular understanding of the nature of their powers and their urge to corrupt, pervert, and blight nature. Toxic spirits summoned by poisoners are twisted into volatile embodiments of pollutants (radioactivity, smog, sludge, acid), mutagens (chemicals, radiation, cancer, etc) and pathogens (diseases).

Reapers

Reapers see metahumanity as a cancer consuming the planet, and themselves as just another malignant tumor. Predatory exploitation, overpopulation, pollution, and other man-made ravages have destroyed the eco-system. Metahumanity has evolved into a parasite that must be eradicated to ensure the planet's recovery. While poisoners revel in environmental pollution, reapers desire the extinction of their own species. Driven by self-loathing and self-destructive obsession, they are fond of devising and employing weapons of mass destructions—nuclear, bio and chemical weapons that will ensure that humans (and sometimes even animals) are annihilated so the Great Mother can heal herself and start anew. Reapers are often found among nihilistic, apocalyptic, and doomsayer cults and radicals who wish to cleanse the world.

Toxic spirits conjured by reapers appear as archetypical forces of destruction such as pestilence (diseases, toxins, and pathogens), genocide (mass killing, violence), environmental pollution, or apocalyptic symbolism (four horsemen, angels of death).

Havocs

A *havoc's* deepest desire is to demolish society and shatter civilization. Some havocs see society as a cancer made of base corruption, moral degradation, and inequality that must be eradicated one piece at a time. Others are acolytes of entropic forces, driven by a sociopathic compulsion to bring down symbols of authority and order and seed chaos and bedlam.

By eliminating the pernicious influence of social hierarchies, mores, and rules through campaigns of mass murder or targeted assassination, the havocs believe that modern civilization will crack under its own weight and give humankind a chance at a new start. Havoc toxics favor insidious strategies and carefully laid plans, working from within to bring chaos and ruin to their targeted groups and individuals. Many havocs follow possession-based traditions. Their spirits mirror the dark aspects of the metahuman soul that havocs despise in society, warping into embodiments of carnage, addiction, vice, repression, and all kinds of perversions.

Sterilists

The rarest of toxics, *sterilists* are just as dangerous. Possibly more than any other type of toxic, sterilist beliefs

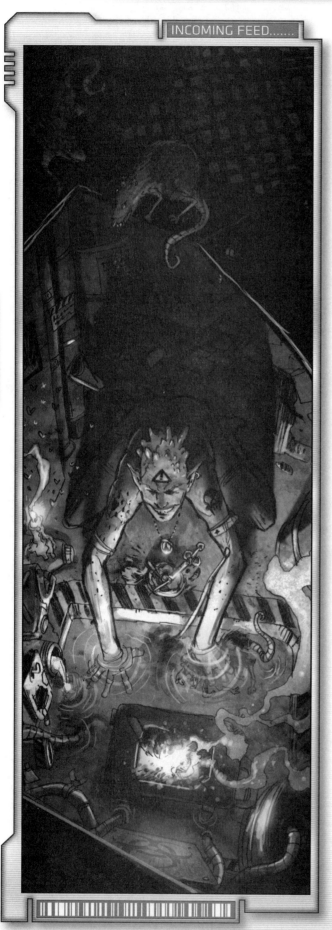

are anathema to the natural order. Even other toxics draw power from life, emotion, and creativity (warped though it may be); sterilists, however, are ultimately cold, detached, and calculating. They devote their existence to the purging of "base" emotions and aspire to machine-like order and impersonal logic.

Sterilists actively seek to force their worldview on others. By infiltrating and subverting the pillars of society, they hope to bring about a world devoid of empathy and emotion, where everyone and everything is merely a cog in a vast mechanism governed by clear and precise parameters. The sooner freedom, impulsiveness, and passion are eliminated, the better and safer the world will be. Their fierce devotion to rationality and efficiency makes even the most intellectual mage uneasy.

Sterilists conjure toxic spirits that are warped into abstract reflections of order (taking on crystalline, fractal, or machine-like appearances), or forms reflecting metahuman spiritual desolation (faceless, featureless humanoids).

TOXIC MENTOR SPIRITS

Though no sane magician has ever encountered toxic mentor spirits and lived to tell about it, toxic magicians are known to associate with such corrupt entities and distorted ideals. Toxic mentor spirits are handled as normal mentor spirits (p. 200, *SR4A*). They come in many different shapes and forms. Toxic magicians that previously had a mentor spirit are often drawn to mentors that pervert or caricature their original affiliation. Havocs tend to favor urban or social mentor spirits, while poisoners lean towards forces and entities that embody pollutants. The following toxic mentor spirits are examples of corrupted animal mentor spirits and abstract toxic archetypes.

Doom

Doom is the apocalyptic prophet that heralds the end times. Toxic magicians following Doom are Armageddon-seeking cultists or radicals who wish to bring about the end of the world by any means possible. Followers of Doom are among the few toxics known to cooperate in groups or cells.

Advantages: +2 dice for toxic spirits of man or guidance spirits (chose one), +2 dice to Con Tests.

Disadvantages: Convinced that the end is nigh, heralds of Doom see no point in maintaining relationships, becoming attached to certain interests, or keeping hold of any possessions that are not of use to their apocalyptic plans. Such magicians must succeed in a Willpower + Charisma (3) Test to take any action that would maintain such unnecessary attachments.

Mutation

Toxics following Mutation believe it embodies the ultimate force of biological development—both natural and unnatural. Mutation represents the drive to forcefully push metahumanity towards its evolutionary potential (whatever that might be to the individual toxic). Followers of Mutation believe mankind and indeed all life must adapt to ascend to its biological birthright by any means possible—even if it means accelerating natural evolution through artificial mutagenesis, be it induced through contact with chemicals, radiation, pathogens, or biogenetic modification. Not all will survive, but those select few that do will carry the seeds and abilities to pass on to their progeny. Mutation magicians almost invariably possess a number of implants, particularly biotech and genetic enhancements.

Advantages: +2 dice for toxic spirits of man or beast (choose one), +2 dice for Health spells.

Disadvantages: Followers of Mutation despise weakness. If the magician should ever exhibit a weakness or prove inferior to another, he suffers a –1 dice pool modifier to all actions until he somehow compensates for the weakness or overcomes his rival (leading many magicians to acquire new implants or other enhancements).

Pestilent Rat

Pestilent Rat is a survivor, forced to live in humanity's waste and to scavenge its spoils for food. Pestilent Rats are disease carriers and plague bearers, spreading pandemics and thriving while humankind succumbs to infection. Followers of Pestilent Rat have no compunction in eradicating whole townships to safely strip the forsaken homes for food, goods, and valuables.

Advantages: +2 dice for toxic spirits of man or beast (choose one), +2 dice to resist pathogens and toxins.

Disadvantages: A Pestilent Rat magician must make a Willpower + Charisma (3) Test to not immediately flee or seek cover whenever caught in a combat situation. If there is nowhere to flee, she is forced to fight.

Pollution

Pollution embodies the defilement and ravaging of the environment. Followers of Pollution celebrate the rape of the world and view Pollution as a fundamental primal force, surpassing all others and pure in itself. It is the taint in the metahuman soul made manifest, released upon the world. Followers of Pollution understand the potency hidden in acid rain, sewage, crude oil spills, over-fertilized soil, waste dumps, and all kinds of poisonous sediments. They are utterly devoted to spreading the taint.

Advantages: +2 dice for toxic water, air, or earth spirits (choose one), +2 dice to resist pathogens and toxins.

Disadvantages: A Pollution magician must make a Willpower + Charisma (3) Test to restrain himself from despoiling or tainting any pristine natural environment in some way.

Rabid Dog

Rabid Dog is a ferocious destroyer of metahumanity, ruining the lives of those he would normally protect. Loyalty and devotion are the antithesis of Rabid Dog's beliefs. A follower of Rabid Dog is a predator who knows nothing but the destruction of those he deems unworthy, working to either poison them with his own bloodlust or savaging them himself.

Advantages: +2 dice for toxic beast or guardian spirits (choose one), +2 to Detection spells.

Disadvantages: Rabid Dog magicians are bloodthirsty, and will take every opportunity to twist the knife or prolong a victim's pain. They must succeed in a Willpower + Strength (3) Test to leave an unfinished victim, to end a victim's life quickly or without pain, or to break off from a predatory hunt.

Radiation

The Children of the Atom see Radiation as the cleansing cosmic fire, both entropy incarnate and the invisible flames of change. The fact that radiation and mana interact in strange and often inexplicable ways on both the physical and astral planes shores their belief and fuels the dream of purging the world in cleansing radioactive fire.

Advantages: +2 dice for nuclear/toxic fire spirits, +2 dice to resist pathogens, toxins, and radiation.

Disadvantages: –1 die for Health spells.

TOXIC METAMAGIC

Initiated toxic magicians are able to learn both normal metamagic techniques and a few toxic metamagics of their own.

Corruption

Corruption metamagic allows a toxic magician to pervert a spirit into a toxic version of itself. To corrupt a spirit, the toxic must first reduce the spirit's services to 0 with Banishing (see p. 188, *SR4A*). The toxic initiate adds his initiate grade to the Banishing Tests. Once the spirit's services are eliminated, but before the spirit departs, the toxic magician makes a Summoning Test (p. 188, *SR4A*) to bring the spirit under his control, adding initiate grade to his dice pool. If the spirit is successfully brought into the magician's service, it immediately transforms into a toxic version of itself (see *Toxic Spirits*, p. 144). Toxic spirits created this way may also be bound into service.

Taint

Taint is the polar opposite of Cleansing metamagic (p. 55). A toxic magician uses Taint to intensify the mana "pollution" in a domain that is already aspected towards toxic magic (see *Domains*, p. 120). Use the rules for standard Cleansing, but consider any hits the toxic magician gets as increasing a toxic background count by the same value as he would have diminished it. Toxic magicians enjoy tainting areas that already have a predisposition for environmental or emotional desolation, such as waste dumps, violent crime scenes, dens of iniquity, slave and labor camps, sterile corporate compounds, shantytowns, ghettos, and z-zones.

Leeching

Prerequisite: Geomancy (p. 56)

This advanced metamagic allows a toxic initiate to draw ambient mana and life-energy out of his surrounding environment to assist him in resisting Drain. The initiate must master Geomancy before attempting to learn this technique. Toxic initiates may use this metamagic during any magical activity that produces Drain, but only in toxic domains. To use Leeching, the magician takes a Free Action and makes a Magic + Essence (3) Test, reducing the Drain Value by the net hits achieved.

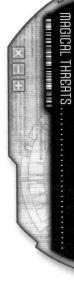

Leeching drains and withers the life force of living things in the immediate environment. This has no effect on characters, spirits, or anything but the smallest critters. Plants, insects, and very small animals, however, will wither and die. Areas that are regularly exposed to Leeching metamagic for prolonged periods of time are gradually strip-mined of life and emotion.

TOXIC SPIRITS

Toxic magicians summon spirits only they can conjure and control. Other magicians can banish toxic spirits, but they are unable to control them with a Summoning Test if the spirit becomes uncontrolled.

Conjuring of toxic spirits is handled as described in the *SR4* core rules, though binding toxic sprits requires a toxic domain (see *Domains*, p. 120) or an appropriate amount (gamemaster's discretion) of toxic materials such as radioactive isotopes, biohazard materials, toxins, or used clinical supplies. Social-oriented toxics often use materials linked to strong negative emotions (murder weapons, snuff clips, pieces or possessions of crime victims) in binding rituals instead.

Toxic great form spirits can be invoked normally (see *Invoking*, p. 57) and exhibit unique powers appropriate to their type—given the variety possible, however, these are left to the individual gamemaster to adapt using the existing unique powers as guidelines. For instance, a great form nuclear spirit could have the power to generate a strong electromagnetic pulse, which would use the rules for the Storm power adapted to damage only non-optical electronics and communications.

Free and wild toxic spirits do exist and are very, very bad news. In addition to possessing the unique powers of their own (see below), a toxic free spirit can engage in a spirit pact with toxic magicians as per the normal rules (p. 108). Numerous incidents have been recorded of toxic spirits appearing of their own accord (see *Wild Spirits*, p. 110), taking up residence in toxic domains, and going on destructive rampages or even pulling strings from behind the scenes.

Each toxic spirit is as unique as its summoner's derangement and as manifold as the corruption that breeds them. A myriad of different toxic spirits exist, many of which seem recognizable while others appear simply alien and menacing. To reflect the fact that such spirits are tainted by both the summoner's insanity as well as environmental blight, *Shadowrun* provides *Toxic Spirit Quick Design* guidelines (p. 147) so that gamemasters can tailor these spirits to their needs. The following six spirits are provided as examples that can be directly used and are linked to the toxic traditions described above.

Abomination (Toxic Spirit of Beasts)

Abomination spirits are the embodiment of toxic beasts, mutated through pollution, genetic tinkering, or evolutionary aberration. Abominations appear as twisted or deformed beasts or hybrids.

B	A	R	S	C	I	L	W	EDG	ESS	M	Init	IP
F+2	F+1	F+2	F+2	F	F	F	F	F	F	F	(Fx2)+2	2

Astral INIT/IP: Fx2, 3
Movement: 10/45

Skills: Assensing, Astral Combat, Dodge, Exotic Ranged Weapon, Perception, Unarmed Combat
Powers: Animal Control (Toxic Critters), Astral Form, Corrosive Spit, Enhanced Senses (Hearing, Low-Light Vision, Smell), Materialization, Movement, Mutagen, Sapience
Optional Powers: Concealment, Confusion, Guard, Fear, Natural Weapon (DV = Force Physical damage, AP 0), Noxious Breath, Search, Venom

Acid (Toxic Spirit of Water)

Acid spirits incarnate the corroding and destructive nature of man's chemical creations. They manifest as amorphous free-floating bodies of acid, sometimes surrounded by acidic fumes, corroding everything they come into contact with.

Street Magic

B	A	R	S	C	I	L	W	EDG	ESS	M	Init	IP
F	F+2	F+3	F+4	F	F	F	F	F	F	F	(Fx2)+3	2

Astral INIT/IP: Fx2, 3
Movement: 10/25
Skills: Assensing, Astral Combat, Dodge, Exotic Ranged Weapon, Perception, Unarmed Combat
Powers: Astral Form, Concealment, Confusion, Energy Aura (Acid), Engulf (Acid damage), Materialization, Movement, Sapience, Search
Optional Powers: Accident, Binding, Elemental Attack, Guard
Weaknesses: Allergy (Clean Water and Fire, Severe)

> ### RADIATION ELEMENTAL DAMAGE
>
> Radiation is a serious hazard to any living creature. A person can absorb radiation slowly over time by being exposed to a radioactive environment or by a short burst of radiation from "hot" sources that apply a high radiation dose at once. High doses of radiation lead to radiation burns and to immediate and long-lasting side effects. Natural radiation of radioactive materials, specific spells (developed by Radiation magicians), and the powers of nuclear spirits may inflict Radiation damage on a living being.
>
> In game terms, Radiation damage is treated as Physical damage. Armor does not help to protect against this kind of attack, while protective measures (such as rad suits) might. Immediate side effects of light radiation poisoning (also called radiation sickness) include nausea (p. 254, *SR4A*), headaches, and blindness. The symptoms of radiation sickness become more serious (and the chance of survival decreases) as the dosage of radiation increases.

Harbinger (Toxic Spirit of Guidance)

Harbingers often appear as emaciated humanoids, ravaged by stigmata and scars and exuding a feeling of doom. Some embody their summoner's personal nightmares, while others are formless, pitch-black shadows or clouds.

B	A	R	S	C	I	L	W	EDG	ESS	M	Init	IP
F−1	F+4	F+2	F	F	F	F	F	F	F	F	(Fx2)+2	2

Astral INIT/IP: Fx2, 3
Movement: 10/25
Skills: Arcana, Assensing, Astral Combat, Counterspelling, Dodge, Intimidation, Perception, Spellcasting, Unarmed Combat
Powers: Astral Form, Confusion, Divining, Fear, Innate Spell (Phantasm), Materialization, Sapience, Search, Shadow Cloak
Optional Powers: Accident, Enhanced Senses (Hearing, Low-Light Vision, Thermographic Vision, or Smell), Guard, Magical Guard, Influence

Harrow (Toxic Spirit of Man)

Like spirits of man, harrows come in a variety of shapes and forms, many hard to spot. Their physical forms are typically leering, spiteful, malevolent humanoids. They haunt metahuman dreams and thoughts, turning peoples' ideals, dreams, and ambitions against them.

B	A	R	S	C	I	L	W	EDG	ESS	M	Init	IP
F	F+2	F+3	F−2	F	F	F	F	F	F	F	(Fx2)+3	2

Astral INIT/IP: Fx2, 3
Movement: 10/25

Skills: Assensing, Astral Combat, Dodge, Perception, Spellcasting, Unarmed Combat
Powers: Accident, Astral Form, Concealment, Confusion, Desire Reflection, Enhanced Senses (Low-Light, Thermographic Vision), Fear, Influence, Materialization, Sapience, Search
Optional Powers: Guard, Innate Spell (any one spell known by the summoner), Movement, Psychokinesis

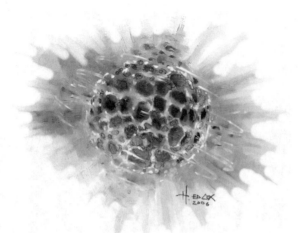

Nuclear (Toxic Spirit of Fire)

Nuclear spirits embody lethal radioactivity and nuclear energy. Spirits of the atom often appear as glowing, radioactive clouds of isotopes or fallout, radiating heat, gamma rays, and x-rays.

B	A	R	S	C	I	L	W	EDG	ESS	M	Init	IP
F+1	F+2	F+3	F	F	F	F	F	F	F	F	(Fx2)+3	2

Astral INIT/IP: Fx2, 3
Movement: 10/25
Skills: Assensing, Astral Combat, Dodge, Exotic Ranged Weapon, Flight, Perception, Unarmed Combat
Powers: Accident, Astral Form, Confusion, Elemental Attack (Radiation), Energy Aura (Radiation), Engulf (Radiation), Materialization, Sapience
Optional Powers: Fear, Guard, Noxious Breath, Search

Sludge (Toxic Spirit of Earth or Water)

Sludge spirits embody the blight of soil or water contaminated by biological or chemical waste. While some sludge spirits can take solid or liquid forms, their appearance usually combines both.

B	A	R	S	C	I	L	W	EDG	ESS	M	Init	IP
F+3	F–1	F+2	F+3	F	F	F	F	F	F	F	(Fx2)+2	2

Astral INIT/IP: Fx2, 3
Movement: 10/25
Skills: Assensing, Astral Combat, Dodge, Exotic Ranged Weapon, Perception, Unarmed Combat
Powers: Astral Form, Anaphylaxis, Binding, Engulf (Water or Earth), Materialization, Movement, Sapience, Search
Optional Powers: Accident, Concealment, Confusion, Corrosive Spit, Elemental Attack, Fear, Guard
Weaknesses: Allergy (Clean Earth and Water, Severe)

TOXIC SPIRIT POWERS

Toxic spirits boast some new powers appropriate to their unnatural and volatile nature.

Anaphylaxis

Type: P • Action: Complex • Range: Touch • Duration: Instant

Anaphylaxis is a massive systemic allergic reaction magically induced by a concentrated burst of pollutants from the toxic spirit. Treat it as an inhalation vector toxin attack (Speed: Immediate; Power: Force; Effect: Physical damage, anaphylactic shock). Armor does not help resist this damage, but gear that protects against inhalation-vector toxins will (see the Toxin Protection table, p. 254, *SR4A*).

Anaphylactic Shock: If the damage is not completely resisted, the victim enters anaphylactic shock, resulting in muscle spasms and systemic failure resulting in death if untreated. The victim takes 1 box of damage each Combat Turn until he dies from cardiovascular breakdown, unless he is treaded by a First Aid + Logic (2) Test with appropriate drugs (i.e. a medkit), or an Antidote, Detox, or Heal spell.

Mutagen

Type: P • Action: Complex • Range: Self • Duration: Sustained

A being can use the Mutagen power to magically enhance its physical body at the expense of its mental abilities. While using the power, it can shift up to a maximum of (Magic) attribute points from Mental to Physical attributes. This power can be used by possessing spirits, shifting Mental attribute points from the spirit to the vessel's Physical attributes. Shifting in or out of a mutated form requires a Complex Action. At the gamemaster's discretion, instead of shifting attribute points this power can instead be used to generate a new physical feature, such as a horn, a tail, or a new sensory organ.

SHADOW SPIRITS

Demons, raksasha, oni, nephilim, yokai, devas, devils—every culture, faith, and mystic tradition has a name for them. Malicious spirits lurk among mankind and prey on the weak and foolhardy. Some are tricksters who simply care nothing for metahuman life or feelings, simply taking joy in manipulating and using metahumans for their own ends. Others harbor a burning hatred for metahumans, with dark appetites that are whetted by suffering and pain. Occultists, paranaturalists, and scholars may puzzle about the origins and diversity of these entities, but the truth is that an unknown number of such dangerous spirits are abroad in the Sixth World. Most are free or wild spirits, taking on forms that range from the innocuous and friendly-seeming to forms that reflect cultural bogeymen or even the restless dead. These are collectively referred to as shadows, but in fact each such spirit is unique.

Many (but not all) shadows have the Energy Drain (Karma) power, allowing them to feed off their victims during moments of powerful emotional outpouring. While the causes of such drastic emotions may vary, shadow spirits seem particularly drawn to the negative emotions that accompany riots, violent deaths, metahuman experimentations, torture, genocide, war, or mass panic, as well as more personal expressions like arrogance, inadequacy, fear, or self-doubt. Shadow spirits often use Compulsion, Influence, and similar powers to provoke situations in which they can drain Karma from their intended victim(s).

SHADOW SPIRIT TYPES

The following examples should be seen as concepts rather than subtypes and are intended to be used as guidelines:

- The **muse** is a creative parasite driven to inspire, then savor the emotional epiphany of artistic creation. Less overtly sinister, the muse is nevertheless an otherworldly being that places little value on the physical needs of metahuman existence (eg. eating, drinking, sleeping, socializing). As a result, manipulated victims are often "damaged" by sleep deprivation, malnourishment, and isolation. The fey and sensuous form the muse assumes is intended to appeal and inspire artists, performers, and other creative types.
- The **nightmare** is a bogey man, a dreadful apparition that delights in horrifying and scaring its victims. The nightmare is a coward and a monster, often choosing children and the elderly as targets. It terrorizes the weak, vulnerable, and innocent, reveling in the fear and helplessness they radiate. Nightmares typically appear in forms drawn straight from horror sims and the darkest mythologies.
- The **shade** is drawn to emotional distress and misery, addicted to sorrow, loss, loneliness, and broken hearts. The shade will invariably seek to aggravate its victims' emotional states, influencing them to commit acts of desperation, abasement, and eventually suicide—often badly carried through, to the additional delight of the shade. Shades are often reported as stern, grey metahuman figures.
- The **succubus** thrives on base sexual energies (e.g. lust, passion, love), shifting between attractive, desirable, and lecherous metahuman forms (male, female, or even androgynous). Hard to distinguish from a normal metahuman, the succubus seduces others to feed from them at the height of the sexual act (though they don't necessarily have to participate themselves), be it a one-night stand or a full fledged orgy. A true sexual predator, the succubus shows disdain for attachments or relationships.
- The **wraith** is the most hostile shadow spirit known. It thrives on violence, destruction, and pain, employing its powers of Compulsion and Fear to inspire hatred, bloodlust, and violence in intelligent beings. The wraith feeds on and enjoys extreme acts of violence, such as torture and rape, and likes nothing better than seeding conflict so it may draw from the suffering of both factions. Wraiths often materialize as a vaguely humanoid cloud of black or gray mist lit from within by a sickly green light, or as a tall dark figure wearing tattered robes and surrounded by mists.

TOXIC SPIRIT QUICK DESIGN

In *Shadowrun*, gamemasters are free to design their own toxic spirits as unique entities, fleshing out their appearances, attributes, and powers fitting the particular beliefs of the toxic summoner. The simplest way to do this is to use the stats of one of the ten basic spirit types as a template and swap out attributes, abilities and powers, replacing them for abilities with appropriate flavor listed in this chapter. As toxic spirits are diverse, gamemasters should not shrink from modifying existing powers and rules when it fits the flavor of the toxic spirit type in their games. Here are a few examples:

Carnage (Toxic Guardian Spirit)

Carnage spirits embody all the aspects of violence and bloodshed: serial killing, homicidal rage, slaughter and massacre, even racial or tribal genocide. They often appear as humanoid or animal figures displaying frenzy, madness, and bloodlust, and may be confused with blood spirits.

Modifications: Using the guardian spirit statistics as a template (p. 96), replace the Confusion power for Compulsion (Homicidal Mania) and add that carnage spirits go berserk when wounded (see Bear Mentor Spirit, p. 200, *SR4A*).

Contagion (Toxic Spirit of Man)

Contagion spirits often appear as feverish humanoids or beasts: plague-ridden, contagious, and covered with carcinoma, pustulent bulges, or pox. They are pestilence in metahuman form.

Modification: Using the spirit of man statistics as a template (p. 303, *SR4A*), exchange the Concealment and Innate Spell powers for Noxious Breath and Pestilence (p. 154).

Smog (Toxic Air Spirit)

Smog spirits normally materialize as brownish-yellow or grayish-white hazes made of noxious air pollutants (nitric oxides, volatile organic compounds, paints, solvents, pesticides, and other chemicals).

Modification: Use the spirit of air as a template (p. 294, *SR4A* and swap Concealment and Confusion powers for Noxious Breath and Weather Control (Acid Rain, Pall of Smog).

Sample Shadow Spirit

B	A	R	S	C	I	L	W	EDG	ESS	M	Init	IP
F+2	F	F+3	F	F	F	F	F	F	F	F	(Fx2)+3	2

Astral INIT/IP: Fx2, 3
Movement: 10/25
Skills: Assensing, Astral Combat, Con, Dodge, Intimidation, Perception, Unarmed Combat
Powers: Astral Form, Banishing Resistance, Influence, Energy Drain (Karma, LOS, Stun damage, see below), Magical Guard, Materialization, Sapience, Spirit Pact
Muse: Compulsion (Creation), Mind Link, Realistic Form
Nightmare: Engulf (as Guidance spirit, p. 100), Fear, Mind Link, Shadow Cloak
Shade: Compulsion (Sorrow), Shadow Cloak, Silence
Succubus: Compulsion (Lust), Desire Reflection, Mutable Form, Realistic Form
Wraith: Compulsion (Homicidal Rage), Confusion, Fear

Shadow Spirit Energy Drain

Shadow spirits use the Energy Drain power (p. 99) to draw Karma from their victims. Rather than draining their targets directly with an unarmed attack, these spirits must instead coerce the victim to commit an emotionally potent act (violence, a burst of creativity, an inspiring speech, panic, sex, etc.) within line of sight so they can tap in and feed off the victim's surging emotions. This version of the power merely exhausts rather than hurting the target, inflicting 1 box of Stun damage for each Karma point stolen.

EXTRAPLANAR MENACES

In the decades that followed the Awakening, the headlong dash to unravel the mysteries surrounding magic led magicians to discover the metaplanes and their spirit inhabitants. While disconcerting and perilous, the dangers encountered by those astral explorers pale when compared to the menaces that awaited mankind beyond the known metaplanes. All too soon, the Sixth World encountered powerful and sinister entities from the astral realms known as the deep metaplanes. The extraplanar entities that were drawn to Earth were unlike any previously encountered in the planes or astral space; their intellects were alien and inhuman, their abilities terrifying. Regrettably for metahumanity, few of these powerful and inscrutable entities have proven friendly, and in fact several have set their sinister sights on Earth.

While these entities are referred to as spirits for convenience and appear at different Force ratings on Earth, they should be considered unique critters similar to wild or free spirits.

EVANESCENCE (WEAKNESS)

Extraplanar entities suffer from a phenomenon known as *Evanescence*, an irresistible fading of form and Force if they remain in Earth's astral space. Unfortunately, these beings have learned to counter such dissipation by anchoring their astral forms to the physical plane, normally through the use of the Inhabitation or Possession powers.

Extraplanar spirits can persist in the Gaiasphere for only a limited amount of time. Once a spirit has found its way to Earth's astral plane (or was conjured, in the case of insect spirits), its astral form begins to dissipate. For each sunrise or sunset that a spirit with Evanescence remains in full astral form, its Force rating is permanently reduced by 1. If the spirit's Force reaches 0, it dissipates (whether it is disrupted or permanently destroyed is unknown). A spirit with this weakness that is bound to a magician, or that goes free, only loses Force at the rate of 1 point per week.

As a side effect of Evanescence, the astral forms of extraplanar spirits are translucent and harder to detect. Apply a –3 dice modifier to all Assensing Tests (see *Astral Visibility*, p. 114 and *Astral Perception*, p. 191, *SR4A*) against any such spirits in full astral form. This insubstantial form also enables them to bypass astral barriers with greater ease (see *Passing Through Barriers*, p. 194, *SR4A*). Apply a +3 dice pool modifier to the spirit for the relevant test.

All effects of Evanescence are negated as soon as the spirit inhabits or possesses a vessel. If it is somehow driven out of the vessel, the spirit's astral form starts to dissipate again.

INSECT SPIRITS

Insect spirits are among the most alien entities the Sixth World has yet encountered and the first of the metaplanar threats to become known. Insect spirits—known as *bugs* by society at large—are so called because of the unexplained resemblance of their astral forms to Earth's insect species. In fact, different insect spirits appear to exist, sharing traits with a variety of terrestrial insects. Insect spirits are hardy survivors, resilient, adaptable, and driven by an overwhelming compulsion to perpetuate their species. Pursuing an implacable impulse to propagate, insect spirits have targeted Earth and begun to infiltrate metahuman society.

Frightening as their insect nature is, bugs are all the more terrifying in that they view all living beings as potential organic vessels with which they can merge. Though other species are apparently compatible and less resistant to incubation, metahumans are the preferred hosts for insect progeny, suggesting that the bugs' strategy is to subvert and replace the dominant species in an eco-system.

Cooperation between various insect species is uncommon though obviously not impossible; most insect spirits will actively avoid clashes with one another over anything other than territory.

Insect Shamans

To bridge the distance between their home plane and Earth, insect mentor spirits seduce and ally themselves with unbalanced or power-hungry metahuman magicians, promising them untold power, unconditional acceptance, and communion with the hive. Known as insect shamans, these magicians are taught how to summon insect spirits to the Earth and form hives or nests.

It is not understood whether insect shamans—who are often loners, eccentrics, and other antisocial personalities—choose to ally themselves with these alien entities or fall prey to the compelling and seductive call of insect mentors. It is suspected that insect mentors are usually the ones to initiate contact with a potential convert, though how they establish contact and develop the shaman's magical ability is unknown. It is also possible, however, that some burgeoning magicians seek out an insect mentor spirit for their own ends.

Like other magicians, insect shamans are able to summon five spirit types. These spirits have little in common with normal spirit types, instead representing functional archetypes or castes of their insect species. The astral forms of these spirits appear as giant insects and reflect the nature of the insect type and species. Insect spirits are only bound to shamans by services until they inhabit a vessel. From then on, they instinctively show their summoner the unwavering loyalty and obedience they offer their queen or mother—at least until the queen or mother commands a shift in loyalties.

Insect Species and Mentor Spirits

The insect spirit "race" consists of a variety of different insect species that exhibit distinct abilities and motivations. Each such species features many of the archetypical characteristics of an entire terrestrial insect species or related-insect family (for instance, Ant reflects all Ant-genera, such as leafcutters or army ants) and is in turn represented by an insect mentor spirit (e.g. Ant, Wasp, Bee, Roach, etc). The insect shaman believes the mentor spirit embodies the essence, personality, and—in the case of hive spirits—the collective conscience of the species.

Insect mentor spirits bestow no special advantages or disadvantages on their shamans, serving as the shaman's tutor in

> **THE INSECT TRADITION**
> **Concept:** The insect shaman draws power from communion with his insect mentor (and in the case of hive species, with the collective of the nest or the hive). By submitting oneself to the greater whole, the shaman is capable of performing magic and calling forth insect spirits from their native plane.
> **Combat:** Soldier
> **Detection:** Scout
> **Health:** Caretaker
> **Illusion:** Nymph
> **Manipulation:** Worker
> **Drain:** Willpower + Intuition
>
> The insect tradition abstracts the incomprehensible magic system taught by their insect mentors to insect shamans. Unlike other magicians, such magicians always adopt a mentor spirit of a certain insect spirit species. Insect shaman spellcasting often resembles gibberish or a clicking, sing-song, alien tongue. Insect shamans often manifest shamanic masks.
>
> Insect shamans are driven by the same compulsion as their patrons and seek to summon forth as many insect spirits as they can and at some point invoke a queen (in the case of hive spirits) or mother spirit (for solitary spirits)—the physical avatar of their mentor spirit.
>
> An insect shaman's magical lodge will invariably be the "breeding ground" of the physical nest or hive, and will include all manner of insect organic materials and by-products (as will his fetishes and foci), most of which will have no significance or potency to a normal magician.

the ways of insect magic and a figurehead for the collective conscience of the species. When the insect population reaches a certain critical mass, the insect shaman invokes a queen or mother from a nymph spirit. If successful, the newborn queen or mother spirit becomes an avatar of the mentor spirit.

Insect spirits (and hence insect mentor spirits) are subdivided into two large groups by their preference for communalism or solitary existence: hive insect spirits and solitary insect spirits.

Insect Inhabitation

Insect spirits require prepared living vessels to ground their astral forms in the physical world and escape the effects of Evanescence (p. 148). The insect shaman may facilitate inhabitation by preparing a host body (see p. 86). Usually this is accomplished by placing the vessel-to-be in a cocoon extruded by the queen or mother—if already present—or constructed from suitable organic materials and detritus by the shaman. Once the vessel is prepared, a summoned insect spirit in astral form may use Inhabitation to merge with the host (see p. 100). Inhabitation immediately stabilizes the spirit's astral form and halts the effects of Evanescence. The spirit's conjurer may influence the result of the inhabitation (by adding Binding skill to either dice pool, as noted on p. 100); if a queen or mother spirit is present, it may help its progeny by adding (Force) dice to either the spirit's or the vessel's dice pool as desired.

HIVE INSECT SPIRITS

Hive insects follow a queen and work to build a hive. The four most common hive insect spirits are ant, locust, termite, and wasp. Though they exhibit individual differences, the hive structure gives them certain similarities. All work for the growth of the hive and the coming of the queen. As long as no queen is present, the shaman is viewed as a surrogate, as he is the only one able to increase the hive. Once the queen arrives, her safety and the prosperity of the hive becomes the primary concern.

Queens do not like sharing power over the hive. The insect shaman is often discarded if the queen deems him unnecessary for the perpetuation of the hive—eliminated or exiled along with any maturing nymphs.

Ant

Highly social beings, ants cooperate exceptionally well within a single hive. Ant hives are composed of numerous workers, scouts, and soldiers along with a smaller number of caretakers and nymphs, often distinguished by their colorings. Ants are builders, constructing complex warrens with multiple levels and no apparent logic by human standards. Their hives are often below ground in areas they have either excavated or heavily modified. The territorial instincts of ant spirits lead to intense rivalry between hives. Ant spirits rarely work alone; the queen or her shaman usually sends them against objectives *en masse*. When subtlety is called for (provided the shaman can convince the queen that rolling out the army will do more harm than good), ant spirits work in small groups of two to four individuals.

Special Abilities: All Physical damage done by ant spirits in melee combat is considered Acid damage (p. 163, SR4A). Ant spirits are particularly vulnerable to the disruption of the link to their shaman/queen and hive through the Hive Mind power. If the shaman is killed and/or the queen disrupted, or the ant spirit is contained behind a mana barrier, the ant spirit becomes disoriented and suffers a –2 dice pool modifier to all tests.

Locust

While locusts don't form a hive in the traditional sense, they organize in gregarious migrating swarms that are effectively analogous to mobile hives. These swarms travel from place to place, ravaging and consuming everything they can in an area before moving on, and halting only to reproduce and restore their numbers. As voracious and infamous as their biblical counterparts, locust spirit swarms are suspected of destroying farmland and encouraging famine in remote areas like Australia, Central Africa, and Central Asia, though there have been no survivors to confirm the accusations. Locusts have an insatiable hunger and can digest almost anything given time.

Special Abilities: All locust spirits possess the skill of Flight and the power of Devouring (p. 154). Locust spirits have such a single-minded impulse to consume that they become oblivious to their surroundings when feeding (–3 dice pool modifier to Perception Tests).

Termite

Termite spirits possess a caste system similar to that of ants. Adept at burrowing, termite workers build cement-hard "mounds" by mixing sand with their saliva to make a fast-setting, concrete-like material with unique properties, which is also often warded for extra protection.

Though less territorial than ants, termites fight ferociously to defend their territory. Termites prefer to build hives above ground, usually inside abandoned human structures to avoid detection, unless they are in an isolated locale. The neat, tidy interior of a termite hive strongly resembles an ant hive. The area outside the hive, however, shows the signs of the termite spirits' presence: discarded materials and scavenged remains of buildings.

Special Abilities: All termite spirits possess the power of Reinforcement (p. 154)

Wasp

Wasp is the descriptor used for the insect spirit species that embodies the essence and characteristics of several wasp-like hymenoptera species (bees, wasps, and hornets, among others). Wasps organize by function and eusocial caste, but express the same five core types of spirits as all insects. Wasp spirits are highly territorial and not overly intelligent, except for nymphs and caretakers who boast a malign intelligence (a trait they share with their earthly cousins) that is especially

Street Magic

prominent in the queen. Wasp soldiers often appear as hornet-like spirits, while worker spirits resemble drones. Wasp hives are far smaller than the hives of other insect spirits, but manage to cram far more spirits into the smaller area. Wasp hives are always built in high places open to the air, such as the upper stories of buildings and other towering structures.

Special Abilities: All wasp spirits possess the skill of Flight (p. 292, *SR4A*) and the power of Venom (p. 297, *SR4A*).

SOLITARY INSECT SPIRITS

Solitary insect spirits, so called because they do not form hives, are often more cunning and adaptable than their communal counterparts. While some establish nests to breed, they feel no strong attachment to a nest and can leave it at will—subject only to the will of the shaman (if one exists). Insect shamans who follow solitary insect mentor spirits eventually feel compelled to summon one or more mothers. Unlike queens, most mother spirits are capable of summoning other mother spirits. This makes solitary insect spirits much more adept at perpetuating their nest and significantly reduces the need to keep the insect shaman around. Solitary insect spirits are also classified by their type and have less class organization. The different types often show different facets of the insect type to which they belong. Beetle, cicada, firefly, fly, mantid, and roach are all examples of solitary spirits.

Beetle

Different types of beetle spirits exist and can be distinguished by their appearance. While soldier spirits appear as horned stag beetles, workers are often similar to scarabs, scouts to longhorn beetles, and caretakers resemble the more common dung beetle. Nymphs and mothers usually appear as a cross between beetle subspecies. Beetles usually dwell in or around nests overseen by one, or occasionally two, mothers. They prefer to tunnel into damp or moist ground and build their own nests rather than occupy existing spaces. Beetle spirits (especially "males") are generally more aggressive than other insect types (also against their own kind) and tend to hunt alone. They are also quite territorial and engage in "sparring contests" with other beetles.

Special Abilities: Materialized beetle spirits possess a degree of tough chitinous armor; increase their Immunity Armor by 4 against normal weapons (see *Immunity to Normal Weapons,* p. 295, *SR4A*), and consider them to have 4/4 armor against magical attacks.

Cicada

Cicadas usually possess small eyes set wide apart on the head and transparent well-veined wings. All cicada spirits produce a loud, infernal buzzing using their abdominal membranes and can amplify the sound to over 100 decibels (the equivalent of the inside of a nightclub). Cicadas are agile and hardy.

Special Abilities: All cicada spirits possess the skill of Flight (p. 286, *SR4A*) and the power of Sonic Projection (p. 154)

Firefly

Firefly spirits appear as soft-bodied, elongated winged beetles that intermittently emit a yellow-green glow from their lower abdomens. Fireflies usually glow only when agitated, for communication reasons, or when within a few dozen meters of a firefly mother. They also flash when their nest mother or shaman is investing new spirits. Fireflies are known to be the least aggressive of the insect spirit species, favoring evasion to conflict when possible. Scouts and nymphs are far more common than soldiers and caretakers.

Special Abilities: All firefly spirits possess the skill of Flight (p. 292, *SR4A*) and the power of Confusion (p. 293, *SR4A*).

Fly

Fly is an umbrella descriptor for a variety of solitary insect spirits that bear similarities to a number of fly-like species, such as mosquitoes, gnats, midges, and houseflies. All such spirits are unclean scavengers living off the refuse of other species, favoring dank, humid, and often pestilent environments. They are gregarious but self-sufficient, forming nests only to mate and feed. Fly nests are chaotic, noisy, unkept messes that reek with the overpowering odor of refuse and garbage.

Special Abilities: All fly spirits possess the skill of Flight (p. 292, *SR4A*) and the powers of Pestilence (p. 154) and Immunity to Disease (p. 295, *SR4A*).

Mantid

Mantids hunt other insects to consume their power and then reproduce. Unusually for insect spirits, mantids always enforce gender selection in their vessels; a male's (invariably caretakers and workers) primary purpose is to serve as a mate and then as sustenance for "females" (soldiers, scouts, and nymphs). Leadership in mantid groupings is normally snatched by the strongest soldier mantid (always females). Though rare, nymph mantids exist and possess a unique status similar to a "seer" or "oracle." While they do form nests, mantids do not have queens or mothers, instead possessing a singular means of reproducing: eating other insect spirits. Mantid spirits are powerful because of their ability to assimilate the Force of a spirit to enhance their own.

Mantids are notoriously hard to control by their shamans (exclusively women) since they are able to reproduce without them. Mantids tend to hide among metahumanity, becoming as much a part of it as their alien nature permits.

Special Abilities: All "female" mantid spirits possess the power of Energy Drain (Force, Insect Spirits Only, Physical damage; see p. 99). Mantids drain Force from other inspect spirits by eating them. Force points consumed by the mantid in this manner can be transformed at a 1:1 ratio into Karma to improve its abilities like free spirits do (see p. 107) or stored internally in what amounts to an "astral womb." When the accumulated stored Force equals the mantid's own, it gives "birth" to a full-grown mantid spirit of equal Force—which may then inhabit a living vessel.

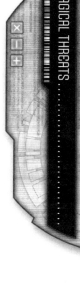

Roach

Cockroaches are scavengers or omnivores that feed from all kinds of garbage. Roach spirits build nests, not because they have to, but because they like to. They cluster around the mother or shaman that "birthed" them, creating the nest. Several mothers can occupy a nest, but more than three rarely share a location. Like their terrestrial counterparts, roaches are also the hardiest insect species, capable of surviving under the most extreme conditions (even radiation).

Special Abilities: Tougher even than trolls, all roach spirits receive a +2 dice pool modifier on all Damage Resistance Tests.

INSECT SPIRIT TYPES

While not all insect spirits boast eusocial hierarchies (i.e. hives or nests), members of known insect spirit species in *Shadowrun* can be assigned to one of five different spirit types. Rather than an elemental or arcane correspondence, these five types reflect specialized expressions, functions, or castes common in the insect world.

Insects with wings can fly in their materialized form, and all insect spirits can crawl along vertical surfaces (such as the side of a building) when materialized.

A Note on Gender: While insect spirits appear to have no real "sex," an analogy is often made with their terrestrial counterparts and eusocial systems. In most insect species, soldiers, scouts, and workers are considered "males," while caretakers and nymphs (and consequently queens and mothers) are exclusively "females." This may or may not affect an insect shaman's choice of vessels for inhabitation, at the gamemaster's discretion.

Caretaker

Caretaker spirits are specialized in taking care of the nest/hive and the spirits going through inhabitation (cocooned and in the pupation). Less common in solitary insect species, caretakers can sometimes be found among roaches and beetles. Caretakers often create protective wards to defend the hive's spawn from enemies or predators.

B	A	R	S	C	I	L	W	EDG	ESS	M	Init	IP
F+2	F+1	F+1	F	F	F	F	F	F	F	F	(Fx2)+1	2

Astral INIT/IP: Fx2, 3
Movement: 10/45
Skills: Assensing, Astral Combat, Dodge, Leadership, Perception, Unarmed Combat
Powers: Animal Control (Insect Type), Astral Form, Guard, Hive Mind, Inhabitation (Living Vessels), Sapience
Optional Powers: Binding, Confusion, Enhanced Senses (Smell, Thermographic Vision, or Ultrasound)
Weaknesses: Allergy (Insecticides, Severe), Evanescence

Nymph

Nymph spirits are juvenile queens or mothers. They resemble weaker and underdeveloped versions of their insect counterparts. Lacking the physical prowess and power they will possess once metamorphosed into a queen or mother, nymphs still make extensive use of all kinds of spell-like and pheromone-based abilities to distract and endanger potential enemies. Insect shamans invariably prefer female vessels for nymphs.

B	A	R	S	C	I	L	W	EDG	ESS	M	Init	IP
F−1	F	F+3	F−1	F	F	F	F	F	F	F	(Fx2)+3	2

Astral INIT/IP: Fx2, 3
Movement: 10/45
Skills: Assensing, Astral Combat, Dodge, Perception, Spellcasting, Unarmed Combat
Powers: Animal Control (Insect Type), Astral Form, Enhanced Senses (Smell, Thermographic Vision, or Ultrasound), Hive Mind, Inhabitation (Living Vessels), Innate Spell (any one Illusion Spell known to the summoner), Sapience
Optional Powers: Compulsion, Fear
Weaknesses: Allergy (Insecticides, Severe), Evanescence

Scout

Scout spirits often operate far afield from the nest/hive to accomplish tasks such as information gathering and reconnaissance. This type of spirit is sent on missions that do not require the brute force approach of soldier spirits. As they are intended to be deployed as infiltrators and observers, queens and mothers will attempt to produce flesh forms for scouts (see p. 100).

B	A	R	S	C	I	L	W	EDG	ESS	M	Init	IP
F	F+2	F+2	F	F	F	F	F	F	F	F	(Fx2)+2	2

Astral INIT/IP: Fx2, 3
Movement: 10/45
Skills: Assensing, Astral Combat, Dodge, Infiltration, Perception, Shadowing, Unarmed Combat
Powers: Animal Control (Insect Type), Astral Form, Concealment, Enhanced Senses (Smell, Thermographic Vision, or Ultrasound), Hive Mind, Inhabitation (Living Vessels), Movement, Sapience, Search
Optional Powers: Confusion, Guard, Natural Weapon (DV = Force Physical damage, AP 0), Noxious Breath
Weaknesses: Allergy (Insecticides, Severe), Evanescence

Soldier

The primary task of soldier spirits is to guard and defend the hive/nest. In solitary species, the soldier is a hunter and predator. They exhibit natural weaponry appropriate to their insect species (mandibles, stings), often have a chitinous exoskeleton, and are more resistant to insecticides.

B	A	R	S	C	I	L	W	EDG	ESS	M	Init	IP
F+2	F	F+1	F+3	F	F	F	F	F	F	F	(Fx2)+1	2

Astral INIT/IP: Fx2, 3
Movement: 10/45
Skills: Assensing, Astral Combat, Counterspelling, Dodge, Exotic Ranged Weapon, Perception, Unarmed Combat
Powers: Animal Control (Insect Type), Astral Form, Fear, Hive Mind, Inhabitation (Living Vessels), Natural Weapon (DV = (Force +2) Physical damage, AP −1), Sapience
Optional Powers: Concealment, Binding, Magical Guard, Noxious Breath, Skill (a soldier spirit may be given an additional Combat skill instead of an optional power), Venom
Weaknesses: Allergy (Insecticides, Light), Evanescence

Worker

Workers are the most common type of insect spirits. Their function is to maintain and expand the physical hive and acquire resources like food, heat, and new hosts.

B	A	R	S	C	I	L	W	EDG	ESS	M	Init	IP
F+3	F	F+1	F+2	F	F	F	F	F	F	F	(Fx2)+1	2

Astral INIT/IP: Fx2, 3
Movement: 10/45
Skills: Assensing, Astral Combat, Dodge, Perception, Unarmed Combat
Powers: Animal Control (Insect Type), Astral Form, Enhanced Senses (Smell, Thermographic Vision), Hive Mind, Inhabitation (Living Vessels), Movement, Sapience, Search
Optional Powers: Concealment, Enhanced Senses (Ultrasound), Venom, Skill (a worker spirit may be given additional Technical or Physical skill instead of an optional power)
Weaknesses: Allergy (Insecticides, Severe), Evanescence

QUEEN AND MOTHER SPIRITS

The queen or mother spirit is an avatar of the insect shaman's mentor spirit. It is the "spiritual" center of the hive or nest.

Metamorphosis Metamagic

The summoning/creation of a queen/mother spirit requires a metamagic technique known as Metamorphosis that is taught exclusively to insect shamans by their mentor spirits. Similar to Ally Conjuration and Invoking metamagic, the insect shaman transforms an already-present nymph spirit into a queen or mother spirit.

To summon a queen/mother, the insect shaman must first create a spirit formula (see *Ally Spirit Formula*, p. 103). The conjuring ritual must be performed in a magical lodge with a Force equal or greater than the desired Force of the queen/mother spirit. The queen/mother is summoned following normal summoning rules (p. 188, *SR4A*); her essence is channeled directly into the nymph, who emerges transformed into a queen or mother spirit with new abilities and powers. If the queen/mother is called into a true form nymph, she will always be a larger-than-human-sized version of the insect form, usually four to six meters long.

Control of the Hive/Nest

As soon as she emerges from her cocoon, the queen/mother becomes the focal point of the hive/nest (though it still operates functionally without her). A queen/mother spirit is a free spirit (p. 106) and is no longer bound by the shaman that called her forth—unless the insect shaman uses her spirit formula to bind her (see *Binding a Free Spirit*, p. 108). Depending on the degree of devotion of the insect shaman to his mentor spirit, the shaman hands over power or vies with the new queen/mother spirit for the control of the hive (normally resulting in the elimination of the impudent shaman). Sometimes queen/mother and shaman enter into a spirit pact (p. 108) out of mutual interest in raising their power. An insect shaman can only ever summon one queen/mother spirit, as it is the embodied avatar of his mentor spirit.

Queen/mother spirits no longer require the shaman to summon new insect spirits from the deep metaplanes, as they can use their Astral Gateway power (p. 98) to bring new spirits across themselves.

If a queen/mother is disrupted, she is cast back to the deep metaplanes and must be brought back by the insect shaman once again using Metamorphosis metamagic. If she is destroyed, the shaman is immediately stripped of his magic (losing his Magician or Mystic Adept quality) and probably becomes a mental/emotional wreck (the gamemaster can assign whatever Negative mental qualities he feels appropriate). Any true form spirits linked to the queen/mother via Hive Mind are disrupted if she is destroyed, while hybrid and flesh forms will become permanently bewildered and insane.

Queen/Mother Spirit

B	A	R	S	C	I	L	W	EDG	ESS	M	Init	IP
F+5	F+3	F+4	F+5	F	F	F	F	F	F	F	(Fx2)+4	3

Astral INIT/IP: Fx2, 3
Movement: 10/45
Skills: Assensing, Astral Combat, Con, Counterspelling, Dodge, Leadership, Negotiation, Perception, Spellcasting, Unarmed Combat
Powers: Animal Control (Insect Type), Astral Gateway, Banishing Resistance, Compulsion, Enhanced Senses (Smell, Thermographic Vision, or Ultrasound), Fear, Hive Mind, Sapience, Search, Spirit Pact

Optional Powers: Concealment, Guard, Natural Weapon (DV = (Force + 3) Physical damage, AP –1), Noxious Breath, Venom, Wealth

Weaknesses: Allergy (Insecticides, Severe)

Note: As free spirits, queen/mothers have the Magician quality. They either have the Astral Form and Materialization powers (if true form); Immunity to Normal Weapons (if hybrid form); or Aura Masking, Immunity to Normal Weapons, and Realistic Form (if flesh form). All queen/mother Spirits additionally possess the Special Abilities of their insect species. Queens/mothers that possess the Wealth power can create (pseudo)biological products according to their insect type—reagents like honey, royal jelly, paper for wasps, etc—that can be sold, consumed, used to make insect tradition magical lodges and foci, etc.

INSECT SPIRIT POWERS

Beside the usual abilities innate to spirits, insect spirits possess a number of powers unique to their kinds.

Devouring

Type: P • Action: Complex • Range: Touch • Duration: Sustained

Insect spirits use the Devouring power to voraciously consume all biomaterial (e.g. crops, wood, vegetation) and most non-living objects in an area. Some flesh and hybrid-form insect spirits actually seem to derive sustenance from this consumption, whereas others regurgitate the material and use it construct parts of their hive. The spirit makes a Force x 2 Test against the Object Resistance threshold (p. 183, *SR4A*) of all possible material/objects within (Magic) meters. If the hits exceed the Object Resistance, the object is affected and devoured. Barriers lose 1 point of Structure rating and vehicles take 1 box of damage per round the power is sustained. Living critters and characters are unaffected. Locust spirits use this power to strip the land of anything remotely edible.

Hive Mind

Type: M • Action: Auto • Range: Special • Duration: Always

All insect spirits of a given species controlled by a shaman or a queen/mother possess a constant telepathic bond which each other. Insect spirits may send a telepathic message to one or more spirits in the hive/nest and/or the shaman as a Free Action. The shaman (or queen/mother) can also use this link to experience any one of the insect spirits' senses (or switch to another) with a Simple Action, in the same way as the Sense Link power (p. 54), but with no range limitation. The Hive Mind power will not work through mana barriers (except those created by the shaman or insects of that hive/nest).

Insect shamans sometimes have difficulty coping with the constant buzz of alien voices in their head, especially if the nest/hive is agitated. In this case the Hive Mind distracts the shaman, and he must succeed in a Magic + Willpower (2) Test to repress the hum of communication if he needs to concentrate on anything, such as fighting or spellcasting.

Pestilence

Type: P • Action: Auto • Range: Touch • Duration: Instant

The critter carries a natural (non-magical), contagious bacterial infection or virus that may infect characters who come into contact with it (or its secretions). Treat this disease as a toxin (p. 254, *SR4A*) with the following attributes: Vector: contact, Speed: 1 day, Power: 8, Effect: Stun damage, disorientation, nausea. Unlike toxins, disease effects last for 1 full day. Each day the disease Power increases by 2 and the character must make another resistance test, until the disease Power is reduced to 0. Note that some critters may carry diseases with different attributes, as noted in the individual descriptions.

Reinforcement

Type: P • Action: Complex • Range: Touch • Duration: Special

Reinforcement is the power to shore up and enhance natural and constructed materials to increase their natural resistance. Fortifying material requires a Force x 2 (square meters, 1 hour) Extended Test. If successful, the Force of the spirit is added to the barrier's Armor and Structure ratings. Multiple applications of reinforcement are not cumulative (only the highest applied effect counts).

Sonic Projection

Type: P • Action: Complex • Range: Special • Duration: Sustained

This power affects everyone able to hear it (except for insect spirits of the same type), creating a highly distracting, deafening, and almost painful infernal buzzing. The spirit makes an Opposed Test using its Force x 2 against each target's Willpower. Sound dampers and spells like Hush/Silence provide additional dice to the defender equal to their rating/hits scored. Each net hit scored by the spirit provides a negative dice pool modifier on all tests for as long as the buzzing is sustained.

THE SHEDIM

Shedim are bodysnatching spirits from the darkest regions of the metaplanar realms. They steal the corpses of the dead and the bodies of imprudent magicians as physical vessels for themselves. Contrary to other threats, who view Earth as a breeding or feeding ground, shedim seem to possess a violent hatred of everything living and exhibit hostility towards metahumans and other spirits.

The first public encounters with shedim took place worldwide during the Year of the Comet, 2061. The dark agendas of these spirits took an even more insidious turn when they were linked to the rise of the New Islamic Jihad a few years later. Their machinations shook the Middle East until 2064, when the master shedim that had seized control of the Jihad's spiritual leader, Ibn Eisa, was revealed. Some fear, correctly so, that the events in the Middle East were merely a prelude to shedim plans to instigate worldwide crisis and widespread death (war, genocide, holocaust).

The Nature of Shedim

Shedim can be considered free spirits (p. 106) and cannot normally be summoned or bound. In fact, as no one has ever found their home metaplane (or at least admitted to it), whether or not they possess true names (spirit formula) remains a matter of conjecture.

On the astral plane, shedim appear as translucent apparitions whose phantom-like forms resemble large, free-floating, jellyfish-like amoeboid entities. Subject to Evanescence (p. 148), the only way a shedim can remain in the physical world is by anchoring itself via possession of a dead vessel—which is why finding a corpse is often the primary concern of shedim newly-arrived on Earth. Shedim also have the disturbing ability to possess the "unoccupied" bodies of Awakened characters who are astrally projecting (treating them as prepared vessels, p. 95).

The levels of intelligence, motivation, and malice observed among individual shedim vary greatly, leading to suspicions that—like insect spirits—shedim may be divided into subspecies or castes. The only distinction thaumaturgic specialists have so far been able to discern is the division of the shedim species into normal shedim (servants or drones) and so-called master shedim, which are even more threatening and powerful.

Since metahumanity has responded to the shedim presence by changing their death rites and protecting cemeteries, crypts, and even morgues with astral defenses such as wards, shedim have developed new tricks to snatch the bodies of metahumans. They have been known to prey on victims of random violence or natural causes shortly after death, and have more than once been found working together to target special victims, kidnap them, and murder them for their bodies.

The powerful entities known as master shedim have also found ways of opening passage to their home metaplane from Earth using the Astral Gateway power (p. 98). They jealously guard this ability as a means to summon and control more of their lesser brethren and appear disinclined to cooperate with other master shedim.

Shedim

B	A	R	S	C	I	L	W	EDG	ESS	M	Init	IP
F	F	F+2	F	F	F	F	F	F	F	F	(Fx2)+2	2

Astral INIT/IP: Fx2, 3
Movement: 10/25
Skills: Assensing, Astral Combat, Dodge, Perception, Unarmed Combat
Powers: Astral Form, Deathly Aura, Energy Drain (Karma, Touch range, Physical damage), Fear, Immunity (Age, Pathogens, Toxins), Paralyzing Touch, Possession (Dead or Abandoned Vessels), Sapience
Optional Powers: Accident, Aura Masking, Compulsion, Regeneration, Search, Shadow Cloak, Silence
Weaknesses: Allergy (Sunlight, Mild), Evanescence

Master Shedim

B	A	R	S	C	I	L	W	EDG	ESS	M	Init	IP
F	F	F+3	F	F	F	F	F	F	F	F	(Fx2)+3	2

Astral INIT/IP: Fx2, 3
Movement: 10/25
Skills: Assensing, Astral Combat, Counterspelling, Dodge, Perception, Spellcasting, Unarmed Combat
Powers: Astral Form, Astral Gateway, Aura Masking, Banishing Resistance, Compulsion, Deathly Aura, Energy Drain (Karma, Touch range, Physical damage), Fear, Immunity (Age, Pathogens, Toxins), Possession (Dead or Abandoned Vessels), Regeneration, Sapience, Shadow Cloak, Spirit Pact
Optional Powers: Accident, Noxious Breath, Search, Silence.
Weaknesses: Allergy (Sunlight, Mild), Evanescence
Notes: Master shedim have the Magician quality (p. 91, SR4A), but may never use Conjuring skills. The gamemaster determines what spells the master shedim knows.

Deathly Aura

Type: P • Action: Simple • Range: Special • Duration: Sustained

The spirit exhibits an aura of primordial fear and decay that taints the surrounding environment. For an area with a radius of (Force) meters around the spirit, the temperature drops by twice the spirit's Force in degrees centigrade. Furthermore, organic materials decay at an accelerated rate (aging by a factor equal to the spirit's Force). This decay is not fast enough to noticeably damage large creatures like metahumans or most critters, but it withers plants and is lethal to insects and small animals like mice. Living creatures are struck by unreasoning terror and must succeed in an Opposed Test between their Charisma + Willpower and the spirit's Force x 2 in order to bring themselves to enter such an area voluntarily.

Paralyzing Touch

Type: P • Action: Complex • Range: Touch • Duration: Special

This is a Touch-range version of the Paralyzing Howl power (p. 296, SR4A). The shedim must touch the target (requiring a successful unarmed attack, which causes no damage).

...GRIMOIRE...

"No, no. That's not it at all. You're never going to get this if you don't concentrate."

Fox Eyes flung his paintbrush across the room. It smacked the wall, leaving a red and disconcertingly blood-like trail down to the floor. It wasn't the first. "I am concentrating!" Swiping her hand across her forehead, she swore when sweat droplets splattered onto her unfinished painting. "You just don't get it! How am I supposed to learn this spell by staring at all those fucking formulae? I feel like I'm back in math class again—and I flunked math class."

Winterhawk sighed, levitating the paintbrush back to Fox Eyes. "Look—I know you don't like it. I know it's not easy for a shaman to learn from a hermetic—or vice versa. Believe me, this is no party for me either. But it seems you need this spell, and it seems that I'm the only one in the vicinity who knows it, so either you're stuck trying to puzzle it out yourself—something I don't think you have time for—or you can put up with me and my mathematical chicken scratchings. What's it to be, then?"

Fox Eyes snatched the brush out of the air and stared down at her painting. The spell was a particularly nasty and specialized combat spell, promising to prove quite useful against what they'd be facing on their upcoming run. The painting indicated this with its harsh lines, violent clashing colors, and angular shapes. She could already see the beginnings of an aura forming around it, the inkling of what it was to be—but it was a long way from done. She might be able to finish it herself at this point, but probably not in time, since she'd still have to learn the spell once she had the formula. "Okay, okay," she said, resigned. She looked up at the old-fashioned whiteboard and tried to make sense of the arcane symbols scrawled over most of its area.

Winterhawk nodded. "All right, then. Now, take a look at the spell's aura again as I cast it, then do ... whatever it is you do." Truth be told, he was as much in the dark about what Fox Eyes was doing as the shaman was about the hermetic process. How were you supposed to represent a spell by making paint splotches on a canvas? He had no doubt that the shaman was in fact doing that—he too could see the power growing in the work—but the process eluded him. Why had he agreed to try to help a shaman translate a spell formula anyway? They'd been at it for what seemed like forever already, with no end in sight. He cast the spell again, and was rewarded by a look of comprehension on Fox Eyes' face, followed by a flurry of rapid and furious brushstrokes.

The door to the lodge opened and a troll poked his head in. "Fox, you getting anywhere yet? We gotta—"

"Out!" Fox Eyes and Winterhawk roared in unison.

Street Magic

SPELL DESIGN TABLE

Spell Category	Threshold	Interval
Combat	12	3 months
Detection	8	1 month
Health	8	1 month
Illusion	12	3 months
Manipulation	16	3 months

Situation	Dice Pool Modifiers
Creating from scratch	–2
Briefly observed aura of same spell	+1
Assessed aura of same spell at length	+2
Translating from another tradition	–1
Modifying an existing formula	+0
Already know a very similar spell	+1
Not using a Magical Lodge	–4
Spirit used to Aid Study	+Force
Mentor Spirit Modifier for that spell category	+variable
Spell attributes	+/–Drain modifier

SPELL DESIGN

This section provides guidelines for players and gamemasters who want to design their own spells. In order to create a new spell (or their own version of an existing spell), a character must first develop a *spell formula* using Arcana skill (see p. 24).

SPELL FORMULAE

A spell formula is the symbolic "code" that defines the workings of a specific spell. These formulae are too complex to memorize, and must be recorded in some medium. In game terms, a spell formula is always the same for a particular spell, but its in-game physical representation differs according to the magical tradition and outlook of the spell designer. A shamanic formula may be an item such as a painting, a carving, a set of runes, or a medicine bag. Hermetic formulae are typically represented as written/digital texts or complex diagrams composed of many arcane equations and symbols. The formulae contain the same concepts but express them in different ways. At the gamemaster's discretion, some traditions may be similar enough that their spell formulae may be interchangeable (for example, hermetics and chaos magicians have very similar ideologies and practices).

Inspiration

There are many ways a character can develop a spell formula. A character who is designing a spell from scratch must know what he wants the spell to do and must have some idea how it should work, whether he dreamed the idea up or is copying it from a scene in his favorite action sim. A character who has assessed a spell's aura may also attempt to replicate it, though this is seriously difficult unless he has had a chance to observe it in detail repeatedly. A character may also copy the formula from a tradition other than his own. A character who wants to modify an existing formula can attempt to reverse engineer a spell's code in order to alter its effects.

The Design Test

Any character who possesses the Arcana skill (see p. 24) can design a spell formula. Though theoretical occultists skilled in Arcana with no magical ability are rare, they do exist, much like pure theoreticians in the physical sciences. They can create a working spell formula but cannot personally test their theories.

A magician does not need to craft the formula within his magical lodge, but using a lodge does help significantly. Mundanes must create the formula according to a particular tradition's outlook; for this reason, using a magical lodge appropriate to that tradition will also benefit their efforts.

Spell design is handled as an Arcana + Logic Extended Test. The threshold and interval are determined by the spell category, as noted on the Spell Design Table. The character's situation and certain attributes of the spell may modify the designer's dice pool. At the gamemaster's discretion, modifiers from the Build/Repair Table on p. 138, *SR4A*, may also apply.

Using the Formula

Once you have a spell formula, you can use it to learn the spell, following the rules given on p. 182, *SR4A*. You can also sell it, publish it as "public domain" magic, and/or give it to your friends or magic group comrades.

Legally buying or selling a spell usually requires a lot of authorization and paperwork—and, of course, a legal SIN. As a result, most shadowrunners deal only with black-market spell formulae.

A spell formula must exist in hard-copy format or be stored via electronic media. The creator of the formula determines the medium used, as appropriate for his tradition. Mages have the advantage here, as shamanic formulae rarely lend themselves to computer storage. A shaman must usually have the actual formula/object, though the gamemaster can allow a digitized image or a hologram to fulfill this requirement for visual formulae such as paintings or mosaics.

SPELL DESIGN STEP-BY-STEP
1. Choose the spell category
2. Choose the type
3. Choose the range
4. Choose the duration
5. Determine effects
6. Calculate the Drain Value
7. Final Touches

Open Source vs. Proprietary

These rules assume that—unlike computer programs—there is no distinction between a spell formula and its "source code." What this means is that anyone who possesses a spell formula can simply copy it. Depending on the formula's medium, this may be difficult—a formula represented as an engraving on a silver plate, for example, may require a skilled artisan to successfully copy. Digital formulae sold by corporations are typically considered proprietary and protected by copyright and usually feature copy protection, though skilled hackers can bypass this (see *Legal vs. Pirated Software,* p. 108, *Unwired*). Many digital formulae, however, are distributed without copy protection as "open source"—particularly Health spells.

DESIGNING NEW SPELLS

The step-by-step procedure described in this section allows players to design spells that maintain game balance while providing plenty of leeway for creativity. All of the spells presented in *SR4* and this book were created according to these guidelines. Gamemasters can use these rules to introduce new spells that are available in their campaigns (or perhaps available to the *bad guys*), just as players can produce new spells specifically for their characters (keep in mind the character will need to develop the spell formula, as described above).

Every choice you make during spell design can affect other elements of the spell. For the most satisfactory results, you should familiarize yourself with all the information in this section first. Having all of the facts in mind when you start will help prevent you from being disappointed with the final results or finding that you have to re-do the spell because you found a limitation that didn't fit your plan. You should also take note of *The Limits of Sorcery* sidebar on p. 159, as this clarifies some specific things that magic in *Shadowrun* simply cannot do.

Step 1: Choose Spell Category

Each spell must be classified according to one of five categories: Combat, Detection, Health, Illusion, or Manipulation (see p. 181, *SR4A*). If the spell heals damage, it is a Health spell; if it kills someone, it is a Combat spell, and so on. Note that *how* a spell accomplishes its effects is more important than the effects themselves for determining its category. For example, if the intended effect of a spell is to kill the target, but the effect is achieved by transforming and manipulating matter (filling the target's throat and lungs with fluids so that he chokes to death), then such a spell would be most accurately created as a Manipulation spell, not a Combat spell. The gamemaster has the final say on what category a spell belongs in.

Step 2: Choose Spell Type

Each spell is either mana or physical (see p. 203, *SR4A*).

Mana spells only affect the mind or spirit of a target, or magical energies. Because they do not have to affect physical objects, mana spells generally cause less Drain. Mana spells cannot affect non-living objects. A mana Illusion spell can fool corp guards within line of sight but has no effect if they are watching via closed-circuit camera from a remote location. Mana spells work against cyber-modified living beings because the cyberware was paid for with Essence and so is considered to be integral to the being's organic system.

Physical spells affect the material form of a target and will work on non-living targets. Physical spells, however, have no effect on the astral plane.

THE LIMITS OF SORCERY

Though spells can create many amazing effects, the power of sorcery in the Sixth World does have limits. Some of these limitations may be inherent in the nature of magic; others may simply be conditions magical theorists have yet to find a way around.

Currently, sorcery obeys the following limitations, which form the base-line assumptions according to which all spells in this and other *Shadowrun* books were created. Players and gamemasters may choose to ignore or alter any or all of these assumptions, but doing so may unbalance their game.

Sorcery Cannot Affect Anything to which the User Does Not Have a Magical Link.

In the case of spellcasting, this link is provided by line of sight: the visual image of the target provides the magical connection between the caster and the target of the spell. For ritual sorcery, a sympathetic link (see p. 28) can provide the magical connection, in addition to standard line of sight or a ritual spotter. Without this link, sorcery cannot affect a target.

Sorcery Cannot Alter the Fabric of the Space/Time Continuum.

Spells cannot directly change distance or the passage of time. Teleportation and time travel are the holy grails of magical R&D departments the world over, but no one has been able to unravel the knotty problem of affecting space or time with magic. Spells can speed up or slow down processes, such as healing or chemical reactions, and allow subjects to move quickly, but they cannot directly alter time or space.

Sorcery Cannot Divine the Future with any Certainty.

Spells are rooted in the same present as their caster and cannot pierce the veil of time to predict the future with any great accuracy. Reliable techniques of long-range precognition do not exist. Spells designed to predict the future only provide clues and hints about possible events, and then only over a short span of time. The further into the future one attempts to divine, the more unreliable the results.

Sorcery Cannot Summon or Banish Spirits.

These abilities are the province of the art of Conjuring. Spells can, however, be used to damage or affect spirits or to create barriers that block or contain them.

Continued on page 160

> **THE LIMITS OF SORCERY (CONT.)**
>
> **Sorcery Cannot Raise the Dead**
> Though spells can heal, once a person has passed away, they are gone forever (though some view conjuring spirits as raising the spirits of the dead).
>
> **Sorcery Cannot Create Magical Items**
> Foci, vessels, and other items imbued with magic may not be crafted with spells; such handiwork requires the hands-on efforts of an enchanter.
>
> **Sorcery Cannot Bridge the Gap between the Astral and Physical Planes**
> Spells only have an effect in the plane on which they are cast. Spells cast on the astral have no effect on the physical, and vice versa. Likewise, spells cast in the astral or physical have no effect on the metaplanes, and vice versa.
>
> **Sorcery Cannot Create Complex Things**
> Though spellcraft can transform energy, spark elemental forces, and even provide nutrition, no magicians have yet determined a way for sorcery to create complex items (such as a gun or even a hammer) from mana alone—despite the best efforts of research corps to date. Sorcery can be used to fix and sometimes transmute complex items, but the days of summoning weapons from nowhere have not yet arrived.
>
> **Magic Is Not Intelligent.**
> Mana only does as it is told when manipulated by Magical skills such as Sorcery. Magical effects do not make independent decisions.

Step 3: Choose Range

Spells can have a range of either touch or line of sight (see *Range*, p. 203, *SR4A*). This determines how the caster "targets" the spell. Some spells may have additional targeting requirements, such as requiring voluntary targets or affecting all of the targets within an area.

Touch: The caster must touch the target in order to cast the spell on it. As noted on p. 203, *SR4A*, touching an unwilling target requires an unarmed attack. This attack succeeds even if the caster and target tie on the Opposed Test. This accounts for the fact that the caster does not actually have to attack and hurt the target, he simply needs to make contact. In fact, this unarmed attack will not cause damage even if the caster succeeds, as he is pre-occupied more with casting the spell than inflicting physical harm.

Line of Sight (LOS): The spell can target anything the caster can physically see or assense, regardless of the distance (see p. 183, *SR4A*). The caster may not target anything that is completely behind cover or otherwise obscured. Since the caster only needs to see part of the target, a Perception Test may be necessary to see if the caster can spot enough of the target to cast. Visibility modifiers apply to the Spellcasting Test. Note that full body armor does not "conceal" the person within and prevent them from being targeted.

Area Effect: As described on p. 183, *SR4A*, area spells affect all valid targets within an area of effect. Area spells cannot affect individuals who cannot be seen, even if they are within the area designated for the effect. Magicians also may not selectively ignore valid targets within the area of effect, including themselves. The base area of effect can be centered anywhere within line of sight and has a radius equal to the caster's Magic in meters.

If an area Illusion or Manipulation spell is sustained, the affected area may be moved with a Complex Action, as long as it remains within line of sight. Characters who "drop out" of the affected area are no longer affected by the spell; characters who are "enveloped" by the area must make a Spell Resistance Test against the effects of the spell as appropriate.

Restricted Target: Some spells are designed to only affect a limited category of targets, such as voluntary targets or a single species (Detect Dwarfs). This helps to reduce the spell's Drain. A spell with the voluntary-target requirement can only be cast on targets that do not resist the spell effects. Targets who are unconscious, under the effects of mind-control, or non-living are always considered voluntary

Very Restricted Target: These spells only affect a very specific type of target, such as the caster or a specific individual or thing. With the gamemaster's approval, this restriction may be applied toward a very limited sub-grouping, such as male trolls, rotordrones, or water spirits. This restriction may not be combined with the Restricted Target Drain modifier.

Step 4: Choose Duration

Spells may be Instant, Sustained, or Permanent (see p. 203, *SR4A*).

Instant spells take effect and end in the same action they are cast. They may have some lasting effects, but the spell itself only lasts an instant. All Combat spells are of instant duration, as are most other spells with damaging effects.

Sustained spells last as long as the caster maintains them; their effects end when the spell ends. Any spell involving sensing, searching, analysis, defense, transformation, or other changes in the world or the way the target of the spell perceives the world should be sustained.

Permanent spells must be maintained for a time, then they become permanent. Only spells that restore the target to its original, natural, unaltered state should be permanent in duration. Spells that heal or repair damage, disease, the effects of drugs, poisons, and so on, for example, are all good candidates. If the spell provides some sort of game bonus (other than restorative), the effect should not be permanent. The gamemaster has the final say on whether it is possible to create a permanent version of a spell.

If a permanent spell is not maintained for the entire time required (Drain Value x 2 Combat Turns), it does not

become permanent and its effect is lost. The caster can reduce the time required for a spell to become permanent by sacrificing net hits from the Spellcasting Test; every 1 net hit spent this way reduces the sustaining period by 1 Combat Turn. Hits used this way do not increase the effect of the spell.

Step 5: Determine Effect

The next step is to determine how the spell affects its target, and what exactly those effects are. The key factor here is whether or not the spell is *resisted*. If a spell is resisted by the target, then it requires an Opposed Test to determine the effect. If the spell is not resisted or affects a non-living target, then the spell simply requires a Success Test, possibly requiring a threshold of hits to be reached.

Beyond the type of test used, the actual game mechanics of how the new spell functions when it succeeds—and how net hits increase the effectiveness—must be carefully thought out in terms of game balance. The best guidance we can give is to have the effects mimic those of existing spells. The gamemaster has final authority on how the spell functions, and should always be careful to limit new spells from being too powerful.

Note that spell effects may sometimes create modifiers that add on to existing modifiers from gear, implants, or adept powers. Unless stated otherwise, these effects are cumulative (though the gamemaster can always rule otherwise). Spell effects do not stack on top of other spell effects, however—only the strongest effect applies.

Resisted/Opposed Test Spells: Any spell that affects an unwilling target can be resisted (see pp. 183, *SR4A*). The spell type determines the attribute used by the target for the Opposed Test: Willpower against mana spells and Body against physical spells. Combat, Active Detection, Negative Health, Illusion, and Mental Manipulation spells are all handled as Opposed Tests (except against inanimate objects, see below).

If the spell requires a voluntary target, any attempt to resist it automatically causes the spell to fail. Unconscious targets do not resist.

For Detection and Illusion spells, unwilling targets (targets who are unaware of the spell) always resist (see *Unaware Resistance,* p. 162).

Success Test Spells: Passive Detection, non-Negative Health, and some Manipulation spells are handled as Success Tests. In most cases, the hits from the Spellcasting Test simply determine the level of effect. Most Passive Detection spells have a threshold determined by the gamemaster, with the net hits determining the results (see p. 205, *SR4A*).

Non-Living Targets: Inanimate objects (including drones and vehicles) do not make Spell Resistance Tests, but the spell does have a threshold to succeed as determined by the Object Resistance Table (p. 183, *SR4A*).

Restricted Effect: Some spells are designed to limit the possible effects. For example, (Critter) Form is a restricted version of Shapechange, as it only allows the tar-

> **UNAWARE RESISTANCE**
>
> It is not uncommon to encounter situations—especially with Detection and Illusion spells—where a character who is *unaware* of a spell must resist the spell. For example, a security guard must roll to resist the effect of an Invisibility spell on a shadowrunner trying to sneak past him. How exactly does this work with Counterspelling and Edge, you might ask? Doesn't the act of resisting in these cases give away the fact that someone is using magic against them? How should a gamemaster handle such circumstances to prevent their players from metagaming? All of these are good questions, and we suggest the following:
>
> **Using Counterspelling**
>
> If a character actively protected by spell defense is targeted by a spell, the Counterspelling applies to the resistance test whether the character is aware of the spell or not. The spell defense must have been actively declared in advance; a magician who is unaware of being targeted by a spell may not use spell defense to counteract it if their spell defense was not already "on."
>
> Note that a magician providing spell defense for a target in these circumstances has a chance to notice that a spell was resisted with a Magic + Intuition (3) Test (see p. 185, *SR4A*).
>
> For each of these tests, the gamemaster should roll the test in secret.
>
> **Using Edge**
>
> Characters who are unaware they are resisting a spell may not *use* Edge on the Spell Resistance Test. If the gamemaster allows it, however, a character may allocate some of his Edge to the gamemaster *in advance* for the express purpose of allowing the gamemaster to use this Edge on his behalf when making secret tests. Edge allocated in this way is considered spent and may not be used for any other Edge purposes, though it does refresh as normal.

get to be transformed into a specific (pre-chosen) animal. Likewise, certain Health spells only address the symptoms rather than the root illness/injury.

6. Calculate Drain Value

The final step is to determine the spell's Drain Value. This is calculated according to a specific formula that takes into account the spell's type, category, range, duration, and effects.

Base Drain Value: All spells except for Curative Health spells have a starting Drain Value of Force ÷ 2 (rounded down). Curative Health spells have a base Drain Value equal to the value of the damage they are healing or effect they are countering.

Drain Modifiers: Certain characteristics of the spell may affect the Drain Value. These Drain modifiers are cumulative and calculated specifically for each spell. The Drain Modifiers Table (p. 163) lists a number of modifiers that are applicable to all spell types. Additional modifiers may apply as noted under the descriptions for each spell category below.

Note that a spell's Drain Value may never be modified below 1.

Combat Spells

Combat spells are either Direct (affecting the target from within) or Indirect (damaging the target by creating an external effect and attacking them with it using ranged combat); see p. 203, *SR4A*. Combat spells are always Instant in duration; they may not be Sustained or Permanent. They may cause either Physical or Stun damage.

Direct Combat spells may be mana or physical, depending on what they target. Direct Combat spells are handled as an Opposed Test (except against nonliving objects).

Indirect Combat spells must always be physical, as they create a damaging physical effect to use against the target. Indirect Combat spells are treated as ranged attacks, so physical armor applies.

Elemental Effects: Elemental spells use the elements of nature to inflict damage (see p. 204, *SR4A*). The specific elemental effect (fire, electricity, etc.) must be chosen for each spell. These elemental spells inflict special types of damage that may also have secondary effects (starting fires, melting equipment, etc). Some of these elemental damage types (Acid, Cold, Electricity, and Fire) are described on pp. 163-165, *SR4A*. A few others are described in the Elemental Effects sidebar on p. 164 of this book. At the gamemaster's discretion, other elemental effects may be allowed, though they should be carefully analyzed and weighed against existing effects. A spell may have more than one elemental effect—each effect adds a +2 Drain modifier, and the elemental effects are combined (though in some cases they may cancel out).

Note that only Indirect Combat spells may have elemental effects (Direct Combat spells may not).

Detection Spells

You must determine whether the sense is directional, area effect, or psychic, as described on p. 205, *SR4A*. Additionally, each Detection spell is either Active or Passive (see p. 205, *SR4A*). Detection spells that detect or analyze physical objects, or that provide a physical sense, must be physical spells. Detection spells that analyze/detect magic, life, or mental conditions are mana spells, as are spells that provide psychic senses.

For Detection spells, the *subject* is the one whom the spell is cast on, and who gains the new/enhanced sense. *Target* is used to refer to anyone the sense is used on, who may resist the spell.

Active Detection Spells are treated as Opposed Tests, except against inanimate objects.

Passive Detection Spells are treated as Success Tests (Perception Tests, more accurately). The Detection Spell Results table on p. 206, SR4A, provides guidelines for how well the sense works.

Extended Range: Detection spells can be given the Extended option, increasing the effective range of the spell to Force x Magic x 10 meters (see p. 206, SR4A).

Health Spells

Most Health spells are curative, healing damage, curing disease, and neutralizing toxins; these are treated as Success Tests, with the net hits determining the effect. Though these spells have a Permanent duration, they do not receive the Permanent Drain modifier because they are restoring the target to his natural health. Most Health spells are mana spells, though spells that affect attribute scores must by physical.

All Health spells (including the Negative Health spells) are *required* to have the Touch range Drain modifier (–2), unless the gamemaster specifically allows otherwise. Health spells may never be area effect, because they must be focused on a specific organic system.

Negative Health spells, which impede the target's health, are treated as Opposed Tests (see p. 207, SR4A).

Illusion Spells

As described on p. 208, SR4A, Illusion spells must be either Obvious (everyone can tell they are fake) or Realistic (seemingly real). They must also be either Single-Sense (affecting only one) or Multi-Sense (affecting multiple/all senses). Mana Illusions only work against living/magical targets, whereas physical Illusion spells will affect technological devices and sensors. All Illusion spells are handled as Opposed Tests, except against inanimate objects.

Illusions that hide or conceal rather than creating sensory input—such as Invisibility—are harder, and so receive a specific Drain modifier.

Illusions cannot cause permanent damage directly to a target, though they may cause a target to act in a way that is damaging.

Manipulation

Manipulation spells must either be Environmental, Mental, or Physical, as

DRAIN MODIFIERS

Characteristic	Modifier
Type	
Mana spell	+0
Physical spell	+1
Range	
LOS	+0
Touch	–2
Restricted Target* (ie, voluntary target)	–1
Very Restricted Target* (ie, caster only)	–2
Area	+2
Duration	
Instant	+0
Sustained	+0
Permanent (does not apply to curative Health spells)	+2
Effect	
Restricted Effect*	–1
Combat spells	
Elemental effect (must be Physical spell with Physical damage)	+2
Physical damage	+0
Stun damage	–1
Detection spells	
Basic Detection (ex: Detect Life)	+0
Complex Detection (ex: Detect Enemies)	+1
Basic Analyze (ex: Analyze Device)	+1
Complex Analyze (ex: Analyze Truth)	+2
Invasive Analyze (ex: Mind Probe)	+4
Improved Sense	+1
New Sense	+2
Psychic Sense (ie, telepathy, precognition)	+4
Extended Area (must already have Area Effect)	+2
Health Spells	
Increases Initiative Passes	+4
Cosmetic Effect	–2
Negative Health Spell	+2
Restricted Effect* (ie, Symptoms Only)	–2
Illusion Spells	
Obvious	–1
Realistic	+0
Multi-Sense	+0
Single-Sense	–2
Illusion Hides or Conceals	+2
Manipulation Spells	
Environmental Manipulation	–2
Mental Manipulation	+0
Physical Manipulation	+0
Minor Change	+0
Major Change	+2
Elemental effect (must be Physical spell with Physical damage)	+2

*Restrictions only stack if one bonus applies to an effect and one applies to a target. You cannot have both a restricted and very restricted target, for example.

ELEMENTAL EFFECTS

Blast

The blast elemental effect is like a hurricane wind or the shockwave of an explosion. Blast damage is treated as Physical damage and is resisted with half Impact armor (rounded up). Characters struck with a Blast damage attack are more likely to be knocked down—add the Force to the damage inflicted when comparing to the defender's Body (see *Knockdown*, p. 161, *SR4A*). Blast damage can also break glass and knock over trees and other objects. At the gamemaster's discretion, objects with a Structure rating less than the Force may be knocked over, shattered, shredded, or otherwise swept away.

Ice

Attacks with the Ice effect cover the target with a slick coating of frozen water. Treat the Ice effect as Cold damage (p. 163, *SR4A*), except that objects or terrain affected will be encrusted with ice. Anyone trying to cross an icy surface may need to succeed in an Agility + Reaction Test to avoid slipping (with a threshold equal to the attack's net hits); vehicles must make a Crash Test (p. 168, *SR4A*). Depending on the local temperature, ice may melt quickly.

Light

Spells with a light effect damage the target with a searing flare. Light damage is treated as Physical damage and is resisted with half Impact armor (rounded up). The brightness of the Light effect will cause any targets to suffer a Glare modifier for one Combat Turn after the attack, unless they are equipped with flare compensation. As a secondary effect, Light damage may cause some highly flammable materials (like gasoline) to catch fire.

Metal

The Metal elemental effect damages the target with small metallic (iron) fragments and shrapnel. This attack is similar to flechette ammunition: increase the DV by +2, but the attacker suffers a +5 AP penalty against Impact armor. Metal damage attacks are resisted with Impact armor. As a secondary effect, Metal damage may shred some easily cut materials like cheap fabric.

Continued on page 165

noted on p. 210, *SR4A*. Some Manipulation spells also have elemental effects in the same manners as some Combat spells.

Environmental Manipulation Spells affect the elements and physical properties of an area, so they are all area spells. They must also be physical spells, unless they are specifically affecting the magical properties of an area, in which case they may be mana spells. Environmental Manipulations are handled as Success Tests.

Mental Manipulation Spells affect the mind and are handled as Opposed Tests. These spells are invariably mana spells.

Physical Manipulation Spells affect specific physical forms, and so must all be physical spells. Few of these are area effect, unless they are intended to affect multiple physical forms in that area. Physical Manipulations are handled as Success Tests.

Mana Manipulation Spells affect specific mana forms, and so must all be mana spells. Few of these are area effect, unless they are intended to affect multiple mana forms in that area. Mana Manipulations are handled as Success Tests.

Step 7: Final Touches

It's possible that you may want to create a spell with effects that simply aren't covered by these rules. In that case, you should approximate existing rules as closely as you can. When in doubt, make up something that seems balanced.

Keep in mind that the gamemaster always has final approval over whether or not a new spell will be allowed into her game.

NEW SPELLS

At the gamemaster's discretion, the following new spells may be available to magicians and mystic adept at character creation or may be learned later in game. These spells follow all the same rules for spells as given on pp. 203–211, *SR4A*.

COMBAT SPELLS

Rules for handling Combat spells are given on pp. 203–205, *SR4A*.

Corrode [Object] (Indirect, Touch, Elemental)
Type: P • Range: T • Damage: P • Duration: I • DV: (F÷2)
Melt [Object] (Indirect, Elemental)
Type: P • Range: LOS • Damage: P • Duration: I • DV: (F÷2)+2
Sludge [Object] (Indirect, Area, Elemental)
Type: P • Range: LOS (A) • Damage: P • Duration: I • DV: (F÷2)+4

Similar to Acid Stream and Toxic Wave (p. 204, *SR4A*), these spells create a blast of corrosive spray that inflicts Acid damage (p. 163, *SR4A*). The acidic effects of these spell, however, only affect the specified objects for which the spell was created—everything else remains unharmed. Each different object requires a separate spell: Corrode Wall, Melt Electronics, Sludge Armor, and so on.

Melt affects a single target. Sludge is an area effect spell. Corrode requires the caster to touch the target.

Firewater (Indirect, Elemental)
Type: P • Range: LOS • Damage: P • Duration: I • DV: (F÷2)+5
Napalm (Indirect, Area, Elemental)
Type: P • Range: LOS (A) • Damage: P • Duration: I • DV: (F÷2)+7

This Indirect Combat Spell combines two elemental effects—fire and water—for a unique effect: burning water. Treat the damage as both Fire damage (may set things on fire; see p. 164, SR4A) and Water damage (increased chance of knockdown and may short out electronics). This damage is Physical damage, resisted with half Impact armor (round up); the fire resistance upgrade (p. 327, SR4A) adds its full rating to the armor value. Armor with a chemical seal, chemical protection, or any other protection against a contact-vector toxin also protects the target.

Firewater is a single-target spell, while Napalm is area effect.

One Less [Metatype/Species] (Direct, Touch)
Type: M • Range: T • Damage: P • Duration: I • DV: (F ÷ 2) – 3
Slay [Metatype/Species] (Direct)
Type: M • Range: LOS • Damage: P • Duration: I • DV: (F÷2)–1
Slaughter [Metatype/Species] (Direct, Area)
Type: M • Range: LOS (A) • Damage: P • Duration: I • DV: (F÷2)+1

These variants of Death Touch/Manabolt/Manaball (p. 204, SR4A) are designed to target a particular species or metatype: One Less Ork, Slay Dragon, Slaughter Spirit, and so on. The target of each spell is designated by the spell formula. These murderous spells can only discriminate based on biological species, not social status or any other quality.

Slay affects a single target. Slaughter is an area effect spell. One Less requires the caster to touch the target.

Ram [Object] (Direct, Touch)
Type: P • Range: T • Damage: P • Duration: I • DV: (F ÷ 2) – 2
Wreck [Object] (Direct)
Type: P • Range: LOS • Damage: P • Duration: I • DV: (F ÷ 2)
Demolish [Object] (Direct, Area)
Type: P • Range: LOS (A) • Damage: P • Duration: I • DV: (F÷2)+2

These variants of Shatter/Powerbolt/Powerball (p. 205, SR4A) only work against a specific inanimate object. Each different type of object requires a separate spell: Ram Door, Wreck Vehicle, Demolish Gun, and so on.

Wreck affects a single target. Demolish is an area effect spell. Ram requires the caster to touch the target.

Shattershield (Direct, Touch)
Type: M • Range: T • Damage: P • Duration: I • DV: (F ÷ 2) – 3

Shattershield is a modified version of Death Touch (p. 204, SR4A) specifically designed to destroy mana barriers (see p. 194, SR4A). The caster must be touching the mana barrier's physical component or astral form. The barrier resists with Force (its Structure rating) + Counterspelling (if anyone happens to be protecting it).

DETECTION SPELLS

Rules for Detection spells are provided on pp. 203–207, SR4A.

To turn any basic Detection spell into an Extended range version, increase the DV by +2. This increases the range of the sense to (Force x Magic x 10) meters.

Most Detection spells require the caster to touch the subject of the spell. To convert touch-range spells into spells

> ### ELEMENTAL EFFECTS (CONT.)
>
> **Sand**
> Sand produces tearing, abrasive, smothering damage, like a sandstorm. Sand damage is treated as Physical damage and is resisted with half Impact armor (rounded up). The secondary effects of Sand damage may jam and damage machinery or weapons that are not fully sealed against the environment.
>
> **Smoke**
> Smoke blasts the target with thick, burning, choking fumes. The victim resists Stun as if from an inhalation vector toxin attack (see p. 254, SR4A). Armor does not protect against this attack, but other protective gear might (see the Toxin Protection table, p. 254, SR4A). Smoke also limits vision, inflicting the Heavy Smoke visibility modifier against the target for one full Combat Turn.
>
> **Sound**
> Sound hits the target with a wave of unbelievably loud noise and gut-churning vibrations. Sound damage is treated as Stun damage. Armor has no effect, but sound dampers and spells like Silence and Hush add their rating/hits to the defender's dice pool (effectively acting like sound armor). If the target suffers more damage boxes than his Willpower, he suffers the effects of nausea (p. 254, SR4A) and is deafened for 10 minutes.
>
> **Water**
> The Water elemental effect is like a high-pressure blast from a firehose. Water damage is treated as Physical damage and is resisted with half Impact armor (rounded up). Characters struck with a Water damage attack are more likely to be knocked down—add the Force to the damage inflicted when comparing to the defender's Body (see *Knockdown*, p. 161, SR4A). Water damage makes the target/area wet and may put out small fires (reduce the Fire DV by the attack's DV) as well as short out sensitive/unwaterproofed electronics.

that will work on subjects within line of sight, increase the DV by +2.

Analyze Magic (Active, Directional)
Type: M • Range: T • Duration: S • DV: (F ÷ 2)

This spell allows the subject to analyze a spell, spirit, astral form, focus, or other magical item/effect within range of the

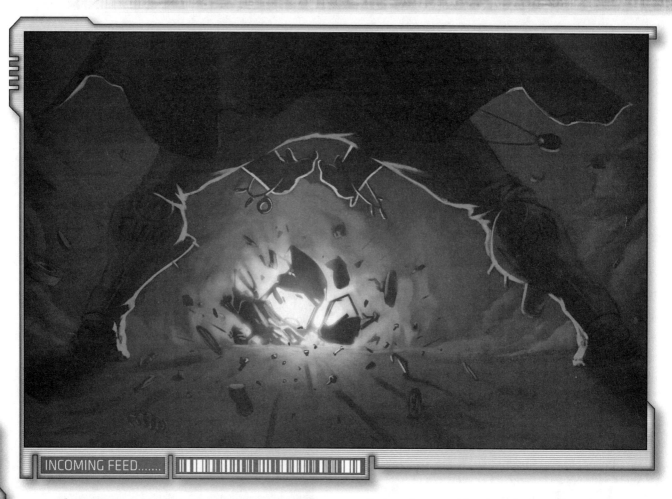

INCOMING FEED.......

sense as if assensing it. To determine the information obtained, note the net hits and consult the Assensing Table (p. 191, *SR4A*). Note that this spell does not confer astral sight, nor does it detect the auras of mundane items or living things. To analyze astral forms or other non-physical astral-only things, the subject must be astrally perceiving or projecting. The caster must touch the subject of the spell.

Astral Clairvoyance (Passive, Directional)
Type: M • Range: T • Duration: S • DV: (F ÷ 2) – 1

This spell works for astral sight as the Clairvoyance spell (p. 206, *SR4A*) works for physical sight. The subject assenses distant scenes as if astrally present at a chosen point within the sensory range of the spell. The "visual point" may be moved to any other point within range of the spell. The subject's normal assensing is "replaced" while using it, nor can the subject use any other senses. Magicians cannot use Astral Clairvoyance to target others with spells.

The caster must touch the subject of the spell, and the subject must be astrally active.

Borrow Sense (Active, Directional)
Type: M • Range: T • Duration: S • DV: (F ÷ 2)
Animal Sense (Active, Directional)
Type: M • Range: T • Duration: S • DV: (F ÷ 2) – 1
Eyes of the Pack (Passive, Directional)
Type: M • Range: T • Duration: S • DV: (F ÷ 2) + 1

Borrow Sense enables the subject to "borrow" a single sense from a chosen target within range of the spell. If the target fails to resist the spell, the subject perceives the target's sense as if it were his own. Any Perception Tests made by the subject using the target's sense are limited to a maximum number of hits as the caster's net hits on the Spellcasting Test. Note that anything sensed by the target does not make a Spell Resistance Test. The caster must touch the subject while casting the spell.

The target of Borrow Sense remains in control of his own actions and senses—the subject is merely along for the ride. The subject cannot make the target focus on anything, and none of the subject's augmented senses (including astral sight) will work through the target's senses. The subject cannot target spells through the target's senses. As long as the caster sustains the spell, the subject can switch from one of the target's senses to another with a Simple Action. Senses that the subject does not normally have can be borrowed (like bat sonar, for example). Note that a target's astral sight is considered a separate sense for purposes of this spell (ie, the subject can borrow sight or astral sight, but not both at the same time).

Animal Sense is a restricted version of Borrow Sense that can only be used to borrow a sense from a non-sapient, non-paranormal animal.

Eyes of the Pack is a variant of Borrow Sense that only works with voluntary targets and only allows the sense of

sight to be borrowed. Switching from the sight of one member of "the pack" to another requires a Simple Action.

Catalog (Active, Area)
Type: P • Range: T • Duration: S • DV: (F÷2)+2

Catalog allows the subject to compile a comprehensive, itemized list of all the non-living items within the area of the spell. The subject can write or dictate a list of the quantity of all items in range of the sense in a manner similar to automatic writing, as long as the caster beats an item's Object Resistance threshold (p. 183, *SR4A*). Net hits obtained indicate the level of detail and description the list provides. Once the spell is dropped, the subject will not recall the exact numbers or items. Items in the area that the subject would not recognize by sight are listed as "unknown." The caster must touch the subject of the spell.

Diagnose (Active, Directional)
Type: M • Range: T • Duration: I • DV: (F÷2)

This spell gives the subject information on the target's general health and any illnesses, injuries, or other medical problems the target might have. The net hits determine the information provided, as noted on the Detection Spell Results table, p. 206, *SR4A*. The caster must touch the subject of the spell.

Enhance Aim (Passive, Directional)
Type: P • Range: T • Duration: S • DV: (F÷2)–1

This spell improves a voluntary subject's aim. Each hit on the Spellcasting Test reduces the Range category for ranged attacks by one level, thus reducing range modifiers (similar to image magnification, see p. 150, *SR4A*). Unlike image magnification, however, the subject does not need a Take Aim action to "lock onto" a target; the spell does that auto-magically. This effect is cumulative with other targeting devices, implants, and abilities (laser sights, scopes, smartlinks, Improved Ability adept power, etc.). The caster must touch the subject of the spell.

Hawkeye (Passive, Directional)
Type: P • Range: T • Duration: S • DV: (F÷2)–1

This spell improves a voluntary subject visual acuity. Each hit on the Spellcasting Test provides a +1 dice pool modifier for visual Perception Tests. This effect is cumulative with other perception aids, implants, and abilities (vision enhancement, adept powers, etc.). The caster must touch the subject of the spell.

SPELL DESIGN EXAMPLES

Here are a few sample spell design formulae, broken down by their Drain modifiers, to give you an idea on how we put these spells together.

Combat
Knockout is a mana spell (+0), touch range (–2), of instant duration (+0), that only causes Stun damage (–1). DV: (F ÷ 2) – 3

Toxic Wave is a physical spell (+1), with LOS/area effect range (+2), of instant duration (+0), with elemental effects (acid, +2). DV: (F ÷ 2) + 5

Detection
Analyze Device needs to be physical to analyze objects (+1), requires touch range (–2), is sustained (+0), and conducts basic analysis (+1). DV: (F ÷ 2)

Combat Sense is a mana spell (+0), touch range (–2), sustained (+0), that provides a psychic sense of precognition (+4). DV: (F ÷ 2) + 2

Detect Enemies, Extended is also a mana spell (+0), touch range (–2) with an extended area effect (+4), sustained (+0), that provides complex detection (distinguishing enemies from others, +1). DV: (F ÷ 2) + 3

Health
Decrease [Attribute] affects attributes so it must be a physical spell (+1), touch range (–2), sustained (+0), which applies a negative effect (+2). DV: (F ÷ 2) + 1

Heal is a mana spell (+0), range of touch (–2), and permanent (+0, since it restores the body to its natural state). Since it is curative, the DV is based on the damage being healed. DV: (Damage Value) – 2

Resist Pain is also a mana spell (+0) with touch range (–2) and permanent duration (also restorative, +0). It is also curative (base DV = damage), but only affects symptoms (restricted effect, –2). DV: (Damage Value) – 4

Illusion
Invisibility is a mana spell (it does not affect sensors, +0) with a LOS range (+0) and sustained duration (+0). It is realistic (+0), single-sense (sight only, –2), and hides its target (+2). DV: (F ÷ 2)

Trid Entertainment is physical (it affects sensors, +1) with a LOS/area effect range (+2) and a sustained duration (+0). It is an obvious (–1), multi-sense (+0) illusion. DV: (F ÷ 2) + 2

Manipulation
Fling is a physical spell (+1) with LOS range (+0) and instant duration (+0) that creates a minor physical change (+0). DV: (F ÷ 2) + 1

Ice Sheet is a physical spell (+1), affecting an area (LOS/area effect, +2), of instant duration (+0). It creates a minor environmental change (–2) with elemental effects (+2). DV: (F ÷ 2) + 3

Mob Mind is a mana spell (affects the mind, +0) with LOS/area effect range (+2) that is sustained (+0) and applies a major mental change (+2). DV: (F ÷ 2) + 4

> **OTHER ELEMENTAL COMBAT SPELLS**
>
> Most Combat spells with elemental effects have the same game characteristics; the only difference is the elemental effect (Acid Stream, Flamethrower, and Lightning Bolt, for example, are all the same). To create a spell with a different elemental effect such as Ice or Sand (see pp. 164–165) is very easy—simply use the same spell statistics, apply the rules for the new elemental effect, and rename it. Here are some examples:
>
> | Elemental Effect | Single Target Spell Name | Area Effect Spell Name |
> |---|---|---|
> | Blast | Boom | Shockwave |
> | Ice | Frost | Blizzard |
> | Light | Laser | Nova |
> | Metal | Frag | Shred |
> | Sand | Dust Devil | Sandstorm |
> | Smoke | Steam | Smoke Cloud |
> | Sound | Screech | Soundwave |
> | Water | Hose | Tsunami |

The Cryptesthesia ("paranormal perception") spell is an advanced form of Clairvoyance and Clairaudience (see p. 206, *SR4A*). Each Cryptesthesia spell allows the subject to utilize a different augmented sense—low-light vision, thermographic vision, enhanced smell, ultrasound, etc.—at a chosen point within the spell's range. The subject does not need to have the sense, it is provided by the spell—but each sense requires a different spell (for example, Sonar Cryptesthesia or Enhanced Vision Cryptesthesia). Magicians cannot use Cryptesthesia to target others with spells. The caster must touch the subject of the spell.

Mana Window (Active, Directional)
Type: M • Range: T • Duration: S • DV: (F ÷ 2)

Astral Window (Active, Directional)
Type: M • Range: T • Duration: S • DV: (F ÷ 2)

These advanced versions of Clairvoyance (p. 206, *SR4A*) and Astral Clairvoyance (p. 166) allow the subject to see or assense past mana barriers (which normally stop Clairvoyance and are opaque on the astral). If the barrier does not resist the spell with its Force, the subject can see/assense distant scenes through the barrier as if physically or astrally present within the sensory range of the spell. Magicians cannot cast spells at targets they see using these spells. Casting these spells does not alert the creator of the mana barrier.

Mana Window bypasses mana barriers on the physical plane with its clairvoyant physical sight. Astral Window bypasses astral mana barriers with its clairvoyant assensing. The caster must touch the subject of the spell, and for Astral Window the subject must be astrally active.

Mindnet (Active, Psychic, Area)
Type: M • Range: T (A) • Duration: S • DV: (F ÷ 2) + 3

Mindnet (Active, Psychic, Extended Area)
Type: M • Range: T (A) • Duration: S • DV: (F ÷ 2) + 5

Mindnet is a version of the Mindlink spell designed to allow telepathic communication between a group of voluntary people. Everyone in the group can freely talk, exchange images, and emote as long as they remain within range of the spellcaster. The number of people participating in the group (excluding the caster) serves as the threshold for the Spellcasting Test.

Night Vision (Passive, Directional)
Type: P • Range: T • Duration: S • DV: (F ÷ 2) – 1

This spell grants a voluntary subject low-light vision like that provided by the low-light cybernetic enhancement (p. 340, *SR4A*). The caster must touch the subject of the spell.

[Sense] Cryptesthesia (Passive, Directional)
Type: M • Range: T • Duration: S • DV: (F ÷ 2)

Spatial Sense (Passive, Area)
Type: P • Range: T • Duration: S • DV: (F ÷ 2) + 2

Spatial Sense, Extended (Passive, Extended Area)
Type: P • Range: T • Duration: S • DV: (F ÷ 2) + 4

Spatial Sense provides the subject with an awareness of his physical surroundings within range of the sense, in terms of landscape, geography, architecture, etc. This layout knowledge lasts as long as the spell is sustained, and is not retained when the spell ends (though the subject can make a map or recite directions before ending the spell). The net hits scored determine how much detail the spell provides—progressing from a general idea of what's where to a rough map to knowing each exit and how secure they are—as noted on the Detection Spell Results table (p. 206, *SR4A*). This spell works in all directions (three-dimensional) and may uncover hidden layout features such as ventilation shafts, secret rooms, and sewer tunnels. It will not detect security features or living things. Areas that are protected by a mana barrier are experienced as "blank spots."

Thermographic Vision (Passive, Directional)
Type: P • Range: T • Duration: S • DV: (F ÷ 2) – 1

This spell grants a voluntary subject thermographic vision like that provided by the cybernetic enhancement (p. 340, *SR4A*). The caster must touch the subject of the spell.

Thought Recognition (Active, Psychic, Directional)
Type: M • Range: T • Duration: S • DV: (F ÷ 2)

Area Thought Recognition (Active, Psychic, Area)
Type: M • Range: T • Duration: S • DV: (F ÷ 2) + 2

A less-intrusive form of Mind Probe, this spell merely scans the target's surface thoughts for a particular word, phrase, sound, or image chosen by the caster when the spell is cast. Rather than digging through the target's brain for information, it merely verifies whether a target has a particular person, place, event, or thing in mind. Investigators use this spell to determine if a target has knowledge of something (such as a murder weapon) that they otherwise wouldn't. Spies use this spell to determine if someone is tailing or looking for them.

Thought Recognition is used on one particular target, Area Thought Recognition scans the minds of everyone within the area.

Translate (Active, Psychic/Directional)
Type: M • Range: T • Duration: S • DV: (F ÷ 2) + 2

This spell sets up a low-level telepathic connection between the subject and a specific target within range of the sense (chosen when the spell is cast), allowing them to understand each other's speech as if the subject spoke the target's native language. The spell generally translates intent better than exact phrasing, and so cannot be used for delicate diplomacy where the tact of a skilled translator is needed, but it does find its uses for international corporate and government types. Translate may be used to communicate with any sapient species that uses language (such as sasquatch or merrow), but may not be used to communicate with non-sapient animals. The hits from the Spellcasting Test determine the quality of the translation. The caster must touch the subject of the spell.

HEALTH SPELLS

Health spell rules are given on pp. 207–208, SR4A. All Health spells require the caster to touch the target.

Alleviate Addiction
Type: M • Range: T • Duration: S • DV: (F ÷ 2) – 4

This spell temporarily reduces the effects of addiction on the target's body and mind (see p. 93, SR4A). Every net hit reduces the addiction level by one (from Severe to Moderate, for example). The spell does not remove the addiction, only alleviates its effects, and it only alleviates the effects of one addiction at a time. The effects of the Addiction return at full force once the spell ends.

Note that this spell does not work against the effects of Focus Addiction (see p. 26).

Alleviate Allergy
Type: M • Range: T • Duration: S • DV: (F ÷ 2) – 4

This spell allows the caster to block or reduce an allergy's effects on the target (see p. 94, SR4A). Every net hit reduces the allergy level by one (from Moderate to Mild, for example). The spell does not remove the allergy, only alleviates its effects, and it only alleviates the effects of one allergy at a time. The effects of the Allergy return at full force once the spell ends.

Awaken
Type: M • Range: T • Duration: S • DV: (F ÷ 2) – 4

Awaken immediately makes an unconscious or asleep target wide awake and alert. The target remains conscious as long as the spell is sustained. At the end of that period, the character relapses into unconsciousness. This spell does not cure Stun damage—it only temporarily mitigates its effects. A character brought to consciousness using this spell still suffers their Stun modifiers. The caster must achieve a threshold equal to the Stun modifiers (or 1 for targets simply asleep).

Crank
Type: P • Range: T • Duration: P • DV: (F ÷ 2)

Crank alleviates a voluntary target's need for sleep. Every hit scored approximates 1 hour of sleep. Popular among student magicians, Crank does have its downside. At the gamemaster's discretion, a character who abuses Crank to avoid actual sleep for long periods may find themselves addicted to magically-aided sleep deprivation (see p. 256, SR4A).

Decrease Reflexes (Negative)
Type: P • Range: T • Duration: S • DV: (F ÷ 2) + 1

This spell decreases the reflexes (Initiative and Initiative Passes) of the target. The target resists with Reaction + Counterspelling. The Force of the spell must equal or exceed the target's Reaction. Every net hit achieved reduces the target's Initiative and Initiative Passes by 1, to a minimum of 1.

Enabler (Negative)
Type: M • Range: T • Duration: S • DV: (F ÷ 2)

The opposite of Antidote (p. 207, SR4A), Enabler increases the target's susceptibility to drugs or toxins. Enabler is popular with wiz-gangers to help themselves and other druggies get a better "high." The target resists with Body + Counterspelling. Each net hit scored reduces the target's dice pool by 1 for the Toxin Resistance Test. Enabler must be sustained until the toxin effect kicks in, otherwise it does not affect the resistance test.

Fast
Type: M • Range: T • Duration: S • DV: (F ÷ 2) – 5

This spell allows a voluntary target to ignore feelings of hunger or thirst for as long as it is sustained. Each hit allows the target to ignore the symptoms of one skipped meal. This does not alleviate the need for food or water, only the desire for them and the symptoms of going without. Wealthy people often use Fast as a "diet spell." Once the spell ends, hunger pains and the effects of not eating and drinking immediately kick in (the gamemaster should apply Fatigue damage as appropriate, and possibly the Disorientation effect, p. 254, SR4A). Use of this spell for more than 72 hours can be highly dangerous.

Healthy Glow
Type: P • Range: T • Duration: P • DV: (F ÷ 2) – 1

This spell brightens eyes and hair, sloughs off dead skin cells, improves circulation, and promotes general well-being. A cosmetic spell, Healthy Glow is popular with the rich as a status symbol and pick-me-up. Though "permanent" in the sense that it does not require sustaining, the effects of the spell do wear off over time, based on the subject's lifestyle, diet, vices, and such. The hits achieved determine how well the target is "cleaned up."

Intoxication (Negative)
Type: M • Range: T • Duration: P • DV: (F ÷ 2)

This spell causes inebriation. The target resists with Body + Counterspelling; any protection the target has against ingestion-vector toxins also applies. Each net hit inflicts 1 box of Fatigue damage (p. 164, SR4A), which represents the target's drunken state. Antidote and Detox can negate the effects of this spell.

Nutrition

Type: P • Range: T • Duration: P • DV: (F ÷ 2)

The Nutrition spell provides a voluntary target with nourishment, allowing them to live off pure mana. One hit is enough to satisfy the target for a few hours, with extra hits increasing the quality of the "meal." This spell prevents starvation and dehydration, but it does have its down side. Those who abuse this spell for long periods of time risk becoming addicted to magical nourishment (see p. 256, SR4A).

Stim

Type: M • Range: T • Duration: S • DV: (F ÷ 2) – 5

This spell allows a voluntary target to ignore the need for rest and sleep for as long as it is sustained. Each hit scored counts as one night of rest that can be skipped. This does not alleviate the need for sleep, only the desire for it and the symptoms of going without. Stim is popular as a study-aid and for getting things done by deadline. Once the spell ends, the effects of sleep deprivation will immediately kick-in (the gamemaster should apply Fatigue damage as appropriate, and possibly the Disorientation effect, p. 254, SR4A). Use of this spell for more than 72 hours can be highly dangerous.

ILLUSION SPELLS

For rules on Illusion spells, see pp. 208–209, SR4A.

Agony (Realistic, Single-Sense)

Type: M • Range: LOS • Duration: S • DV: (F ÷ 2) – 2

Mass Agony (Realistic, Single-Sense, Area)

Type: M • Range: LOS (A) • Duration: S • DV: (F ÷ 2)

Agony inflicts an illusion of terrible pain on the target. Each net hit scored by the caster temporarily inflicts 1 box of Physical damage on the target. This is not actual damage, only a measure of the effect of the spell. If the target's damage boxes are filled, he is racked with pain, unable to move or act. Once the spell is ended, the pain and damage boxes immediately go away.

Agony affects a single target, Mass Agony is area effect.

Bugs (Realistic, Multi-Sense)

Type: M • Range: LOS • Duration: S • DV: (F ÷ 2)

Swarm (Realistic, Multi-Sense)

Type: M • Range: LOS (A) • Duration: S • DV: (F ÷ 2) + 2

These spells make the target believe that small bugs of various persuasions are crawling over their entire body, biting them, scurrying about, and crawling into orifices. The bugs look, feel, smell, and taste real. This illusion is usually enough to make any target who fails to resist freak out and do everything they can to get the insects off. Characters who suffer through with the sensation and carry on suffer a –1 dice pool modifier to all actions for each net hit scored by the caster for as long as the spell is sustained. At the gamemaster's discretion, any character who suffers a dice pool modifier larger than their Willpower simply loses self control (the gamemaster determines the character's actions).

Bugs affects a single target, Swarm is area effect.

Camouflage (Realistic, Single-Sense)

Type: M • Range: LOS • Duration: S • DV: (F ÷ 2) – 2

Physical Camouflage (Realistic, Single-Sense)

Type: M • Range: LOS • Duration: S • DV: (F ÷ 2) – 1

This spell colors the subject in a camouflage pattern that mimics his surroundings. The camouflage coloring adds a –1 dice pool modifier to standard visual Perception Tests and ranged combat attacks made against the subject for each net hit scored by the caster. Camouflage works against living viewers, Physical Camouflage also works against technological sensors.

Chaff (Realistic, Multi-Sense)

Type: P • Range: LOS • Duration: S • DV: (F÷2)

Flak (Realistic, Multi-Sense, Area)

Type: P • Range: LOS (A) • Duration: S • DV: (F÷2)+2

Chaff is a version of Chaos (p. 209, SR4A) that only affects non-living sensor devices. The sensor is bombarded with a storm of input; for each hit scored over the Object Resistance threshold, the sensor's rating is reduced by 1.

Double Image (Realistic, Multi-Sense)

Type: M • Range: T • Duration: S • DV: (F÷2)–3

Physical Double Image (Realistic, Multi-Sense)

Type: P • Range: T • Duration: S • DV: (F ÷ 2) – 2

Double Image creates an exact image of the subject that appears next to him and mimics everything he does. The caster must touch the person who is being "duplicated." The caster has limited control of the double and can adjust its movement (to keep it from walking through walls and so forth), though in tight quarters this may be difficult. A character who does not resist the spell will not be able to tell the original and double image apart—the double sounds, smells, and looks like the original. The double is insubstantial; bullets and melee attacks will go right through it. Physical Double Image affects technological sensors as well.

Dream (Realistic, Multi-Sense)

Type: M • Range: LOS • Duration: S • DV: (F ÷ 2) – 1

The caster may craft any type of dream sequence (including visuals, sounds, emotions, etc.) and transmit it to a sleeping target. The dreams cannot cause actual harm but may entertain, relax, or frighten. The caster's net hits determine the dream's vividness and complexity. Targets who have severe nightmares do not recover Stun damage while they persist, and any rest during that time is lost. The target will vividly remember the dream when awakened. The Dream spell is often cast using ritual spellcasting (p. 184, SR4A) as a means of sending warnings, threats, or torment to an enemy. It is also used in modern psychological and therapeutic counseling involving directed dreaming.

Foreboding (Realistic, Multi-Sense)

Type: M • Range: LOS (A) • Duration: S • DV: (F ÷ 2) + 2

This area spell gives any living beings who enter its range feelings of imminent danger, fear, and unease. Characters will simultaneously feel chilled and nervous; their hackles will rise, and they'll feel slightly panicked. Any character that does not resist the spell who wishes to stay in the area will suffer a –1 dice pool modifier to all actions for each net hit scored by the caster, representing their shaking, fear, and nervousness, for as long as the spell is sustained. At the gamemaster's discretion, characters who suffer a dice pool modifier greater than their Willpower may be unable to stay in the area, or may simply curl up into a gibbering ball.

Hot Potato (Realistic, Single-Sense)

Type: M • Range: LOS (A) • Duration: S • DV: (F ÷ 2) – 1

This area-effect spell creates the illusion that all metal within the range is extremely hot to the touch. Characters who do not fully resist the spell will feel like any metal they are in contact with (weapons, armor, implants, piercings, etc.) is burning them. If the character does not drop, remove, or otherwise disengage contact from the metal, they will suffer a dice pool modifier equal to the caster's net hits to all actions as they are distracted by the "burning" sensation.

Orgasm (Realistic, Single-Sense)

Type: M • Range: LOS • Duration: S • DV: (F ÷ 2) – 2

Orgy (Realistic, Single-Sense, Area)

Type: M • Range: LOS (A) • Duration: S • DV: (F ÷ 2)

Orgasm envelops the target in the stimulating throes of sexual climax. A favored weapon in the private arsenal of many magicians' personal lives, this spell is also a great way to distract your enemies without them wanting to kill you in the morning. Each net hit scored by the caster applies a –1 dice pool modifier to all of the target's actions as they gasp and gush. At the gamemaster's discretion, a character who suffers a dice pool modifier higher than his Willpower is completely incapacitated and pre-occupied.

Orgasm affects a single target, Orgy is area effect.

[Sense] Removal (Realistic, Single-Sense)

Type: P • Range: LOS • Duration: S • DV: (F ÷ 2) – 1

Mass [Sense] Removal (Realistic, Single-Sense, Area)

Type: P • Range: LOS (A) • Duration: S • DV: (F ÷ 2) + 1

These spells strip the target of a specified sense (sight, hearing, taste, etc.) Each sense requires a separate spell. The target suffers a –1 dice pool modifier to all Perception Tests involving that sense for every net hit scored by the caster. Implants and other technological sensors that use that sense are also affected. [Sense] Removal affects a single target, Mass [Sense] Removal is area effect.

Stink (Realistic, Single-Sense)

Type: M • Range: LOS • Duration: S • DV: (F ÷ 2) – 2

Stench (Realistic, Single-Sense, Area)

Type: M • Range: LOS • Duration: S • DV: (F ÷ 2)

These spells create an illusion of a sickening, gut-wrenching stench. Every net hit scored by the caster applies a –1 dice pool modifier to all of the target's actions as they gag and retch. At the gamemaster's discretion, a character who suffers a dice pool modifier higher than his Willpower is completely incapacitated and pre-occupied with throwing up.

Stink affects a single target, Stench is area effect.

Sound Barrier (Realistic, Single-Sense, Area)

Type: P • Range: LOS (A) • Duration: S • DV: (F ÷ 2) + 3

A variant of the Silence spell (p. 209, SR4A), Sound Barrier creates a perimeter of silence around the area of effect (rather than creating a mass area of silence). Those inside cannot hear outside noises but can hear sounds within the globe and vice versa. Only sounds crossing the border are affected, in the same manners as the Silence spell. This spell also affects technological devices, infrasound, and ultrasound.

Vehicle Mask (Realistic, Multi-Sense)

Type: P • Range: T • Duration: S • DV: (F ÷ 2) – 2

This version of the Physical Mask spell (p. 209, SR4A) is specifically used to mask vehicles and drones. The vehicle must be masked to look like another vehicle of roughly the same size. This spell can also affect the vehicle's sound, smell, and other characteristics. This spell can also modify a vehicle's Signature (see p. 171, SR4A); each net hit scored by the caster can be used to raise or lower the vehicle's Signature modifier by 1. The caster must touch the vehicle being masked.

MANIPULATION SPELLS

Rules for Manipulation spells are on pp. 210–211, SR4A.

Mana Manipulations: This new category of Manipulation spells includes mana spells that specifically affect mana forms, much as Physical manipulations affect physical forms.

Alter Memory (Mental)

Type: M • Range: LOS • Duration: P • DV: (F ÷ 2) + 2

This spell allows the caster to add, alter, or erase a single memory. The net hits scored by the caster determine how detailed and complex the affected memory can be. Every (Force) months—or anytime a character is presented with evidence that the memory is false (gamemaster's discretion)—the victim may roll a Willpower (only) Test; each hit reduces the hits on the caster's original Spellcasting Test. If the spellcaster's net hits are reduced to 0, the spell no longer affects the target and the memory returns.

Alter Temperature (Environmental, Area)

Type: P • Range: LOS (A) • Duration: S • DV: (F ÷ 2) + 1

This spell changes the ambient temperature in an area, increasing or decreasing it by 5 degrees centigrade for every hit. The gamemaster may judge any effects of extreme temperature on the area affected, but usually sufficiently high or low temperatures might cause characters without proper protec-

tion to suffer Cold damage or Fatigue. The temperature may also interfere with the operation of some machines.

Animate (Physical)
Type: P • Range: LOS • Duration: S • DV: (F ÷ 2)
Mass Animate (Physical, Area)
Type: P • Range: LOS (A) • Duration: S • DV: (F ÷ 2) + 2

This spell causes inanimate objects to move. The object moves according to its structure (balls can roll, rugs may crawl, humanoid statues can walk, and so on). The spell imparts a limited flexibility, allowing solid objects such as statues to move as if they had joints. The caster must achieve enough hits to beat the object's Object Resistance threshold (p. 183, SR4A); larger items (over 200 kg) should have threshold adjusted accordingly. Controlling the object takes only a Simple Action; objects can also be ordered to maintain a movement while the caster directs his attention elsewhere. The caster only has a rough control over the object's movement and cannot manipulate individual parts or components (finer control requires a spell like Magic Fingers, p. 211, SR4A). The maximum movement rate for objects is (Force) meters per turn, subject to the gamemaster's discretion. If the object is held, the caster must win an Opposed Test using Force x 2 against the holder's Strength + Body to break free. If fastened, make this Force x 2 Success Test against an appropriate gamemaster-determined threshold.

Animate affects a single non-living object, Mass Animate is area effect.

Astral Armor (Mana)
Type: M • Range: LOS • Duration: S • DV: (F ÷ 2) + 2

This is an astral version of the Armor spell (p. 210, SR4A). It protects a single subject from astral combat attacks and only works in astral space. Each hit provides 1 point of mystic armor.

Bind (Physical)
Type: P • Range: LOS • Duration: S • DV: (F ÷ 2) + 1
Net (Physical, Area)
Type: P • Range: LOS (A) • Duration: S • DV: (F ÷ 2) + 3
Mana Bind (Mana)
Type: M • Range: LOS • Duration: S • DV: (F ÷ 2)
Mana Net (Mana, Area)
Type: M • Range: LOS (A) • Duration: S • DV: (F ÷ 2) + 2

The target of the Bind spell is constricted by invisible bands of magical energy that wrap around and impede the movement of his limbs. The target resists with Strength + Counterspelling; every net hit reduces the target's Agility by 1. If Agility is reduced to 0, he is bound and unable to move his limbs. The target may not move or act normally, but may attempt to crawl or hop short distances (at one quarter their normal movement rate). The target may still defend and dodge against attacks, but suffers a dice pool modifier equal to the caster's net hits. The target can attempt to break free of the bindings by making an Opposed Test, pitting Strength + Body against the spell's Force x 2.

Bind works on single targets, Net is area effect. Both spells may be used against inanimate objects such as drones to restrict moving or rotating parts, though this may not stop some drones and vehicles, depending on their method of propulsion. Mana Bind only works on a single living or magical target, Mana Net is area-effect against living/magical targets.

Calm Animal (Mental)
Type: M • Range: LOS • Duration: S • DV: (F ÷ 2) – 1
Calm Pack (Mental, Area)
Type: M • Range: LOS (A) • Duration: S • DV: (F ÷ 2) + 1

Calm Animal calms any non-sapient creature (normal or paranormal), making it non-aggressive while the spell is sustained. Calm Animal affects a single creature, Calm Pack is are effect. Affected animals will still defend themselves if attacked.

Catfall (Physical)
Type: P • Range: LOS • Duration: S • DV: (F ÷ 2)

Catfall slows a target's fall to help him land without injury. Multiply the caster's hits by the spell's Force to determine the maximum distance in meters the target may fall without danger of injury. If the target falls a greater distance, subtract the maximum distance of the spell before calculating damage.

Clean [Element] (Environmental, Area)
Type: P • Range: LOS (A) • Duration: P • DV: (F ÷ 2) + 2

This area spell clears all impurities out of the volume of a particular element within range. Each element requires a different spell (Clean Air, Clean Water, etc). For example, Clean Air could be used to cleanse a room of toxic fumes, or Clean Water could purify a drinking supply. The caster's hits determine how thoroughly the element is cleaned; slightly muddy water would require only 1 hit to clean for example, whereas contaminated runoff could require 4 or even 5 hits to make it drinkable.

Compel Truth (Mental)
Type: M • Range: LOS • Duration: S • DV: (F ÷ 2) – 1

This spell forces the target to speak only the truth. The target can say something he or she believes to be true, even if it is not. The subject may choose not to speak or to withhold information but cannot directly lie.

Some jurisdictions (like the UCAS) consider the use of this spell by law enforcement authorities to be a violation of a suspect's right against self-incrimination. Others have been known to use this spell (among others) to get to the truth in legal cases.

Control Animal (Mental)
Type: M • Range: LOS • Duration: S • DV: (F ÷ 2) + 1
Control Pack (Mental, Area)
Type: M • Range: LOS (A) • Duration: S • DV: (F ÷ 2) + 3

These variants of Control Thoughts and Mob Mind (see p. 210, SR4A) only work on non-sapient animals (both normal and paranormal). The caster seizes control of the animals minds and actions, issuing commands with a Simple Action (or the same command to a group). Control Animal affects a single creature, Control Pack is are effect.

Deflection (Physical)
Type: P • Range: LOS • Duration: S • DV: (F ÷ 2) + 1

Deflection protects the target by turning aside ranged combat attacks. Every hit scored gives the target a +1 dice

pool modifier for defending against ranged physical attacks. The effects of this spell are subtle enough to be discounted as a missed shot or poor aim (at least at first).

[Element] Aura (Environmental)
Type: P • Range: LOS • Duration: S • DV: (F ÷ 2) + 3

This spell creates a rippling aura of elemental energies around a subject's body. Each element requires a different spell (Flame Aura, Electrical Aura, Cold Aura, etc.). This fiery aura does not affect the subject, but increase the DV of any melee attacks by the caster's hits. Attacks are treated as Cold, Electricity, Fire, or some other elemental damage (see pp. 163–165, *SR4A*, and pp. 164–165 of this book), as appropriate to the aura, and are resisted with half Impact armor.

Any successful physical melee attack against the subject also means that the attacker must resist similar damage from the aura. The aura's Damage Value equals the spell's Force.

[Element] Wall (Environmental, Area)
Type: P • Range: LOS (A) • Duration: S • DV: (F ÷ 2) + 5

This spell creates a wall composed of the specified element; each element requires a different spell (Fire Wall, Ice Wall, Smoke Wall, etc). This wall has a height and length up to the spell's Force in meters, or it can be crafted as a dome with a radius and height equal to half the Force in meters. The width of the wall can be up to one meter. The caster may adjust this size as he would adjust any area effect radius (see p. 183, *SR4A*).

Anyone coming into contact with the wall suffers special damage as appropriate to the element (see pp. 163–165, *SR4A,* and pp. 164–165 of this book) with a DV equal to the spell's Force. Note that some elemental walls (fire, smoke, etc.) are not solid and will not block attacks, though they may inflict Visibility modifiers as determined by the gamemaster. Solid walls (earth, ice, etc.) have an Armor and Structure rating equal to the caster's Spellcasting hits.

Fashion (Physical)
Type: P • Range: T • Duration: P • DV: (F ÷ 2)

This spell instantly tailors clothing, transforming garments into any fashion the caster wishes. The hits measure the degree of style in the tailoring. The spell cannot change clothing's protective value, only its cut, color, pattern, and fit. The weight of the clothing does not change, and it must cover approximately the same amount of area (a jump suit can't be converted into a bikini). The caster must touch the clothing.

Fix (Physical)
Type: P • Range: T • Duration: P • DV: (F ÷ 2) + 1

The Fix spell repairs damage to non-living materials, including drones and vehicles. The caster must touch the object and must achieve enough hits to beat the item's Object Resistance threshold (p. 183, *SR4A*). Fix can repair any item with a weight equal to the Force x the spellcaster's hits in kilograms or less. It can only repair broken items when all the pieces are present. Each hit scored repairs 1 point of Structure rating or 1 box of damage. The Fix spell can only be used once to repair any set of damage.

Gecko Crawl (Physical)
Type: P • Range: T • Duration: S • DV: (F ÷ 2) − 1

The Gecko Crawl spell allows the subject to walk along vertical or overhead surfaces at a movement rate equal to Force x hits in meters per turn. The subject is still affected by gravity and will fall if separated from the surface. The gamemaster may require Climbing Tests in order for the subject to climb especially slick surfaces. The caster must touch the subject of the spell.

Glue (Physical)
Type: P • Range: LOS • Duration: S • DV: (F ÷ 2) + 1

Glue Strip (Physical, Area)
Type: P • Range: LOS (A) • Duration: S • DV: (F ÷ 2) + 3

This spell bonds the target to any one surface to which it is currently in contact, with a Strength equal to the spell's Force. The caster must beat the surface's Object Resistance threshold (see p. 183, *SR4A*). Pulling the two surfaces apart requires an Opposed Test between the spell's Force x 2 and the separator's Strength + Body. If a target or surface has a Body or Structure rating lower than the spell's Force, the skin/surface will be torn apart in the process of being separated (suffering DV equal to the difference). Glue affects a single target, Glue Strip is area effect.

Interference (Environmental, Area)
Type: P • Range: LOS (A) • Duration: S • DV: (F ÷ 2) + 3

Interference creates a barrage of static in the electromagnetic spectrum, jamming radio and wireless signals. This spell jams all signals in the area of effect with a Signal rating less than the hits scored by the spellcaster, just like a jammer (p. 329, *SR4A*).

Lock (Physical)
Type: P • Range: LOS • Duration: S • DV: (F ÷ 2)

This spell telekinetically holds any door, portal, hatch, closure, or other similar blockade closed with a Strength equal to the Force. The caster must beat the item's Object Resistance threshold (p. 183, *SR4A*). Opening the portal requires an Opposed Test between Strength + Body and the spell's Force x 2.

Mana Static (Environmental, Area)
Type: M • Range: LOS (A) • Duration: P • DV: (F ÷ 2) + 4

This area-effect spell creates a background count of 1 for every hit scored by the caster. As with normal background count, the mana static impedes magical activities (see p. 117). Once the spell is made permanent, the background count from this spell recedes at a rate of 1 point per hour. Mana Static affects everyone, including the caster.

Makeover (Physical)
Type: P • Range: T • Duration: P • DV: (F ÷ 2)

This spell creates a complete makeover for a voluntary subject, including cosmetics, hair, and nails. It even polishes teeth and eliminates plaque. Changes are as permanent as those made in a beauty salon. The number of hits measures the degree of style in the makeover.

Mist (Environmental, Area)
Type: P • Range: LOS (A) • Duration: I • DV: (F ÷ 2) + 3

Mist creates a thick fog that fills the entire area of effect. The mist is dense and difficult to see through, imposing a visibility modifier equal to the hits scored by the caster. Because the spell is not sustained, the mist dissipates quickly, based on the surrounding temperature and winds; reduce the vision modifier by 1 per Combat Turn.

Offensive Mana Barrier (Environmental, Area)
Type: M • Range: LOS (A) • Duration: S • DV: (F ÷ 2) + 3

This amped-up version of the Mana Barrier spell (p. 211, SR4A) takes it a step further by "zapping" any spirits, dual beings, or astral forms that come into contact with it. The barrier inflicts Physical damage with a DV equal to its Force. Otherwise, this spell functions the same as Mana Barrier.

Preserve (Physical, Area)
Type: P • Range: T • Duration: P • DV: (F ÷ 2)

Preserve prevents inert organic matter from drying out, decaying, or putrefying. It can be used on such mundane things as food and drink, but it is most often used by forensic spellcasters to protect cadavers from decay before autopsy, or to preserve small organic samples (hair, skin) taken from a crime scene for use as a material link (see p. 28). The material's rate of decomposition is reduced by a factor equal to the number of hits scored; 4 hits would preserve a substance for 4 times as long as it would normally last.

Pulse (Environmental, Area)
Type: P • Range: LOS (A) • Duration: I • DV: (F ÷ 2) + 3

Pulse sends out a brief, highly-charged burst of electromagnetic energy. This spell will erase standard RFID tags and may also affect other non-optical and non-hardened electronic circuit systems within the area of effect. Most electronics in 2070 are optical-based, but the spell might affect some archaic devices and power systems. The caster must beat the item's Object Resistance threshold (p. 183, SR4A). Affected systems may suffer data loss, power outages, or burn out entirely at the gamemaster's discretion; use the hits scored by the spellcaster as a guideline. Pulse will also disrupt wireless reception and radio communication for a brief instant.

Reinforce (Physical)
Type: P • Range: LOS • Duration: S • DV: (F ÷ 2) + 1

This spell increases the structural integrity of an object no larger than caster's Magic in square meters. Each hit increases both the Armor and Structure rating by 1 for the duration of the spell.

Shape [Material] (Environmental, Area)
Type: P • Range: LOS (A) • Duration: S • DV: (F ÷ 2) + 3

This spell allows the caster to move and shape a volume of a specified element or material (air, earth, water, fire, mud, lava, plasteel, concrete, tar, etc.) within range. The caster must beat the material's Object Resistance threshold (p. 183, SR4A). The material can be moved and reshaped in any way the caster desires, at a maximum Movement Rate of (net hits) meters per turn. Loose material can be moved and re-shaped easily, but material that is connected or reinforced (such as walls or other material part of a structure) must be broken apart by reducing its Structure rating by Force points per Combat Turn. This spell allows the caster to rapidly dig holes, redirect streams, fill balloons, create a path through a fire, construct a barricade, or create a doorway where one didn't exist before. Each element/material requires a separate spell (Shape Sand, Shape Ice, Shape Wood, Shape Concrete, and so on). Elements or materials reshaped by the caster remain in that form when the spell ends. If that form cannot be supported by the material, it will collapse. The material/element can also be spread out, extinguished, or evaporated; for example, a fire could be extinguished by reducing the Power by the caster's Spellcasting hits each turn.

Spirit Barrier (Environmental, Area)
Type: M • Range: LOS (A) • Duration: S • DV: (F ÷ 2)

Spirit Zapper (Environmental, Area)
Type: M • Range: LOS (A) • Duration: S • DV: (F ÷ 2) + 2

This modified version of the Mana barrier spell (p. 211, SR4A) only works against spirits and spirit powers. When cast on the physical plane, it will impede materialized spirits. It has no effect on spells, foci, or non-spirit dual beings and astral forms.

Spirit Zapper is a similar restricted variant of the Offensive Mana Barrier (p. 174).

Sterilize (Physical, Area)
Type: P • Range: LOS (A) • Duration: I • DV: (F ÷ 2) + 2

This area-effect spell kills bacteria and other microorganisms and destroys material such as skin flakes, stray hairs, and spilled blood. Organic material affected by this spell cannot be used as a material link (see p. 28). Because the spell does not affect biomaterial attached to a living being, it does not kill the various helpful and harmful microorganisms living inside a creature. Each hit scored by the caster inflicts a –1 dice pool modifier to any skill tests made to collect and use sterilized biomaterial for forensics or material link purposes. Shadowrunners often employ this spell to eliminate incriminating trace evidence, especially if blood has been spilled.

NEW ADEPT POWERS

The following adept powers are intended to round out and diversify the possibilities available to adept characters of all varieties in *Shadowrun*. For additional powers, see pp. 195–197, SR4A.

Analytics
Cost: .25 per level

Analytics improves the adept's logical ability to detect and analyze patterns, puzzles, and ciphers. It is especially useful for clue-hunting and evidence analysis, providing the subject with amazing deductive powers. This power provides a +1 dice pool modifier per level to any test involving pattern recognition, evidence analysis, or solving puzzles or logical problems.

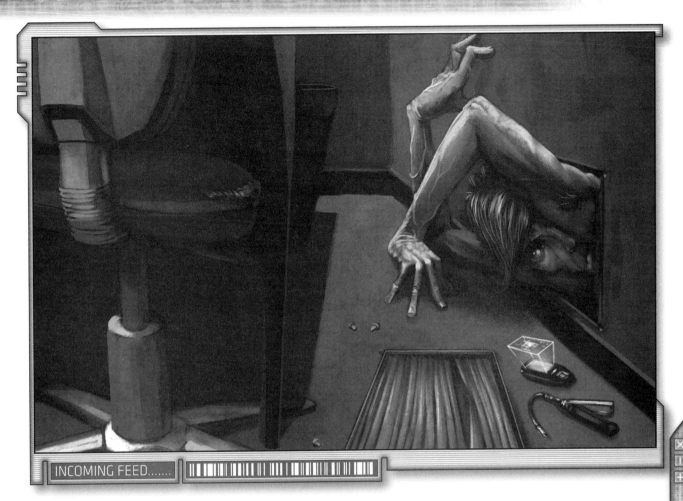
INCOMING FEED.......

Note that gamemasters should not allow this power to be an instant problem solver. While it may certainly help a character to isolate an overlooked fact, decipher a coded message, or identify an area of research not yet pursued, it may also introduce possibilities that are unlikely or red herrings. It is also possible that a puzzle may not be solvable simply because crucial information has not been uncovered (though it may make the subject aware of this).

Animal Empathy
Cost: .25 per level

An adept with this power gains a preternatural affinity with non-sapient animals (both normal and paranormal). Each level of Animal Empathy adds one die to the character's dice pool for tests involving the handling of animals, as well as attempts to frighten or intimidate animals.

Berserk
Cost: 1

A character with the Berserk power has the ability to voluntarily trigger a berserk state (with a Free Action) and enhance his physical abilities at the cost of a temporary loss of mental faculties and sensory acuity. While under the effect of the Berserk power, the adept is subject to frenzied bloodlust and will go after opponent(s) without regard for his own safety. Berserk adepts gain +1 to all of their Physical attribute ratings but also lower all of their Mental attribute ratings by 1 (to a minimum of 1) for (Magic) minutes. All relevant dice pools and Physical and Stun damage tracks are modified for the duration of the power. After Berserk wears off, the character's attributes return to normal. Adepts or mystic adepts who also possess the berserker disadvantage from a mentor spirit will find this power triggers automatically when they become berserk.

Blind Fighting
Cost: .5

A character with Blind Fighting has a mystical "sixth sense" that allows him to fight effectively even when deprived of vision. Blind Fighting reduces the penalties for full darkness modifiers to –4 (rather than –6). Any applicable cover and movement modifiers remain in effect.

Cloak
Cost: .25 per level

The adept who develops Cloak is able to shroud their presence from magical detection. Add a dice pool modifier equal to the adept's level in this power to Opposed Tests to resist detection by *active* Detection spells (p. 205, *SR4A*) or the Search power. Cloak does not hamper attempts to read the character's aura through astral perception or otherwise spot the character directly from astral space; it just makes him difficult to "lock onto" to with detection magic.

Street Magic

Commanding Voice
Cost: .25

This power channels the adept's magic into his voice to enhance the modulation and pitch, subliminally influencing the actions of any listeners. The adept takes a Complex Action to give a simple but forceful command (five words or less) to the target, making an Opposed Test with Leadership + Charisma against the target(s) Willpower + Leadership. If the adept succeeds in the test, the target uses his next action to either carry out the command or stands confused (gamemaster's choice, but the more net hits achieved the more likely he will obey the adept's command). Such commands carry no weight beyond the immediate impetus, and the affected characters will quickly reassert their wits, returning to their original course of action. If multiple individuals are targeted, use the largest dice pool among the defenders and add +1 dice per additional target (max. +5).

Commanding voice may only be used on metahumans who can directly hear *and* understand the adept's words. It has no effect when the voice is amplified or broadcast via technological means (eg. wireless transmission, loudspeaker, etc). It is also less effective on subsequent uses against the same target. Apply a cumulative –2 dice pool penalty for each use within the preceding 24 hours.

Cool Resolve
Cost: .25 per level

Cool Resolve makes a character inhumanly self-assured and unflappable in social exchanges, whether these be delicate negotiations or an interrogator's grilling. Each level of the power adds one die to the adept's dice pool for Opposed Tests involving Social Active skills in which he is the target/defender.

Counterstrike
Cost: .5 per level

Counterstrike allows an adept to seamlessly spring from a successful defense in melee combat to a powerful offense, turning the attacker's force against him. To use this power the adept *must* first successfully *parry* or *block* a melee attack (p. 156, SR4A). The character's level in Counterstrike plus any net hits achieved during the *parry* or *block* are added to his next melee attack roll—as long as he retaliates in his next available action. If the adept opts to dodge or make a full defense maneuver other than *parry* or *block,* Counterstrike is ineffective.

Distance Strike
Cost: 2

This power allows an adept to "transmit" an unarmed physical attack over a short distance to strike a target with concussive force. The power's range equals the adept's Magic attribute in meters, and it inflicts damage as normal (this may include the effects of Killing Hands but not Elemental Strike). Though the attack is rolled as a normal unarmed attack (ignoring Reach modifiers), the defender resists the attack as if it were a ranged attack (ie. the defender may just roll Reaction or go on full defense). Cover modifiers apply and the strike is unable to pass through solid objects. Targets on the other side of mana barriers cannot be affected by this power.

Eidetic Sense Memory
Cost: .5

An adept with this power has the ability to memorize all types of sensory input. Besides perfect photographic visual memory, the adept can recollect sounds, textures, tastes, and smells—and any combination thereof. The adept can recall these sensory impressions at will, and will remember who or what they have memorized in future encounters. The adept can also photo-read, greatly increasing their reading speed.

Elemental Strike
Cost: .5

This power can only be developed by characters who already possess the Killing Hands power (p. 196, SR4A). Elemental Strike enhances the effects of Killing Hands with an elemental effect (see pp. 164–165 of this book and pp. 163–165, SR4A). The specific elemental effect must be chosen at the time the power is bought, though an adept may take this power more than once to achieve different elemental effects (only one elemental effect may be applied per strike). While active, the power wreathes the adept's hands with a visible effect appropriate to the chosen element. Activating Elemental Strike is a Simple Action, after which the effect lasts for (Magic attribute) Combat Turns. Given the focus it demands, Elemental Strike may not be combined with Distance Strike.

Empathic Healing
Cost: .5

This power allows an adept to heal another person by transferring some or all of their wounds to himself. The adept rolls a Magic + Willpower Test. Each hit transfers 1 box of damage from the target to the adept's own damage track. Only Physical damage may be transferred in this manner. As with magical healing by spell, characters with implants are harder to heal: the subject's lost Essence (rounded down) is applied as a negative dice pool modifier to the adept's test. The transferal process takes 2 full Combat Turns per box of damage to complete and the adept must maintain physical contact with the target during the entire process. Empathic Sense may only be used once on any particular set of wounds.

Enthralling Performance
Cost: .5

To utilize this power, an adept must have an artistic skill such as Artisan or Gymnastics. The power only applies to that specific skill, though the adept may purchase this power more than once, applying it to different skills. If the gamemaster allows, it, this power may also apply to Unarmed Combat (Martial Arts) or Con (Impersonation).

This power infuses the adept's performance of his chosen artistic ability with magic. While exercising his art (whether painting, dancing, performing katas, or acting), the flow of his movements and the thrill of his virtuosity mesmerizes the audience into a mild hypnotic state. The adept makes an appropriate skill + Magic Test. The adept's hits serve as a threshold modifier for any Perception Test his audience might make during the performance. Entranced audience members who are subject to sudden stress (such as being knocked over or actively threatened) or are subject to obtrusive environmental distractions (such as an unsilenced gunshot) will automatically be released from the trance. The maximum period an adept can keep subjects entranced is equal to his Charisma x 10 minutes.

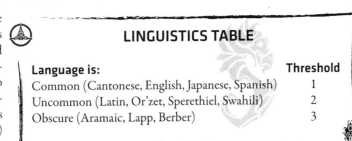

LINGUISTICS TABLE

Language is:	Threshold
Common (Cantonese, English, Japanese, Spanish)	1
Uncommon (Latin, Or'zet, Sperethiel, Swahili)	2
Obscure (Aramaic, Lapp, Berber)	3

Facial Sculpt

Cost: .25 per level

An adept with this power may change his facial features through slight shifts in muscle build, bone structure, and cartilage. Each level adds a +1 dice pool modifier to any Disguise Tests (p. 133, *SR4A*). An adept is able to maintain his new face for (Magic) hours.

Possible changes include: raising or lowering cheek bones, thickening or thinning of the lips, stretching the eyelids, altering the height or shape of the ears, squaring or rounding the chin, or drawing up or fattening of the nose. It can alter the character's perceived metatype (at least in the face), though depending on the character's body mass this may look odd.

Flexibility

Cost: .25 per level

Flexibility makes an adept's limbs unusually supple and limber, able to twist and bend beyond the metahuman norm. Flexibility also helps the adept squeeze through small openings and tight passages, which would otherwise prove difficult for a normal person of his size (such as transoms, ventilation ducts, and other tight fits). Each level increases the adept's dice pool for Escape Artist tests (p. 133, *SR4A*) by one die. The bonus applies to any test made to escape handcuffs, ropes, and other such bindings, as well as tests to escape Subduing attempts (p.161, *SR4A*). The gamemaster should adjust the threshold to reflect particularly tight quarters or difficult contortions.

Freefall

Cost: .25 per level

For each level of Freefall taken, a character may reduce the effective distance he falls by 2 meters for the purpose of calculating falling damage (see p. 164, *SR4A*). For example, if an adept with Freefall at level 3 falls 8 meters, he takes damage as if he had fallen only 2 meters. While this power protects from falling damage, the adept may still take damage if he falls onto a dangerous surface such as a glass shard-riddled balcony or a burning floor (gamemaster's discretion).

Gliding

Cost: 1

This power allows an adept to run up to (Magic) meters across a tangible surface that would normally be unable to hold his weight, such as a fragile tree branch, thin ice, or water. Any attempts to run longer distances require breaking points or landings between uses of Gliding. Any attempt to use this power for acrobatic maneuvers (such as jumping from the surface or performing a Gymnastics dodge) is considered a difficult maneuver, and subtracts 3 dice from the relevant dice pool. Secondary effects of the adept's motion, such as sound or vibrations, are still noticeable (leaves shake and water ripples) unless the adept also uses the Traceless Walk power (p. 180).

Inertia Strike

Cost: .5

Inertia strike allows an adept to channel his power into a potent melee or unarmed attack focused on knocking his opponent off of his feet. The use of this power requires a Free Action to focus before the attack test. The adept may add half his Strength (round down) to the number of boxes of damage done solely for the purpose of determining whether Knockdown occurs (p. 161, *SR4A*).

Iron Gut

Cost: .25 per level

This power allows an adept to digest nearly anything and pass it without harm (gamemaster's discretion). Each level of Iron Gut adds a +1 dice pool modifier for Resistance Tests against ingested toxins.

Iron Lungs

Cost: .25 per level

Iron Lungs grants an adept a dramatically enhanced lung capacity. Each level of Iron Lungs increases the amount of time an adept can hold her breath by 30 seconds (10 Combat Turns). Additionally, each level adds a +1 dice pool modifier for Body or Strength Tests to determine when fatigue sets in (p.164, *SR4A*).

Iron Will

Cost: .25 per level.

Iron Will makes an adept's mind resistant to external influences. The character may add the power's level in bonus dice to tests to resist magical mind control or alteration—including Mental Manipulation spells and some critter and adept powers.

Linguistics

Cost: .25

The Linguistics power combines enhanced memorization and mimicry to allow an adept to pick up a new language after minimal exposure—no Karma expenditure or test required. After (10 – Magic) hours of contact to the new language in use, the adept makes an Intuition + Logic Test using a threshold as noted on the Linguistics Table. If successful,

the adept develops the Language skill at Rating 1 at no Karma cost. Increasing the skill beyond this point requires normal Karma expenditure, but the base learning time for the adept is halved.

Living Focus
Cost: 1

Living Focus allows the adept to physiologically adjust his body to channel mana in order to sustain a spell cast solely on him (in effect becoming a metahuman sustaining focus). The magician who cast the spell need not sustain it; this power allows the adept to do so with a little concentration. The Force of the spell sustained in this manner may not exceed the adept's Magic, and the adept may only sustain one spell at a time. The adept suffers a –2 dice pool modifier for all actions for the duration he sustains the spell.

Magic Sense
Cost: .5

This power grants the adept extra sensitivity to the ebbs and flows of mana in his vicinity. The adept can sense magical activity on the same plane within (Magic x 10) meters of his person. This power will detect active foci, spells, mana barriers, dual-natured beings, and mana anomalies; on the astral it will also detect astral forms. Treat this power as the Detect Magic spell (p. 207, SR4A), with a Force equal to the adept's Magic.

Melanin Control
Cost: .5

An adept with Melanin Control has the ability to alter his hair or skin color within the limits of normal skin tone for the character's ethnicity/metatype. For instance, a caucasian's skin could go from albino skin to dark tropical tan but not to black. For the purpose of this power, skin tone is simplified to five standard varieties (albino, caucasian, tan, brown, and black) and the same with hair color (white/gray, blonde, red, brown, and black). Use of Melanin Control requires a Complex Action to shift either hair or skin color one grade. Therefore, to shift albino skin to rich brown would require three Complex Actions. The effect lasts the adept's Magic in hours.

Metabolic Control
Cost: .5

This power grants an adept exceptional control over his metabolism, giving him the natural power to reduce the effects associated with extreme wounds by stabilizing and suspending his body's organic processes. Metabolic Control allows the character to enter a meditative trance state in which bodily processes are slowed, thereby reducing the rate of breathing and bleeding, but also limiting his need for food, water, and air. The character's metabolism is reduced by a factor equal to his Magic (therefore also delaying the effects on a set of toxins, poisons, and diseases). For example, a character with Magic 5 will have his metabolism decreased by a factor of 5. While in this state, the character cannot act as normal (though he can break out at any time).

This power activates automatically if the adept goes into Physical damage overflow (see p. 153 and 253, SR4A), placing the adept's body into a suspended state. In this case, the adept will only take additional overflow damage at the rate of 1 box per (Body) *hours*.

Missile Mastery
Cost: 1

Even the most harmless of items such as pens, coins, and playing cards become deadly weapons in the hands of an adept with Missile Mastery. Such is the character's knack for throwing weapons that he adds +1 to the Damage Value of any non-explosive thrown weapon he uses. Improvised thrown weapons (such as playing cards, glasses or pens) have a Damage Value of (STR ÷ 2)P (round up) in the adept's hands. At the adept's discretion, thrown weapons that normally inflict stun damage may instead inflict physical.

MOTION SENSE TABLE

Moving Thing Is:	Threshold
Smaller than dog/cat	3
Smaller than average metahuman (dwarf)	2
Average metahuman (human, elf, ork)	1
Larger than average metahuman (troll)	0

Motion Sense
Cost: .5

This power grants the adept a magical sense of minute disturbances in the ambient mana, allowing him to subconsciously detect the motion of objects, people, or animals within (Magic) meters, even when he would be unable to detect them through normal senses such as sight, sound, or smell. The adept makes a Perception + Magic Test with a threshold based on the Motion Sense table. If the target is detected, reduce the dice pool modifiers for visibility or blind fire by 2. This power cannot detect movement through astral barriers.

Multi-Tasking
Cost: .5

Multi-tasking grants the ability to simultaneously process information from multiple senses. For example, an adept with this power could read data off multiple vid-screens and simultaneously hold a conference call over his commlink or hold a conversation while watching the trid, providing full attention to each. In game terms, Observe in Detail (p. 147, SR4A) counts as a Free Action for the character. The adept is also hard to distract (for instance, they would suffer no modifiers in a crowded nightclub or an AR spam zone). Additionally, an adept with Multi-tasking gains two Free Actions per Initiative Pass when not directly involved in combat.

Nerve Strike
Cost: 1

This power allows an adept to inflict a paralyzing attack, temporarily crippling an opponent, by targeting vital nerve

Street Magic

clusters. The adept declares he is using the power and makes a normal unarmed melee attack. Instead of inflicting damage, each net hit reduces his opponent's Agility or Reaction (attacker's choice) by 1. Lost Agility and Reaction returns at a rate of 1 point per minute of rest. If a character's Agility or Reaction is reduced to 0, he is paralyzed and unable to move. Nerve Strike is most effective against metahuman opponents; when used against critters, reduce Agility or Reaction by 1 for every 2 net hits instead. Targets that lack a functional nervous system such as spirits, drones, and zombies are immune to this power.

Nimble Fingers
Cost: .25

Nimble fingers allows the adept to perform simple reflex and timing tricks more efficiently and effectively. It adds a +1 dice pool modifier to Palming and other slight-of-hand tests involving manual dexterity. Additionally, Insert Clip, Pick Up/Put Down Object, Remove Clip, and Use Simple Object are considered Free Actions for the adept.

Pain Relief
Cost: 1

Using a technique similar to Nerve Strike, Pain Relief allows an adept to channel mana through his hands and apply it to chi or chakra points on a target (the adept cannot use Pain Relief on himself). Integral to many Asian holistic traditions such as Reiki, acupuncture, Quijong, and Shiatsu, this technique allows the adept to dissipate fatigue, muscle tension, and pain—effectively healing Stun damage. The adept makes a Magic + Agility (2) Test, healing a number of boxes from the Stun damage track equal to the number of net hits achieved. As with Health spells, modifiers for healing targets with implants apply (see p. 207, SR4A). This energy manipulation takes 5 minutes per damage box healed, and the adept must maintain physical contact for the duration. Any interruption means all progress is lost and the process must be restarted. The target draws no benefit from further applications of Pain Relief until the remaining Stun damage is healed naturally.

Penetrating Strike
Cost: .25 per level (maximum 3)

This power allows the adept to channel the force of an unarmed combat attack a short distance forward, thereby bypassing the target's armor. This power gives the adept's unarmed strikes a negative AP equal to the Penetrating Strike's level (max. 3). This power can be combined with Killing Hands, but not with Distance Strike or Elemental Strike due to the extra focus these already require.

Piercing Senses
Cost: .25 per level

Piercing Senses makes an adept more resistant to illusions. Each level gives an adept a +1 dice pool modifier on tests to resist Illusion spells and illusion-based critter powers (such as Concealment and Mimicry).

Power Throw
Cost: .25 per level

Each level of this power adds 2 to the character's effective Strength solely for the purpose of determining range and damage of thrown weapons and objects.

Quick Draw
Cost: .5

The adept may use the Quick Draw rules (p. 147, SR4A) to draw any weapon, not just pistols. An adept may draw and use a single melee weapon, missile weapon, throwing weapon, or firearm in one action, and need not spend two actions to draw and ready the weapon and then attack: drawing and readying occur in the action used for the Attack Test. If attacking with the weapon requires a Complex Action, the adept may still draw and attack in a single Action Phase. If attacking with a weapon that requires only a Simple Action to use, the adept may draw and make two attacks in a single Action Phase. The adept must succeed in an appropriate weapon skill + Reaction (2) Test to Quick Draw.

Rooting
Cost: .25 per level

By taking a Simple Action, an adept with the Rooting power can become an immovable object. Each level adds a +1 modifier to Body solely for checking for knockdown (p. 161, SR4A) and also adds a +1 dice pool modifier to any tests to resist being knocked down, thrown, levitated, or otherwise moved against his will. While rooted, the character cannot move at all from where he stands. He may otherwise act normally with his arms and upper body (including making attacks) but may not dodge and suffers a –3 dice pool modifier to combat parries and blocks. The power's effect can be cancelled with just a thought.

Smashing Blow
Cost: 1

An adept with this power may focus his magic to break through obstacles. Multiply his base DV by 2 when performing an unarmed strike on a barrier or other static structure (p. 166, SR4A).

Sustenance
Cost: .25

This power allows an adept to replenishes the same amount of energy and health from three hours of sleep and one solid meal a day, as a normal person would with eight hours of sleep and three meals. Additionally, Sustenance enhances digestive and metabolizing processes, and therefore the adept requires only one trip to the restroom each day.

Temperature Tolerance
Cost: .25 per level

An adept with Temperature Tolerance gains a degree of resistance to extremes of cold and heat. Each level of this power adds a +1 dice pool modifier for tests to resist the effects and damage of exposure to extreme temperatures. This power also extends to resisting the magical effects of elemental fire or cold.

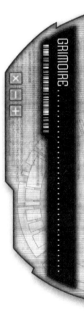

THREE DIMENSIONAL MEMORY TABLE	
Time passed	Threshold Modifier
Less than 24 hours	+0
Less than a week	+1
Less than a month	+2
Less than a year	+3
Over a year	+4

Three-Dimensional Memory

Cost: .5

An adept with Three-Dimensional Memory can use a Complex Action to memorize an area he has viewed first-hand in ultra-clear detail. At a later time, the character may make a Magic + Perception Test to call up the "stored" memory and walk through the "scene," exploring it as if he was walking through the location for the first time. The adept may not interact or disturb anything in the recalled scene, he may only review things he actually saw or sensed, even if only incidentally at the time. For instance, the adept cannot review the contents of a drawer unless it was open when the adept memorized the scene.

Scenes memorized in this manner must be no greater than the adept's Magic x Magic in cubic meters. An adept may memorize a number of areas equal to his Magic attribute. The threshold for the Perception Test itself is modified by the time elapsed since the memory was "registered," as noted on the Three-Dimensional Memory Table.

Traceless Walk

Cost: 1

The adept with this power may move over surfaces—including soft or brittle surfaces such as snow, sand, or thin paper—without leaving visible traces. He makes no noise through contact with the floor (though movement may still cause other sounds), and any hearing-based Perception Tests to detect him suffer a –4 dice pool penalty. The adept will not trip ground-based motion or pressure sensors. The adept cannot walk across liquid surfaces (but can walk across deep snow without sinking) and can still be tracked by non-visual cues such as scent and sound.

Wall Running

Cost: 1

This power allows the adept to run up sheer walls or other vertical surfaces. The adept makes a Strength + Running Test, with hits indicating the number of meters he may climb. Attempts to run up longer distances require stops or landings and additional uses of Wall Running. Any move that requires a Gymnastics Test (such as jumping from one wall to another) performed while using this power suffers a –2 dice pool modifier. Secondary effects of the adept's motion still occur, such as resulting sound or tracks, unless combined with the Traceless Walk power.

NEW MENTOR SPIRITS

The following mentor spirit rules expand upon those detailed on p. 200, SR4A.

MENTOR SPIRIT ARCHETYPES

These additional archetypes are common throughout the globe, but are not intended as the final word on possible mentor spirit types. Gamemasters and players should feel free to develop more mentor spirit archetypes using these as a guide, but be careful to remember that mentor spirits tend to represent the archetypes of vast cultures rather than individual people.

Adversary

Wherever there is a cosmological order, there is an entity who wishes to overthrow it. Adversary is the original rebel working to thwart the mythical Powers-That-Be. Whether he acts out because of his own selfishness or because he is helping those less privileged, free will and cynicism are his trademarks and tools. In some Judeo-Christian traditions, Adversary is the fallen angel who has spurned God's will, while some North American and Asian shamanic traditions see Adversary as a trickster figure and manipulator who brings change.

Advantages: +2 dice for Manipulation spells, +2 dice to either Counterspelling or Banishing Tests (player must choose one).

Disadvantages: Adversary magicians have issues with authority. If the Adversary magician is given orders or instructions which do not match his own desires and intentions, he must make a Willpower + Charisma (3) Test or refuse the order, going with his own decision instead, regardless of the consequences.

Artificer

Artificer is the inventor, craftsman, and smith; the true symbol of humanity's ingenuity and resourcefulness. His tools, and those of his followers, empower mankind to conquer all obstacles. He is not always as skilled at understanding people as he is at analyzing the world, however, which may make him and his followers difficult to deal with or easy to manipulate. Mythical figures such as Hephaestus and Daedalus are common interpretations of Artificer, as are the Celtic Goibhniu and Norse Weland.

Advantages: +2 dice for Manipulation spells, +2 dice to Enchanting Tests.

Disadvantages: Artificer magicians are easily distracted by new and unusual finds or a persistent problem. When faced with something he has never seen before or a problem he can not easily solve, the Artificer magician must make a Willpower + Charisma (3) Test to resist examining the situation at length. The magician will not put his life in danger just to examine a new device, but he will take the next safe opportunity to do so.

Bull

Bull is a symbol of strength, fertility, and masculine vitality that originates in the most ancient of Earth's civiliza-

tions. In the past, Bull's people built vast empires on top of lifeless scrubland, and he is no less demanding of his followers in this age. He may be stern and demanding, but Bull is also fiercely caring of his charges. Bull has always been popular in the Eastern Mediterranean and among the druids of Tir na nOg, but he has also gained a following in the Americas.

Advantages: +2 dice for Combat spells, +2 dice for Leadership Tests.

Disadvantages: Bull magicians are impatient and stubborn, and insist on getting their way. If the Bull magician does not get what he wants, he must make a Willpower + Charisma (3) Test or stubbornly dig in his heels and demand compliance.

Crocodile

Crocodile is the cruelest of gift-bringers, capriciously doling out life and death. It is Crocodile who brings the rains that flood the fields with precious water, ensuring a fertile bounty, but Crocodile also brings drought and disease and pulls victims to their watery graves between his jaws. Those who follow Crocodile understand how precious and precarious life is.

Advantages: +2 dice for Health spells, +2 dice to Survival Tests.

Disadvantages: Crocodile's magicians understand that everything comes with a price. They are truly mercenary in their outlook and must make a Willpower + Charisma (3) Test to offer anything without compensation, no matter how small.

Dark Goddess

In ancient times, the creative power of fertility was often as frightening as it was awesome. The power of creation was linked with the power of destruction in a necessary cycle that forever fed itself. Early goddess-figures of the earth and fertility were therefore also tied to the destruction of war and death, as two sides of the same coin. Ishtar, the primordial Mesopotamian goddess of fertility and war, is an example of a Dark Goddess figure. As is Kali, the Hindu source of rebirth and death, and Morrigan, the Celtic queen of war and doom, whose origins trace back to the dark and rich soil of the earth. Lilith, the cursed first woman of Hebrew myth, also has a large following among female magicians of the Sixth World.

Advantages: +2 dice for Combat and Health spells.

Disadvantages: Ruled by extremes of both creation and destruction, followers of the Dark Goddess often relish in confrontation. They must make a Willpower + Charisma (3) Test to avoid escalating a conflict, no matter how small, into a major clash, whether physical, mental, or social.

Dragon

Dragon is a sly ruler, slow to act and slightly cruel, but undeniably powerful. His regal demeanor hides a scheming mind and his dark lair hides endless riches. In China he is the Dragon Emperor, one of the pair of creatures that represents the balance of yin and yang. In North America, the actions of Dunkelzahn and Ghostwalker have revitalized the worship of this mighty creature. Wherever they are found, Dragon's followers are confident individuals striving for power and influence.

Advantages: +2 dice for Manipulation spells, +2 dice for Negotiation Tests.

Disadvantages: Dragon magicians are single-minded and confident to a fault, as well as sore losers. A Dragon magician must make a Willpower + Charisma (3) Test to follow advice or orders that are not their own, or to accept a defeat gracefully.

Great Mother

The Great Mother supports all living things from her generous bounty and lives to embrace her children. She provides for the livelihood of her followers and heals their bodies and souls. She is fertility unbound, but she is vulnerable to those who would take her gifts for granted. Some of her modern followers have been deemed extremists, but many feel it is those who spoil the Earth who have gone to the extremes.

Advantages: +2 dice to Health spells, +2 dice for earth or plant spirits (player must choose one).

Disadvantages: –1 die for Combat spells.

Gryphon

The Gryphon is an amalgam of the king of the earth (the lion), and the king of the skies (the eagle). It is the guardian of nobility and a symbol of valor and royalty. Though the creature originally appeared in the Middle East, guarding the first kings of Man, the proud beast has come to represent leaders throughout the world. Gryphon expects nothing less than greatness from its followers; they are lords among men.

Advantages: +2 dice for Binding Tests, +2 dice for Leadership Tests.

Disadvantages: Gryphon magicians must have a Charisma attribute of 4 or greater and are expected to be skilled and wise leaders. Gryphon magicians must make a Willpower + Charisma (3) Test to attack anyone other than the most potent adversary in combat, or to accept any assistance in defeating that foe.

Horned Man

Though interpreted in many ways by many cultures, the Horned Man is always a symbol of masculine energy, wild behavior, and vegetation. To the Celts he was Cernunnous, the god of the hunt. To the Greeks he was Dionysus, the god of the vine and revelry. He and his followers live outside the normal constraints of civilization, whether deep in the wild or deep in enthusiastic debauchery. Either way, they know that there are mysteries beyond the fringes waiting to be unlocked by those who would seek them with reckless abandon.

Advantages: +2 dice for Illusion spells, +2 dice for guidance spirits or plant spirits (player must choose one).

Disadvantages: Horned Man magicians know no boundaries for acceptable social behavior. As such, they suffer –1 die on all Social Tests unless they are dealing with those who are just as free-thinking.

Horse

Horse, whether followed by the Plains Amerinds or Central Asian tribes, represents freedom in all its forms. He shares a bond with mankind, at least those who understand nobility, liberty, and the majesty of roaming the Earth freely. Horse will not stand for being bound or restricted and can become irrational in the face of captivity. But to those who respect Horse's need for limitless freedom, he can be a true and loyal friend.

Advantages: +2 dice for Health spells, +2 dice for beast spirits.

Disadvantages: Horse magicians do not tolerate confinement or isolation well. If bound to one location, either physically or through coercion, or otherwise cut off from others for an extended period, the Horse magician must make a Willpower + Charisma (3) Test or become irrational and self-destructive for 3 turns minus 1 turn per hit gained. While irrational, the Horse magician will do all they can to escape the confinement.

Lion

Lion is a proud hunter and a skilled warrior, but Lion also represents the fringes of the world, where unknowable things threaten mankind. Lion stalks this dark hinterland, protecting civilization by attacking the things that would threaten it. Lion is not an altruistic beast, however; she will just as readily cull the weak from mankind. The ancient Egyptian goddess Sekhmet is identified with Lion, as is the demon-hunting Hindu goddess aspect Durga.

Advantages: +2 dice for Combat spells, +2 dice for Banishing Tests.

Disadvantages: Lion magicians refuse to back down from challenges. A Lion magician must make a Willpower + Charisma (3) Test to forgive a slight, back down from a fight, or refuse a challenge.

Oak

Oak is the strongest and oldest of trees, patient and noble. He protects others, shielding moss and small plants from the elements. Strong shields, buildings, and ships are made from oak. He is the guardian of sacred places, and wise in the ways of nature.

Advantages: +2 dice for Plant spirits, +2 dice for Arcana Tests.

Disadvantages: If an Oak magician fails to protect or guard someone or something important to him, he suffers a –1 dice pool modifier on all actions until he atones for the failure.

Owl

Owl features in mythologies all over the globe as a symbol of wisdom, prophecy, death, and as a guide to the afterlife or spirit world. Owl maintains vigilance throughout the night and has gleaned wisdom from the darkness. He perches between this world and the next, able to foretell the future of man and guide his spirit after death. Owl magicians are wise, quiet, and perhaps a bit creepy, aware of secrets hidden in the darkness beyond.

Advantages: +2 dice for Perception and Assensing Tests, +2 dice for spirits of man or guidance spirits (player must choose one).

Disadvantages: –1 die for Combat spells.

Phoenix

Phoenix is the ultimate expression of creative energy, to the extent that it is reborn from its own ashes in a fiery display. It symbolizes vibrancy, resurrection, and the life-giving energy and cyclical nature of the sun. The Phoenix is beautiful, regal, and honest, and in Chinese mythology she is the Phoenix Empress, the counterpart of the Dragon Emperor and symbol of the balance of yin and yang. Phoenix magicians are often vibrant, energetic, and creative individuals who can not be slowed down.

Advantages: +2 dice for Health spells, +2 dice for fire spirits.

Disadvantages: –1 die for Binding Tests.

Sky Father

The Sky Father rules from the dome of the heavens, high atop his mountain throne. He is the male counterpart to the Great Mother, the ultimate patriarch of early civilization. He rules all he can see and there is little that escapes the Sky Father's gaze from his high vantage point. One must be careful not to offend Sky Father though, for his pride edges towards hubris and his temper is quick to rain thunder and lightning down from the heavens.

Advantages: +2 dice for Detection and Manipulation spells.

Disadvantages: Pride is the greatest weakness for followers of Sky Father. If insulted in any way, they must make a Willpower + Charisma (3) Test or they will aggressively confront or retaliate against the source of the slight. Sky Father magicians are also vulnerable to flattery, and suffer a –1 dice pool modifier for resisting Con attempts.

Spider

Spider weaves the web of worlds and waits patiently for all things to come to her. Her mood may be dark and fearsome, but she takes a curious interest in her followers and will protect them behind her web, ruthlessly capturing invaders who might do them harm. From the center of her web she is the mistress of schemes and conspiracies, but she does not appreciate surprises that manage to slip past her silken strands.

Advantages: +2 dice for Detection and Illusion spells.

Disadvantages: Spider magicians are not quick on their feet. They must make a Willpower + Charisma (3) Test to make any quick decisions in situations they have not planned for.

Sun

Sun is excellence, shining brightly in the sky. Sun appreciates those who strive for perfection, whether in one craft or a thousand. He is a fearless protector of kings, illuminator of the divine, and caretaker of visionaries. Much is required of those who follow the Sun, but these heroic magicians have felt the light and warmth of the heavens and would have it no other way.

Advantages: +2 dice for fire spirits or guardian spirits (player must choose one), +2 dice for Combat spells or Healing spells (player must choose one).

Disadvantages: Sun expects perfection from his followers, or at least a harsh lesson for them if they fail. Sun magicians must spend 2 points of Edge to negate a glitch or downgrade a critical glitch.

THE MANY FACES OF MENTOR SPIRITS

Mentor spirits represent mythological or psychological archetypes common to mankind, found in many different cultures that span the globe. Because of their universality, the ideas they represent translate to dozens of cultures and mythologies, though the names these cultures use to identify them differ. Below are a number of sample cultural mythologies and how they interpret the presented mentor spirit archetypes. These examples are not exhaustive; there are many cultural figures they do not cover, nor do they even come close to describing the many interpretations of mentor spirits in the Sixth World.

Aztec

The Aztec gods of the Fifth Sun are often seen as dark and cruel, despite efforts by the nation of Aztlan and Aztechnology to highlight the deities' self-sacrifice to prevent a global cataclysm. In spite of the image problem, the Aztec pantheon has gained global recognition through the ascension of Aztlan and the gods are recognized throughout the Americas.

Significant Aztec deities include: **Quetzalcoatl,** the feathered serpent (Snake); **Huitzilopochtli,** the hummingbird of war (Thunderbird); **Tlaloc,** the god of rain (Crocodile); **Tlazolteotl,** the eater of filth (Seductress); **Xipe Totec,** the flayed god of rebirth (male interpretation of Dark Goddess).

Celtic

What is typically called the Celtic pantheon is actually more of a loose confederation of local and tribal gods common to the lands of Western and Central Europe. What is known of the major gods shared by these people mostly comes through records kept by the Roman Empire and medieval scholars, but this has not harmed the popularity of these deities among druidic traditions of Europe.

Major Celtic deities include: **Dagda,** the All-Powerful (Wise Warrior or Bull); **Lugh,** the Shining One (Fire-bringer or Sun); **Morrigan,** the Terrible Queen (Dark Goddess, Wolf, or Raven); **Epona,** the horse goddess (Horse); **Cernunnos,** the Horned One (Horned Man).

Chinese

The Chinese Celestial Bureaucracy still features heavily in the fractured nation-states of former China and Chinese cultural enclaves in major cities all over the globe. Unlike Japanese mythology, which has adapted itself to the trappings of the modern world, Chinese mythology is still very culturally inclusive and is therefore rare in other societies. However, the ancient power of the Chinese dynasties means that variants of the Chinese mythological figures are common in mythologies throughout Asia.

Common Chinese deities include: **Ti-Tsang Wang,** savior of lost souls (Owl); the **Jade Emperor,** ruler of Heaven (Dark King); **Nuwa,** creator of humanity (Great Mother); **Huang Di,** the Yellow Emperor (Wise Warrior); **Lei Gong,** the duke of thunder (Thunderbird); **Matsu/Tin Hau,** goddess of the sea (Sea).

Classical

The classical deities of ancient Greece and Rome are powerful symbols that are regaining popularity in the Sixth World, especially in small mystery cults located throughout the Mediterranean and the Balkans. In addition, many hermetic magicians in the Western world interpret their mentor spirits through classical ideals, deeply rooted as they are in the origins of Western civilization.

The most well-known Classical deities include: **Zeus/Jupiter,** the lord of the sky (Sky Father); **Poseidon/Neptune,** god of the sea (Sea); **Hades/Pluto,** god of the underworld (Dark King); **Apollo,** god of light (Sun); **Aphrodite/Venus,** goddess of love (Seductress); **Ares/Mars,** god of war (Wolf); **Athena/Minerva,** goddess of war and the city (Wise Warrior); **Artemis/Diana,** goddess of the wild (Bear); **Dionysus/Bacchus,** god of the vine (Horned Man).

Egyptian

Strangely, the Egyptian pantheon is more widely followed outside of Egypt than within the land of its birth. Fundamentalist Muslim officials in Egypt have attempted to suppress the ancient cults' reappearance, but outside of Egypt the old gods are embraced by hermetics who trace some of their tradition's roots to ancient Egyptian techniques.

The more widely accepted Egyptian gods include: **Ra,** the sun god (Sun or Phoenix); **Osiris,** god of the underworld (Dark King); **Isis,** Queen of the Throne (Moon Maiden); **Set,** god of the desert (Wolf); **Thoth,** inventor of writing (Artificer); **Horus,** patron of kings (Eagle); **Bast,** the temple guardian (Cat); **Sobek,** the crocodile god (Crocodile).

Hindu

Hindu adherents typically see mentor spirits as different aspects of the universal spirit Brahman. As each of these aspects is divine in its own way, however, each is worthy of worship and imitation. Mentor spirits are extremely common among magicians of the Hindu tradition, but they are also openly respected by the non-Awakened. It is not at all unusual to see shrines to various deities and mentor spirits on any street in India or in Indian enclaves within cities throughout the world.

Major Hindu deities include: **Brahma,** the creator (Artificer); **Vishnu,** the preserver (Sun); **Shiva,** the destroyer (male interpretation of the Dark Goddess); **Devi,** the divine mother (Great Mother); **Krishna,** the supreme person (Wise Warrior); **Ganesha,** the lord of hosts (a less grim interpretation of the Dark King); **Hanuman,** the monkey king (Dragonslayer).

Japanese

The stories of the "Eight Million Kami" of Japanese mythology have enjoyed resurgence along with Japan's national imperialism. Today the myths are well known not only in Japan but throughout the world, especially along the coastal cities of the Pacific Rim. Often tied to Japan's economic might, it is not unusual to see the most popular kami respected even in straight-laced boardrooms.

Well-known kami include: **Amaterasu,** the sun goddess (Fire-bringer, Phoenix, or Sun); **Izanagi,** the creator god (Dark King); **Izanami,** the dead goddess (Dark Goddess); **Tsukuyomi,** the moon god (a male version of Moon Maiden); **Susanoo,** god of sea and storms (Sea or Shark); **Maneki-neko,** the beckoning cat (Cat); **Hachiman,** divine protector of Japan (Wise Warrior).

Norse

The Norse pantheon reappeared in strength in Scandinavia after the Awakening. Since then, however, cults dedicated to the Norse deities have spread throughout Northern Europe and the Baltic Sea region. Unfortunately for many Norse magicians, these cults have also recently been linked to violent criminal organizations and the international terrorist organization Winternight.

Popular Norse deities include: **Odin,** the All-Father (Sky Father); **Thor,** god of thunder (Dragonslayer or Thunderbird); **Freya,** the lady of fertility (Great Mother); **Loki,** god of strife (Raven or Trickster); **Tyr,** the one-handed god of war (Wise Warrior); the **Norns,** weavers of fate (Spider).

Voodoo

The Voodoo loa may be most popular in the Carib League, but their followers can also be found around the North American Gulf Coast, in the nations of South America, and as far away as the African micro-states. Like the followers of the Norse pantheon, Voodoo houngans have been on the defensively lately; their magic often being wrongly blamed for the appearance of the shedim.

Major Voodoo loa include: **Agwe,** the Lord of the Sea (Sea); **Damballa,** the Great Serpent (Snake); **Erzulie,** the Passionate Woman (Seductress); **Ghede,** the Undertaker (Dark King); **Legba,** the Old Man of the Crossroads (Owl); **Obatala,** King of the White Cloth (Eagle); **Ogoun,** the Loa of Iron and Fire (Wise Warrior); **Shango,** the Loa of Thunder (Sky Father or Thunderbird).

GEAR TABLES

Magical Goods	Cost	Availability
Orichalcum, per unit	50,000¥	12
Quickening Materials	Force x 1,000¥	Force x 4
Ritual Sorcery Materials	Force x 500¥	Force x 2
Talisman	100¥	—

Metamagic Foci	Cost	Availability
Anchoring Focus	Force x 10,000¥	(Force x 6)R
Centering Focus	Force x 15,000¥	(Force x 6)R
Masking Focus	Force x 10,000¥	(Force x 6)R
Shielding Focus	Force x 5,000¥	(Force x 6)R
Symbolic Link Focus	Force x 2,500¥	(Force x 6)F

Focus Formulae	Cost	Availability
Anchoring Focus	Force x 2,500¥	As spell category
Banishing Focus	Force x 1,000¥	(Force x 4)R
Binding Focus	Force x 1,500¥	(Force x 6)R
Centering Focus	Force x 2,500¥	(Force x 8)R
Counterspelling Focus	Force x 1,000¥	As spell category
Masking Focus	Force x 2,500¥	(Force x 8)R
Power Focus	Force x 2,000¥	(Force x 8)R
Shielding Focus	Force x 2,500¥	(Force x 8)R
Spellcasting Focus	Force x 1,000¥	As spell category
Summoning Focus	Force x 1,000¥	(Force x 4)R
Sustaining Focus	Force x 1,500¥	As spell category
Symbolic Link Focus	Force x 2,500¥	(Force x 8)F
Weapon Focus	Force x 2,000¥	(Force x 8)F

Enchanting Tools	Cost	Availability
Talislegger Kit	100¥	4
Assaying Kit	500¥	8
Enchanting Shop	50,000¥	12
Alchemy Microlab	100,000¥	12R

Renting an Enchanting Shop	Cost	Availability
Per hour	25¥	8
Per day	100¥	9
Per month	1,500¥	10

Reagents	Raw	Cost, per unit — Refined	Radical	Availability
Animal*				
Blood, Fur, Scales, Skin	50¥	100¥	200¥	4/6/8
Silk	75¥	150¥	300¥	4/6/8
Intact Pelts	100¥	200¥	400¥	4/6/8
Ivory	300¥	600¥	1,200¥	4/6/8
Venom	600¥	1,200¥	2,400¥	4/6/8
Herbal*				
Sap, Petals, Leaves, Bark	50¥	100¥	200¥	4/6/8
Cotton	75¥	150¥	300¥	4/6/8
Fruit	100¥	200¥	400¥	4/6/8
Rare Hardwoods	600¥	1,200¥	2,400¥	4/6/8
Metal				
Iron	50¥	100¥	200¥	4/6/8
Copper	100¥	200¥	400¥	4/6/8
Silver	300¥	600¥	1,200¥	4/6/8
Mercury	600¥	1,200¥	2,400¥	4/6/8
Gold	10,000¥	20,000¥	40,000¥	4/6/8

MAGICAL GOODS (CONT.)

Reagents	Cost, per unit			Availability
	Raw	Refined	Radical	
Mineral				
Crystals	50¥	100¥	200¥	4/6/8
Fossils	75¥	150¥	300¥	4/6/8
Obsidian	100¥	200¥	400¥	4/6/8
Semi-Precious Gems	200¥	400¥	800¥	4/6/8
Precious Gems	500¥	1,000¥	2,000¥	4/6/8

*Parts of endangered plants or animals may be Restricted or Forbidden by eco-conscious governments.

Magical Compounds	Cost	Availability
Sage	1,300¥	10R
Spirit Strength	2,800¥	16F
Witches' Moss	1,300¥	10F

ADEPT POWERS TABLE

Power	Cost	Reference	Power	Cost	Reference
Analytics	.25 per level	p. 174	Linguistics	.25 per level	p. 177
Animal Empathy	.25 per level	p. 175	Living Focus	1	p. 178
Astral Perception	1	p. 195, SR4A	Magic Sense	.5	p. 178
Attribute Boost	.25 per level	p. 195, SR4A	Melanin Control	.5	p. 178
Berserk	1	p. 175	Metabolic Control	.5	p. 178
Blind Fighting	.5	p. 175	Missile Mastery	1	p. 178
Cloak	.25 per level	p. 175	Missile Parry	.25 per level	p. 196, SR4A
Combat Sense	.5 per level	p. 195, SR4A	Motion Sense	.5	p. 178
Commanding Voice	.25	p. 176	Multi-Tasking	.5	p. 178
Cool Resolve	.25 per level	p. 176	Mystic Armor	.5 per level	p. 197, SR4A
Counterstrike	.5 per level	p. 176	Natural Immunity	.25 per level	p. 197, SR4A
Critical Strike	.25 per level	p. 195, SR4A	Nerve Strike	1	p. 178
Distance Strike	2	p. 176	Nimble Fingers	.25	p. 179
Eidetic Sense Memory	.5	p. 176	Pain Relief	1	p. 179
Elemental Strike	.5	p. 176	Pain Resistance	.5 per level	p. 197, SR4A
Empathic Healing	.5	p. 176	Quick Draw	.5	p. 179
Enhanced Perception	.25 per level	p. 195, SR4A	Penetrating Strike	.25 per level (max 3)	p. 179
Enthralling Performance	.5	p. 176	Piercing Senses	.25 per level	p. 179
Facial Sculpt	.25 per level	p. 177	Power Throw	.25 per level	p. 179
Flexibility	.25 per level	p. 177	Rapid Healing	.25 per level	p. 197, SR4A
Freefall	.25 per level	p. 177	Rooting	.25 per level	p. 179
Gliding	1	p. 177	Smashing Blow	1	p. 179
Great Leap	.25 per level	p. 195, SR4A	Spell Resistance	.5 per level	p. 197, SR4A
Improved Ability	.25 or .5 per level	p. 196, SR4A	Sustenance	.25	p. 179
Improved Physical Attribute	1 per level	p. 196, SR4A	Temperature Tolerance	.25 per level	p. 179
Improved Reflexes	2, 3, or 5	p. 196, SR4A	Three-Dimensional Memory	.5	p. 180
Improved Sense	.25	p. 196, SR4A	Traceless Walk	1	p. 180
Inertia Strike	.5	p. 177	Wall Running	1	p. 180
Iron Gut	.25 per level	p. 177	Voice Control	.5	p. 197, SR4A
Iron Lungs	.25 per level	p. 177			
Iron Will	.25 per level	p. 177			
Killing Hands	.5	p. 196, SR4A			
Kinesics	.5 per level	p. 196, SR4A			

SPELL TABLE

Key

Name is self-explanatory. Spells marked with an asterisk (*) appear in SR4; the rest appear in this book.
Type is either Mana (M) or Physical (P). See p. 203, *SR4A*.
Test is either O (Opposed Test, resisted with the noted attribute + Counterspelling), or S (Success Test). Spells marked S (OR) must beat the Object Resistance threshold (see p. 183, *SR4A*).
Range is either line of sight (LOS) or touch (T). Spells with an (A) are area effect. For Detection spells, the notation after the slash refers to the range of the sense: a directional (D) sense like sight or an area (A) sense detecting targets in all directions; (EA) is an extended area effect. Spells with a (V) require a voluntary subject.
Damage is either Physical (P) or Stun (S).
Duration is either Instant (I), Sustained (S) or Permanent (P). See p. 203, *SR4A*.
Drain is the Drain Value (p. 203, *SR4A*).

Combat Spells	Type	Test	Range	Damage	Duration	Drain
Acid Stream (Indirect, Elemental)*	P	O (REA)	LOS	P	I	(F ÷ 2) + 3
Ball Lightning (Indirect, Elemental)*	P	O (REA)	LOS (A)	P	I	(F ÷ 2) + 5
Blast (Indirect)*	P	O (REA)	LOS (A)	S	I	(F ÷ 2) + 2
Clout (Indirect)*	P	O (REA)	LOS	S	I	(F ÷ 2)
Corrode [Object] (Indirect, Elemental)	P	S (OR)	T	P	I	(F ÷ 2)
Death Touch (Direct)*	M	O (WIL)	T	P	I	(F ÷ 2) – 2
Demolish [Object] (Direct)	P	S (OR)	LOS (A)	P	I	(F ÷ 2) + 2
Fireball (Indirect, Elemental)*	P	O (REA)	LOS (A)	P	I	(F ÷ 2) + 5
Firewater (Indirect, Elemental)	P	O (REA)	LOS	P	I	(F ÷ 2) + 5
Flamethrower (Indirect, Elemental)*	P	O (REA)	LOS	P	I	(F ÷ 2) + 3
Knockout (Direct)*	M	O (WIL)	T	S	I	(F ÷ 2) – 3
Lightning Bolt (Indirect, Elemental)*	P	O (REA)	LOS	P	I	(F ÷ 2) + 3
Manaball (Direct)*	M	O (WIL)	LOS (A)	P	I	(F ÷ 2) + 2
Manabolt (Direct)*	M	O (WIL)	LOS	P	I	(F ÷ 2)
Melt [Object] (Indirect, Elemental)	P	S (OR)	LOS	P	I	(F ÷ 2) + 2
Napalm (Indirect, Elemental)	P	O (REA)	LOS (A)	P	I	(F ÷ 2) + 7
One Less [Metatype/Species] (Direct)	M	O (WIL)	T	P	I	(F ÷ 2) – 3
Powerball (Direct)*	P	O (BOD)	LOS (A)	P	I	(F ÷ 2) + 3
Powerbolt (Direct)*	P	O (BOD)	LOS	P	I	(F ÷ 2) + 1
Punch (Indirect)*	P	O (REA)	T	S	I	(F ÷ 2) – 2
Ram [Object] (Direct)	P	S (OR)	T	P	I	(F ÷ 2) – 2
Shatter (Direct)*	P	O (BOD)	T	P	I	(F ÷ 2) – 1
Shattershield (Direct)	M	O (Force)	T	P	I	(F ÷ 2) – 3
Slaughter [Metatype/Species] (Direct)	M	O (WIL)	LOS (A)	P	I	(F ÷ 2) + 1
Slay [Metatype/Species] (Direct)	M	O (WIL)	LOS	P	I	(F ÷ 2) + 1
Sludge [Object] (Indirect, Elemental)	P	S (OR)	LOS (A)	P	I	(F ÷ 2) + 4
Stunball (Direct)*	M	O (WIL)	LOS (A)	S	I	(F ÷ 2) + 1
Stunbolt (Direct)*	M	O (WIL)	LOS	S	I	(F ÷ 2) – 1
Toxic Wave (Indirect, Elemental)	P	O (REA)	LOS (A)	P	I	(F ÷ 2) + 5
Wreck [Object] (Direct)	P	S (OR)	LOS	P	I	(F ÷ 2)

Detection Spells	Type	Test	Range	Duration	Drain
Analyze Device (Active, Directional)*	P	O (WIL)	T/D	S	(F ÷ 2)
Analyze Magic (Active, Directional)	M	O (WIL)	T/D	S	(F ÷ 2)
Analyze Truth (Active, Directional)*	M	O (WIL)	T/D	S	(F ÷ 2)
Animal Sense (Active, Directional)	M	O (WIL)	T/D	S	(F ÷ 2) – 1
Area Thought Recognition (Active, Psychic)	M	O (WIL)	T/A	S	(F ÷ 2) + 2
Astral Clairvoyance (Passive, Directional)	M	S	T/D	S	(F ÷ 2) – 1
Astral Window (Active, Directional)	M	O (Force)	T/D	S	(F ÷ 2)
Borrow Sense (Active, Directional)	M	O (WIL)	T/D	S	(F ÷ 2)
Catalog (Active)	P	S (OR)	T/A	S	(F ÷ 2) + 2
Clairaudience (Passive, Directional)*	M	S	T/D	S	(F ÷ 2) – 1
Clairvoyance (Passive, Directional)*	M	S	T/D	S	(F ÷ 2) – 1
Combat Sense (Active, Psychic)*	M	O (WIL)	T/A	S	(F ÷ 2) + 2
Detect Enemies (Active)*	M	O (WIL)	T/A	S	(F ÷ 2) + 1
Detect Enemies, Extended (Active)*	M	O (WIL)	T/EA	S	(F ÷ 2) + 3
Detect Individual (Active)*	M	O (WIL)	T/A	S	(F ÷ 2) – 1
Detect Life (Active)*	M	O (WIL)	T/A	S	(F ÷ 2)
Detect Life, Extended (Active)*	M	O (WIL)	T/EA	S	(F ÷ 2) + 2
Detect [Life Form] (Active)*	M	O (WIL)	T/A	S	(F ÷ 2) – 1
Detect [Life Form], Extended (Active)*	M	O (WIL)	T/EA	S	(F ÷ 2) + 1
Detect Magic (Active)*	M	O (WIL)	T/A	S	(F ÷ 2)
Detect Magic, Extended (Active)*	M	O (WIL)	T/EA	S	(F ÷ 2) + 2
Detect [Object] (Active)*	P	S (OR)	T/A	S	(F ÷ 2) – 1
Diagnose (Active, Directional)	M	O (WIL)	T/D	I	(F ÷ 2)
Enhance Aim (Passive, Directional)	P	S	T/D (V)	S	(F ÷ 2) – 1

SPELL TABLE (CONT.)

Detection Spells	Type	Test	Range	Duration	Drain
Eyes of the Pack (Passive, Directional)	M	S	T/D (V)	S	(F ÷ 2) + 1
Hawkeye (Passive, Directional)	P	S	T/D (V)	S	(F ÷ 2) − 1
Mana Window (Active, Directional)	M	O (Force)	T/D	S	(F ÷ 2)
Mindlink (Active, Psychic)*	M	S	T/A (V)	S	(F ÷ 2) + 1
Mindnet (Active, Psychic)	M	S	T/A (V)	S	(F ÷ 2) + 3
Mindnet, Extended (Active, Psychic)	M	S	T/EA (V)	S	(F ÷ 2) + 5
Mind Probe (Active, Directional)*	M	O (WIL)	T/D	S	(F ÷ 2) + 2
Night Vision (Passive, Directional)	P	S	T/D (V)	S	(F ÷ 2) − 1
[Sense] Cryptesthesia (Passive, Directional)	M	S	T/D	S	(F ÷ 2)
Spatial Sense (Passive)	P	S	T/A	S	(F ÷ 2) + 2
Spatial Sense, Extended (Passive)	P	S	T/EA	S	(F ÷ 2) + 4
Thermographic Vision (Passive, Directional)	P	S	T/D (V)	S	(F ÷ 2) − 1
Thought Recognition (Active, Psychic/Directional)	M	O (WIL)	T/D	S	(F ÷ 2)
Translate (Active, Psychic/Directional)	M	O (WIL)	T/D	S	(F ÷ 2)

Health Spells	Type	Test	Range	Duration	Drain
Alleviate Addiction	M	S	T	S	(F ÷ 2) − 4
Alleviate Allergy	M	S	T	S	(F ÷ 2) − 4
Antidote*	M	S	T	P	(Toxin DV) − 2
Awaken	M	S	T	S	(F ÷ 2) − 4
Crank	P	S	T (V)	P	(F ÷ 2)
Cure Disease*	M	S	T	P	(Disease DV) − 2
Decrease [Attribute] (Negative)*	P	O (attribute)	T	S	(F ÷ 2) + 1
Decrease Reflexes (Negative)	P	O (REA)	T	S	(F ÷ 2) + 1
Detox*	M	S	T	P	(Toxin DV) − 4
Enabler (Negative)	M	O (BOD)	T	S	(F ÷ 2)
Fast	M	S	T (V)	S	(F ÷ 2) − 5
Heal*	M	S	T	P	(Damage Value) − 2
Healthy Glow	P	S	T	P	(F ÷ 2) − 1
Hibernate*	M	S	T (V)	S	(F ÷ 2) − 3
Increase [Attribute]*	P	S	T (V)	S	(F ÷ 2) − 2
Increase Reflexes*	P	S	T (V)	S	(F ÷ 2) + 2
Intoxication (Negative)	M	O (BOD)	T	P	(F ÷ 2)
Nutrition	P	S	T (V)	P	(F ÷ 2)
Oxygenate*	P	S	T (V)	S	(F ÷ 2) − 1
Prophylaxis*	M	S	T (V)	S	(F ÷ 2) − 2
Resist Pain*	M	S	T	P	(Damage Value) − 4
Stabilize*	M	S	T	P	(Overflow damage) − 2
Stim	M	S	T (V)	S	(F ÷ 2) − 5

Illusion Spells	Type	Test	Range	Duration	Drain
Agony (Realistic, Single-Sense)	M	O (WIL)	LOS	S	(F ÷ 2) − 2
Bugs (Realistic, Multi-Sense)	M	O (WIL)	LOS	S	(F ÷ 2)
Camouflage (Realistic, Single-Sense)	M	O (WIL)	LOS	S	(F ÷ 2) − 2
Chaff (Realistic, Multi-Sense)	P	O (INT)	LOS	S	(F ÷ 2)
Chaos (Realistic, Multi-Sense)*	P	O (INT)	LOS	S	(F ÷ 2) + 1
Chaotic World (Realistic, Multi-Sense)*	P	O (INT)	LOS (A)	S	(F ÷ 2) + 3
Confusion (Realistic, Multi-Sense)*	M	O (WIL)	LOS	S	(F ÷ 2)
Double Image (Realistic, Multi-Sense)	M	O (WIL)	T	S	(F ÷ 2) − 3
Dream (Realistic, Multi-Sense)	M	O (WIL)	LOS	S	(F ÷ 2) − 1
Entertainment (Obvious, Multi-Sense)*	M	O (WIL)	LOS (A)	S	(F ÷ 2) + 1
Flak (Realistic, Multi-Sense)	P	O (INT)	LOS (A)	S	(F ÷ 2) + 2
Foreboding (Realistic, Multi-Sense)	M	O (WIL)	LOS (A)	S	(F ÷ 2) + 2
Hot Potato (Realistic, Single-Sense)	M	O (WIL)	LOS (A)	S	(F ÷ 2) − 1
Hush (Realistic, Single-Sense)*	M	O (WIL)	LOS (A)	S	(F ÷ 2) + 2
Improved Invisibility (Realistic, Single-Sense)*	P	O (INT)	LOS	S	(F ÷ 2) + 1
Invisibility (Realistic, Single-Sense)*	M	O (WIL)	LOS	S	(F ÷ 2)
Mask (Realistic, Multi-Sense)*	M	O (WIL)	T	S	(F ÷ 2)
Mass Agony (Realistic, Single-Sense)	M	O (WIL)	LOS (A)	S	(F ÷ 2)
Mass Confusion (Realistic, Multi-Sense)*	M	O (WIL)	LOS (A)	S	(F ÷ 2) + 2
Mass [Sense] Removal (Realistic, Single-Sense)	P	O (INT)	LOS (A)	S	(F ÷ 2) + 1
Orgasm (Realistic, Single-Sense)	M	O (WIL)	LOS	S	(F ÷ 2) − 2
Orgy (Realistic, Single-Sense)	M	O (WIL)	LOS (A)	S	(F ÷ 2)
Phantasm (Realistic, Multi-Sense)*	M	O (WIL)	LOS (A)	S	(F ÷ 2) +2
Physical Camouflage (Realistic, Single-Sense)	P	O (WIL)	LOS	S	(F ÷ 2) − 1
Physical Double Image (Realistic, Multi-Sense)	P	O (INT)	T	S	(F ÷ 2) − 2
Physical Mask (Realistic, Multi-Sense)*	P	O (INT)	T	S	(F ÷ 2)
[Sense] Removal (Realistic, Single-Sense)	P	O (INT)	LOS	S	(F ÷ 2) − 1
Silence (Realistic, Single-Sense)*	P	O (INT)	LOS (A)	S	(F ÷ 2) + 3
Sound Barrier (Realistic, Single-Sense)	P	O (INT)	LOS (A)	S	(F ÷ 2) + 3

SPELL TABLE (CONT.)

Illusion Spells	Type	Test	Range	Duration	Drain
Stealth (Realistic, Single-Sense)*	P	O (INT)	LOS	S	(F ÷ 2) +1
Stench (Realistic, Single-Sense)	M	O (WIL)	LOS (A)	S	(F ÷ 2)
Stink (Realistic, Single-Sense)	M	O (WIL)	LOS	S	(F ÷ 2) – 2
Swarm (Realistic, Multi-Sense)	M	O (WIL)	LOS (A)	S	(F ÷ 2) + 2
Trid Entertainment (Obvious, Multi-Sense)*	P	O (INT)	LOS (A)	S	(F ÷ 2) + 2
Trid Phantasm (Realistic, Multi-Sense)*	P	O (INT)	LOS (A)	S	(F ÷ 2) +3
Vehicle Mask (Realistic, Multi-Sense)	P	O (INT)	T	S	(F ÷ 2) – 2

Manipulation	Type	Test	Range	Duration	Drain
Alter Memory (Mental)	M	O (WIL)	LOS	P	(F ÷ 2) + 2
Alter Temperature (Environmental)	P	S	LOS (A)	S	(F ÷ 2) + 1
Animate (Physical)	P	S (OR)	LOS	S	(F ÷ 2)
Armor (Physical)	P	S	LOS	S	(F ÷ 2) + 3
Aspected Mana Static (Environmental)	M	S	LOS (A)	P	(F ÷ 2) + 4
Astral Armor (Mana)	M	S	LOS	S	(F ÷ 2) + 2
Bind (Physical)	P	O (STR)	LOS	S	(F ÷ 2) + 1
Calm Animal (Mental)	M	O (WIL)	LOS	S	(F ÷ 2) – 1
Calm Pack (Mental)	M	O (WIL)	LOS (A)	S	(F ÷ 2) + 1
Catfall (Physical)	P	S	LOS	S	(F ÷ 2)
Clean [Element] (Environmental)	P	S	LOS (A)	P	(F ÷ 2) + 2
Compel Truth (Mental)	M	O (WIL)	LOS	S	(F ÷ 2) – 1
Control Actions (Mental)*	M	O (WIL)	LOS	S	(F ÷ 2)
Control Animal (Mental)	M	O (WIL)	LOS	S	(F ÷ 2) + 1
Control Emotions (Mental)*	M	O (WIL)	LOS	S	(F ÷ 2)
Control Pack (Mental)	M	O (WIL)	LOS (A)	S	(F ÷ 2) + 3
Control Thoughts (Mental)*	M	O (WIL)	LOS	S	(F ÷ 2) + 2
[Critter] Form (Physical)*	P	S	LOS (V)	S	(F ÷ 2) + 1
Deflection (Physical)	P	S	LOS	S	(F ÷ 2) + 1
[Element] Aura (Environmental)	P	S	LOS	S	(F ÷ 2) + 3
[Element] Wall (Environmental)	P	S	LOS (A)	S	(F ÷ 2) + 5
Fashion (Physical)	P	S	T	P	(F ÷ 2)
Fix (Physical)	P	S (OR)	T	P	(F ÷ 2) + 1
Fling (Physical)*	P	S	LOS	I	(F ÷ 2) + 1
Gecko Crawl (Physical)	P	S	T	S	(F ÷ 2) – 1
Glue (Physical)	P	S (OR)	LOS	S	(F ÷ 2) + 1
Glue Strip (Physical)	P	S (OR)	LOS (A)	S	(F ÷ 2) + 3
Ice Sheet (Environmental)	P	S	LOS (A)	I	(F ÷ 2) + 3
Ignite (Physical)*	P	O (BOD)	LOS	P	(F ÷ 2)
Influence (Mental)*	M	O (WIL)	LOS	P	(F ÷ 2) + 1
Interference (Environmental)	P	S	LOS (A)	S	(F ÷ 2) + 3
Levitate (Physical)*	P	S	LOS	S	(F ÷ 2) + 1
Light (Environmental)	P	S	LOS (A)	S	(F ÷ 2) – 1
Lock (Physical)	P	S (OR)	LOS	S	(F ÷ 2)
Magic Fingers (Physical)*	P	S	LOS	S	(F ÷ 2) + 1
Makeover (Physical)	P	S	T (V)	P	(F ÷ 2)
Mana Barrier (Environmental)*	M	S	LOS (A)	S	(F ÷ 2) + 1
Mana Bind (Mana)	M	O (STR)	LOS	S	(F ÷ 2)
Mana Net (Mana)	M	O (STR)	LOS (A)	S	(F ÷ 2) + 2
Mana Static (Environmental)	M	S	LOS (A)	P	(F ÷ 2) + 4
Mass Animate (Physical)	P	S (OR)	LOS (A)	S	(F ÷ 2) + 2
Mist (Environmental)	P	S	LOS (A)	I	(F ÷ 2) + 3
Mob Control (Mental)*	M	O (WIL)	LOS (A)	S	(F ÷ 2) + 2
Mob Mind (Mental)*	M	O (WIL)	LOS	S	(F ÷ 2) + 4
Mob Mood (Mental)*	M	O (WIL)	LOS (A)	S	(F ÷ 2) + 2
Net (Physical)	P	O (STR)	LOS (A)	S	(F ÷ 2) + 3
Offensive Mana Barrier (Environmental)	M	S	LOS (A)	S	(F ÷ 2) + 3
Petrify (Physical)*	P	O (BOD)	LOS	S	(F ÷ 2) + 2
Physical Barrier (Environmental)*	P	S	LOS (A)	S	(F ÷ 2) + 3
Poltergeist (Environmental)*	P	S	LOS (A)	S	(F ÷ 2) + 3
Preserve (Physical)	P	S	T	P	(F ÷ 2)
Pulse (Environmental)	P	S (OR)	LOS (A)	I	(F ÷ 2) + 3
Reinforce (Physical)	P	S	LOS	S	(F ÷ 2) + 1
Shadow (Environmental)*	P	S	LOS (A)	S	(F ÷ 2) + 1
Shapechange (Physical)*	P	S	LOS (V)	S	(F ÷ 2) + 2
Shape [Material] (Environmental)	P	S (OR)	LOS (A)	S	(F ÷ 2) + 3
Spirit Barrier (Environmental)	M	S	LOS (A)	S	(F ÷ 2)
Spirit Zapper (Environmental)	M	S	LOS (A)	S	(F ÷ 2) + 2
Sterilize (Physical)	P	S	LOS (A)	I	(F ÷ 2) + 2
Turn to Goo (Physical)*	P	O (BOD)	LOS	S	(F ÷ 2) + 2

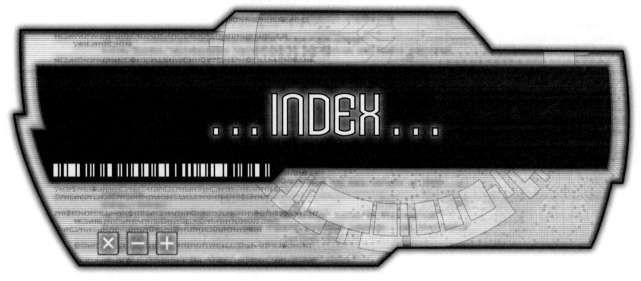

INDEX

A
Abomination spirit, 144
Aboriginal tradition, 35
Absorption, 59
Adept
- centering 53,
- geasa and, 27, 31
- metamagic, 53
- powers, 174–180
- quality, 23
- twisted, 139
- ways, 44–45

Acid spirit, 144–145
Alarm ward, 125
Alchemix, 18
Alchemy, 81–82
Alchera, 115–116
Ally conjuration, 53
Ally spirit, 51, 103–105
Anchoring, 59–60
- trigger conditions, 60

Arcana skill, 22, 24, 30
Area effect spells, 160
Artificing, 82–84
Asceticism ordeal, 51
Aspected enchantments, 83
Aspected Magician quality, 26, 31
Astral constructs, 112–114
Astral Earth, 144–115
Astral forms, 112
Astral plane, 112–114
Astral rifts, 116
Astral security, 122–127
- patrols, 126
- wards, 123–125
- tools, 126–127

Astral shadows, 112
Astral shallows, 116
Astral Sight quality, 24
Astral Visibility, 114
Athlete's way, 44
Attack of will, 94
Attunement (Animal), 53–54, 55
Attunement (Item), 54
Auras, 112
Aura Noise, 114
Avengers, 138
Awakened ivy, 127
Aztec tradition, 35–36
Aztechnology, 17

B
Background count, 117–119
- aspect, 118–119
- magic and, 118

Bear Doctor Society, 69–70
Benandanti XXV, 70
Black magic tradition, 36
Blood magic, 139
Blood spirits, 139–140
Brotherhood of the Iron Crescent, 70
Buddhist tradition, 36

C
Cannibalize, 140
Carnage spirits, 147
Cermak Blast Zone, 122
Channeling, 54–55
Chaos magic tradition, 37
Charged ward, 125
Christian theurgy tradition, 37–38
Cognition, 55–56
Combat spells, 162, 164–165, 168
- Direct, 162
- elemental effects, 162, 168
- Indirect, 162

Contagion spirits, 147
Corps cadavre, 95
Corruption, 14
Crater Lake, 120
Crystalwell, 128
Cursed quality, 26

D
Dead Warlocks, 70
Deep Lacuna, 116
Deep metaplanes, 129–130
Detection spells, 162, 165–169
- active, 162
- passive, 162
- extended range, 163

Disruption, 94, 133
Divining, 56
Domains, 117–119, 120–121
Drain
- Conjuring, 30
- healing and, 30
- modifiers, 162, 163
- Value, 162

Druidic tradition, 38
Dweller on the Threshold, 130–131

E
Elemental effects, 162, 164–165, 168
Emergence Lake, 130
Empower Animal, 60
Enchanting skill, 22, 24, 30
Enchanting, 78–88
- shops, 78–79
- tools, 79

Evanescence, 148
Exotic reagents, 83
Extended Masking, 60–61

F
Faustian mages, 138
Fetishes, 81

Street Magic

Filtering, 61
Flesh form spirit, 100
Flux, 61
Flourescing Astral Bacteria, 126–127
Foci, 84–85
Focus Addiction quality, 26–27
Focus formula, 82–83
Free spirit, 106–110
    powers, 109–110
    types, 92–93

G

Geas quality, 27–28, 30–31
Geasa, 29–31, 51
Geomancy, 56–57
Gladio, 71
Glomoss, 127
Great Ritual, 57
Guardian spirits, 96–97
Guardian vines, 127
Guidance spirits, 97

H

Harbinger spirit, 145
Harrow spirit, 145
Haven lily, 127
Havocs, 141
Health spells, 163, 169–170
    Negative, 163
Hermetic Order of the Auric Aurora, 72
Hindu tradition, 38–39
Hive insect spirits, 150–151
Hive, the, 131
Hybrid form spirit, 100

I

Illuminates of the New Dawn, 72
Illusion spells, 163, 170–171
Infusion, 61
Inhabitation merges, 100
Initiation
    groups, 50, 67
    rites, 50
Initiatory ordeals, 50–52
    asceticism, 51
    deed, 51
    familiar, 51
    geas, 51
    meditation, 51
    metaplanar quests, 51, 133
    oath, 51
    sacrifice, 52
    suffering, 52
    thesis/masterpiece, 52
Insect tradition, 148–149
    mentor spirits, 149–150
Insect spirit, 149–154
    hive, 150–151
    powers, 154
    queen/mothers, 153–154
    solitary, 151–152
    types 152–153
Instant spells, 160
Invoking, 57,
    blood spirits, 139–140
Islamic tradition, 39
Invisible way, 45

J, K, L

Jamil Islamyah, 72
Karma, 24, 107
Korean tradition, 46–47
Latent Awakening quality, 23–24
Leeching, 143
LOS range spells, 160

M

Madness, 46
Magic
    corps and, 16–18
    cyberware and, 23
    education and, 12–13
    in the shadows, 19
    law and, 13–14
    Matrix and, 23
    media and, 9–11
    religion and, 14–16, 35, 46
    urban legends, 11
Magic loss, 31
Magic traditions, 34–43, 46–47
Magical compounds, 88
Magical goods, 76–88
Magical groups, 62–74
    avatar, 65
    benefits, 67
    bond, 65
    creating, 69
    customs, 64
    finding a, 68–69
    founding, 69
    initiation, 67
    joining, 69
    patron, 68
    purpose, 64
    rank and status, 65
    resources and dues, 68
    strictures, 65–67
    violations, 65–66
Mana, 111, 117
Mana ebbs, 120
Mana spells, 159
Mana storms, 122
Mana surges, 121–122
Mana warps, 121
Manadyne, 18
Manipulation spells, 163, 171–174
    Environmental, 163
    Mana, 164
    Mental, 164
    Physical, 164
Masking ward, 125
Material links, 28
Maya Cloud, 124
MCT Research Unit 13, 73
Mentor spirits, 180–184
    as magical group avatar, 65
    toxic, 142–143
    twisted, 137
Metamagic, 52–59
    enchantments, 85
    insect, 153
    learning, 52, 133
    toxic 143
    twisted, 139–140
Metamorphosis, 153
Metaplanes, 128–133
    deep, 129–130
    metaphor, 128
    metaplanar forms, 129
    spirit shortcut, 94
Metaplanar quests
    Dweller on the Threshold, 130–131
    goals, 131–133
    ordeal, 51
    magical groups and, 68
    metamagic and, 52
    trials, 131
Miracles, 46
Mitsuhama, 17
Mystic Crusaders, 73

N, O

Norse tradition, 39–40
Nuclear spirit, 146
Orichalcum, 81–82

P

Path of Blood, 138
Path of Maho/Demons, 139
Path of the Dead, 139
Path of the Wheel, 40
Pathfinders, 73
Permanent spells, 160
Physical spells, 159
Plant spirits, 98
Poisoners, 141
Polarized ward, 125
Possession-based traditions, 34
Power Bleed, 140
Psionics, 45
Psychomtry, 57

Q, R

Qabbalist tradition, 40
Qualities, 23, 24–28
    Adept, 23

Magician, 23
    Mystic Adept, 23
Radiation, 145
Rat Pack, 74
Reagents, 80, 81, 82, 83
Reapers, 141
Reflecting, 61
Resisted spells, 161, 162
Restricted effect spells, 160
Restricted target spells, 160
Ritual magic, 31, 68
Ritual Spellcasting, 28–29

S

Sacrificing, 139
Saeder-Krupp, 17
Sensing, 58
Shadow spirits, 146–148
Shamanic way, 45
Shedim, 155
Shinto tradition, 41
Sister of Ariadne, 74
Sludge spirit, 146
Smog spirits, 147
Solitary insect spirits, 151-152
Somatic Control, 58
Sons of Thunder & Sea, 74
Speaker's way, 45
Spell
    Combat, 164–165
    category, 159
    duration, 160
    Detection, 165–169
    effect, 161
    Health, 169–170
    Illusion, 170–171
    Manipulation, 171–174
    range, 160
    type, 159
Spell design, 158–164
    examples, 167
    Sorcery limits, 159–160
Spell formulae, 158
Spell/Spirit Knack quality, 25, 31
Spirit Pact quality, 26
Spirit pacts, 108–109, 110, 132
Spirits, 89–110
    appearance, 96–97
    ally, 103–105
    combat, 94
    destroying, 133
    disruption, 94
    Edge and, 31, 95
    form, 90–92
    formula, 103, 107, 133
    free, 92–93, 106–110
    insect, 149–154
    intellect, 90
    long-term binding, 94
    movement, 94
    perception and, 95–96
    powers, 98–103
    services, 94–95
    shadow, 146–148
    shedim, 155
    toxic, 144–146
    vessels and, 95, 100, 102–103, 110
    wards and, 124–125
    watcher, 95
    wild, 93, 110
Sterilists, 141–142
Sustained spells, 160
Symbolic links, 29, 58
Sympathetic links, 28–29, 58
Sympathetic Linking, 58

T

Taint, 143
Talismans, 81
Talismongering, 76–78
Task spirits, 98
Telesma, 83
Touch range spells, 160
Toxic
    mentor spirits, 142–143
    metamagic, 143
    paths, 141
    spirits, 144–146, 147
Trap wards, 125–126
True name, 107
Twisted, 136–141
    adepts, 139
    corrupted, 137
    mentor spirits and, 137
    metamagic, 139–140
    paths, 137
    spirits and, 137
Traditional or hedge witchcraft, 41–42
True form spirit, 100

U, V, W, X, Z

Unique radicals, 88
Very restricted target spells, 160
Vessels, 86–87, 88, 95, 100, 102–103, 110
Voids, 119–120
Voodoo tradition, 42
Wards, 123–125
    advanced, 125–126
    fooling, 124
    physical anchor, 124
    shape, 124
    spirits and, 124–125
Warrior's way, 44–45
Watergate Rift, 118
Way of the Burnout, 31
Wiccan tradition, 42–43
Wild spirits, 93, 110
Wuxing (megacorp), 117
Wuxing tradition, 43
Xerxes Positive Research, 18
Zealots, 138
Zoroastrian tradition, 43

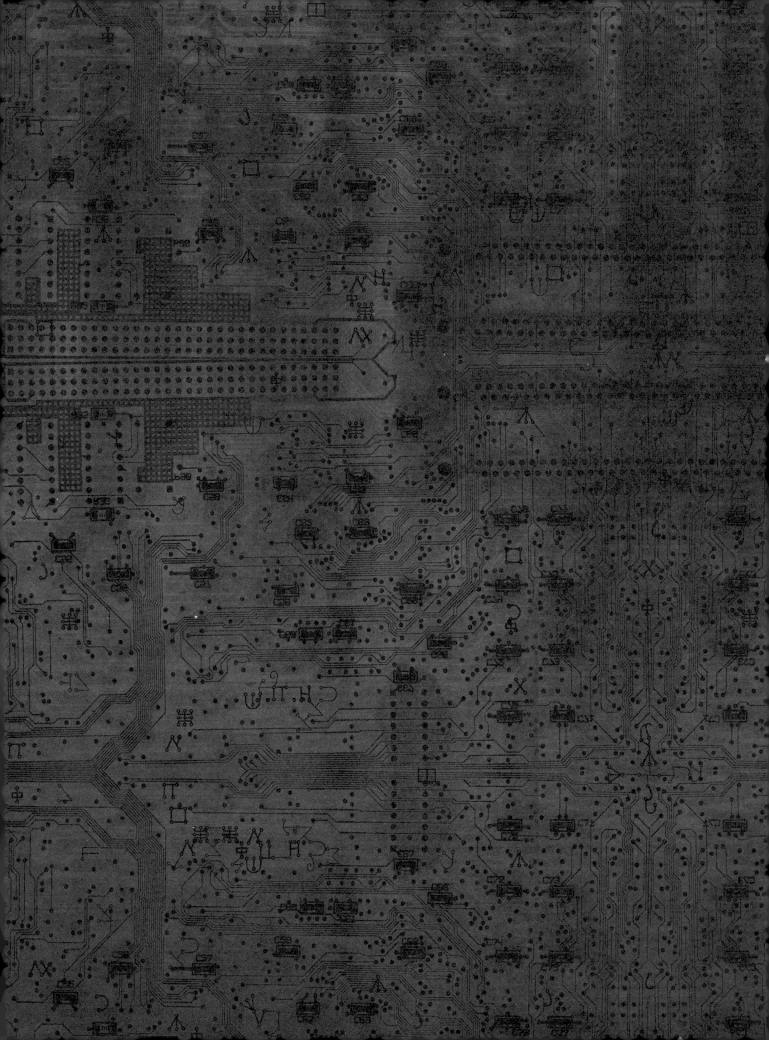